ALL
WHO WANDER
ARE LOST

· AN ICARUS FELL NOVEL ·

BRUCE BLAKE

Comments?

Contact Bruce at: bruce@bruceblake.net

Visit Bruce on-line at www.bruceblake.net for free stories, to stay updated on news and new releases, and to purchase signed copies

ISBN 978-0-9868811-7-6

Cover by MiblArt

All Who Wander Are Lost

Bruce Blake

"Never regret thy fall,
O Icarus of the fearless flight
For the greatest tragedy of them all
Is never to feel the burning light."
- Oscar Wilde

Chapter One

WHEN YOUR GUARDIAN ANGEL and her friend, the archangel Gabriel, tell you to stay put, it's probably a good idea to listen. I should have, but I have inexplicable difficulty with authority figures. It gets me in trouble. A lot.

An old Buick sat to the right of my motel room door looking like it hadn't moved in a decade or so, and it certainly hadn't budged since I checked in; a few other cars were parked in the motel's lot but there were no people. I stepped across the threshold and closed the door behind me, the click of the lock firecracker-loud in the winter night.

I paused. Still no one around. I breathed deep and stepped away from the door, the first time I'd been outside the dingy, musty-smelling room in weeks.

A month ago, the police found a tranny prostitute named Dante Frank dead on a bed in a five-star hotel, hairy chest and hairless vagina exposed for the world to see along with the biblical references his killer carved in his flesh. Dante, whom I'd known as Danielle Francis, was the last victim of the serial killer dubbed the Revelations Reaper by the media. The police had a suspect in the string of killings: me.

I didn't kill any of them but, if the truth be told, their deaths were on me.

Forget the angels telling me to stay indoors, the fact the local news had been flashing an unflattering picture of my face on the screen every night until a week ago should have kept me inside my seedy room. But you know what they say about common sense...it ain't so common.

Icarus Fell: living proof.

I didn't think that because they finally stopped plastering my face all over the six o'clock news they'd stopped looking for me. Every cop in the city likely still carried my picture like they were at war and I was their girl waiting for them back home, but after four weeks in my motel-room-prison, the prospect of remaining inside held as little appeal as being girlfriend to a bunch of cops. I'd spent every moment of the last month thinking about my role in the deaths, wishing things were different. Another minute trapped alone with my guilt might prove one too many.

I slipped away from the motel and down a side street, disappearing in shadows and down alleys wherever I could. The taste of impending snow in the early December air fortified my lungs.

As I ranged farther from the motel, the garbage strewn on the streets and graffiti tags spray-painted on walls—'Big Turk Wuz Here' and other poetic gems—became less frequent until they disappeared completely. I'd made my way to a neighborhood where people cared, a fact which should have rang alarm bells in my head and made me more careful, but the lack of hookers and drug dealers lifted my spirits and my worry ebbed taking caution along with it.

Dumb ass.

I paused at the intersection, the lights of an approaching car reflecting on the frost-rimed pavement as I waited to be sure it would obey the stop sign. Without the fresh air loosening my wits, I'd have waved him through, but freedom made my head light in the way of a non-smoker after a few drags on a cigarette. The car's brakes squeaked as it rolled to a halt. I stepped off the curb and raised a hand in thanks, squinting against the lights, but couldn't see the driver. Hand replaced in pocket, I continued on my way, thinking nothing of it until I heard the hum and chatter of a power window in need of repair.

"Hey, you."

The words weren't spoken with the timbre of someone in need of directions. The caution and worry the beautiful night had leeched from me flooded back; I quickened my pace.

"Stop."

I broke into a run before his engine roared and tires chirped. Cutting across a well-manicured lawn, I hopped a fence, ran through a back yard dominated by an inter-locking brick patio and an in-ground pool emptied for the winter, then vaulted another fence into a rear lane, cursing my stupidity with every step.

Despite a house between us, I heard the car's engine rev and labor as the driver gave chase. I dove through a line of tall shrubs, their branches scratching my face, and into another yard, keeping my flight to places the car couldn't go. Ten minutes of fence-jumping and shrub-diving later, I emerged on a sporadically lit street. Familiar graffiti scrolled across the side of a building; Big Turk and his poor spelling were back. Close to my motel. My lungs labored, the cold air hurting my chest instead of refreshing it as a stitch in my side dug in and grabbed hold. I stopped to catch my breath, bent at the waist, hands grasping knees like the world's worst marathoner run out of steam, but rest didn't last long. A siren wailed behind me and I forced my legs back into action.

I darted into an alley and the all-too-familiar stink of garbage and piss, depression and decay hit me immediately. I'd lost so many days and nights of my youth in alleys like this, sleeping off a bottle of vodka or poking a needle in my arm. I forced the thought from my mind. This was no time to self-analyze by way of shitty memories.

Tires screeched at the mouth of the alley. I didn't look back, my attention taken by a figure stepping out of the shadows into my path. A Carrion, I assumed—a human-shaped demon sent to collect souls and make my life difficult—but I quickly realized the silhouette was smaller and more feminine, leaving two possible people. Angels, really. I halted a few paces beyond arm's-reach in case I was wrong.

"Hey, mister. Long time, no see."

I recognized the voice immediately. The angel stepped into the light and I saw her gingerbread hair, glimpsed the freckled skin of her cheek.

"Gabe."

The Archangel Gabriel is the messenger. She brings scrolls with my assignments inscribed on them: who's scheduled to pass, where, when, and where to take them when it's done.

I couldn't think of a worse time for her to show up.

"Did you miss me?"

Her pure voice echoed off the alley walls and a chorus of swallows which always accompanied her, but that I couldn't see in the dark, chirped and chittered on a fire escape overhead.

"Don't have time right now, Gabe," I said breathlessly and glanced over my shoulder. The alley remained empty, but it wouldn't for much longer.

"Here."

She offered a scroll which hadn't been in her hand a second before.

"Really, Gabe? I don't—" I gestured toward the alley at my back, offered a pleading look. She shook the scroll at me and raised an eyebrow.

I'd learned the hard way that harvesting wasn't the kind of job you could slack off at; the hard way seems to be how I learn pretty much everything. I gave in without any real fight.

My finger brushed hers as I grasped the rolled parchment and an electric charge prickled the hairs on my arm, bringing with it a longing to spend time with her, to be in her presence as long as possible. I nearly forgot the man chasing me.

"Gabe, I—"

She smiled and shrugged. "You don't have time, remember?"

Swallow wings beat the air above my head as she walked away. I stared after her for a second before pulling myself from the angel-induced stupor to look at the scroll in my hand. This was my second assignment since everything went down: the deaths, the media frenzy, the explosion at the church. What happened to souls during my seclusion? Did they make other arrangements or were they okay with everyone going to Hell for a few weeks while I got my wits about me? Great vacation for me, but kind of sucked for everyone else.

Unrolling the scroll unnerved me. After being given one inscribed with my son's name, I couldn't help but hold my breath. Probably would every time I did it.

Shaun Williams.

I set my captive breath free. Didn't know him. The address scrawled on the yellowed parchment wasn't familiar either, but I knew the city well enough to recognize it was close. I read the time of death, then checked my watch.

Two minutes from now.

The sound of shoes hammering pavement reverberated off the alley's brick walls. I got my legs moving again and took a corner, feet tangling in a pile of garbage bags and spilling me to the pavement.

My shoulder hit hard and I skidded a couple of feet along the damp ground, filth snow-plowing onto my jacket. I scrambled to my feet, glanced ahead and behind as the footsteps grew louder, and realized the futility of my flight. Facing my pursuer seemed the only option. Maybe I could talk my way out of it before my appointment came and went.

Damn it.

Bad things happen to good people when I miss appointments. And to bad people; also, the Swiss.

I backed down the alley and didn't have to wait long for the man chasing me. He rounded the corner, avoided the garbage bags which had tripped me, and skidded to a halt in a pool of light cast by a security light mounted high overhead. The dress pants he wore looked a year or so beyond their best-before date; a long wool coat covered a rumpled dress shirt which may never have made a dry cleaner's acquaintance. I might have noticed more but the gun in his hand distracted me.

"Mr. Fell," he said between panted breaths. "If that's really your name."

"It's the name the bastard gave me," I muttered glancing from gun to a face I'd met a few times and seen many more on the news. The muscles in my jaw clenched and released as I silently counted the passing seconds in my head. "We seem to meet under awkward circumstances, don't we, Detective?"

"Sometimes happens between serial killers and cops."

"I didn't kill anyone."

"Right." He leveled the gun, his eternally tired eyes unwavering. "And I'm Serena Williams. Put your hands behind your head."

A little firework went off in my brain, interrupting my mental countdown. He obviously wasn't Serena Williams—wrong sex, wrong skin color, and he didn't look like much of a tennis player—so why pick her out of a thousand possible celebrities to use sarcastically? I chanced pissing him off and stole a peek at my watch: t-minus one minute. My gut wrenched one twist to the right.

If I don't get out of here quick—

The thought cut off half-formed, bullied aside by another. The detective was the lead investigator in the Revelations Reaper case, the guy the newscasts interviewed no matter how uncomfortable he looked on camera, so I'd seen his face a hundred times on TV. And every time they showed him offering his oft-quoted 'no comment', they emblazoned his name on the screen in white letters.

How did I miss it?

Detective Shaun Williams.

I raised an eyebrow. "Detective Williams?"

"Yeah, that's right. Now that we've been properly introduced, put your fucking hands behind your head before I shoot you."

I peered past him, then to both sides. With his name on the scroll in my back pocket, there had to be someone waiting to ambush this man scheduled to die in about forty-five seconds.

"You need to get out of here," I said, eyes still searching the shadows. "You're in danger."

"Me?" He stretched his arm toward me, pushing the barrel closer. "If you don't get your hands up right now, you'll never walk again."

The seconds ticked off in my head, echoing down the hallways of my mind. I gritted my teeth, fought the compulsion to try and save him.

Not my job.

They sent me to retrieve his soul after his death, not prevent it. But so many already died because of me and my poor choices. Maybe this was an opportunity to make amends—with myself, if no one else. My eyes found his and held his gaze for a second; I didn't have much more than that.

"You'll thank me for this later," I murmured and darted toward him, moving faster than he expected an out-of-shape-almost-forty guy like me could.

He squeezed the trigger but I was on him before he got the shot off. The gunshot nearly deafened me, the explosion echoing through my head, ringing in my ears. My arms encircled him, pinning his at his sides, and inertia carried me forward, driving him to the ground. Breath whooshed out of his lungs when we hit, but I didn't let go.

"This is for your own good," I said into his ear. His body jerked but my grip held. The last few seconds counted down in my head.

Five...four...three...two...one.

When I reached zero, I held on a few seconds longer in case my timing was off or my watch was slow. Nothing happened. No gunshot, no one jumping from the shadows; a grand piano didn't drop from a balcony. Nothing.

I leaned back, a hand on his gun arm to prevent him from shooting me. Some thanks that would be for saving his life. I gripped his wrist expecting him to squirm away, but he didn't. His lack of movement should have tipped me something was wrong, but I was too concerned with making sure we weren't about to be attacked to notice. Nothing moved in the shadows, no one approached down the alley.

Could the scroll have been wrong?

Unlikely, but it happened before, when other forces manipulated events. How did I know the same wasn't the case this time?

I didn't.

A small movement caught my eye and I looked left to see a figure standing five yards away. Fear forced bitter, electric saliva into my mouth like I'd bitten down on a piece of aluminum foil, and I snatched the gun from Detective Williams' hand, jerked it toward the silhouette. The man didn't react, but simply stood watching. His presence made a knot form in my stomach which worked its way quickly into the back of my throat. The figure stepped forward into the light and the muscles in my forearm tensed, my finger brushed the trigger. It only took a second to realize he wasn't as opaque as he should be.

This wasn't a man, but a dislodged soul.

"What—?" I began but the lump in my throat got the better of my voice.

My brain finally registered the detective's lack of movement and I looked from the soul to the detective's face. His tired eyes stared up at me blankly; a dark circle of fluid spread across the grungy pavement beneath his head.

"No, I—"

The sight of his glazed eyes hit me like a spinning kick to the gut, stealing my breath and energy. My gun arm sagged, the police-issue .38 resting against my thigh, forgotten. I resisted the urge to shake him by the lapel of his wool coat or slap him awake, call out his name. I already knew what the result would be. The overhead light reflected in the pool of liquid around his head making a grisly halo.

I was responsible for another death.

I shook my head in disbelief and looked back at the spirit. There were no black bags under its eyes or worry lines at the corners of its mouth, but there was no mistaking to whom the soul belonged: except for the felt fedora tilted over the soul's left eye like he'd stepped out of a Mickey Spillane novel, the spirit wore the same clothes.

"I didn't—"

My words stuck again. Or maybe I didn't want to complete the sentence because it would make what happened real. No need to worry, the ghost took care of that piece of business for me.

"You killed me."

Chapter Two

M Y HEAD DIDN'T WANT to stop shaking, like it would change things, reverse time like Superman flying counter-clockwise around the earth to save Lois Lane. I must have looked like one of those bobble heads they give away at baseball games.

"You killed me," the spirit said again and I bit back a spark of anger. *No need to rub it in.*

"But how?" I glanced at the pool of blood under the detective's head and figured I knew how, but my mouth spoke ahead of the thoughts in my head. "I only tackled you."

The apparition crouched beside his former body, two feet separating us, and reached toward the corpse's face but his ethereal hand passed through without effect. Freshly released souls forget such details. A look of frustration crossed his face.

"Do you mind?" The soul gestured toward its earthly head.

"Sure."

Hesitant, I lay the gun down on the pavement beside the detective, suddenly unconvinced that danger had passed. My fingers touched the detective's cooling cheek as I turned his head. The sharply pointed rock it had struck when I tackled him was still embedded in his cranium. I sucked a whistling breath through my teeth.

"Man, I'm sorry." My statement felt woefully inadequate, but it was all I could think of to say.

The spirit shrugged. "An accident."

I nearly opened my mouth to ask why he wasn't angry, but I didn't. I'd seen enough dead people to know they all react differently.

"Yeah, but you're still dead." I removed my hand from the detective's head and let it roll back, the murder weapon protruding out the back stopping it halfway. "And I still killed a cop."

The spirit was staring at me, his gaze sending lancets of guilt through my chest, but he didn't say anything, so I didn't either. We stayed there for probably two minutes, him staring at me and me glancing away and back, away and back, like someone who'd done something wrong and couldn't bear to hold his gaze.

How appropriate.

During the pause, my mind raced: what would Mikey think about this? How badly did I screw up? And, more importantly, what would the repercussions be? Mike sent me on a brief trip to Hell for botching a job once, a trip I didn't like so much. I thought of Gabe and Poe and all the people whose souls ended up condemned because of me. The spirit watched my head swivel back and forth a few times like he really was Serena Williams and I was watching him play a tiny, invisible tennis match, then he tapped me on the shoulder as best a ghost can.

"What do we do now?"

I must have stared at him like he'd spoken some indecipherable ghost language because he felt compelled to rephrase the question.

"What happens next?"

I finally focused on him, grabbed the gun from where I'd set it down, and stood, feet straddling his corpse. The spirit stood, too.

"Now you go to Heaven."

I started down the alley, but after a few steps, realized he hadn't followed, so I stopped and looked back over my shoulder.

"*You're* going to take me to Heaven?"

His disbelieving tone irked me a bit—*why shouldn't it be me who takes him to Heaven?*—but I attempted to keep my irked-ness from showing in my response. Accident or not, I'd just killed the man; he deserved some compassion.

"Sort of. I do the earthly part." I resumed walking. "You better come, there might be others looking for you, and they're not as nice as me."

An ominous statement coming from the guy who just killed you.

With the gun held in front of me like they do on all the cop shows, I peeked around the corner, worried I'd thrown the cosmic plan out of whack and an assailant would jump us at any moment. None did. We emerged onto a side street empty of traffic and, glancing both directions, hurriedly crossed to the shadows on the other side. We walked in silence for a while, the dead policeman's soul trailing a step or two behind, following uncertainly. After a few blocks, enough time and distance had passed that I figured we were safe, so I lowered the gun and decided to break the uncomfortable silence.

"Sorry about what happened back there," I said over my shoulder hoping he'd take my attempt at conversation as an invitation to walk with me. Having a dead guy walking at my heels made me a little uncomfortable.

"Everyone's time comes," he answered nonchalantly, stepping up beside me.

"Yeah, but it doesn't happen that way."

"Really? How do you know?"

"It's not what I do. I'm a harvester not a...Hell, I'm the guy who collects the crops, not the one who chops them down."

"Maybe this time was different."

I stopped and he strode a step farther before realizing and doing the same.

"Look, killing ain't my business. They give me a scroll, I collect the soul." It sounded like I might have come up with a slogan, though the one about the crops sounded more manly. This one rhymed, though. "Simple."

"Twenty-five years of police work taught me things are rarely simple." He scratched his stubbly chin, probably a left over habit since I couldn't imagine a spirit having an itch. "This scroll tells you how the person will die? Who kills them?"

I gritted my teeth. The answers coming to mind lacked a certain politeness, so I held them at bay behind my lips. Sometimes I try new things.

"Not everything's a crime to solve."

Fucking detectives, I wanted to add. Our conversation ended abruptly, leaving me feeling lonely. After a month in solitary, it was good to hear a voice which didn't belong to me or a television character. Another part of me rejoiced at the end of the discussion—he'd voiced some things already on my mind, things I'd avoided asking. Things like:

Where was the guy who was supposed to kill Detective Shaun Williams?

There wasn't a soul—living or otherwise—within blocks when I ended the man's life on the fortuitously-placed sharp stone. That small detail hadn't escaped my notice amongst worry of repercussions; I'd chosen to ignore it. Now he'd fucked that up for me.

Gabe wouldn't have set me up, would she?

I considered it. The archangel didn't seem to have a nasty bone in her body, assuming angels had bones. Between her love for time spent in human form and the delicate swallows that followed her everywhere, imagining her as anything but gentle and kind was difficult.

No, not Gabe. Michael.

Anger stirred in me and I realized it was the first time I'd thought of him like that: Michael instead of Mike or Mikey. I'd transformed his name back to fullness the way a parent uses their child's middle name when they're angry. It never happened to me—no parents, and no one bothered giving me a middle name to use so they could illustrate their dissatisfaction. But the act of elongating his moniker fit as I thought about what the head archangel may have done, the way I might have been manipulated.

"I'm sorry I didn't believe you."

I only half-heard the detective-soul's words. When I looked at him, the muscles in my jaw bunched as I strained to contain the anger bubbling into my throat.

Not his fault.

"What?"

"When you were in jail, I didn't believe you. I'm sorry."

"Why would you?" I shrugged, his words distracting me from the conclusion to which I'd jumped. "How often do you meet someone who's been dead six months?"

He chuckled. "Not very often."

A couple of blocks passed beneath our feet as I related my story, at least the after-death part. No point telling him all the sordid details of my life, he probably discovered them while working the case, anyway. My story included his head connecting with the sharp rock but stopped short of my suspicions about Mike. He listened, nodding occasionally, until I finished, then we walked in silence for a while.

"Do you take me right to the pearly gates?"

"Don't know if there are any." My turn to chuckle. It must have seemed odd to him: an agent of Heaven who's never been there. "Judging by the address they gave me, it seems I'm taking you to a warehouse."

· · · ● · ● ● · · ·

I guessed right. The address for the drop was a patio furniture storehouse. We wandered past stacks of colored plastic chairs and folded umbrellas, tables piled together like building blocks placed by the hands of a giant child, and cases of cushions reaching almost to the ceiling. The detective's soul walked beside me wearing a look nearer to the disappointment end of the scale than to wonder. Understandable, but he should have seen the motel where I first met Mikey. At least no one turned tricks in the warehouse.

It didn't take long to find the angel assigned to escort Detective Williams on the rest of his journey. The corner of the huge room where the angel sat on a green molded plastic chair was more brightly lit than the rest of the storage area, whether because of the pristine white of his Mr. Clean-style clothes and pale skin, or because celestial beings actually glow, I couldn't say. The angel stood as we approached.

"Welcome, Shaun Williams," the close-to-albino said in his sing-song voice.

The escorts—they probably had a more suitable label that made them sound less like high-priced prostitutes, but I hadn't bothered to learn it—all looked identical: snow-white duds, snow-white hair, translucent skin. They functioned only to take souls I delivered the rest of the way to Heaven and, judging from the discussions I'd attempted in the past, they were interested in little else.

Try again.

"Tell Mikey I want to see him."

The angel gazed at me, a question plain in his eyes. He didn't move or speak.

"Michael. You know, the archangel? Second in charge? Tell him Icarus Fell wants to see him."

Detective Williams' soul went to the angel's side and turned to me.

"Thank you," he said. I stared at him a second, confused, then the anger and guilt roiling inside me spilled over like a pot of potatoes left to boil with the lid on.

"You're thanking me?" My throat clamped down on the words, compressing them until they came out like short, squat men wielding hammers. "I killed you, don't you understand that? Someone—or something—manipulated me like a goddamn puppet with their hand up my ass and now you're dead, Detective."

The spirit shrugged and smiled, increasing my ire. "I had nothing left but my work; someone else will do it. They won't miss me. Thank you."

The angel took Detective Shaun Williams' soul by the arm like he intended to lead him away, but they didn't move. Instead, their forms wavered like on a television with poor reception, then they started to fade.

"Tell Michael I want to see him," I yelled. In my final glimpse of them before they disappeared, the angel raised his arm and pointed over my shoulder.

"Tell him yourself."

I didn't turn around immediately. The hair on my arms, on the back of my neck, stood up; hyperactive butterflies fluttered madly in my gut, crashing into the walls of my stomach. Did I really want to see Mikey after all?

No point putting it off.

I pivoted slowly, drawing out the movement.

I'd have felt his unmistakable presence if I didn't give in to anger, but I did, and the pressure pushing against me, the warmth bordering on uncomfortable, went unnoticed until I looked upon him.

The archangel stood ten feet away, thigh-sized arms crossed in front of his chest. The buttons of his button-down collar were undone; the blond hair draped across his shoulders glowed against the stop-sign red shirt. His shirttail hung loose over black dress pants; black-and-red wing-tip shoes completed his questionable fashion statement. All this received only brief consideration because his expression captured my attention.

The archangel Michael—the biblical right hand of God—looked pissed.

Chapter Three

I N THE TIME SINCE I'd seen Mikey, I'd forgotten what an imposing figure he was. Last I saw him, he was wielding a golden sword as big as me, protecting me from the angel of death, something one would normally not fail to recall. He didn't look any worse for wear after the epic battle with Azrael at the church: his blond locks flowed in waves over his shoulders; his muscles strained against the silk of his shirt as though Michelangelo had sculpted a tribute to David's bigger, body-building brother. His presence both scared the shit out of me and thrilled me to my spine.

"You were looking for me."

His voice came out flat, something which took considerable effort for an angel. His words sounded more statement than question.

"Yes."

He spread his arms in a 'here I am' gesture. I parted my lips but my lungs refused to aid my vocal chords in forming words. My mouth snapped shut, teeth clicking, and I sniffed a deliberate breath through my nostrils, forcing my lungs to do the work they're employed to do. The fresh pumpkin pie smell of the archangel tested my resolve, but my vocal chords gave in to my wishes on the second attempt.

"Did you send me to kill Detective Williams?"

He regarded me with flickering golden eyes. The pause wasn't to give him time to formulate the proper response—I didn't believe for a second Mikey or any other angel was ever at a loss for words—he wanted a different effect. I shivered a little, giving it to him.

"It matters not how a man's body dies when it is the soul's time to go on."

"That doesn't answer my question."

"Does it not?"

I bit down hard enough that the cords in my neck stood out. The prickle on my skin vanished taking with it the thrill in my stomach and the shortened, excited breath the archangel's presence brought. Their disappearance left anger and guilt alone to brood over my actions, my decisions. And Mike's.

"This isn't what I signed up for," I seethed between clenched teeth. "I'm not your goddamned tool."

"No, Icarus Fell, you are my God-saved tool."

His comment spun my brain in a tight little circle. It took a moment to regain my equilibrium as a wave of nausea swept through my midsection.

"I'm supposed to save people, not kill them," I said, much of the gusto gone from my voice. "Too many people died because of me."

"You did save him." Mikey tipped his head indicating the spot where the detective and his escort were a minute before. "What is the problem?"

"The problem is: if I didn't kill him, I wouldn't have needed to harvest him."

The archangel appeared to take one step but suddenly stood directly in front of me, his chest brushing mine. The fierce heat radiating from him brought sweat to my brow instantly. I looked up into his face; I'd estimated Mikey at six and a half feet tall but, as he stood before me, he seemed considerably taller. His heat leaked into my chest, seeped through my clothes and flesh, warmed my internal organs, and threatened to boil my blood.

Did he mean for it to calm me or discourage me? It accomplished both. And more.

"God's universe is a place of give and take, but it is He alone who gives and takes. You, like all others, are part of the mechanism He uses to do so."

"I'm no killer," I snapped and, before putting thought to my action, shoved against Mike's chest with both hands.

Really bad idea. I may as well have pushed the Empire State building. Michael remained stationary as the shove jammed my wrists back painfully, then sent me to the floor directly on my tail bone, rocketing a flare of pain up my spine. When I looked up a second later, the archangel already loomed over me.

"Every effect has a cause." He knelt in front of me and the fire in his eyes felt like lasers burning into mine. "Every action a result. Do you think nothing you do has consequences? Do you think you live this second life—this gift I gave you—without connection to any other living being?"

I stared at him, breathless. My head might have moved in a gesture signifying I didn't think that was the case, but I was trying so hard to keep from shaking, I couldn't be sure. I searched desperately for a sarcastic response but came up lacking. Between the jarring impact of falling on my ass and the archangel's proximity, my senses were rattled almost to the point of uselessness. He could have told me Martians had invaded New Orleans or that the *Titanic* was a rowboat and I'd have agreed with him.

"Get up," he said as he stood.

I scrambled to my feet wanting nothing more at that moment than to make him happy with me. He grabbed my arm, his fingers hot as embers, but they didn't burn. Instead, electricity coursed through me like I'd been struck by lightning. My body stiffened, eyeballs rolled back in their sockets. My eyes closed and I felt as though we were moving.

When I pried my eyelids open, the patio furniture warehouse was gone and I had to squint against the daylight. We stood on a busy street corner, a place downtown I'd have recognized if the archangel's mode of transportation hadn't left my head spinning.

"Where...where are we?" I ventured through dried lips.

He raised his finger and pointed. Across the street, obscured by traffic flowing past, a woman with long, chestnut hair stood holding hands with a five-year-old boy. She watched the cars zipping by, waiting for a break so they could cross; the boy held a small toy, something tiny enough for him to conceal in his left hand.

Should I know these people?

I didn't think so. Why would he bring me here?

"Why are we here?"

The words were barely clear of my lips when the boy dropped his toy—a red dinky car, it turned out. It tumbled from his hand, bounced once on the edge of the curb, pirouetted in the air, and came to rest in the street. The boy released his mother's hand and bent to retrieve it but over-balanced. The woman shrieked as her son fell in front of traffic. She leaped from the curb and caught the boy under his arms, threw him clear of the on-coming car which struck her before the driver had time to remember his car had brakes. The impact catapulted her ten yards, flying over the boy, until her head impacted a light post and flipped her body three hundred-and-sixty degrees like a rag doll caught in a wind storm.

My mouth fell open.

Pedestrians jumped away from the woman's body, one man narrowly avoiding contact with her ruined head. The boy lay on the sidewalk wailing, his arm scraped when his mother threw him to safety, no idea she'd given her life to save him. As her body came to a stop in a jumbled heap, her soul separated from it and a man in a black trench coat and hat pulled down over his eyes stepped out of the crowd. He ignored the child and the woman's corpse, instead making his way toward the woman's soul where she stood halfway between the boy and her body, looking from one to the other, unsure what to do.

I recognized the man immediately.

"Carrion," I blurted and went to step off the curb.

I didn't think I'd get there before him to rescue her from a trip to Hell, but I'd give it my best try. Or would have if Michael's hand on my arm didn't stop me. The shock of his touch stiffened my body again and the world went blank.

Upon the return of my senses, I found the sun still shining, but the harsh smell of car exhaust had been replaced by the bite of brine in the air. I turned to ask Mikey what-the-Hell happened, but the words never formed. Water stretched around us in every direction—water, water everywhere as Samuel Taylor Coleridge said in his poem, or Bruce Dickinson from Iron Maiden quoted in their Mariner-inspired song. I glanced at my feet and was shocked to find water beneath us, too.

"How...?"

No point finishing the question—what do silly things like the laws of nature mean to an archangel? I might not know an angel's full capabilities but by now you'd think I'd at least expect the unexpected. No quick learner, me; another of my shortfalls.

I searched the horizon and saw nothing: no boats, no land, no wayward surfers or swimmers; nary a threatening shark fin cut through the water.

Maybe he brought me here for the view.

"There."

I'd have referred to the craft plummeting toward the ocean as a Cessna, but I don't know much about planes. A plume of black smoke trailed behind the single engine, concealing the cockpit and leaving a widening smudge across the sky like squid ink in water. As it plunged seaward, I imagined how the pilot must feel watching death approach, knowing he couldn't prevent it. Sort of how I'd felt with a gorilla-sized mugger on my back plunging a knife into my kidneys.

Nice to have something in common with the people you work with.

The plane hit two hundred meters away with the biggest splash I've ever seen, like a mechanical giant belly-flopping from the high-diving board. We rose and dipped with the wave but my shoes remained dry—the pilot wasn't so lucky. The impact obliterated the craft, sending pieces of airplane shooting into the sky. When the wave settled, a million pieces of debris bobbed on the surface of the sea, one of them the body of a man.

"We should help him."

I said the words already knowing they were meaningless. It's not my job to help not in the paramedic sense of the word, but I meant his soul, not his body. Mikey remained silent. Seconds later, a not-quite-opaque figure sat up from the dead pilot, using his corpse as a life raft. I looked from the spirit to Mike and back. I hadn't received a scroll with the man's name, but that didn't mean he should be left to...whatever happens to souls left alone too long.

I took one step away from the archangel and went headlong into the sea; salt water filled my mouth and nose, gagging me; cold assaulted my flesh. I thrashed and struggled, so surprised by the need to swim that I forgot how. My head broke the surface giving me a second to gulp a breath past the briny taste in my mouth before I went under again. The first time I died, the knife wounds were unexpected and painful, but drowning was an entirely different kind of trauma. I kicked and stroked as my mind reeled, wondering if I could die again.

Michael pulled me out with one hand, dangling me above the water like a fishing trip trophy—the one he wished had gotten away. I sputtered until my lungs cleared and breath filled my chest again.

"There is nothing you can do."

I barely heard his words above the buzzing in my ears. After hanging there shaking my head to clear the water, I realized the noise wasn't an audio reaction to my near-second-death experience, but the sound of an outboard motor.

Mikey set me back beside him and I looked across the still-undulating sea at a speed boat which, in keeping with its name, approached rapidly. Its black hull cut through the water; two black-clad men piloted the boat toward the crash site and its floating non-survivor.

Carrions. Again.

The boat pulled up beside the soul floating on his corpse-canoe and one of the Carrions leaned over the side and offered his hand. The man's spirit accepted eagerly, like a drowning man offered a hand, strangely enough. If he knew where his rescuers intended to take him, he probably wouldn't have been so keen. They pulled him in, the motor roared, and they sped off toward the horizon.

With the boat's wake lapping beneath our feet, I turned to demand an explanation, but the world wavered before I opened my mouth, then faded to black. In the darkness, I wondered if the world would return or if this was my final punishment.

•••••••••••

I paced, amending my path occasionally to avoid errant umbrella stands and waterproof cushions fallen from their piles. Anger and guilt roiled and twisted in my gut; I breathed deep, attempting to control it. There was nothing to gain by venting my ire at the archangel, I'd learned that lesson. Michael stood nearby, arms crossed, waiting. Finally, I stopped and faced him, mimicking his pose.

"Why didn't you let me help them?"

"They were beyond help."

"But I was right there. I could've done something."

"Their time has passed, Icarus. They died while you hid in your motel."

"Will you call me Ric, for Christ's sake?"

He glared at me—presumably for taking the name of the boss' son in vain—but didn't respond. I held his gaze feeling like a man engaged in a staring contest with a cat. Time crawled past, my discomfort increasing as each second ticked by.

"Why? Why would you show me that?"

"So you would see that death happens, Icarus Fell. Whether you are there or not, death happens."

"I know that. I can't be everywhere, I'm not God."

"You most certainly are not."

I fought the urge to smack the smug look off his face, which might equate to committing suicide-by-archangel. Instead, I bit down hard on my back teeth so my next words came out poorly enunciated.

"But there are souls who went to Hell because of me. That's not right."

Mikey shrugged and the action of his shoulders rising and falling acted like a pump inflating my anger.

"What is it you humans say? 'Shit happens'?"

"But they wouldn't have died if I'd harvested the priest's soul, like I was told. It's my fault."

He looked like he might shrug again and I gritted my teeth, readying myself in case I had to slap him and he had to hurt me. Lucky for both of us, he chose to speak instead.

"Every decision we make, good or bad, yields a consequence."

"Will you stop fucking saying that!?"

I yanked my gaze back from his and paced again, feet hammering the concrete floor like a child denied dessert. I realized I could do nothing on my own to correct things, but that didn't mean nothing could be done. If anyone possessed the ability to do it, the blond-haired behemoth occupying the lawn furniture warehouse with me was the guy.

I stopped and faced him.

"Help me get them back."

His features softened; he tilted his head slightly to the right and reached his hand out to me like a peace offering.

"Icarus." He spoke slowly, like he provided explanation to someone with a severe mental issue. My hackles stirred. "You have seen Hell before. You cannot possibly want to go again."

"I don't *want* to; I *have* to."

"No."

My hands bunched into fists but his expression didn't change.

"You have to help me."

"I *have* to do nothing."

He crossed the space between us, his hand stretched toward my shoulder in a fatherly gesture. I dodged to avoid his touch but his fingers found me. The electric shock of his touch flowed down my arm, spilled into my chest, exciting nerve endings and spasming muscles.

"You will go back to your motel and await Gabriel's scrolls. You will do nothing else but wait."

He squeezed my shoulder and a vision flashed before me: a lake of souls writhing in agony, their moans gathering to a cacophony threatening to burst my ear drums. He let the pressure off and the vision faded but the cold sweat it brought to my forehead remained.

"Do you understand?"

I nodded minutely—all I could manage. I suddenly knew what it was like to be the hapless *Star Wars* stormtroopers: 'these aren't the droids you're looking for.'

Mikey stepped back, his form wavering in the dim warehouse. My nerves tingled for a few seconds before the excitement subsided leaving a gap in my being which ached for his touch to fill it. It was always that way with an angel's touch: impossible to get used to, impossible to avoid, impossible to do anything but want more. My shoulders sagged and it required effort to keep my head from lolling forward. When the last shadow of him disappeared, my chin drooped and I collapsed onto a conveniently placed stack of cushions.

Minutes ticked by while I lay there, each of them tugging at me to get up and get on with my death. I'd seen what happens to unharvested souls; I knew Mikey's intention in showing me the vision was to scare me off the idea of going to Hell, but it had the opposite effect.

I wasn't responsible for every soul sent south—I couldn't save them all—but there was the matter of the ones who'd been damned because of my poor decisions, my laziness, my ego. I couldn't let them stay there.

As I reclined, staring up at the girder-and-pipe-filled ceiling from the not-too-comfortable cushions, recovering from the archangel's touch and the latest episode of Hell-o-vision, I didn't know how I'd go about getting them back, only that I would.

Somehow.

Chapter Four

P OE KNOCKED AGAIN AND waited. Someone walked by on the sidewalk and cat-called her but she ignored the man's slurred words. The first snowflake of the season floated lazily past her nose making her smile: she had loved snow since childhood, and the love carried on beyond life into the sweet hereafter. She peeked over her shoulder at more big, puffy flakes drifting down. The sight relaxed her.

She turned back to the door and knocked a third time.

A minute later she stepped away, looked up and down the street, some of the calm brought by the snowflakes gone. The man who had cat-called her leaned against a lamp post a block down, vomiting; the street was otherwise empty.

Where is he?

Poe died too young to have a child, but being guardian angel for Icarus Fell, she thought she knew how it felt. Michael had left no doubt he wasn't to leave his room, yet here she stood, wondering where Icarus was. There were only a few possibilities: restaurant, cafe, bar, or Trevor's. She glanced at her watch: eleven-thirty pm.

Too late for a cafe or to see his son. She tapped her chin with her index finger. *I hope he's not drinking again.*

Michael said he might be upset—the reason she was looking for him—but could it be bad enough for him to hit the bottle again? Not with Trevor back in his life.

What would upset him?

Michael didn't say; he considered the detail above her pay-grade.

Unsure where to go, she headed left down the street; searching was better than waiting. The snow continued with flakes the size of cotton balls. Poe caught one on her tongue, one of life's joys an angel rarely gets to appreciate. The last time she'd experienced snow while in human form was eight or nine years before, when Icarus passed out in someone's back yard. She'd dragged him out of the yard and onto the sidewalk for someone to find and call 911. He'd been a dead weight, and she remembered being thankful for the packed snow under him lending aid. Snow: helpful and beautiful.

Poe's first destination lay at the end of the next block, and as she breathed deeply, inhaling the snow's crisp freshness, the odor of fried food encroached—a sure sign she neared the Denny's Icarus liked to frequent before his motel arrest.

Traffic sent the massive snowflakes swirling, hurling exhaust and noise into the winter-crisp, fried-food night. Halfway down the block, the urge to turn and run, to find a place away from traffic and people and responsibility, grabbed Poe. She'd daydreamed about lying in a field, snowflakes falling on her until they buried her, transforming her into a hill in the landscape of winter instead of a cog in Heaven's machine. No more worries, no pressure, no responsibility.

And no Michael. Or Icarus.

Poe shook her head as she reached to pull the restaurant's door open, clearing snowflakes from her blond hair and silly fantasies from her thoughts. Escaping sounded wonderful, but could she desert Icarus? Could she bear never seeing Michael again?

No to both.

Crossing the threshold into the restaurant was like passing through a force field separating calm from chaos. Behind her, traffic hummed rhythmically past, its cadence constant, while ahead glasses clinked, silverware jingled, people chatted—loud, inconstant, nerve-jangling. Somewhere near the back of the restaurant a plate crashed to the floor eliciting a sarcastic cheer from a few patrons. Poe let the door swing shut behind her and stepped into the clamor, her nerves set on-edge by the noise. She glanced around the room and observed a man leaning forward on his table, apparently asleep; a group of teens sneaking sips from a bottle hidden inside a brown paper bag; tables-full of men and women talking, eating, laughing. In the far corner, away from everyone else, she spied Icarus Fell sprawled alone across the bench of a booth designed to seat six, a full cup of coffee untouched on the table in front of him. She waved, but despite the fact he looked right at her, he didn't acknowledge her.

Maybe he didn't see me.

Poe breathed deep, nearly choking on the greasy odor of French fries, fried eggs and superbird sandwiches. She crossed the floor, breath held, the thought of speaking with Icarus and ordering an extra-thick chocolate shake pushing her on.

"Hey, stranger," she sing-songed as she slid onto the bench across from him. Icarus looked at her but didn't smile.

"Hey."

"What's going on?"

Icarus glanced down at the coffee cup, wiped away a line of coffee which had run down the side with his thumb, but didn't answer.

"Michael said I should drop by and see you. Why aren't you in your room?"

"Michael," Icarus repeated, disdain plain in his voice. A knot of dread crept into Poe's chest. "What does he care?"

"He cares. He just shows it his own way."

"Right."

Poe glanced over her shoulder, searching for a server from whom to order a shake and interrupt the unenjoyable conversation. She disliked it when Icarus spoke badly of Michael or vice-versa.

"I need your help."

She turned to find Icarus had abandoned the survey of his mug in favor of her; his gaze on her brought a giggle to her lips.

"That's what I'm here for, silly. I'm your guardian angel."

"Good."

"Did you want to talk about something? Is it Michael?"

"Not Mike. He wouldn't help, that's why I need you."

"He wouldn't? Why not?"

"Because I want to go to Hell."

Poe felt the blood drain from her face; her fingers and toes went cold. She opened her mouth with no intention of speaking. When she realized it happened, she forced it shut again. Images flashed through her mind of winged things with twisted limbs and melted faces. She closed her eyes to make them leave.

"What can I get you?"

The server's words startled her. She opened her eyes and looked up into the woman's plump, fifty-something face, half-expecting the face of a monster to be waiting to take her order. When it wasn't, she still struggled to find words to answer.

"She'll have a chocolate shake. Extra thick."

"Anything else?"

"That's it."

The woman left and Poe looked back at Icarus, her lips quivering, finally forming a word.

"Why?"

"Because there are souls condemned to an eternity of torture who shouldn't be there. They're in Hell because of me, not because they deserve to be there."

She grasped the edge of her seat hard enough that her knuckles went white. She made herself relinquish her grip and breathe a steady breath through her nose.

"This is why Michael thought you'd be upset. He told you not to go."

"He said he wouldn't help."

"Then you can't go."

"But I am." He leaned forward, elbows resting on the table, and she sniffed to see if he'd been drinking. It didn't smell like it, but the odor of coffee and fried food made it difficult to be sure. "And you're going to help me."

"No," she said. A whisper. "I can't."

"You have to."

She shook her head; Icarus' eyebrows canted toward his nose, lines formed on his forehead. Poe leaned away from him, her back pressed against the booth's cushion.

"You said it yourself: you're my guardian angel. It's your job to help me."

"It's my job to keep you safe, but not...not there. Not if Michael said no."

Icarus slammed his open palm against the table slopping coffee over the edge of his mug; the impact made Poe jump. She pushed herself harder against the seat back.

"Damn it, Poe. Whose side are you on?"

She forced her lips into a thin, taut line for fear if she opened her mouth the word 'Michael's' might come out and anger him further. But her silence provided the same effect. Icarus rose from the booth, hip bumping the corner of the table and spilling more coffee. Standing, he leaned toward her, hands braced on the end of the table. Poe fought the urge to cower.

"I'm going with or without you. Will you help?"

The guardian angel stared at him, eyes wide, unwilling to answer. The muscles in his jaw bulged and she thought he'd get angry with her. Instead, he straightened, turned toward the door and stomped away. Poe shifted in her seat to watch him pick his way between the tables before being slowed by a crowd milling about near the door.

"Here's your shake, sweetie."

Poe looked at the waitress and ventured an unsuccessful smile.

"Is your friend done?"

She nodded.

"He barely touched it. Spilled more than he drank, I think."

The woman picked up the mug and used a cloth hanging from her apron to clean up the spilled coffee. She took a step to leave then stopped.

"Are you alright?"

This time Poe forced the corner of her mouth to turn up a bit and nodded.

"Well, let me know if you need anything else, honey."

The waitress left and Poe turned to look for Icarus again. He was gone. She sank back into her seat and contemplated her milk-shake: the curly-cue of whipped cream topping it, the patina of frost on the side of the metal overflow cup. She considered going after him but realized that she had no idea where he might go, what he might do. After all the years she'd watched over him, all the things they'd been through, this time she felt out of her league. She'd seen Hell and it was too big and too bad a problem for her.

She didn't feel like drinking a chocolate shake anymore.

· · ●·●●·● ● · ·

The faces differed, but the setting remained unchanged. A foursome of men in their twenties occupied the table by the huge television where Marty, Todd, Phil and I used to sit. Countless nights passed as we drank and debated whatever sport was in season, back before a mad man raised from the dead took their lives. Before two of them went to Hell because of me. Before the Giants somehow managed to beat the Patriots for the Superbowl for a second time.

Fucking Eli Manning.

Sully, the bar's namesake, was conspicuous by his absence. A woman I'd never seen before concocted my vodka sodas with a lime wedge from behind the bar normally patrolled by the red-headed bar owner. I picked up my current drink—the fifth double—and swirled the oily-looking lime juice floating atop the vodka into kaleidoscopic patterns, searching for meaning in it like it was an alcoholic Rorschach test. I raised the glass toward my lips but stopped part way.

I shouldn't be doing this.

The liquor burned my throat as I gulped it down then waved the bartender over.

"Another one, please."

"Good enough."

She poured my drink, set it on the tattered coaster in front of me, then took the ten spot I offered. She made change as I picked up the drink and twirled on my stool to survey the room. I didn't recognize anyone. Even if I did, none of them would recognize me, it had been that way since Mike brought me back to harvest souls. My ex-wife, my drinking buddies, even my son hadn't known me. Sister Mary Therese was the only person who saw through the facade shrouding me from those who once knew me, and she'd ended up dead, too. Because of me.

At least I saved her from damnation.

I squeezed the lime wedge over the vodka soda and dropped it in, then licked juice from my fingers. Poe would be disappointed if she knew I was here, but she could have stopped it by agreeing to help. What good is a guardian angel who's unwilling to keep you safe when you decide to go to Hell?

I downed half the drink in one gulp and savored the feel of it muddling my head.

I don't need her anyway.

But Poe would be looking for me; she wouldn't leave me to take a cruise through Hell without at least trying to talk me out of it. It wouldn't work, though. Eight people died because of me, and although I harvested three, five souls languished in Hell who didn't belong there. Maybe Hell wasn't all biblical fire-and-brimstone, but it wasn't unicorns-and-blowjobs, either.

I finished my drink and thumped the empty glass on the bar. I determined to leave the change as a tip, then stood and required the edge of the bar to keep me from wobbling.

Maybe I shouldn't have ordered doubles.

"Are you all right, sir?"

"Fine."

"Can I call you a cab?"

I wondered briefly if, when I told her I did, she'd say 'you're a cab', then waved my hand dismissively and only stumbled once on my way to the door. Outside, a dusting of snow had collected on the ground, and the white stuff continued to fall. I hiked my collar up and wondered how, in this winter wonderland, a guy might find his way to Hell.

Chapter Five

THE SNOW STOPPED DURING the night but, since I didn't crawl out of bed until after noon, I couldn't say exactly when it did. The guy behind the desk of the motel I stumbled into after leaving Sully's tried to charge me for a second day—check out time was eleven—but I convinced him a couple of bucks for his own pocket was a better choice.

Two inches of fluffy powder crunched under my feet and billowy clouds hung over the city threatening more. By the time I reached the park, it was criss-crossed by tracks marring the winter wonderland, but a layer of untouched snow covered the bench next to the pond. I cleared a spot for my ass and sat down to commune with the ducks, the bag of bread I'd bought on the way dangling in my hand.

My banishment had precluded me from visiting the place where Father Dominic took Sister Mary Therese's life. I stared out at the pond, the ducks amending their paths toward me, and felt thankful I'd gotten the Sister in time; I couldn't have forgiven myself if the woman who'd been so good to me—to everyone in the world—went to Hell because I was a vindictive prick.

I shifted on the bench and felt snow melting through my pants as I looked over my shoulder at the near-empty park. No one was in the meadow rolling balls of snow into Parson Brown yet: too early in the year.

I shouldn't be here.

The police would likely consider me the prime suspect in the death of Detective Williams. I didn't care. Soon, I'd be gone to Hell to reverse what I'd done. Somehow.

And I might not come back.

Heart brimming with remorse, I leaned forward and tossed a chunk of bread onto the webfoot-trampled snow at the edge of the pond. Three green-headed drakes and two brown females flapped and quacked to retrieve the food. The sound reverberated in my aching head.

One more excellent reason not to drink.

This spot was Sister Mary-Therese's favorite, feeding the ducks one of her most-loved pastimes. Whether the ducks survived the winter without her donations didn't worry me—I was here because feeding them made me feel connected to her, so I threw another piece of bread despite my hangover's protestations. My choices for connection were lacking these days, so feeling connected to someone—even someone dead, even ducks—seemed particularly important.

A tiny avalanche started in the upper limbs of the ancient willow over-hanging the pond, the tumbling snow collecting and growing as it sieved through the lower branches. I looked up and saw the flutter of wings amongst the latticework of branches, but couldn't see the bird causing the disturbance. I squinted, shielded my eyes, and saw movement in the top of the tree; about a dozen birds had taken up perches high in its branches. Their presence lifted my mood as I sensed someone on the bench beside me.

Gabe.

I faced her, happy to have someone to talk to, though her arrival meant another scroll, another death, more work. When I saw the woman seated beside me, the greeting tickling the edge of my tongue died an early death.

Instead of Gabe's pixie-cut gingerbread hair, golden eyes and freckles, the woman beside me wore her black hair long and straight, framing her blue eyes and pale cheeks. A stud shone below her lower lip and part of a tattoo that looked like it might be the end of a dragon's tail coiled around the top of her bare arm. I didn't know who she was, but her lack of warm clothes on a chilly day told me what she was.

"Hi," she said smiling.

"Who are you?"

A bird perched in the tree squawked as if chastising me for my lack of politeness. The woman didn't take the same offense and extended her hand.

"Piper."

"Piper. As in—"

"Like the Pied Piper. I'm not too fond of rats, though. Or children."

"And you're an—" I glanced around to ensure no one was within earshot. "An angel?"

"Oh, see? They said you were a smart one, and they were right."

In spite of the sarcasm smothering her words like an excess of butter on a slice of toast, a blush came to my cheeks.

"Why are you here?"

She leaned back, one arm draped across the back of the bench, and gazed into my eyes. I couldn't have looked away if my clothing was on fire.

"They sent me."

"They who?"

"You know...them." She raised her eyes skyward.

My eyes flickered toward the billowy clouds, then back. She didn't mean the clouds, I was pretty sure. No surprise there; only one question remained.

"Why?"

"To watch out for you. They feel your current guardian isn't doing the job well."

My heart jumped. "Poe?"

"Right. Poe."

"I don't understand."

She admired her manicure, keeping me in suspense a few seconds. I leaned toward her, drawn in like a boy scout waiting for the scary part of the campfire story.

"I'm not in the know on this sort of thing, but I've heard rumors she's not always there for you."

"That's ridiculous. She's my guardian angel. She's always there, watching over me."

"Yeah? How did life go for you?"

"Well—"

"Mmm hmm. And what about when the priest died?"

"She was there when I went to harvest Father Dominic."

A knot formed in my gut: guilt and worry and now suspicion, too. If this kept up, my future surely involved an ulcer.

"Yes, she was."

I opened my mouth, fully intending to mock her for her ludicrous accusations, but her expression showed no sign of jest, no hint of putting me on. I hesitated, thinking about what she'd said.

Why didn't Poe make sure I took his soul? She could have prevented everything.

The knot expanded, forcing itself through my midsection, constricting my chest. I wanted to look away from the woman, maybe turn and run from her words, but the way the light glinted on the stud below her lip held me rapt. She waited for me to speak but my reeling mind failed to remember a stitch of the English language, so she carried on.

"Frankly, whenever she's there, things go awry. Isn't it odd Carrions show up to so many of your harvests?"

I felt my forehead crease.

"I—I never..."

My words ran out. A few birds perched in the tree took to the air around the willow, then settled back in. Sometimes I'd thought Poe wasn't the best guardian angel, but I assumed Carrions always showed up when someone died, assigned to the case like me.

Piper leaned closer and spoke in a whisper. "You know she's been to Hell, don't you?"

"She's hinted about her past, but—"

"That's why she won't help. It's also why I'm here."

I stared at her a few seconds, my insides twisted with emotion and confusion. Poe never seemed to intentionally wrong me and always appeared to have the best intentions. I'd grown to like her in spite of her penchant for always doing what Mikey said. But what this Piper woman said made some sense. Some.

"What do you mean 'it's why you're here'?"

A bird fluttered out of the tree and landed on her shoulder; it was of similar size to the swallows which accompanied Gabe, but lacked the color. Instead of a dazzling blue-green back and white breast, this bird was a uniform black with a sharp beak, like a miniature raven. It eyed me; I expected it to utter a tiny 'nevermore'.

"I'm going to help you rescue your friends."

I shook my head to clear whatever clogged my ears and made me hear her incorrectly. The guilt and worry bundled in my gut loosened in favor of a nervous excitement.

"You're going to help?"

She nodded.

"Why'd Mikey change his mind?"

"Don't know." She shrugged and the bird bobbed up and down with her shoulders. It let out a peep of protest and she reached up to stroke its head.

Curiosity begged me to pursue this line of questioning, but I stopped myself. Why look a gift angel in the mouth? I'd already found archangels were at least as fickle as my ex-wife.

I stood and the bird on her shoulder took to the sky. The others in the tree followed.

"What do we need to do?"

"Nothing now."

She stood and I saw she was only three inches shorter than my six-foot-two. The snow where she'd sat hadn't melted, yet when she touched my arm, it gave me the same electric charge as when other angels touched me. The feel of her touch differed slightly, hurt a little.

"Meet me at the church at five."

She walked away, ducks waddling out of her path as she went. I didn't need to ask her which church, there was only one church in my life.

And it was only a few weeks ago I'd caused its destruction.

· · • • • • • • · ·

I gaped at the sight before me as I approached the church. I'd seen pictures on the news, but the grainy, off-color image on the cheap television in my motel didn't do justice to the wreck left in the wake of an archangel MMA brawl.

Yellow police tape encircled the church grounds, torn bits of it fluttering in the wintery breeze like a wind sock at a community airstrip. Beyond, the church was unrecognizable as a house of God. The explosion created when Mikey and Azrael clashed had toppled the steeple and knocked over three of its outer walls, leaving only the south-facing one standing. Incredibly, a stained-glass window in the wall remained intact, its depiction of the virgin Mary whole and untouched. I'd heard about this on the news, too; media and church officials called the window's survival a miracle and it had become almost as popular as the image of Jesus burnt into a grilled cheese sandwich. Even at dinnertime on a Wednesday, the sidewalk nearest the stained glass image was jammed with people beseeching the virgin to solve their problems. They huddled inside their snow jackets, some with their faces turned Heavenward, some with their heads hung in prayer, others holding candles.

Seeing them made me want to throw a rock through the window.

If only they knew what I know.

I ducked under the police line and scurried across the lawn in a clandestine crouch to avoid being seen by the sheep on the sidewalk. As I hurried past the churchyard's oak tree—also undamaged by the explosion—my jaw unconsciously tightened. It was the spot where muggers killed me during a spring rain storm, transforming my shitty life into a shitty after-life.

Why couldn't the explosion have burnt the damn tree to the ground?

I skirted the debris scattered across the churchyard, some cast as far as the iron fence bounding the cemetery to the north, and averted my eyes from the oak and its unpleasant memories as I scampered toward the graveyard, putting the still-standing wall and its miracle window between me and the religious lemmings. From the edge of the rust-spotted fence, I approached the ruined church, unsure where the woman meant for us to meet. Twilight dimmed the ruins to a charcoal-pencil smear of tumbled walls and burned-out pews. I squinted and picked out a much more shapely figure standing amidst the rubble. She raised a hand, beckoning.

"Over here, Icarus."

"Ric." I made my way through the labyrinth of charred wood and broken rock. "Why the Hell can't you people call me Ric?"

She didn't respond—they never do. Something about angel physiology rendered them incapable of shortening my name to something I found bearable. My name, Icarus Fell, was a joke, a punishment. Truthfully, I'd rather be called something classier—like dickhead.

"Are you ready to go?"

I raised an eyebrow. Was she asking if I remembered to pack my toothbrush and a change of underwear?

"We're going to Hell. Is anyone ever ready for that?"

She shrugged. "Some more than others."

She stepped up on a fallen chunk of wall and I looked up into her blue eyes, luminescent in the waning daylight—another angelism. I tore my gaze away and surveyed the scatter of church pieces, searching for a portal to Hell; there was no blurry spot or black hole, like in the movies, no gap in the earth beneath which the river Styx flowed. The ruined church organ lay by the wall, but with my lack of keyboard-playing talent, I wouldn't be able to play my way to Hell, though the possibility of my off-key singing one day earning me a ticket south certainly existed. I suppressed a shudder.

"What do we do now?"

She smiled, stepped off her perch, and grabbed my hand. Her angelic energy shot up my arm and into my chest, an electric tingle with an underlying heat that straddled the line between painful and euphoric. Pictures of naked flesh and exploring hands jumped into my mind; I shook my head to dispel them and concentrate on the task at hand without success. To regain control of my waylaid brain, I recalled Marty and Todd, Elizabeth Elton, Tony McSweeny—all of whom currently resided in Hell because of me—but each time I brought one of them to mind, their faces morphed into Piper's, dark hair cascading down her long neck, across her smooth shoulders. I couldn't control my thoughts as long as her hand was on mine.

I pulled away, hands draped strategically in front of my crotch.

"What's happening?" I asked.

She halted and faced me, an innocent smile tugging the corners of her mouth, a knowing playfulness flickering in her eyes. I struggled against the urge to reach out and stroke her cheek, to pull her to me, embrace her.

"Whatever do you mean, Icarus?"

I opened my mouth to explain but found I could only blush when I tried, like a teenager too shy to ask out the most popular girl in high school.

I wonder if Trevor is going through this?

"How...how will we get there?" I bumbled instead of explaining what I'd felt for fear of... embarrassment? Rejection?

"Just follow me."

She didn't take my hand this time and I sighed with relief. The reprieve allowed some of the blood which had been diverted from my brain to return. Unfortunately, the lack of her touch also allowed realization of what we were doing to creep into me, frigid fingers entwining with my spine and sending a shiver and goose bumps up my neck.

We crossed the nave, passed the unscathed altar where Father Dominic had threatened my son's life a month before, and stopped at the base of the still-standing wall. I pulled up beside her and gazed at the blackened stone. When she didn't do anything, I touched the stone wall, found it as solid as ever.

"I don't get it."

She didn't respond, surveying the wreckage around us instead. After a moment, she strode to a charred but mostly-whole pew and picked it up like it weighed nothing. She brought it to where I stood and propped it against the wall beneath the stained glass Virgin Mary.

"Ready?"

"You asked me that already. The answer's still: not really."

She shrugged, smiled, and started climbing, using the pew as a ladder to the window. When she reached the top, she stepped onto the window ledge and motioned for me to follow. I breathed deep, gathering my nerves.

Do I really want to go to Hell again?

The answer was no, I didn't *want* to. I had to.

I struggled my way up the charred pew with less dexterity than Piper but made it to the top. She offered her hand and helped me onto the ledge, a bolt of electricity and a wayward lustful thought shooting through me. I shook free of her touch.

We stood there a few seconds, inches from the miracle window, and I wondered what the people gathered on the sidewalk watching for miracles would think when we burst through the glass. But when she took a step toward it, the glass didn't break. Instead, her foot passed through it as though she stepped through one of those seventies beaded curtains. Bit by bit, she disappeared.

I hesitated.

Piper was gone, vanished through the window like Alice through the looking glass. I could have turned and left; I wanted to. I looked back at the pew leaning against the wall, at the debris-strewn church, and started to turn, but a sound stopped me. A voice.

The voice of a woman.

Was it one of the miracle-seekers crying out to the Heavens? Piper prompting me to follow? Maybe it was Beth Elton calling for help all the way from Hell.

I drew a fortifying breath and my foot went through the window like it didn't exist, then my hand, my arm, and finally my torso and head. The chilly night disappeared, replaced by searing pain, confusion, agony. I saw the people standing on the sidewalk for a second; the murmur of their prayers thundered in my ears, the light of their candles blinded me. Then they faded from view. A pressure mounted in my head, threatening to over-inflate it to the point of bursting.

And then blackness overcame all.

Chapter Six

I OPENED MY EYES, half-expecting everything to be ablaze. It didn't disappoint me to find it wasn't the case. The gray sky looked like an average overcast day threatening rain, though I couldn't discern any clouds, just gray. I breathed deep through my nose but didn't smell brimstone or sulfur, only the earthy smell of the first rain after a lengthy dry spell.

"About time, sleeping beauty."

My neck creaked as I turned my head and gazed into the eerily blue eyes of Piper kneeling beside me. She smiled.

If this is Hell, count me in.

"How long?"

"A minute or two. Not long enough for brain damage."

"I'll have to come up with another excuse."

She stood and offered her hand, but I struggled to my feet on my own rather than risk the visions her touch was sure to insert in my mind. They weren't unpleasant, but I'd rather have my wits about me in Hell than walk around with an erection. As I gained my feet I surveyed the area around us: a medium-sized stream burbled on our left, stretching to the horizon; a forest of twisted trees clogged our right. We stood on a swath of earth which accounted for all else.

"Where are we?"

"Hell," she said as casually as if she'd told me 'the grocery store.'

"You sure? Doesn't look like Hell."

"You were expecting a lake of fire, something like that?"

"No, actually. Last time I visited, it was a deserted apartment building."

She shrugged. "To each his own."

She looked away and took a few paces toward the stream, leaving me to feel as though I'd lost a friend. My eyes followed her, and when I managed to tear them away, I noticed a small city perched on the far bank.

That wasn't there before.

"Is that where we're going?"

"I think so."

"You don't know?"

She looked back over her shoulder with an expression of mock disdain.

"I'm an angel, Icarus. Why should I know anything about Hell?"

"Right. I'm sorry. I didn't mean—"

"You've been here more times than I have."

That shut me up. Still, I didn't know anything about the place, my exposure being limited to a fiery hallway in an abandoned apartment building and a few rooms which didn't look like they belonged in Hell. Hardly detailed knowledge.

I walked toward the edge of the stream, fully intending to step in and make my way across. I enjoyed Piper's company, but the sooner this expedition got underway, the sooner we'd get the Hell out of here, pardon the pun. My right foot was hovering over the water when her hand on my shoulder sent a shock through my spine.

"Don't go in the water."

I returned my foot to dry land and shook my head as I dragged myself from her touch before all the blood left my brain. I blinked a few times to clear the mud from my thoughts.

"Why not? I thought you said to go to the city."

"We do, but you can't touch the water of the River Styx."

I stared at her for a moment, looked at the stream, then back at her, trying not to laugh—I didn't know if doing so would hurt her feelings—but couldn't stop myself.

"The River Styx. Really? Disappointing."

She raised an eyebrow.

"I expected something bigger, a bit more...torrential."

I gazed back at the over-sized creek, searching the flowing water for signs of damned souls sliding by under its surface, eyes blank, mouths open in eternal screams. Think I saw one of those ornamental Japanese goldfish—koi. Big, but I didn't notice any teeth.

"How do we get to the other side?"

She looked left, then right. "I suppose we have to find the ferryman."

The second the word cleared her lips, a solitary puff of fog appeared on the far bank. It roiled and moved in place for a minute, then struck out across the creek, misty tendrils trailing behind. A minute and a half later, it reached us. The fog cleared to reveal a flat-bottomed raft bearing a stooped old man with long pole in hand. A black patch covered one of his eyes, the other bulged and stared beside his hook nose; long, stringy hair hung past his shoulders. He looked enough like Marty Feldman's rendition of Igor in *Young Frankenstein* that I expected Mel Brooks to shout: 'Action!'.

Piper took a step toward the boat but I caught her by the sleeve of her shirt, stopping her.

"Whatever you do, don't pay him 'til we get to the other side."

She looked at me like she thought she'd been wrong about the brain damage.

"Come on...Chris de Burgh. 'Don't pay the Ferryman'. You must know it."

She shook her head.

"'The Lady in Red'? 'Spanish Train'? 'Patricia the Stripper'?"

A blank stare.

"You guys need better tunes up in Heaven."

Nothing worse than funny references your audience doesn't understand. It felt like I was talking to my ex-wife—she never appreciated classic rock humor, either.

"Are you done?"

I paused a second before nodding. She stepped onto the raft, making it rock gently; I hesitated but followed. The bent ferryman stared at us with his one eye but didn't push off. I looked at him expectantly—this was his job, he should know what to do—then turned my gaze on Piper, who was staring across the stream toward the city. I sidled up beside her.

"What are we supposed to do now?" I asked out of the corner of my mouth, one eye on the ferryman.

"You can't wait until the other side to pay him, no matter what this de Burgh fellow told you."

Her mouth crinkled up in a smirk and I almost laughed aloud, but the urge dissipated quickly as the man's unblinking eye bore into me. He extended his hand. I patted my pockets and found them as empty as when I'd set out to feed the ducks.

Shouldn't have left all my change to tip the barkeep.

"Pay him what?"

"I don't know, I'm an angel. Ask him."

I took a hesitant step toward him. The wrinkles in his cheeks and forehead were deep enough to be crags; I thought, if I looked close enough, I'd find tiny mountaineers scaling them. I didn't want to look that close.

"Excuse me, sir. We need to reach the other bank."

He stared at me, mouth pulled down in a scowl. I swallowed the lump forming in my throat and rephrased the question, not liking how this was proceeding. I gestured across the stream.

"What will it cost to get there?"

His palm up, expectant hand turned, the exaggerated knuckles folding all but one of his twig-like fingers back until his hand quaked in my direction. The lump returned to my throat.

"Me?"

He nodded. I backed away a step and whispered to Piper.

"Ah, a little help here?"

I didn't look at her—didn't want to take my eye off the wizened man—but felt her gaze. Its effect didn't match her touch, but it brought goose bumps to my neck and courage I wouldn't have found on my own.

"Give him what he wants."

I didn't want to look away from the ferryman for fear it would be the last thing I ever did, so I clenched my teeth instead of giving her the disbelieving look her statement deserved.

I raised my hand tentatively toward him. Our hands drew closer and I felt an uncomfortable warmth radiating from his flesh. Then, with enough speed to make a mongoose jealous, his fingers encircled my wrist.

As soon as his flesh touched mine, I saw it wasn't really a man stooped in front of me, but a wolf-shaped beast—the huge, misshapen werewolf from 'An American Werewolf in London' come to life. Terror froze me. The wolf-beast jerked me toward him and lurched forward; its jaws found my shoulder, fangs dug into muscle. I screamed.

The thing shook its head once, rending my flesh. It reared back, a chunk of me in its teeth, my blood running between its jaws. A wave of nausea overtook me, spinning my head, dizzying me. I stumbled away and the beast released its hold on my wrist. My feet tangled and my tail bone struck the raft's deck hard enough to click my teeth together. A second later, Piper knelt beside me.

"Are you alright?"

My lips moved but no sound emerged. I registered the concern in her eyes, then returned my gaze to the man-wolf.

Gone.

The stooped ferryman stood at the back of the raft working his pole as he guided us across the stream. I jerked my head around expecting to find the beast behind me, but the raft held only the three of us.

"Did you see what happened?" I asked, breathless.

"Yes. You asked him what it would cost to cross, shook his hand, then you stumbled. Did you hurt yourself?"

I shook my head and brought my hand up to the shoulder where the beast took a chunk out of me. No pain. When I looked at my fingers, they were free of blood.

What the fuck?

"You didn't see it?"

Piper shrugged. "See what?"

I opened my mouth to tell her about the wolf-thing, its bite, but the instant my lips moved, my cheeks burned with embarrassment.

I must have imagined it.

I couldn't admit to this beautiful woman—angel—that a mirage made me panic.

"Nothing. Never mind."

She offered her hand to help me up off my ass but I chose again to do it without the aid of her skin against mine. I climbed to my feet, head feeling like the Hindenburg—lighter than air but about to explode.

"Are you sure you're alright?"

I nodded, then promptly vomited over the side of the raft. A group of huge goldfish like the one I'd seen earlier gathered and made a meal of my spew. The sight made me gag again but I retained the rest of the contents of my stomach and stood on unsteady legs.

The ferryman stared straight ahead, his one bulging eye fixed on his goal of the other shore. Over his shoulder I saw the bank we'd left receding.

Good.

I wanted to get off this raft as quickly as possible, leave the man with his craggy face and long pole behind. And whatever-the-hell-it-was that bit me. Pivoting on my heel, I faced Piper. An amused smirk had usurped her expression. I wanted to tell her how it's not polite to laugh at the folly of others, but the far bank caught my eye.

It was no closer.

"What the...?"

I spun back toward the spot we'd left, saw it was farther away, then looked back to our destination which looked the same distance as before.

"What's going on, Piper?"

She shrugged. "It's Hell," she said, unconcerned. "We'll get there eventually."

I slouched down onto the deck of the raft, sitting cross-legged—what Trevor's kindergarten teacher called criss-cross applesauce—and breathed deep, attempting to quell my shaking hands.

An hour later, I'd shifted position a few dozen times—criss-cross applesauce is fine for kids but gets uncomfortable quickly when you're in your fourth decade. A warm wind rose from the direction of our goal, which was no closer; waves lapped the side of the raft. I peered into the water and saw the school of giant goldfish swimming along-side, their tails working but getting them no further ahead than us. Piper sat at the front like a monk deep in meditation. I stared a few seconds at her dark hair hanging to the middle of her back, at the smooth whiteness of the flesh of her arms, then finally at the distant city, still as far away as when we began the trip across the river Styx.

"Enough," I said.

I climbed to my feet, knees aching, and approached the ferryman. He remained fixed on our destination, so I stepped into his line of sight but stayed far enough away he couldn't reach me.

"What's going on here? You got the payment you wanted, when will we get to the other side?"

I'm not sure what the payment had been—probably didn't want to know—but felt he'd taken something from me. Behind him, the far bank had disappeared, leaving a stretch of churning water between us and our point of departure. How-the-hell a stream could grow into a small sea was beyond me, then I realized the answer to my query.

Hell.

The ferryman's eye shifted and he stared at me for a full minute before returning to his survey of the far shore. As much as I didn't want to deal with this man—this thing—it was time for answers.

"Look at me." I moved again to block his view. "When will we—"

The raft struck something solid spilling me onto my tail bone for a second time. Perhaps we'd hit one of the enormous koi. I righted myself and saw the ferryman pointing past me, gnarled finger extended toward the shore. Piper came to my side.

"We're here," she sing-songed.

The edge of the raft made contact with the rocky shore. A few hundred yards away, the city overtook the landscape, its buildings rising taller than I'd thought, many reaching hundreds of stories toward the ashen sky. Monolithic, ultra-modern slabs stood shoulder to shoulder with cathedrals which looked like they were erected a thousand years ago. The skyscrapers stretched the length of the shore as far as I could see.

I opened my mouth to ask 'what-the-hell' again but closed it without posing the question. This was Hell, after all: apparently I'd have to get used to a little strangeness.

Chapter Seven

WE TRUDGED ALONG THE boulevard leaving footprints in the half-inch layer of ash covering its surface.

"Now what?" I looked away from the pale gray buildings to Piper; she didn't look at me.

"You keep asking me that. Aren't you the one who wanted to come to Hell?"

Our words bounced from skyscraper to citadel, cathedral spire to tower, but we heard no other sounds, saw no other prints in the dust. It seemed we had the entire city to ourselves. I breathed deep, collecting my thoughts, and gagged at the taste of the ash on my tongue—God only knew what had been burned to produce it; the answer might be beyond even His knowledge.

"We've got some souls to find."

"Okay. Any ideas how to do that, Sherlock?"

I stopped and surveyed our surroundings. Buildings rising on all sides were surprisingly tidy and in good repair; the road stretching on seemingly without end did so free of garbage or debris. Each side street we came to looked exactly the same. With no real plan, I strode to the doors of the closest hi-rise and found a glassed-in case set on the wall to the left. The glass protected a black board and white plastic letters.

"Hey. Come look at this."

The little white letters were arranged to form names, each one set beside a number which presumably corresponded to an apartment number. I stared, open-mouthed.

"It can't be what it seems."

Piper shrugged—her favorite gesture.

"Never know until you try."

There were easily a thousand names on the list. Luckily, and somewhat unbelievably, they were in alphabetical order. I browsed from the a's, watching for recognizable names, only slightly deterred by occasional missing letters, fallen from their spots to collect in the bottom of the case like an alphabet soup sucked dry of its broth.

I finger-traced a path through the b's and c's, a few names catching my attention—surely it couldn't be *the* Ray Charles—before reaching the e section and a name on the list because of me.

"Elizabeth Elton," I whispered.

Piper stepped up beside me, her chin an inch from my shoulder.

"Who?"

"She used to be my...neighbor. Father Dominic killed her."

"What luck." She clapped me on the shoulder and that small touch sent a jolt coursing straight for my groin. "With all the people who've gone to Hell, what were the chances we'd find someone you were looking for on the first try?"

"No shit." My finger traced a line from Beth's name to the apartment number. "It says she's in twenty-eighteen."

There was no buzzer beside the board. I looked high and low, then went to the opposite wall looking for it, watching for some secret door hiding a phone to call up and get buzzed in.

Nothing.

"Damn it." I turned to Piper still standing by the board watching me with the amused expression she liked almost as much as shrugging. "I don't know how to get in."

She tilted her head at me and smiled, then walked the two steps to the front door, grabbed the handle and pulled the door open.

"Should we try this?"

"Smart ass."

She bowed her head and swept her arm toward the open door, ushering me through. I went sheepishly, thinking how different Piper was from Poe. When I first met Poe, she was shy and nervous and had become only marginally less so over the last few months. This woman was the opposite: outgoing, playful, fun to be with. Too bad she was an angel and not a woman I met in a bar.

We entered a massive foyer with crimson walls. No ash covered the smooth gray floor; our footsteps echoed up to the ceiling forty feet above. Other than four walls, a door, a ceiling and a floor, there was nothing—no light fixtures, no comfy places for visitors to rest, no mailboxes. Only the elevator doors set into the far wall broke the monotony of emptiness. I strode across the slate tile floor, the oppression of the dark walls and floor and the dim light weighing on me with each step. I glanced over my shoulder to make sure Piper was following and found her two paces behind me, walking with the quiet grace of a careful cat.

Halfway across the lobby, I stopped.

"Did you hear that?"

She paused, listening. "I don't hear anything."

We remained there a few seconds, a look of concentration on my face so she'd know I was listening. I'd thought I heard a sound like rock scraping against rock hidden amongst the echoes of my footsteps, but now, listening for it, I heard nothing. We waited a few seconds longer, then I borrowed a page from Piper's book and shrugged.

"Guess I'm hearing things."

We set out again, and after a few steps, the sound returned.

"There it is again," I said without stopping this time. "Do you hear it?"

"No."

She increased her pace and looped her arm through mine. The electricity of her touch filled me immediately, its buzz in my ears hiding any sound I may have heard. Piper guided me—a little dazed and more than a little aroused—to the elevator doors where she punched the call button, then gazed up at the lighted numbers above the sliding doors. I took the opportunity to peruse the smooth curve of her neck, the drape of her hair across her shoulder, the fullness of her lips. She hummed a tune at the back of her throat as she waited and it sounded to me like the most beautiful music I'd ever heard.

The doors slid open and she stepped through, letting go of my arm.

I crashed back to earth or, in this case, Hell. The murmur in my bones disappeared leaving me feeling empty, alone. She stood in the elevator facing me; my body ached to say something to her, tell her she made me feel like no one ever had, beg her to come back to me.

"Are you coming, silly?"

Her words broke the spell. I shook my head to clear the cobwebs and dragged my sleeve across my mouth in case my open-mouth gape left drool on my chin, then stepped into the elevator and pushed the twenty button.

"It was twenty-eighteen, right?" I asked, my voice quaking slightly.

The doors slid closed. At first, I stood close enough to feel the heat radiating from her hand and part of me wanted to hold it, go back to the exotic place her touch took me. Another part knew that if I did, I might never return. I side-stepped a little farther away as the muzak version of Barry Manilow's 'Mandy' assaulted us from a tinny-sounding speaker hidden in the elevator's ceiling.

Now I know I'm in Hell.

The trip felt like it took an eternity, but Piper's close proximity bringing a light sweat to my brow may have been as much responsible for the feeling as the torture of Mr. Manilow or some Hellish trick like our raft ride across the River Styx. At least I didn't have to pay the elevator-man.

At last, the number twenty above the door illuminated with a co-inciding electronic ding. A second later the doors slid open. I went to step out but hesitated, peeking through the doors first.

"Holy shit."

Instead of the apartment building hallway I expected, our elevator opened on a rough-hewn subterranean passage. Guttering torches set in sconces at regular intervals along the walls threw flickering illumination along the passage.

"This is more like what I thought Hell would be," I said and stepped out of the elevator.

Piper followed. "Which way should we go?"

I glanced one way along the hall, then the other. No signs like in a hotel or apartment building indicated what number-range of rooms lay in which direction. Frustrating.

"Your guess is as good as mine."

"Let's go this way, then," she said gesturing to her right.

We set out down the passage and, as we approached the first torch, I noticed the sconce was shaped like a human arm: well-muscled, sun-bronzed, the torch held in its fist.

Creepy. A little cliché, but creepy.

The next sconce was a smaller, more feminine arm. We passed a wooden door, fiery roman numerals blazing on its surface: MMI. It took me a moment to recall my schooling and recognize it as two thousand and one–twenty-oh-one.

"Looks like you chose the right way."

We continued past a more doors and more sconces, each arm different than the previous. One was considerably smaller than the others, created in the image of a child's. It sagged at an awkward angle, as if it had trouble bearing the weight of the torch. I examined it as we went by and realized it quivered with effort; as I watched, it went slack. The torch dipped, flaming oil dripping onto the stone floor, then I heard a whip crack and a muffled cry of pain. The torch came up to level again.

I hurried to catch up to Piper.

She'd stopped in front of a door, the numerals MMXVIII emblazoned on its surface.

"Here it is," she said.

"Here it is," I agreed.

Neither of us reached for the door knob. The air in the passage suddenly seemed thick, filled with the smoke of the torches. I raised my hand toward the knob with more effort than it should have taken, as though I lifted a great weight along with it. I felt Piper's eyes on me and my cheeks went red, embarrassed at having trouble completing such a basic task in front of this beautiful woman.

Open the damn door.

My fingers brushed the brassy knob—warm to the touch but not unbearable. I gripped it, cranked it, and threw the door open, each movement pronounced like a stage actor ensuring the people at the back of the theater saw my actions.

A sickly-sweet smell wafted from the room, a mix of flowers and something rotten. I hesitated before crossing the threshold. I hadn't seen Elizabeth Elton in many years, since I was nineteen, when I had scraped together enough money for a less-than-modest basement apartment in the cheapest part of town. Beth was twenty years older than me and lived upstairs with her abusive boyfriend and two children born of different fathers—neither of them him. We got to know each other one day when her man was gone on a multi-day drinking binge. Sometimes I watched the kids for her while she was earning money however she could; sometimes I shared her bed when the boyfriend was away. I don't know if he found out, but one morning I woke up and they were gone.

She was the first woman I ever loved.

We stepped into the room and closed the door because there's no telling what might come traipsing down a hallway in Hell. An orange couch which looked like it had been rescued from the side of a road sat against one white wall streaked with smears of dirt. A coffee table and two end tables provided resting places for half a dozen vases of flowers: roses, carnations, and other blossoms of types I couldn't name. The flowers drooped, loose petals shed onto the dingy beige carpet. Magazines with dog-eared covers spilled across the tables and a picture of a sailing ship navigating a stormy sea, its captain lashed to the mast, hung askew on the wall over the couch.

"A waiting room in Hell?" I asked rhetorically.

Piper provided her now customary shrug and went to the door in the left wall. Four long scratches marred its surface, the curls of wood carved from it littering the floor below. I didn't want to meet whatever made the marks.

"It's locked," she said jiggling the knob.

"Let me try."

I coaxed her out of the way, careful not to touch her, and tried the door myself. Locked, like she said. I threw my shoulder against it. Nothing.

"We're not getting through this without a key."

"What do you want to do, then?"

I looked from Piper's bluer-than-blue eyes to the couch and the disarrayed magazines. "I guess we wait."

We sat on the couch necessarily closer than I felt comfortable with to avoid some questionable-looking stains. I felt heat from her thigh and shoulder only inches from mine and picked up a magazine to distract myself from the probable rise of lust it would cause. The issue I chose seemed like it would do the trick: the spring 2008 issue of *Torturer's Quarterly*. An overhead photo of a man, his limbs humorously elongated as four horses pulled him to pieces, adorned the cover.

Who knew Hell had its own publisher? Everything I'd ever read about the publishing industry suggested it shouldn't be a surprise. We'd probably find a few used car lots down here too, and a plethora of law firms.

I flipped through the pages, curious but trying not to look too closely at the pictures. Piper sat straight and motionless beside me, staring at the door. I turned pages and fidgeted, sometimes brushing her thigh and feeling a wave of static electricity flowing through me. I scooched myself as far away as the stain beside me—definitely not a coffee spill—would allow.

After an indeterminate amount of time measurable only by the flipping of one-hundred-and-twelve pages of stomach-turning pictures and articles explaining how best to insert bamboo under fingernails, the lock on the door clicked. I put the magazine down over the ugly stain and we both stood as the door swung open and a young woman in a nurse's uniform, her features disfigured like she'd had a facelift go horribly awry, poked her head into the room.

"Ms. Elton will see you now."

Piper and I looked at each other—me with a disbelieving expression plastered on my kisser, her looking like she wondered if I'd be chivalrous and offer for her to go first. I was tempted, given we didn't know what lay on the other side of the door, but I couldn't bring myself to let her take the lead. Given the fact that those muggers murdered me some months ago, perhaps chivalry is dead.

We stepped through the door and traded the flowery-rotten smell for a rotten-flowery one. The room was larger than the waiting room but with earthen walls and no furnishings, decorations or trappings. A pit I couldn't see into from where I stood opened in the center of the dirt floor; Beth huddled against the far wall, shivering. At the sound of our entrance she curled herself into a tighter ball, face hidden in the crook of her elbow.

"Beth?"

I took one step forward before electricity shot up my arm as Piper put her hand on me, halting me. Elizabeth peeked out from behind her arm and her eyes widened, her shivering stopped.

"Icarus? Is that you?"

"Ric. Yeah, it's me."

She stood and I saw blood smeared on her thin, bare arms and the flesh of her legs showing through the tatters of what once was a sun dress. Despite her condition, it didn't seem she was injured, and I wondered to whom the blood belonged.

"What are you doing here?"

"I came for you."

The look on her face changed. She'd never been a beautiful woman, but the smile helped things a bit.

"Really?"

She walked toward me, shoulders back and toes of her bare feet dragging along the floor the way dancers walk during a performance. I didn't remember her walking that way when I knew her; perhaps they gave dance lessons in Hell.

"Really," I said glancing at Piper who watched passively. I guess I'd hoped she'd look a little jealous with the exchange. She didn't.

When Beth had crossed halfway to me, a bell rang—not an alarm bell or someone summoning the butler, but the brassy clang of a ring bell at a boxing match. Her smile vanished and revealed terror hiding beneath. She turned away like she'd forgotten me and went to the edge of the pit where she sat with her legs dangling over the edge. I raised an eyebrow at Piper; not surprisingly, she shrugged. We watched and, a few seconds later, the growl of a dog boiled up out of the pit. A second growl made it a chorus.

"Beth?" I took one step toward her.

As disconcerting as the growls were, it was the small, high-pitched voice which halted my step.

"Mama?"

"Luke!"

Beth's youngest child; three-years-old last time I saw her. Her other boy had been five.

What was his name again?

"Brandon!"

That's it.

The growls turned vicious and one of the boys cried out. Beth screamed. I wanted to rush to her but didn't, my head spinning. Nearly twenty years had passed; I didn't need to be a mathematician to realize her sons should be adults.

"Help her," Piper prompted, touching my elbow. The shock of it jolted me into action.

Everything became a blur. The children screamed, their cries overwhelmed by the snarling dogs. Beth cried and screamed, stood and cursed at the dogs.

"Leave my boys alone, you fuckers!" Her hands were balled into fists at her sides, all the sinewy muscles beneath her skin pulled tight as she leaned forward.

"No."

I reached for her and my fingers brushed the fabric of her shabby dress as she jumped into the pit. Stumbling, I went head first to the dirt floor and would have tumbled into the pit after Beth if Piper hadn't grabbed me. I looked at her and nodded my thanks then pulled myself to the lip of the pit to see if I'd be able to salvage Beth's soul.

I wasn't ready for what I saw.

Both the boys—aged near what I remembered them—were awash in blood. The dogs were backing away from Beth, tails between their legs, and she held her sons one under each arm. She sat with a puff of dust, pulled them both onto her lap. The youngest, Luke, mewled like a kitten unable to draw milk; Brandon silent and unmoving. Sobs tremored through Beth's shoulders as she wrapped her fingers around her sons' throats and squeezed.

"Beth! Wait, no."

I scrambled to go over the edge of the pit but Piper stopped me. I reached toward Beth, fingers clutching empty air. A minute passed; Luke pulled at his mother's grip, but his struggle soon stopped. After three minutes, Beth let go and stood.

The dogs growled and stalked toward her.

"Give me your hand," I yelled. She didn't face me.

The dogs leaped at her; she didn't raise her arms in defense. They rode her to the ground, one with its jaws wrapped around her arm, the other gnashing at her throat. Seconds later its teeth found their mark. I looked away, unable to watch.

"Damn it." I rolled over and sat up, head hung between my knees. "We almost had her."

"Almost," Piper repeated and brushed hair out of my eyes, the tip of her finger caressing my forehead. Images jumped into my head: naked flesh, writhing limbs, droplets of sweat. I scuttled away, crabwise. After what I'd just seen, this was no time for lust.

"It always happens like that," a voice said from behind Piper. "If I don't finish them off, the dogs do. It looks more painful when the dogs take them."

I shifted to see past the angel. Beth stood by the door through which we'd entered, the disfigured nurse with her, sewing up the gash on her neck with a wicked needle and flesh-colored thread. Beth's expression was weary, beaten.

"Beth." I got to my feet feeling shocked, sickened and relieved.

"They'll be back in a few minutes."

"You won't be here."

I went to her, took her hand in mine. I felt Piper close behind me as the nurse finished up her ministrations and stepped back. My eyes flickered between Beth's face and the nurse, expecting her to reveal herself as a demon and jump us, preventing us from rescuing Beth's soul.

"We're going to take you where you should have gone in the first place."

She looked up into my eyes and I saw hope in them, but it was tempered; she probably suspected we were another aspect of her punishment and torture.

"But I can't leave my boys."

"They're not really here," Piper said and stroked her arm.

Beth pulled away from her touch like she'd been brushed by the clammy scales of a snake. She looked toward the pit, her bottom lip quivering. I saw in her eyes where her mind went: as awful as experiencing the pit and the dogs and her sons' deaths over and over was, at least she got to see her boys.

"This is no place for you," I said and guided her toward the door while looking sideways at the nurse. "Are you going to try and stop us?"

The nurse shook her head and the little nurse's hat canted to the left.

"Can I come with you?"

I'd assumed her a demon, a thing of Hell, not another soul living out her damnation. I opened my mouth to tell her she could but stopped and looked at Piper first. She gestured me closer.

"We don't know who she is or what she's done," she said, her breath warm in my ear. "I don't think it's a good idea."

She was right—this woman might be a serial killer or a dealer or perhaps she'd played a bit part in *Ishtar*, the worst movie ever. We shouldn't bring someone with us and expect Heaven to take them when we didn't know anything about them. I looked back into her pleading eyes and shook my head.

"I'm sorry."

I reached for the door as the bell sounded again and the first snarls spilled from the pit. Elizabeth took a step back toward the center of the room but I caught her by the elbow and guided her through the door. She resisted but, once we closed the door behind us, she came back into herself. Her mood lightened, the stress and pain in her face waned.

We crossed the decrepit waiting room and reached the outer door. I paused with my hand on the knob and looked at Piper.

"What do you think?"

She shrugged.

I took a deep breath and opened the door, all the muscles in my arms and legs gathered and ready to choose between fight and flight. I didn't imagine for a second it would be easy getting out of Hell.

Chapter Eight

MANNY WAS THE SAME height as Trevor but a year older and thirty pounds heavier. His curly black hair hung in front of his eyes and the corners of his mouth were set in a perpetual sneer.

"Why don't you go home to your Mommy, freak?"

The other boys gathered around them snickered, but Trevor paid them no attention. Instead, he concentrated on the bigger teen. He knew where this was going and was already tensing the muscles in his legs and body. At his side, his fists clenched and released, clenched and released.

Manny shoved Trevor in the shoulder and he fell back a step.

"Come on, pussy. Don't you have anything to say for yourself?"

Trevor did his best to hold his expression passive despite the way his insides boiled. He didn't respond.

"Fuck you then, freak."

This time, Manny shoved him in the chest with both hands. Trevor stumbled back three steps before landing ass-first on the muddy field. The boys gathered around laughed and pointed; Manny sneered like he was proud of his accomplishment. Trevor made no move to get back to his feet. If he did, it would only be worse, so he stayed down and let mud soak through his jeans.

"Hey! What's going on over there? Trevor?"

The sound of the high-pitched voice made him cringe. There couldn't have been a worse time for his mother to show up to pick him up from school. Manny looked toward her voice then back toward Trevor.

"Your mama's here to save you this time," he said. He stomped his foot on the muddy field, splashing dirt across Trevor's shirt and onto his face. Trevor flinched. "See you next time."

He led the other boys away. As they left, Trevor looked across the field at his mother rushing toward him. She looked ridiculous picking her way through the mud in her high heels. Before she got to him, Trevor got up from the field and brushed mud from the back of his jeans. Anger and embarrassment clamped his jaw tight even as he told himself he didn't care. How could anything matter anymore when you've been in the grasp of an archangel?

"Trevor, are you okay?"

His mother slowed her pace as she approached, careful not to slip or splash dirt on her new skirt. She didn't know where the envelope of money that had shown up in their mailbox one day had come from, but Trevor did. He smiled at the thought of the money, and his father, and how surprised she had been.

"What happened? Were those boys picking on you?"

"We were just playing, Mom. What are you doing here?"

"I told you I'd pick you up today."

Trevor wiped his dirty hands on his thighs. "Yeah. In the parking lot, not on the field."

"I saw those boys around you. It didn't look friendly, so I thought I'd help."

"I don't need your help."

I was nearly killed by a dead priest and met an archangel, he wanted to say. *What help could you give?*

He'd wanted to say things like that many times since what happened at the church, but he always kept his mouth shut like Icarus had told him. Nothing good would come of telling people, unless you considered being institutionalized good.

"Don't be like that. We all need help sometimes."

She pulled a hanky out of her purse and wiped at the mud on the back of his jeans. Trevor danced away.

"Stop that."

"You can't sit in the car like that."

"Fine. I'll change into my gym gear."

He broke off the conversation and began walking toward the school hoping his mother would take the hint. She didn't. He heard the splash of her heels in the mud following him.

"I'll meet you at the car, Mom. Don't make it worse than it already is."

He kept walking as the sound of her footsteps stopped. A part of him buried deep inside wished that she would have kept after him, insisted on helping. It was the same part that had been relieved to see her wobbling across the field toward him, but he couldn't let her know that part existed. He wasn't a boy anymore. Since the church, he hardly felt he was human anymore.

When he was almost to the school, he looked back and saw her crossing the field toward the parking lot. Her shoulders were hunched forward as she watched her feet, avoiding as much of the mud as she could. He'd hurt her feelings, he knew, but there was no helping it lately. How could he live a normal life after what had happened?

He needed to talk to someone about what happened. He needed to see his father, but he was in hiding. They wanted to blame Icarus for the deaths, probably for the explosion at the church, so he understood why he hadn't been able to see him. That didn't make Trevor miss him any less.

Trevor stopped with his hand on the door handle, hesitating before he entered the school.

When was the last time I missed him?

Years, that's how long. Enough time that he didn't cry when muggers killed his father, though by then he'd been convinced Icarus wasn't really his father.

He knew better now.

He yanked the door open and slouched through into the hall, headed for his locker and the dry, if not clean, gym shorts in it. He had to get out of this place, away from these people.

It was time to see his father.

Chapter Nine

G ETTING OUT OF HELL turned out to be easier than expected.

At Piper's suggestion, we took a left down the passageway—I did my best to distract Beth from the arms holding the torches—and followed it to the end where we found a heavy metal door with a glowing exit sign above. The door opened easily and we stepped through into the familiar patio furniture warehouse where I'd seen Mikey. Who knew?

We passed the tallest tower of plastic chairs imaginable and arrived at the open spot where I'd handed off the detective's soul. No one there. Not Mikey, not a generic, white-tressed angel dressed like Mr. Roarke, the enigmatic host on *Fantasy Island*.

"Where are they?" I glanced around the patio-furniture clearing.

"Where's who?" Beth asked.

My heart ached at the quiver of emotion in her voice. I couldn't have been easy for her to leave her sons behind, even in Hell. I had an idea what she was going through—I'd experienced it.

"The esc...the courier," I said. "This is as far as I take you. An angel who looks kind of like Mr. Clean after he's joined a heavy metal band takes you the rest of the way."

Her eyes darted back and forth between piles of plastic-wrapped umbrellas and boxes of dismantled tables as she probably wondered 'what an odd place to meet an angel and travel to Heaven'. Couldn't say I'd blame her for thinking it.

"What does it mean if they're not here? Do I have to go back?"

"No." Piper put a hand on Beth's arm and she pulled away. "They just didn't know we were coming."

I rubbed my chin: hadn't thought about that. Until now, angels seemed to appear whenever I needed them. And sometimes when I didn't. Once I'd summoned Poe by yelling her name, but I didn't need her this time, nor did I want her involved. The only idea which occurred was to hide Beth until I had to harvest someone else, then pawn her off with the other soul; a two-for-one deal.

"We may have to wait a while," I said keeping the pawning-off plan to myself—not very flattering.

"I'll take it from here," Piper said. "I've got some contacts. It shouldn't take long."

"Okay." I pulled a folding chair with thick, all-weather cushions toward us and offered it to Elizabeth. "May as well get comfortable."

She took the offered seat and I began looking for two more when Piper interrupted my search.

"I've got this covered, Icarus."

"Ric."

"Why don't you go get some food and rest. I'll find you when she's gone."

"No, I—"

Her palm touched my cheek and instead of seeing flesh and lust, visions of hamburger platters and soft beds came to mind. My stomach gurgled and my eyelids fluttered with fatigue.

"It's okay, she's in good hands."

She removed her hand and I opened my mouth to speak but the hunger pangs and tiredness didn't dissipate with her touch; apparently they were real. I nodded and went to Beth who looked more relaxed than a few minutes ago. I knelt beside her and took her hand in both of mine.

"I'm going to take care of some other business." Not exactly a lie. "Piper will make sure you get where you're supposed to go."

"Are you sure that's okay?" Her eyes flickered to the angel standing ten feet from us then back. Some of her former nervousness returned.

"It's fine. She's been doing this a lot longer than I have." I laughed and looked down at my hands. "Shit, I can barely find the moving sidewalk to purgatory, never mind the stairway to heaven. Piper has a direct connection."

Beth put her free hand on top of mine and squeezed; I looked up to see tears gleaming in her eyes.

"Thank you for this, Icarus. Thank you for everything." She leaned forward and kissed my cheek.

If she knew the circumstances surrounding her trip to Hell, she might not be so thankful.

I didn't say anything, only nodded in case my conscience went rogue and let the cat out of the bag. When I stood and turned to leave, I laid my hand on Piper's shoulder, partially to show appreciation for her help, partially out of a desire to feel the electricity touching her sparked in me. It didn't this time.

"See you soon," she said with a bright smile. I felt like she meant the smile and lack of shock therapy to tease me; it opened a hole in my chest.

"Yeah," I managed before redirecting my attention to the task of finding a way out of the maze of outdoor furniture, fatigue, hunger and empty longing in tow.

· · · ● · ● · · · ·

I walked right by my usual haunt: Denny's. Poe had found me there too many times, I didn't want to chance it if she was looking for me. A few blocks north and a couple west brought me to the door of a charming little place called 'Benny's BBQ Pit'. And when I say charming, I mean kind of dirty and peopled by overweight men looking for plates heaped with meat slathered in barbecue sauce.

A great place to disappear.

Half-way through my plate of Jack Daniels-infused pulled pork, baked beans and coleslaw—the weight of it in my belly increasing my fatigue—the little bell above the diner's door chimed. Normally, I don't bother looking up at such things, but this time I did. I'd like to say the sight of Poe standing in the doorway surprised me, but I'd be lying. She has a knack for finding me when I don't want to be found.

The server stepped up to seat Poe as my guardian angel saw me attempting anonymity jammed against the wall in the back-corner booth. She pushed past the young lady without a word of explanation or apology, a very un-Poe-like action, and approached me with jaw set and golden eyes blazing. Her blond hair was down and the way her eyebrows angled toward her nose gave her an unfamiliar intensity. It actually made her more attractive. I threw on a smile in the hope of disarming her apparent irritation and wondered how much barbecue sauce I had smeared on my face.

"Hey, Poe. What are you doing here?"

She stomped across the restaurant, halting at my table, arms crossed and nostrils flared.

"Where have you been?" she demanded without benefit of salutation.

I shrugged. "Around."

I swallowed the beans in my mouth and looked down at the partially demolished pile of meat left on my plate, picked at it with my fork. Poe sat down across from me, angry heat radiating from her.

"Around where?"

"Just around."

She remained silent for a minute, waiting me out. I looked up again and saw the muscles in her jaw bunched. In my experience, Poe's emotions were generally limited to happy/enthusiastic or nervous/scared. This angry thing was new and it kind of scared me.

"Do I have to report every movement to you?" Hide fear with attitude.

"If you're going to Hell, yes."

I put my fork down and leaned forward, doing my best to keep my own temper under control. I'd caused enough scenes in enough restaurants over the years and I thought the pork plate here quite tasty, so I didn't want to ruin it for future visits.

"I told you I'd go with or without you. What did you expect?"

"Michael expects you to do as you're told."

"Fuck Michael."

Poe's eyes widened and I felt the urge to look over my shoulder to ensure the archangel wasn't standing behind me. When I didn't feel an electrified, gorilla grip on my shoulder, I assumed I'd gotten away with it. A minute passed in silence. Poe's gaze remained steady on mine—another curiosity, she usually found it difficult to maintain eye contact. She drummed her fingers on the table.

"Would you like a menu?"

The waitress stood beside the table, pen and pad at the ready in case Poe wanted to order. The guardian angel didn't look at her.

"No, she's fine," I answered on her behalf. "In fact, she's just leaving."

Noticing the tension between us, the woman nodded, told us to yell if we needed anything, then retreated. The fingers of Poe's left hand continued drumming: dut, dut dut, dut, pause, dut, dut, dut, dut.

"I'm not going anywhere."

"There's nothing you can do. We found Beth Elton and brought her back. She's on her way up right now."

"*We?*"

I cleared my throat, suddenly wondering if I'd said too much. I was in no danger from Poe—it's my guardian angel's job to keep me safe, not to hurt me—but might I be getting Piper in shit?

"Yeah, we."

Apparently, she saw no humor in my lack of forthrightness. Her eyes narrowed.

"Who took you to Hell?"

"Just someone."

Her fingers ceased drumming and she slapped her open palm on the table, startling me and making the salt and pepper shakers dance a brief jig. I looked to see if the noise had upset our server, but she stood near the register polishing silverware and glanced away when she saw me looking.

"Dammit, Icarus, will you tell me what's going on?"

Now she swears, too.

I sighed. Seeing Poe angry wasn't as much fun as I might have thought. In fact, I felt a little bad.

"Piper," I said finally. "Piper helped me get there. She's with Beth right now, waiting for an escort."

"Piper? Who's Piper?"

"A guardian angel, like you. You must know her."

The expression on her face changed, grew angrier, and it occurred to me that telling a guardian angel you're hanging out with another guardian angel might be akin to telling your girlfriend you had sex with someone else.

"I've never heard of her," Poe said through clenched teeth. "Where did you find her?"

"We bumped into each other at the park."

"At the pond where the nun died?"

"Yeah."

"I don't like this, Icarus."

"Ric."

She leaned back and her expression softened from rageful to angry.

"I didn't want you going in the first place, I certainly don't want you to go with someone I don't know."

I crossed my arms and bent one corner of my mouth up in an 'it's-your-fault' kind of smirk.

"Maybe you should have come with me, then."

"Maybe I should have," she said, her voice so quiet I barely heard her. She looked down at her hands fiddling in her lap—more like the Poe I knew. She glanced up at me then away. "I don't trust her."

"You don't know her."

"Exactly."

"Then you take me back."

She shook her head, looked back down at her hands. A few seconds passed before she spoke again, a touch of sadness in her voice.

"I'm going to have to tell Michael what's going on."

I bit down against the anger her words stirred in me. I didn't want to lash out now she'd become vulnerable Poe again.

"He's going to be pissed," she added.

As she spoke, the bell over the door jingled. My eyes flickered that direction and I saw Piper stride into the restaurant. When the server offered to seat her, she simply pointed at our table and sauntered our direction.

"Do what you want," I said looking past Poe. "We're not going to be here very long."

She glanced over her shoulder at Piper coming toward us.

"Is that her?"

"Yeah."

Poe slid out of the booth and stood, looked at me for a second, then left without a 'good-bye', 'be careful', 'take care' or 'fare-thee-well'. My gut twisted a bit that she hadn't shown some final concern for my well-being; I had to stop myself from calling after her, though I'm not sure what I would have said.

As she and Piper passed in the aisle between tables, their shoulders bumped and the restaurant crackled briefly with the snap of static electricity. They faced each other for a fraction of a second and I saw Piper's lips move minutely, then Poe continued out of the restaurant. Piper slid into the seat where Poe had been.

"Was that Poe? She warmed the seat for me."

I nodded. "She said she doesn't know you."

"We've never met."

She reached across the table and plucked a small slab of pork off my plate, popped it into her mouth. I looked at her with raised eyebrow as she chewed the piece of meat.

"Mmm, that's good."

"How come you don't know each other? You're both guardian angels."

Unsurprisingly, she shrugged. "Different districts. And, frankly, most of the others don't want to hang around the ones like her."

My eyebrows joined the rest of my face in creating a frown.

"What do you mean?"

"You don't know?"

"Know what?"

"I can't believe she didn't tell you."

"Tell me what?"

Piper sighed and leaned against the red vinyl back of the booth seat. "She's under investigation."

"Investigation?" *What the Hell was she talking about?* "What the Hell are you talking about?"

"Certain people are suspicious," she answered with more nonchalance than the subject appeared to warrant. "They think she might be playing for the other side."

My frown disappeared and I laughed out loud.

"Poe? Ridiculous."

"Really? What about all the Carrions around when you harvest a soul?'

I'd been thinking about the Carrions since Piper mentioned it before and couldn't deny I seemed to attract them like kids to an ice cream truck.

"Why do you suppose they keep showing up, Icarus? Do you think Gabriel's sloppy with the scrolls?"

Gabe always seemed quite casual but I guessed one didn't get to be an archangel by being bad at their job.

"I just thought the Carrions always showed up."

"No one gives them scrolls when someone's dying. They show up if they get wind of it on the streets, if someone leaks the info."

I leaned forward, elbows on the table, and propped my chin on my fists.

"Poe. I don't believe it."

Piper shrugged again and rose from her seat.

"Why do you think she's nervous all the time? Why do you think she's so afraid of Michael?"

"Yeah, but—"

"It's time for us to go, there's souls a-waitin'. Pay the lady."

She walked out of the restaurant leaving me pondering her words. I looked longingly one last time at the pork left on my plate—I usually maintain a strict policy of 'no meat gets left behind,' but we did have things to accomplish. I left a twenty on the table and followed the angel out, my head spinning with her revelation.

Had Poe been setting me up all this time?

Chapter Ten

WE ENTERED HELL THROUGH an abandoned warehouse near the water this time and, upon our arrival, found no river Styx to cross. Instead, a wide chasm separated us from the city. I stepped up to the edge and peered down the sheer side at a swirl of mist hiding the bottom. Mind you, this was Hell, so who knew if a bottom lurked down there or not.

"This doesn't look good," I said doing my Captain Obvious impression.

"There must be some way across."

Piper wandered off to the right and I watched her go—clearly no way across in that direction. I looked the other way and saw the fissure stretching away to the distant, hazy horizon. On our side of the gap, the land was desolate and barren, on the other, the city seemed to go on forever. With the chasm too wide to jump, the sides too sheer to climb—not that I'd have climbed down into the eerie mist, anyway—there seemed no way to get there from here.

"Icarus. Look over here."

A hundred yards along the ravine, Piper stood at the end of a decrepit bridge of rope and wood planks. It swung gently over the gap despite the stillness of the air.

That wasn't there a minute ago.

A shiver wiggled its way up my spine. Something about this made me several steps beyond nervous, but I joined Piper by the bridge, anyway.

"I don't feel good about this," I said.

"What's there to feel good about? This is Hell. Do you want to find your friends or not?"

Good point. Nothing would be easy down here; frankly, it surprised me we weren't being melted or something.

"You're right. Let's get on with it."

I put one tentative foot on the first wooden plank, testing its strength. When I looked across to the other side, I saw a man standing mid-bridge, a black cowl hiding his face.

He wasn't there a minute ago.

"Shit."

"What is it?" Piper asked.

I pointed to the figure as she stretched to peer around me.

"Hmm, bridge-keeper," she said.

"Great. He's not going to ask me the air-speed velocity of an un-laden swallow, is he?"

"What?"

"*Monty Python and the Holy Grail.* You angels should rent more movies, you're really missing out."

"I'm more a *Meaning of Life* fan."

I stared at her for a second before laughing, but the merriment died quickly as I took a step onto the bridge, the plank beneath my foot creaking, as expected. Two more steps set the bridge rocking slightly. I stared ahead at the figure blocking my way—he seemed unconcerned by my presence or the motion I created.

"Wait here until I deal with him," I said over my shoulder. Piper made a noise of agreement.

I took a few more steps, choosing my footing carefully to avoid slipping through the gaping spaces between some boards. The rope sides of the bridge made stretching sounds, the way they do in thrillers to indicate their impending break.

Great.

A few yards short of the bridge keeper, I stopped and regarded him. His black outfit hung to the wooden planks, hiding his feet, while the cowl left his face shadowed. I felt like I'd either run into the grim reaper who'd left his sickle at home, or I'd been transported into Dickens' *A Christmas Carol* and this fellow was to show me my Christmases yet-to-be. Didn't like the sound of either.

"Hello," I ventured.

No reply.

I took another step toward him, the bridge trembling along with my knees, my knuckles white as I gripped the rope sides. One more step and the figure extended his arm, the black robe falling away to reveal an old-yet-unremarkable hand –no skeletal fingers, hook or stump.

I began breathing again. Until I realized he wanted payment.

"Payment," I said without intending to verbalize the thought.

A gust of wind rose from nowhere, stirring the keeper's hood to look as though he nodded. I reached my hand toward his, willing it to keep from quivering.

This time, when our hands touched and the figure transformed, I was ready.

The cowl and cloak melted away from a hog-like head with flat nose, bulging eyes and short tusks. The beast lunged at me with its mouth full of yellow, misshapen teeth agape, but I zigged. Its jaws snapped closed in surprise and, before it recovering its balance, I jammed my shoulder into its solar-plexus and toppled it over the side.

The bridge rocked wildly as it somersaulted over the side, pitching into the chasm below. It fell silently, cloak snapping in the air as it fell—no cursing my name, no scream of fear or hate. I grabbed one side of the bridge with both hands, holding on for my after-life until the motion of the bridge settled. When it did, I straightened, faced Piper with a smile and gave her a confident wave.

She didn't smile back, giving me a look of concern instead. My smile faded as she pointed over my shoulder, warning me. The hairs on the back of my neck stood on end.

I turned, but the beast didn't give me time for fancy moves. It lowered its head and surged forward, the two short tusks digging into my gut. The force lifted my feet off the planks; pain shot through my gut, swirled into my head. My upper torso leaned precariously over the side and I stared into the abyss. For the first time, I saw shapes swirling in the mist, indistinguishable yet undeniably huge and dangerous. I struggled to right myself.

The beast's forward motion stopped and I fell to the splintered boards as it pulled its tusks free; it felt like my entrails followed them. Hands clutching my mid-section, I rolled onto my side and peered into the mist again as it swirled and roiled with the flap of great wings. Teetering on the edge of oblivion, I closed my eyes and waited to die.

• • • • • • • • • •

Piper's electric touch woke me from what felt like a short, fitful sleep. She'd rolled me onto my back to keep me from going over the side and I stared up at a solid gray sky; lightning streaked through it like glowing veins in the mottled skin of the underworld. When she leaned over to check on me, the world became blue eyes and black hair.

Much better.

"Is it gone?"

"It?"

"The hog-thing. Don't tell me you didn't see this one, either."

"I saw a man in a black cloak. He touched you and you fell. I was worried you might go over the edge."

"Yeah, me too."

I attempted to sit up but intense pain in my gut like I'd done too many crunches—which for me was about twenty—stopped me. My hand instinctively went to my stomach looking for blood where the creature had gored me but it came away dry. Relief sighed through my lips.

"Is he gone?"

"He disappeared after you fell."

"Good. I don't think he'd have been able to withstand any more of my onslaught."

She smiled a smile which suggested she thought me more pathetic than amusing.

"Are you okay to go?"

"Yeah."

She stood and offered her hand. I didn't want to take it but my attempt at sitting didn't go so well, so I slipped my hand into hers. The charge immediately jolted me: manicured nails raking a bare back, teeth nibbling an earlobe too hard, expressions of ecstasy and pain.

And then I was standing and my hand was my own again.

The lust and excitement and hint of fear brought by her touch drained out my feet like water from a tub and I stared at her open-mouthed. Her lips formed words my ears couldn't figure out how to decipher.

"Icarus," she repeated. "Are you alright?"

"Ric. I'm fine. Let's go."

I let her lead so I'd have time to catch my breath. I'd found it by the time we reached the end of the bridge without further incident.

A fifteen foot swath of dusty earth separated the gaping chasm and the city limits. As we crossed it, the sound of rushing water made me glance back to see the bridge swept away as the misty canyon filled with murky water. A huge goldfish jumped, its jaws snapping empty air. What would a kid have to feed a fish to make it grow to that size? I put it from my mind and directed my attention back to the city ahead us. We stepped off bare dirt onto hot sidewalk.

The city presented itself differently this time: crowds filled the sidewalks, cars crept along the streets, horns blaring. Other than the outlandish gargoyles keeping vigil over the crowds from the corners of every building, this might be any city in America. I pointed to a particularly hideous monstrosity overhanging the street from a fifties-styled office building of about forty floors.

"Those weren't there last time, were they?"

"No."

As if responding to my reference, the gargoyle's head pivoted toward us, the red-glowing eyes set in its cockatrice face locating us at the edge of the crowd. It shifted position to see us better.

Shit.

"Let's get out of here," Piper said, mercifully catching me by the sleeve instead of touching me directly.

We melded with the flowing crowd, ducking our heads to avoid the gargoyle's stare. As we moved away from the building-mounted beast, I noticed no one in the crowd made eye contact; they all stared straight ahead, eyes glazed, more than one person bumping us unapologetically. We weaved our way through the press of zombies stepping on toes and bumping arms. Three blocks passed under our feet before I looked back to see the gargoyle had settled back into place, but one on the nearest building watched us from beneath hooded lids.

"They're still watching," I whispered.

"Yes."

We fell into the rhythm of the crowd and with each building we passed I wondered if we should check its directory for a name I recognized. Piper faced straight ahead, walking like she knew where to go.

"Where are we going?"

"I don't know," she replied.

I was looking at a building when she answered, but I'd bet she shrugged.

The people we passed during the next half-hour didn't look exactly alike, but extremely similar: ashen complexions, drab gray clothes, blank eyes, mouths pulled taut out of fear or extreme constipation. The latter might explain the sulfurous smell permeating the city.

While checking out our fellow commuters, I noticed a stir in the crowd across the street. I stopped to see what it was and the crowd flowed around me like a stream around a rock. I stood on tippy-toe to locate the cause of the disturbance.

"Hey, Pipe. What's going on over th—"

A head popped out of the throng, halting my last word before it made it over my lips. I recognized the head.

Marty.

Another lucky coincidence? Possible...but in Hell?

Maybe God's not the only one who works in mysterious ways.

"Hey," I yelled without waiting to see if Piper had heard me. "Marty!"

I pushed through the crowd, bumping a dozen people on the way. When I reached the edge of the sidewalk, I stopped, waiting for a break in the bumper-to-bumper traffic. None came, so I took a page out of an action flick and jumped onto the hood of the closest car, intending to leap from one to the next and make my way across the road like the frog in that old arcade game.

It wasn't as easy as it looked in the movies or playing 'Frogger'.

As soon as my foot hit metal, I lost my balance and left an ass-shaped dent in some blank-faced guy's hood. I scrambled to my feet and stumbled to the next car, wobbled momentarily, then jumped to the next, arms extended like a tightrope walker.

Imagine how difficult this would be if they were going faster than three miles-per-hour.

Horns blared. One guy jammed on his brakes when I landed on his hood and I almost slid off the front and under his wheels. I righted myself and flipped him the bird; he stared back with empty eyes and taut lips. From its place on the nearest corner, a gargoyle stretched its wings. By then, only one lane separated me from my goal. I looked up and saw Piper standing on the curb, hand extended, encouraging me. I leaped from the last car landing awkwardly beside her without help. Maybe if I'd accepted her assistance, I wouldn't have twisted my ankle.

"How'd you get here?"

She shrugged. "Angel stuff."

"Hmph. Could you have helped me?"

"Yes."

"Why the Hell didn't you?"

"You didn't ask."

I glared at her, wanting to be angry, but the thought of having found Marty—and therefore, probably Todd—made it difficult to be mad. That and her blue eyes.

"Did you see—?"

She pointed over my shoulder.

"That way."

I forced my way through the robotic crowd, keeping an eye on Marty's head bobbing amongst them. The black coats he and Todd wore made them easy to pick out of the gray crowd. They weaved their way through the horde keeping a consistent distance ahead. If we sped up, they sped up; if we slowed, they did, too.

I broke into a run and they did the same, right on cue.

Damn it.

I tried to dodge a blank-faced little old lady but failed, mowing her down. A pang of guilt made me look back over my shoulder to see if she was all right, but she'd already regained her feet and carried on as if nothing happened. I turned back in time to see Marty and Todd disappear down some stairs, but didn't give myself enough time to either stop or adjust my gait to the concept of descending stairs.

I went down them, anyway.

My hip hit the stairs first, flipping me over and smacking my shoulder next. I attempted to stop myself and, when I couldn't, went for the old tuck-and-roll—also with little success. My right arm got caught between my body and the edge of a stair and pain exploded as I heard a snap.

My spill down the stairs ended flat on my back, head propped on the bottom step, staring at the ceiling. I groaned loudly at the pain in my arm and squeezed my eyes shut. Seconds later, I felt a presence at my side.

"Are you okay?"

I opened my eyes and looked up at Piper bent over me, mild concern showing on her face. I bit back the urge to curse.

"I think I broke my arm."

I struggled to a sitting position and looked at what I expected to be a subway station but turned out to be a locker room.

"Couldn't you have done something? What kind of guardian angel are you?"

"Not yours. Your guardian angel wouldn't come to Hell with you, remember?"

"Right."

She grabbed me by the collar and pulled me up as I held my arm gingerly against my chest.

"Let's have a look at that."

Her fingers brushed my flesh and the buzz of static electricity followed it, standing the hairs on my arm on end. After a second, she grabbed my forearm on either side of the break. I felt the ends of the bone grate together and sucked a breath through my teeth as I bit back the urge to scream in pain. I wanted to pull away, but the pain subsided, replaced by warmth and a tingling like I'd slept on the arm wrong and woken with pins and needles. The sensation was pleasant and uncomfortable all at once. In my mind, I saw the ends of the bone knitting themselves back together under her touch. I put up with it as long as I could, pulling away after a minute. My arm didn't hurt as much.

"We don't have time for this right now. Where did Marty and Todd go? Did you see?"

I wobbled and she put a hand under my armpit, steadying me.

"No."

Something caught her attention and she stopped, listening, fingers buried in my pit sending a tickle into my chest. I brushed her hand away.

"What is it?"

"Someone's coming."

I surveyed the room quickly—it looked like the locker room of a high school: wooden benches, double banks of short lockers painted different colors, sinks, toilet stalls, and an open shower area. There was a blue door with a metal pull handle in the farthest wall I suspected might lead to a gym, and a second door with a locking knob in the wall to our right, across from the showers.

"In there," I said moving toward it with my arm cradled against my chest, though it felt considerably better.

I twisted the knob and found it unlocked, barely making it through as the other door flew open and the sounds of sneakered feet slapping tile floor and the hoots and hollers of a team of teenagers flooded the room. I twisted the lock on the knob and we leaned against the door, listening to see if we'd been noticed. It didn't seem as though we had.

"I think we're okay," I said, ear pressed against the door. My angel-friend didn't answer. "Piper?"

I pivoted from the door and found her staring across the room. I expected to see we'd found refuge in a storage closet, but my expectation was incorrect. Instead, we'd entered an office. I'd never heard of anyone keeping an office off a boys' locker room, but I also wouldn't have expected to find a locker room at the bottom of stairs normally leading to a subway platform or a dog-fighting pit behind the door of a doctor's office waiting room, either. Seems Hell is full of surprises.

I took in the office with a quick glance: a four-drawer metal filing cabinet stood against one wall, basketballs of different brands filled a rolling rack nearby. A box in one corner over-flowed with whiffle balls and the scoops for throwing them; orange mesh pull-over tops used for differentiating teams spilled over the side of a second, smaller box, tossed in by careless hands. A simple desk with two drawers sat against the far wall, a man at it perched on the edge of a wooden desk chair, his back to us. He didn't seem to notice we'd entered.

I stepped up beside Piper and she raised her hand, stopping me. She extended a finger toward the desk, pointing out the one thing I hadn't noticed: a closed-circuit television.

It looked like one which might have been found performing security duty in a 7/11 sometime in the eighties, the screen no more than twelve inches across, the picture in grainy black and white. I couldn't tell what was on the screen from where we stood, so we edged closer, trying not to betray our presence. After a few steps, I saw multiple figures moving around on the screen but still couldn't tell who or what, nor get an inkling of where the camera on the other end might be. Intent on the screen, the man didn't notice us.

Piper must have realized what he watched before I did because she averted her gaze, put her hand on my chest to stop me from getting any closer and shook her head. A spark flared in my heart at her touch but I brushed her hand aside and took two more steps, less concerned about the man noticing my presence after seeing her reaction.

The picture cleared: the boys in the locker room. Most of them were shirtless, changing out of their gym clothes; a few had already stripped to hit the showers, also clearly in view of the camera's placement. One boy stood at the center of the locker room, staring up at the camera as if he looked through it and out the other side.

I looked away and into the face of the man for the first time. He was older than I remembered; his hair had receded a few inches from his forehead, contacts replaced the wire-rimmed glasses he'd worn. He stared intently at the screen, an unsettling look on his face.

"Tony?"

He didn't hear me. The wooden chair creaked beneath him as he leaned forward awkwardly, getting a better look, and I noticed his arms were tied to the chair. He licked his lips and leaned back, his eyes flickering down to his lap. My gaze followed his to the bulge in his red gym shorts with white stripes down the side. He looked back up to the screen and I recognized the unsettling look on his face as a mix of desire and desperation—a staple of Hell's punishments.

My stomach did a somersault, anger and disgust exploding in my chest. My foot lashed out kicking the edge of the chair and sending it skittering across the room on squeaky wheels.

"What the fuck are you doing?"

The man who was once my youth soccer coach—and who also coached my son—looked up, surprised. It made me angrier to see he didn't seem to have any guilt mixed in his expression.

"Who are you?"

I clamped my teeth together, grinding my molars.

"Ric Fell," I said, anger compressing my name. A sliver of pain shot up my broken arm as my hands balled into fists. I ignored it in favor of righteous rage. "What the fuck are you doing?"

"Icarus? Oh my God. Icarus! Those men told me you'd come. Are you here to save me?"

His words caught me off-guard: *those men told me you'd come,* but I ignored their implications for the time-being.

"What's going on here?"

He glanced at the small screen then at himself. Guilt finally made an appearance on his face, though I'm sure being caught caused it, not his actions. He pulled at his arms, showing me they were tied down as if to say it wasn't his fault. I didn't think for a second the ropes were meant to keep him in front of the video feed—he obviously enjoyed watching—but to keep his hands out of his lap. Another sickened feeling rose from my belly into my throat.

"Help me."

I pulled my uninjured arm back, hand open, fully intending to slap the man silly, but Piper caught my wrist before I let loose, the prickling shock of her touch interrupting me. I turned toward her.

"This is Hell, Icarus. The man is being punished already."

"Not enough."

"We can't stay. Bring him or leave him, but we have to go."

Piper's expression remained placid, neutral. She really didn't care whether or not we brought him. I looked back at the man lashed to the chair and caught his eyes flickering back to me from the screen. The urge to punch him welled up again but I lowered my arm: Piper was right, the longer we hung around, the worse things might potentially get. I hadn't forgotten Tony's comment about 'those men' or the way the gargoyles had kept their eyes on us. Neither seemed a good sign.

I tried to sort through the situation. On the one hand, I'd come here to bring back the souls I was responsible for sending to Hell, Tony McSweeny among them. But I didn't expect to find this.

He coached my son.

I struggled my anger back into place and tried to remain logical. On our last visit to Hell, I'd watched Beth kill her children, an act I knew didn't happen in the real world. Just because he was strapped to a chair watching teenage boys undress and shower didn't mean he did the same thing in life.

Did it?

It would be easier to convince myself if he didn't keep glancing back at the monitor.

"Icarus," Piper prompted.

"Alright."

I untied my former soccer coach. He flinched and sucked air in through his teeth as I pulled the ropes away, purposely doing it in an un-gentle fashion in case he deserved it.

"Thank you," he said as he stood.

"You ended up in Hell because of me, Tony," I said doing my best to sound threatening. "I better not get you out of here to find you really should have spent the rest of eternity dry-humping the inside of your own jeans."

"You won't," he said shaking his head. "I don't know what all this was about. Thank you."

I shook off his thanks and moved to the door. Piper had already opened it a crack to peek through.

"We can't go that way," I said casting a look over my shoulder at Tony. "Wouldn't be right."

"It's empty."

A quick glance at the monitor confirmed that no boys remained in the locker room. Removing Tony from the chair dispelled his punishment.

"Okay. Let's go."

Piper led the way out the door and I shuffled Tony out behind her. We made it a couple of steps out of the small office before stopping. The room we stepped into wasn't the locker room, but the subway platform I'd originally expected.

And a subway train was pulling up to the station.

"Crap."

Chapter Eleven

T HE GROUP OF PEOPLE did precious little milling for a crowd its size. Trevor stood off to the side, separated from the group, watching them as they stared at the unbroken stained-glass window. A wide variety of people made up the crowd: the youngest looked to be a five-year-old strapped into one of those dog-leash like contraptions as his mother whispered prayers toward the miraculous glass; the oldest must have been giving ninety a run for its money. Men, women and a number of different ethnicities. The one thing they might have in common was their faith—if this window survived the explosion, it must surely be a testament to God's power.

If they only knew.

He only remembered glimpses of what happened within the church's walls as he'd spent most of his last visit here thankfully un-conscious. What he did remember kept him awake most nights. Being fifteen and having been party to a battle between archangels as well as having one almost steal your soul would give anyone nightmares.

Trevor shuffled his feet and looked away from the crowd. The yellow police tape ringing the devastated church in a rough circle flapped in the breeze and he had the uneasy feeling it gestured to him, beckoned. He stepped off the sidewalk onto the damp grass and circled around to the far side, under the branches of the oak tree, away from the miracle-seekers. A little after seven p.m., winter's shortened days made it fully dark. When he reached the spot directly opposite the window, Trevor ducked under the police tape and approached the ruins.

Chunks of broken stone wall littered the blackened grass. He hadn't been here when the explosion happened, but even unconscious, he'd felt the power of the archangels enough that the extent of the destruction didn't surprise him. He stepped past charred pews and over a chunk of marble which may once have been part of the altar, though he knew too little of religion and its trappings to say for sure. His father always insisted on *not* going to church. Funny he'd lost his life in this very churchyard and Trevor came so close to losing his here, too.

Coincidence?

The rubble formed a small mount in the middle of the former church and Trevor climbed to the top, picking his way nimbly from stone to chunk of wood to another stone. Each step brought a memory which couldn't possibly be his: Icarus fighting a man covered in scars and blood; Poe lying unconscious amongst flames; two brawny men he knew to be archangels locked in a battle, one with a flaming sword, one with a sword of shadow; and finally Icarus carrying him in his arms, taking him away.

Trevor reached the top of the pile and gazed down in disbelief—the church appeared whole again, each pew in place with copies of the bible and hymnals in their places in the compartments on their backs. Tapestries which had been burned to ash hung on the walls near the altar, the organ sat ready to play. He looked around, taking it all in, the re-formed building lit by a dim glow.

The pile of rubble under Trevor's feet had been replaced by red carpeting as he stood in the middle of the church's main aisle near the altar as though awaiting the opportunity to give away the bride. He knew each part of the church had a name—he'd watched enough TV and seen enough movies to know that—but he never remembered the nave from the chancel. It never seemed important.

He moved toward the stained glass window depicting the Virgin Mary, on the other side of which he knew a crowd watched. The only thing which looked out of place in the church was the charred pew leaning against the wall beneath the window. Trevor reached it and looked at it curiously. The wood was blackened but not turned to charcoal; chunks torn from the wood formed handholds and steps. He leaned against it, testing the strength of the pew, and finding it solid, placed his foot in the first divot.

The wood creaked beneath Trevor's weight but didn't buckle as he climbed toward the stained glass without knowing why he did. He wanted to stop and chastised himself for falling prey to the same mania as the crowd gathered on the sidewalk to see the miracle window, but each step closer filled him with more excitement. Inexplicably, he wanted nothing more than to be close to the woman in the glass, the Virgin Mary.

He reached the top of the pew and stopped, the bench wobbling slightly under him. The window ledge looked wide enough to accommodate his feet so he stepped onto it, bracing himself against the sides to keep his balance. His face was on the same level with the savior's mother's face, his eyes staring into hers.

Half-a-minute passed before he felt the heat at his back. A gentle, comfortable heat, like the sun warming his skin while lying on a beach. After a moment, he realized a light accompanied it, growing brighter and brighter, and a smell: apple pie, cinnamon, cloves. Trevor stood, arms spread, and leaned his head back, basking in the glow until it overtook him, filled him, leaving nothing in his world but light and warmth.

· · · ● · ● ● · ● ● · ·

The man raised his eyes from his whispered prayer, asking for his father's health back, for God to forgive him whatever he'd done and take away the pancreatic cancer leeching the life out of him. He didn't know why he'd stopped mid-prayer to glance up at the miracle window but he'd suddenly, inexplicably felt the need. He saw from the corner of his eye that the man beside him—the one praying for his baby grandson born prematurely—had done the same, and the woman in front of him with her child in a harness.

They stared at the window together, along with the rest of the congregation, as a glow gathered behind it, dim at first, then brightening.

"Dear God," the man whispered, adding to the murmur of the crowd.

The light grew brighter, the colored panes glowed brilliantly, mesmerizing him. Then the shadow appeared around the Virgin, an outline of a man standing behind her, arms outstretched as if to embrace her.

"Oh my Lord," the man said, louder this time.

The others added their own exclamations.

"The light..."

"It's so beautiful..."

"My God."

"Jesus Christ," the woman with her boy on a leash screeched suddenly, startling the man. "It's Jesus."

The light brightened until it blotted out the colors of the window and the shape of the Virgin Mary, brightened until only the outline of the man remained, a dark shadow-crucifixion framed in the window.

Then the light went out.

The man blinked and saw the shape every time his lids closed, the image temporarily burned into his retinas, the memory etched indelibly in his memory and his soul. Tears spilled down his cheeks and he pushed through the crowd, desperate to call his father and see how he felt.

· · · ● ●● ● ● · ·

Trevor opened his eyes and stared up at the ceiling: white, plain, a cobweb dangling in one corner. Could be any ceiling, but not the ceiling of his bedroom—no Lamb of God poster pinned over the bed. He sat up, half-expecting it to be a struggle and his body full of aches and pains. It wasn't.

A quick glance around the room and he realized he was in a motel room: generic dresser, nondescript art on the walls and possibly the last remaining tube TV in the known universe. Knowing his locale did little to ease his nerves.

A sound caught Trevor's attention: running water. He shifted on the bed and looked toward the bathroom door which stood ajar half-an-inch, a sliver of light shining through. He swung his legs over the edge of the bed, not sure whether he intended to creep to the bathroom door and attempt to see who was behind it, or if he would creep right on by, out the front door and find his way home.

Before he stood, the decision was wrested from him.

The bathroom door swung open and a man stepped through—tall and broad, big by any standards, and wearing a black shirt open at the throat, black dress pants and a red blazer. His blond hair hung past his shoulders and he held a hand towel, drying his hands after washing.

"Ah, you're awake," the man said and smiled. His white teeth and golden eyes glimmered.

Trevor nodded once in reply but said nothing. He felt a familiarity about the man, like he'd met him before, but it eluded him. A friend of his Mom's? A parent of a classmate? Neither option felt right.

Then who?

The man tossed the towel over the worn arm of the desk chair and spread his arms in a welcoming gesture.

"You look confused, Trevor. Don't you remember me?"

The teenager looked at him for a full minute, scouring his memory while discovering nothing but the feeling you get when you hear a song and know the title but can't quite fish it out of the bowels of your brain. Finally, he shook his head.

"I'm not surprised, really. You weren't in the best condition last time we met." The man crossed the last two paces to stand in front of Trevor, hand extended expectantly. "I'm Michael."

Trevor's eyes widened and he sucked a whistling breath in through his teeth.

The archangel.

Chapter Twelve

Boarding a subway car in Hell didn't seem like the best idea. I'd seen too many horror flicks and read too many stories in which shitty things happen to people who ride subways: *Jacob's Ladder*, *The Midnight Meat Train*, *Another Man's Shoes* and a whole raft of others. Subways are famous for providing havens for demons and ghouls of all sorts.

Piper took a step toward the train's open doors.

"I don't know, Pipe."

"We don't have much choice."

I looked up and down the platform. The subway station ended in a blank wall at each end of the train with no doors, windows, alcoves or flights of stairs in between. Not so much as a line of graffiti marred the white surface; the door through which we'd come was gone. It seemed my angel friend was correct in her assessment.

"This place is fucked," I commented, not really intending to do so aloud. Piper looked at me and raised a sarcastic half-smile.

"No kidding, Sherlock."

"The phrase is 'no shit, Sherlock'."

"Whatever."

Tony looked nervous standing between us. His eyes darted side to side as he shifted from one foot to another like a kid who needed to pee. "Can we get out of here, guys. I got a bad feeling."

"There's nowhere else to go," Piper said taking a half-step toward the doors.

"That's what worries me." I breathed deep, collecting myself as the other two watched, awaiting a plan. How a guy like me ended up being the leader of a rescue team making their way through Hell is beyond me. Actually, I know exactly how it happened, but that still didn't make it a good idea.

"Fine. Let's go."

I grabbed Tony by the elbow and led him through the train's doors with Piper close behind. Every nerve in my body tingled, ready for whatever nightmare the subway might throw at us. But no door in Hell seems to lead where you think it should. It looked like we were stepping onto a brightly lit subway car and we ended up in a dark room.

"What the...?"

I turned back to see if the platform was still there, but the door slid closed behind us, locking us in before my eyes registered what room it was. I tried the door: gone. My hand still gripped Tony's arm and I felt a presence to my left—Piper, by the feel of it—so it seemed we'd all made it through. Better check, anyway.

"Piper?"

"I'm here."

"Where are we?"

I swear I heard her shrug.

I breathed deep, looking for a little courage from the air, but found only the dank smell reminiscent of a basement. With Tony's sleeve bunched in my fist, I stretched my other arm out before me, waving it in the empty air, and followed that up by sliding my toe forward, scraping it along a bare floor. When I determined the floor remained solid beneath my shoe, I completed the step then repeated the procedure.

Pitch, inky, absolute; no night was ever this dark. A line of cold sweat formed on my forehead as I moved, never knowing what I might touch or when the floor might run out beneath my feet. In the still of the darkness, my breath sounded a monsoon in my ears, my pulse beat like a Japanese Taiko drum ensemble. The noise fouled my brain almost as completely as the blackness robbed me of my vision. I wiped the sweat on my forehead away with my sleeve.

The monsoon roared, the drummers hammered away and paranoia built in me like water threatening to overflow a dam. I rubbed my fingers together to feel the cloth of Tony's shirt, hoping it would anchor me to reality, but I felt only the fleshy pads of my fingertips and realized it had been a very long time since I heard the sound of my companions' footsteps through the din in my head.

"Still with me, Pipe?"

"I'm here, Icarus."

The sound of her voice quieted my brain. "Ric."

"Piper."

"Whatever. Keeping up okay, Tony?"

No answer.

"Tony?"

Nothing. I stopped and Piper walked into the back of me, throwing me off balance and sending the usual jolt up my spine.

"Tony," I called, louder this time, and looked around at the same black in every direction. "Where are you?"

My voice echoed from unseen walls then died away, replaced by what I'd describe as a grumble. Not an 'I don't wanna eat my peas, Dad' grumble, but the grumble of distant thunder or the sound of a minor earthquake.

"What the fuck is that?"

Piper grabbed my arm in answer and rushed me into the impenetrable dark. I resisted but the shock of her energy flowing through me precluded anything except obeying her every wish.

Death and torture filled my head instead of lustful visions. Panic clogged my throat and I gave up any idea of resisting. If the panic I felt flowed from her to me, I harbored no desire to know its cause.

We stumbled forward and the rumble followed, creeping slowly closer with each step. Out of habit, I glanced over my shoulder, but saw nothing beyond the gory images Piper's touch planted in my head. I followed her blindly.

We slowed and Piper jolted like she ran into something. The sound of metal scraping metal followed, overwhelming the grumble at my heels, and a gust of cool air against my cheek startled me. Piper pulled me ahead and my feet caught, spilling us through the emergency exit door she'd opened and onto pavement developing a rime of frost. My injured arm smacked the ground sending a lance of agony through me.

The door slammed shut behind us.

"Shit." I sat up cradling my arm against my chest. "That fucking hurt."

"Sorry."

I forced the pain from my mind and looked around feeling a bit frantic.

"Where's Tony?"

"I don't think he made it."

"Dammit."

Logically, I should have been disappointed—all that work for nothing—but relieved was how I really felt. After what we saw of him in Hell, the decision of Tony's salvation had been wrested from me. Did I actually want to bring him back, send him to Heaven?

"Maybe he shouldn't have been brought back," Piper said echoing my thoughts.

"Maybe."

She rested her hand on my injured arm, filled my limb with warmth and forced dueling regret and relief from my head. No illicit thoughts or torture scenes this time; instead the electricity concentrated on one spot, clung to the break in my bone. The pain eased, overwhelmed by warmth. I looked at her hand, half-expecting a glow radiating around it, a pulsation, the sound of a choir singing. There were none of those.

When I looked up, she was staring into my face.

She smiled.

I smiled.

Like a scene out of a chick-flick Rae made me watch once upon a time, we leaned toward each other, static electricity jumping between us. After losing Tony, I didn't know if this was the right thing to do. That, but also because she was an angel and the powers-that-be might not feel good about me fishing off the company dock.

But I couldn't stop myself.

Didn't really want to.

She leaned closer and I felt her breath on my lips. The tip of her nose touched mine sending a tiny shock into my face. We readjusted our angle.

Closer.

Closer.

Our lips touched and an indescribable feeling washed into my face and down my body like the tide overtaking the shore.

Suddenly, I thought I knew what it would be like to go to Heaven.

· · · ● ● ● ● ● ● · ·

The street lamp buzzed, flickered, then went out. Poe glanced up, neither startled nor afraid; street lights often malfunctioned when she was near, though she didn't know exactly why. A result of her energy, she guessed.

She looked back to the plain, gray exterior wall of the warehouse. No signage announced its contents, but she knew it contained stacks of low-end patio furniture awaiting shipment to discount department stores. She'd been here before, as an observer, like this time, but this felt very different. Last time, when Icarus brought the detective, she only kept her eye on him, ready to keep him safe if anything went wrong—just doing her job. This time, however, a feeling with which she'd been unfamiliar for decades hung over her: dread.

She leaned against the brick wall of the building kitty-corner to the warehouse and crossed her arms in front of her chest. Half an hour passed as she waited, her mind examining the events of the last few days, forming questions.

Why did Icarus want to go to Hell so badly? What happened there? Who is Piper?

She didn't have the answers, found herself unable to divine the motivations of a man like Icarus Fell even after all the years watching him, protecting him. Beneath all the questions and concerns about her charge lurked the one question she was afraid to put to words:

Why is Michael angry with me?

Maybe she wasn't always the best guardian, wasn't always around when Icarus needed her. She'd carried the guilt of his death with her every second since it happened, but everything turned out for the best. If muggers hadn't killed him, who'd harvest souls? Wasn't the balance better maintained with how things happened?

She couldn't shake the feeling there was more at play here than she knew.

The clang of the fire exit door slamming open startled Poe, jarring her thoughts. Two figures stumbled through the doorway and tumbled onto the ground. From across the street, Poe heard the man grunt and recognized Icarus' voice. She took one step, intending to rush to his aid, but stopped when she saw the second figure was a woman: Piper. She eased back into the shadows.

The two of them righted themselves, Icarus holding his arm against his chest, like it was injured. Her heart jumped and the urge to rush to him sprang back to her limbs but she contained it. It was her job to keep Icarus safe, but she didn't trust the woman, and her purpose for being here was to observe. She couldn't interrupt.

The woman put her hand on Icarus' shoulder and a shudder ran up Poe's back—not cold or fear, but like a piece of her had been pulled free, yanked from the base of her spine and out the top of her head. Her head spun and she struggled to keep focus.

They leaned toward each other and she decided to make them stop. There was something wrong about this woman. Poe opened her mouth, intending to call out a warning, but no sound came from her throat. Her legs wouldn't carry her forward. She watched, voyeuristic as their lips touched; her stomach coiled in a knot like watching Icarus die all over again.

It wasn't my fault.

As they pulled apart—Icarus' eyes closed, lost in the moment—the woman glanced across the street and made eye contact with Poe, the corners of her mouth curving up in a look-what-I-did grin. Fire flashed in her eyes.

Poe threw her hands in front of her face and fled up the street without looking back.

· · · ● · ● · ● · · ·

Poe disliked few people, places or things, but the motel Michael favored for use as his earthly office made the list. She supposed the things which made her dislike the place were exactly why he chose it: a dirty, run-down haven for prostitutes and junkies in a part of the city regular folk feared to travel through, let alone stop in. Who'd expect to find the archangel Michael here?

He met her in the dimly lit lobby. There was a small TV mounted near the ceiling in one corner facing a tattered couch, the sound of the shopping channel muted. A rack of out-dated brochures and fliers, most of them advertising tattoo shops or massage parlors long-since busted and closed, dominated another wall. Behind the plexi-glass barrier protecting the check-in-er from the check-in-ees, a scrawny man who could have been one of the junkie-residents rather than the proprietor sat in a chair, chin resting on his chest as he snored quietly and drooled on the front of his shirt. Michael lounged on the couch dressed in a black suit and white shirt open at the throat, a red rose in the lapel of his jacket, looking very much like she'd interrupted his evening of ballroom dancing.

"So?"

Poe tip-toed across the room, though she suspected the man behind the counter wouldn't have woken if she'd brought a marching band. If the substance causing his slumber didn't keep him from waking, Michael's influence certainly would. She perched on the edge of the couch, as far from the archangel as space allowed.

"He's been to Hell," she said, her voice a whisper. She didn't meet Michael's eyes.

"I know. We have one extra soul in stock: one Elizabeth Elton. A former neighbor of our harvester's, I believe."

She nodded but said nothing. Michael's tone held its usual calm, but she sensed something underlying it which made her want to get up and leave before she found out what it was.

"What else?"

"He went a second time."

"And?"

"He didn't bring anyone back."

Poe's eyes flickered to him as Michael's narrowed, searching her face. She looked away.

"You are sure?"

Poe nodded again.

Michael leaned forward, elbows resting on his knees, and looked up at the TV. Poe followed his gaze and saw a pretty woman with dark hair modeling a cubic zirconia necklace. When she looked away from the model, Michael was scrutinizing her again. Panic and regret exploded in her chest; she nearly fell to her knees to beg the archangel's forgiveness without knowing what she should be forgiven for. She'd let him down in some way, that was obvious—something she'd never want to do given all eternity with which to work—and she wanted to make it up to him, no matter what it was.

"This is your fault."

Poe's breath caught in her throat.

"But...I..."

"It is your job to keep the harvester from trouble and harm." He leaned back and threw his arm along the back of the couch. Normally, Poe would have struggled against the urge to snuggle in against him, bask in his energy. Not this time. "You have failed him, and you have failed me."

Her airway tightened as she struggled to hold back tears. Her lower lip quivered.

"While he is indulging his whims, others are lost because he is not here to do his job." He flipped his hair out of his face with a quick flick of his head. "Someone needs to get him back to work."

"I've tried," Poe said, her words coming in a rush. "He's determ ined...to bring them all...back. He won't stop...until he has. There's this woman...a woman helping him. Piper. She's making things worse. She—"

Michael held up his hand and Poe stopped speaking immediately.

"Who is this woman?"

"I don't know. She says she's a guardian."

"Perhaps she will do a better job than you did."

Poe looked away, afraid his accusatory glare might burn her soul.

"At any rate, souls need to be harvested. Any suggestions?"

Michael rose without waiting for an answer. He crossed the lobby to the door marked 'stairs' and glanced back before going through. Poe didn't need him to speak to know he wanted her to follow. The man behind the plexi-glass barrier stirred as she passed, but didn't wake. She pushed through the door and into the stairwell and picked her way through the garbage littering the steps. Two flights up, a door swung closed. Poe chewed her lower lip, dreading further confrontation with the archangel but knowing she had no choice but to follow.

On the third floor, Poe went down the hallway with its peeling wallpaper and worn carpeting to the door Michael had left open. She paused before stepping through. All these years she'd done her best. For Icarus, for Michael. As she stepped across the threshold, her life—the life she'd lost—passed before her eyes.

She couldn't bear the thought of losing this one, too.

Michael stood at the end of the short hall blocking the sleeping area of the room. The laugh track of a television sit-com came from behind him. Poe closed the door.

"There have been rumors about you, Poe."

She froze, eyes wide. *What kind of rumors could there possibly be?*

"I...I don't understand."

"Question about your loyalties. You have been on both sides."

"No, I—"

Michael held up his hand again and again she fell silent though her mind worked feverishly. She'd worked so hard for so long...

"Your words are unnecessary. It is your actions which will set you free. As problematic as the harvester's choices have been, his timing may have worked in your favor."

The feeling of dread returned to Poe with enough force to make her head feel light. She put her hand against the wall to steady herself.

"What do you mean?"

"You will do the harvester's job until he returns on his own accord or you convince him to come back. And you will take him with you."

Michael stepped aside and gestured toward a figure lying on the bed watching TV. The motel's neon sign shone through the open curtains, turning the person into silhouette. Poe took a few uncertain steps down the hall and saw the man's unkempt hair and youthful features as she drew closer. When she stepped into the room, he faced her and she saw him in the glow of the television.

"Hi, Poe."

The world wavered before her eyes.

"Trevor."

Chapter Thirteen

T HEY STOOD ON THE sidewalk looking up at the window, mimicking the worshipers and miracle-seekers pressed close around them.

"Are you sure this is where we need to be? I was here before." Trevor looked at the faces in the crowd. "A lot more people now."

Poe looked from the window to Trevor's narrow face, into his washed-out brown eyes.

He looks a lot like Icarus.

"I'm sure. What do you think drew you here?"

"I don't know. Because this is where shit went down, maybe."

"Maybe. Or maybe because this is where your father went through."

Trevor looked at her and she averted her eyes back to the stained glass Madonna.

"'Went through'? Went through what? Where?"

She raised a finger toward the window. It *was* amazing it survived the blast; she understood why all these people were gathered on the sidewalk to beseech their creator.

"Went through there," she said, then lowered her voice. "To Hell."

Trevor grabbed Poe's arm, but let go immediately, surprised by the shock the touch gave him. He gestured for her to follow and stepped out of the crowd.

"What do you mean Hell? The big guy said he's out of town. We're supposed to harvest a soul while he's away."

"Trevor." Poe took him by the shoulders, saw the look in his eyes as her energy flowed into him. She tried to limit it. "Your father is in Hell."

The teenager's eyes stared blankly for a moment then, slowly, he looked back toward the window.

"Hell," he repeated.

"Yes. I couldn't live with myself if something happened to him. I have to get him back."

"But what about Michael? He'll be pissed."

Poe sighed heavily, her shoulders slouched. She didn't want to anger the archangel further but the weight of her responsibilities pressed on her. If she'd done her job, been a better guardian for Icarus, he wouldn't be in this situation, probably wouldn't have met the woman, Piper.

Piper.

Her name stirred the memory of the kiss she saw them share and her gut clenched like someone ringing out a dishcloth. Something about the woman made her angry and afraid, but she didn't know what or why. Was it something wrong? Was it jealousy?

No.

Trevor's elbow prodded her side, pulling her from her thoughts, and she realized he'd spoken.

"What?"

He answered by pointing up the block to a white van; black, two-foot-high lettering identified it as belonging to TV19 news. A pudgy, balding man was pulling a camera out of the van while a pretty woman wearing a gray blazer smoothed creases out of her black skirt. Poe looked back to the crowd, which had grown since their arrival, and saw two policemen near the back, their police hats bobbing above the heads of the worshipers.

"We can't do this now, can we?" Trevor asked.

We? Poe didn't bother telling him he wouldn't be going, not yet.

"No. Too many people."

"What do we do?"

Poe knew many paths to Heaven, but the ways to Hell changed constantly—they wouldn't be easily discovered. Many years had passed since she last trod them and the ones she'd known would be long gone. She scratched her elbow, pondering the possibilities, and an idea occurred to her.

"We'll do as Michael asked."

"Harvest a soul? But what about my Dad?"

Poe started down the sidewalk, excusing herself as she passed the cameraman and news lady. Trevor followed a step or two behind.

"Don't worry about your father."

· · · • • • • • · · ·

It didn't take long for the swallows to find them and, as always, Gabriel appeared soon after. As she approached, Poe fought the urge to hide behind Trevor. It wasn't fear which made her want to take cover every time she saw Gabriel, but awe, like she was in the presence of a movie star. Awe and jealousy—she wished mortals reacted to her the way they did to the archangel.

"Hello, Poe," Gabriel sing-songed.

Poe raised a hand and fluttered her fingers in response.

"And who do we have here?" The archangel nodded toward Trevor.

Poe looked at the teen and saw his mouth agape and eyes wide, the same sort of reaction most males experienced upon meeting Gabriel.

"Trevor. He's Icarus' son."

"Of course. I see the resemblance."

Poe shifted her weight from one foot to the other, uncomfortable with Gabriel's gaze on her. She wiped sweaty palms on her thighs.

"Icarus isn't here," she said.

"I know."

"Michael sent me to do the job."

"I know."

Poe tried to look the archangel in the eyes but her gaze kept skittering away regardless of what she wanted. Enthralled by the angel, Trevor neither moved nor spoke. Poe wondered if she should check and make sure he remembered to draw breath.

"Do...do you have a scroll for me?"

Gabriel produced a roll of parchment from behind her back, smiled, and held it out to Poe. Unconsciously, the guardian angel took a step back and half a step to the side, partially hiding behind Trevor.

"You know what to do?"

Poe didn't sense condescension in her voice, but after the things Michael had said, she didn't know if Gabriel spoke out of concern or something else. She suppressed the urge to snatch the scroll away, instead allowing the angel to place it on her outstretched palm.

"Yes. I've seen it a few times."

A swallow flitted between them, a streak of blue-green barreling through the air. Trevor finally showed some reaction by following its path with his eyes.

"You don't have much time."

"Okay."

Gabriel nodded once and lifted her arms skyward like she intended to embrace the entire firmament. A cloud of swallows Poe hadn't noticed rose from branches of trees and roofs of buildings, swirling into a tornado of blue and white. They darted about performing aerobatics, following Gabriel as she walked away and disappeared between two buildings. As soon as she was gone, Trevor became aware of the world again, like he'd woken from a deep sleep.

"Who was she?"

Poe stepped out from behind him and looked at the roll of parchment. She'd seen Icarus with scrolls before but never held one herself; energy radiated from it making her palm itch. It built as she stared at it imagining her flesh reddening beneath, bumps and welts forming, blisters bursting.

"Poe?"

"Take it," she said breathlessly. "Please take it."

Trevor took the parchment and she rubbed her palm vigorously on her leg before regarding it. No marks left behind, no open sores; the itch disappeared as soon as the paper no longer contacted her flesh.

"Are you okay?"

"I think so."

She rubbed her hand on the thigh of her pants again, just in case.

"What did you ask me?"

"I asked you who she was."

They walked, though they hadn't unrolled the scroll yet and didn't know where they should go. Poe didn't want to stay there and chance seeing Gabriel again.

"The archangel Gabriel."

"Really? Wow. Two archangels in one day."

"You may not remember it, but you've met Raphael, too." She glanced back over her shoulder—there were no swallows to be seen.

"Cool. And does this scroll tell us who's going to die?"

Poe nodded. "Gabriel said we didn't have much time. You better open it."

They paused in the middle of the sidewalk as Trevor unrolled the parchment. It wouldn't contain the name of anyone she knew—anyone she knew was long since dead—but she held her breath anyway.

·········

She'd seen worse deaths, but Poe worried the sight of blood might disturb Trevor. It turned out teenage boys hadn't changed much since her time on earth.

The man—a forty-eight year old father of two named Clayton Dillinger who'd been married to his high school sweetheart for twenty-two years—extended himself too far while installing Christmas lights on the eaves of his bungalow. The fall itself would have hurt but probably not killed him except for the collection of garden gnomes his wife had arrayed in the flower garden the spring before. One smiling gnome with a particularly pointy hat broke a couple of Clayton's ribs, driving one clear through his heart and out his chest.

"Oh, gross," Trevor exclaimed with a note of enthusiastic joy in his words—the sound of a young man who'd watched too many horror movies.

Seconds after Mr. Dillinger's life expired, a semi-opaque second Mr. Dillinger sat up, separating himself from the first. The specter stood and gazed down at the lifeless body, then looked up expectantly, waiting for what came next.

"There he is. Let's go get him." Trevor took a step to cross the street but Poe put her hand on his arm, stopping him. He looked back at her over his shoulder.

"Wait."

She pulled him back into the shadows and watched a figure approach from down the street. Poe had first sensed they were being followed when they got on the bus to make their way to Mr. Dillinger's house but had done nothing to dissuade their tail. If it was who she suspected, their pursuer would have the same purpose as they did. Unfortunately, this man wouldn't lead Mr. Dillinger to Heaven; he would lead Poe to Hell, though.

The man closed in, raised a hand to Mr. Dillinger, and called out a greeting. Poe recognized him –his shaven head, black trench coat and neatly trimmed beard. As she realized he was the same Carrion who had nearly killed her a few months back, he looked her way and grinned a devilish grin, eyes flashing red fire.

And then he spoke with Mr. Dillinger.

"Who's that?" Trevor asked.

"Carrion."

Poe felt Trevor's eyes move to the two men across the street and back again without removing her gaze from their conversation. It took all her self-control not to run across the road and push herself between the two men. She'd dedicated herself to protecting mortal souls for decades and found it difficult to give one up without a fight.

It's for the greater good.

"Carrion? But don't they take souls to Hell?"

Poe nodded.

"We can't let him. Hey!"

Trevor took another step but this time when Poe touched his arm, she concentrated on her touch, sent her energy into him. He stiffened with it; she let him go, guilt tickling the lining of her stomach.

"We have to help him," he wheezed, his breath gone.

"Trust me."

He settled beside her, watching the proceedings outside the Dillinger house. Clayton and the Carrion stood beside the ladder looking at the gnome-skewered body, the blood soaking his shirt and jacket, a string of icicle lights dangling from the eaves. They spoke quietly, then Mr. Dillinger shook the Carrion's hand and they started down the block together. The Carrion shot another look over his shoulder at them, grinning like a schoolyard bully who'd won the game by cheating and knew they wouldn't do anything about it. When he looked away, Poe grabbed Trevor's arm and pulled him down the street.

"Wha...what are we doing?" he asked sounding dazed from her last touch. "He's gone. The Carrion got him."

She stopped and turned the teen to face her, holding him by both shoulders. Though only fifteen, he stood nearly a foot taller than her and she had to tilt her head back to meet his eyes.

"I'm following him to Hell to find your father."

Chapter Fourteen

I RUBBED MY CALF—THE latest body part missing a piece due to a foul-looking hell-beast's bite—and was surprised at how good my arm felt. Hard to believe Piper healed it so quickly.

Poe never healed me.

"What do we do this time?" she asked.

A hot wind blew down the empty street, swirling gray dust into miniature tornadoes. The gargoyles on the corners of the buildings stared straight ahead, ignoring us, as Piper's words echoed from building to building.

"Not sure," I replied, straightening. "Where did everyone go?"

She shrugged—of course—then took my hand and led me down the street. Her touch electrified me, as always, but this time it called more peaceful and soothing visions to mind. I wondered who determined how her touch affected me: her, me, or someone higher up? As we walked, it felt like we were lovers enjoying a stroll rather than a mother leading a child, as it might have before.

My mind strayed to the feel of her lips on mine.

"Pipe, about what happened."

"Piper," she said and stopped. "I think something's going on over there."

I looked down the boulevard in the direction she'd indicated. In the distance, a haze hung above the street; it might have been mist but seemed more likely ash kicked into the air by many feet.

"A crowd," I said.

"Or a mob."

"We're not going to find anyone we're looking for if no one's around."

She shrugged. "You want to go?"

"I don't know. Do you want to go?"

With words like this being spoken, it couldn't have been anything but a date. Put us somewhere else and we'd have sounded like a couple deciding between Italian and Chinese.

"Let's go."

Our fingers remained entwined as we made our way down the empty street. The buildings and the gargoyles perched at their corners ignored us, but I still felt like our echoing footsteps called unwanted attention our way. I peered in windows and doorways and saw no one.

Where did everyone go?

We heard the crowd before we saw them. Their voices combined to a tumultuous roar hanging over their heads like the cloud of ash kicked up by their shuffling feet, like a rock concert without the rock. Though, given the way most rock stars lived and died, Hell would probably put on quite a show.

As we drew closer, we saw people shoe-horned together, bodies writhing and twisting to get a view over those in front of them. The crowd at the end of the boulevard was huge, big enough we couldn't see past them to find out what held their attention. I stood on my toes, stretched to my fullest, to no avail.

"Come on," Piper said pulling me forward.

Thirty feet from the mob, a small group of people broke off and headed toward the closest building. Six men, bare-chested and heavily muscled, encircled two figures like a cadre of body guards protecting a politician. I strained to see who they protected and caught a glimpse of a boy—the boy I'd seen staring at the camera when we found Tony. On his right, a woman held his hand, dark hair flowing down her back. When we reached the edge of the crowd, she glanced back at me: high cheek bones, angular jaw, dark eyes.

My mother.

I dragged my feet trying to stop Piper's forward motion, tugged hard to free my hand of her grasp. My lips parted, to call out to the woman who gave birth to me, to beg Piper to stop, but the crowd swallowed us; their clamor drowned any words I might have spoken.

The crowd closed around us, cutting off my view, and Piper forced a path between the gathering of damned souls. As we moved, it became apparent that personal hygiene is not a high priority in Hell. The stench of tens of thousands of bodies unwashed for—weeks? Years? Centuries?—stuck to the inside of my nostrils and throat threatening to choke me, urging my last meal up into my chest. I swallowed hard to put it back where it belonged.

"My God, these people reek."

The ones closest to us ceased moaning and chanting and faced me, their expressions moving from vacant to annoyed. Who knew they'd be so easily offended?

Piper pulled me close. "This may be the wrong place to use the lord's name in vain. Or any other way."

"Right." I smiled weakly and nodded at the faces around us. "Sorry about that. Force of habit."

They returned to their mindless noise-making and we went back to finding our way through the crowd—no harm done. I shuffle-stepped closer to Piper.

"I saw my mother," I shouted to be heard above the commotion. "Did you see her?"

"No."

"She was with the kid I saw before."

She didn't respond.

"Who is he?"

A patented Piper shrug. "I don't know. Do you want to stop and ask someone?"

I glanced at the zombie faces around us.

"No. Think I'll pass."

Ten minutes passed and we still hadn't reached the front of the crowd. Stinking bodies rubbed against me, loose hands groped me unenthusiastically. Foul breath, distant stares, filthy flesh. I held my breath like a child driving through a tunnel, desperate to keep the air in his lungs until the other end to earn the right to make a wish. When my lungs wouldn't cooperate anymore, I'd let it out and draw another with a whoosh, each time wishing for fresh air.

Many members of the crowd were naked, some of them engaged in sexual activities. This might sound exciting, but not in Hell. It was ugly sex, and if any of these people were attractive in life, Hell beat, burned and crushed it out of them.

As we finally neared the front of the crowd, the din became louder. I caught a glimpse of an empty platform, nothing else. Piper turned her head toward me and said something, at least I assume she did. I saw her lips move but the words she spoke disappeared in the noise.

"What?"

She moved away, unaware I'd spoken.

"Piper," I yelled. No reaction.

Then her hand slipped out of mine.

The crowd swallowed her in an instant, like the whale taking Geppetto in the story of *Pinocchio*. One second she was there, the next... gone.

"Piper!"

I no longer tried to hold my breath as I gasped air in and out, eyes darting from face to face, searching for my angel.

"Piper!"

I fought my way through the crowd, pushing aside slack-limbed people who didn't care they'd been pushed aside. Frantic, I bulled my way forward.

How did she disappear so quickly?

And then I was at the front of the crowd.

The ramshackle platform stood a couple of feet high and looked thrown together from scrap pieces of wood, duct tape and bent metal. A woman stood in the middle of it attempting to hide her nakedness behind a slim lectern but it was too narrow to keep her sagging breasts from view. She shuffled some papers on the stand, cleared her throat.

They say some people fear public speaking more than death—before me stood the living-dead proof.

A sheet of paper fluttered to the platform and she attempted a smile, but her nervousness and the tears on her cheeks ruined the effort. The woman bent at the waist to retrieve it and a tomato flew out of the crowd to splatter against the dirt-streaked flesh of her right buttock. Surprised, the woman stumbled a step but didn't fall. I chuckled a little at that, then immediately felt guilty as she straightened and faced the crowd again.

More projectiles struck her: another tomato, a head of lettuce, a shapeless blob which may have been mud or feces, and finally a rock which caught her in the left cheek, drawing blood to add to the flow of tears. She flinched each time a projectile struck her but held her ground, taking her punishment for being so audacious as to think she could stand before a group of people and give a speech.

Any urge I'd had to laugh was long gone. We all had our own Hells to go through. My heart ached for her, but I kept myself from jumping in front of her.

A second rock struck her chest, then a third caught her in the eye. I couldn't watch anymore and diverted my gaze. To my surprise, I saw a familiar face standing at the front of the crowd, staring at me. The man looked more tired than I'd seen him in life, his suit more rumpled. At first, I didn't believe my eyes; it must be some sort of Hell illusion.

Detective Williams.

The last time I saw him, I left him with a white-clad angel to take him to Heaven. Given those circumstances, this must be his twin—the real Detective Williams would be lounging on a billowy white cloud enjoying the hereafter.

He raised his hand in greeting.

I waved back hesitantly and mouthed the words 'what happened?' He responded by changing his wave to a different sort of gesture. I watched for a second, confused, unaware he meant it as a gesture of warning until the black cloth bag covered my face and a cord cinched around my neck.

Chapter Fifteen

T HEY WATCHED FROM THE shadows as the Carrion took Clayton Dillinger down the back alley, away from the bustling avenue. The closer they got to the goal, the worse Poe felt. Her stomach churned like a supernova swirled within her. Her nerve endings tingled, she rubbed sweat from her palms; she hid it from Trevor, didn't want to scare him. Truthfully, she didn't want him to be here at all, but she might need his help getting to Hell.

And it was good for someone to know she'd gone.

At the end of the alley, the Carrion crouched, stuck his fingers into the holes in a manhole cover, and lifted it as though it was made of cardboard. A light emanated out of the sewer access, flickering and glowing as if all the shit and gases in the sewer were on fire. The Carrion gestured and Mr. Dillinger's soul hesitated. The man in black gestured again, insistent, but Mr. Dillinger shook his head and backed away a step. A few seconds passed, the situation appearing to be a stalemate until the Carrion took a deep breath and grabbed the spirit by the front of his jacket. Dillinger struggled a moment, but he was no match. The Carrion stuffed him down the manhole and quickly climbed down after him.

And left the manhole cover off.

Poe fidgeted in the shadow, staring from manhole cover lying on the ground to the glow emanating from below.

"Should we go?" Trevor sounded more excited than nervous.

Poe watched for another second, suspicious. Nothing happened.

Maybe he's forgetful. She half-stood, stretching to see further down the hole. Nothing. *Not bloody likely.*

Whether she'd stumbled on a careless Carrion or he'd left the cover off to entice her down was irrelevant. Her goal was to get to Hell and this was the way. She stood and Trevor was at her side in an instant, nervous excitement radiating from him.

"You're staying here," she said looking at him.

He shook his head. "He's my dad, Poe. I'm not losing him again."

"You have to stay and let Michael know I've gone." She reached up and put her hand on his cheek. "And I can't risk both of you."

He looked back at her, the muscles in his jaw clenching and un-clenching. His eyes flickered to the manhole and back and, for a moment, Poe worried he might be considering going anyway. Then he let out his breath and the tension left his body. Poe relaxed, too, and in that second, Trevor bolted for the manhole.

"No!"

Her fingers brushed the back of his jacket as he dove through the opening, then he was gone.

Poe stood for a few seconds, hands pressed against her eyes, and drew a shuddering breath.

Hell.

She went through the opening.

· · · ● · ● · ● · · ·

Heat.

I don't remember it being this hot.

Poe glanced at Trevor but the temperature didn't seem to affect him. He sauntered along, hands in pockets, like any other fifteen-year-old slouching their way down the street on a sunny afternoon. He didn't notice Poe looking at him, the sheer cliff rising on their right holding his attention.

"Are you doing okay?" It wasn't what she wanted to ask—that would have sounded more like 'what the Hell were you thinking?' But there was no point chastising him now. And, truthfully, she felt safer having him there.

"Fine."

"What about the heat?"

"I'm good."

She wiped sweat off her forehead with the back of her hand and in turn wiped her hand on the leg of her pants. Her legs quivered as they walked the path with the cliff looming over them to the right and an expansive plain free of grass or shrubs stretched to their left. She might have imagined the surface of Mars to look like this.

Except Mars wouldn't have had the desiccated souls making their way across the rocky plains, hands and ankles bound together by chains.

"Wow," Trevor said looking skyward. "What's that?"

Poe looked up at the swirling gray clouds and saw what Trevor meant: a winged creature made its way across the bleak tapestry of sky. More followed in a loose flock, flying past, then circling back on the same path.

"Keepers," Poe responded feeling suddenly breathless.

"Keepers?"

She nodded. "Exactly what it sounds like." Her lungs burned.

"This is exactly how I imagined Hell. Just like in the movies."

"For now."

Poe stopped and bent at the waist, hands resting on her knees like she'd set a personal best in the Boston Marathon. Trevor continued a few steps before realizing she'd stopped. He turned back, the youthful enthusiasm of his voice disappearing.

"Are you alright?"

"Have...to...catch...my...breath."

"I'll try to find some water."

She caught him by the wrist.

"No. Don't drink...or...eat anything."

"Sure." He shook his hand away and looked around. "What can I do?"

"Need...rest."

Poe sank to the dusty ground and sat cross-legged, head hung, elbows resting on her knees. She concentrated on filling her lungs, but they wouldn't cooperate. A droplet of sweat rolled down her nose and clung to the tip. She watched it, eyes crossing, as it shivered, lengthened, fell. It hit the ground in a puff of dust which grew up toward her, blurring her vision. Poe blinked to clear it away, but the world grew hazy.

"Poe?"

She tried to raise her head to look at Trevor, assure him she was okay, but the task felt like raising a medicine ball at the end of a yard stick.

"I...," she managed.

The world went black.

· · · · ·· · · · ·

Trevor jumped forward and caught the guardian angel before she struck the ground.

"Poe?" he said shaking her a little. "Poe."

Her open eyes stared blankly toward the roiling sky and one of the keepers screeched high overhead. Trevor leaned his face toward Poe's and felt her breath on his cheek.

"Passed out," he said aloud and smiled with relief. "If you can't take the heat, get out of the abyss."

Poe had complained about the heat, but he didn't feel it. Maybe the nether world affected mortals and angels differently.

Maybe it doesn't affect me because I'm supposed to be here.

He didn't really remember his abduction by Azrael, but between what he did recall and what his father told him, he thought it might be time for a healthy dose of fear.

If Poe didn't recover, how would he get out of here?

He looked up at the keepers wheeling through the sky above. They appeared closer now, close enough he saw them as man-shaped creatures with wings rather than birds. Gargoyles.

Are they coming closer because of us or is it a coincidence?

He didn't want to hang around to find out.

Trevor lay Poe down, careful not to bang her head on the stony ground, then walked to the cliff; its sheer face looked an impossible climb without equipment, even without an incapacitated angel on his hands. He thought about leaving her to search for help, but he banished it immediately. Forget what might happen to her, what kind of help would he find in Hell?

Trevor turned from the cliff and looked across the boulder-strewn plain toward the chain-gangs of damned souls marching across it. They trudged slowly, like they had no real destination or desire to get there. They also didn't look dangerous, not with their hands and feet chained, at least.

"That way."

He returned to Poe, checked her breathing, then worked his arms under her shoulders and knees. Before standing, he took a couple of breaths, preparing himself for the strain of her weight, but when he stood, he found her quite light. And touching her didn't bring the same sensation he'd felt before.

"Not good."

He put it from his mind—worrying wouldn't help.

His first steps carrying Poe were unsteady, but he soon found his footing. He dragged his feet as he walked, sending loose rock and gravel skittering ahead, and he glanced up frequently, tracking the keepers as they flew overhead.

Closer. Definitely closer.

He increased his pace to as fast as he dared, careful not to lose his footing on the loose stones. The rocks his steps sent clattering across the ground sounded unnaturally loud, each impact of stone against stone echoing in his head like a bowling ball thundering down the alley. Ahead of him, the lines of damned souls looked to have heard the ruckus and amended their path to intercept him.

"That's not good."

Trevor veered further to his right to avoid the creatures he presumed had once been healthy, and perhaps happy, living things. Despite their languid pace, the distance between them closed. A keeper screeched above, too close for comfort; Trevor forced himself not to look up and veered harder right.

He almost walked over the edge of the canyon before he noticed it.

A chasm capable of making the Grand Canyon blush with inadequacy stretched out at his feet. The far side looked miles away, the bottom hidden by a swirl of thick, white mist—if a bottom existed at all.

"Shit."

Trevor looked back. Impossibly, the souls were ten yards away. He shuffled away from the edge and from the chain gang, his breath short, nervous bursts from the effort of carrying Poe.

And fear. This wasn't like doing a back flip off your friend's garage or eating something unstomachable on a dare. This was damnation, eternity.

The first hand on his shoulder startled him. He pulled away jerkily, teetering on the edge of losing his balance as Poe's dead weight shifted in his arms. Then the others were on him and he saw their unspeakable despair. Their mouths drooped in exaggerated expressions like ghostly Halloween masks, their eyes burned into him, pleading for help, for relief. Their uniformly gray skin looked like steak gone bad; their bodies and limbs were strangely elongated as though they'd been stretched on a rack.

Trevor gasped air in through his mouth, tried to pull away from their groping, but they outnumbered him too badly.

"Get away," he yelled, twisting and turning. "Leave us alone."

Long fingers brushed Poe's hair, stroked her cheek, caressed her arm. Shoulders bumped him, hands pushed him, but none sought to touch him directly. They all wanted to contact the angel in his arms.

"P-p-p-," one of them stuttered with a mouth unused to forming words.

"Oh," another groaned. "Oh."

The others in the group surrounding them—thirty, maybe more—added their unpracticed voices, increasing the volume and settling into a chant.

"P-p-p-," the first group stuttered.

"Oh. Oh," the second groaned.

Trevor looked frantically from one slack face to another, glanced over his shoulder. Nowhere to go but down.

How will we get out? Where can I go? What—

The cadence of the souls' chant interrupted his thoughts. The syllables connected in his head.

"P-p."
"Oh. Oh."
"P-p."
"Oh. Oh."

"P."

"Oh."

"P."

"Oh."

The creatures weren't stuttering and moaning, they were combining their voices to speak as best they could.

They're saying her name!

He jerked her away from their reaching hands, the aching muscles of his arms suddenly aware of the weight he carried. His feet stirred a low cloud of dust as he shuffled away until his heel hung over the edge of the chasm.

Nowhere else to go.

His pulse hammered in his ears, nearly drowning the chant of the damned souls. They pressed toward him and he could only hold his ground as they pawed he angel, touching her, caressing her. They didn't seem to want to hurt her, but how could he be sure?

"P."

"Oh."

One of them wrapped its long, gray fingers around her arm and tugged, testing his hold. Another grabbed her ankle, another her wrist. Together they pulled and Trevor stuttered forward a step trying to keep them from wrenching her from his grip. He should have been relieved to take a step away from the abyss, but the prospect of losing Poe to this mob—losing his guide, his way out and possibly his father's last hope—sent relief skittering into the clutches of fear and panic.

"No."

He pulled back and the hands gripping Poe let go, making him stumble back a step, two. With the second, his foot touched empty air.

The fall happened in slow motion. Trevor canted backward, his gaze locked on the souls directly in front of him. Their expressions didn't change—no surprise, shock, or regret—only maybe deeper disappointment in their eyes as what they saw as their possible redemption slipped over the edge.

Trevor tumbled backwards, the gray, despairing faces vanishing, replaced by angry clouds that made him miss the sun. He closed his eyes as the stinking air enveloped him, pulled him down toward the mist he knew swirled below hiding...what? Rocks? Monsters? Nothing?

Death.

Wind flapped his hair by his ears, and he imagined his mom and dad—not his parents how they were now, but how he remembered them: together and happy, as far as he'd known. He thought of the Tinker Toys he and Ric spent hours playing with, building cars and towers, simple structures for a young boy to enjoy. He thought of his mother taking him to soccer practices—a time he'd loved in his youth but lost interest in as he grew.

Why do things have to change?

And then the falling stopped.

He gripped Poe tighter against his chest and opened his eyes. The tortured sky hovered above; the sheer chasm wall floated beside him; his hair no longer whipped his cheeks. He felt arms under him—powerful, muscular arms supporting him the way he held Poe—and he glimpsed black wings flapping on either side of him, each stroke pulling them up out of the abyss.

Trevor kept his eyes fixed on the canyon wall sliding past as they rose. He didn't want to see what held him. In Hell, it couldn't possibly be better than falling to his death.

They floated up past the edge of the cliff and he saw the faces of the souls who had inadvertently caused their fall. This time, he saw their expressions change, the slack-cheeked desperation and despair shifting to fear bordering on terror. The souls shuffled away from the cliff, their chant ended, the chains binding them at ankle and wrist clanking.

Whatever carried Trevor and Poe lifted them thirty feet beyond the cusp of the canyon and the souls threw their heads back to watch. From above, Trevor saw how wrong he'd been about their numbers; where he thought the damned numbering thirty or forty, there were thousands of gray, fearful faces staring at them and the creature holding them.

The thing sank back toward the ground, its descent sending the souls shuffling back with a clatter of chains. It landed and set Trevor down, Poe still in his arms. The teenager stumbled away and the crowd of souls gasped, but he kept his balance and resisted the urge to turn and gaze upon his rescuer for fear it might also be his executioner.

Or worse.

"P," half the crowd before him began quietly.

"Oh," the other half answered.

"P."

"Oh."

The chant grew progressively louder until it echoed across the plain like a soccer match jeer. The ground trembled with it. Trevor looked at the angel unconscious in his arms and wondered if giving her to them might be the only way to save himself.

The creature behind him didn't give him the opportunity to give the idea serious thought.

The screech it emitted was loud enough he almost dropped Poe to cover his ears and protect his brain from scrambling. The soul-mob fell instantly silent.

It took a few seconds for the ringing in Trevor's ears to subside, leaving silence. He swallowed hard, the sound of saliva squeezing down his fear-constricted throat the first sound his ear drums comprehended. Then the cadence of his heart beating frantically in his chest. Finally, he felt as much as heard breath chuffing behind him, like a bull preparing to charge.

Trevor's body stiffened as he realized he could no longer ignore whatever stood behind him. Facing it might mean his death, but if that was the case, then not facing it would likely yield the same result. Wouldn't it be better to know it was coming than stand blindly in fear of it?

He thought so until he saw it.

Chapter Sixteen

THE BAG OVER MY head smelled like someone's high school gym shorts—ones brought the first day of school and unwashed until the last. I did my best not to inhale the stench as two men gripping my arms hard enough to hurt pulled me away. On the bright side, the bag smelled marginally better than the crowd of zombies.

My feet skittered across the ground finding no purchase to impede the men, so I gave up, stumbling along as they dragged me. If I fought them, I'd end up out of breath, gasping, and I didn't want to increase the taste of crotch already entering my mouth, so I decided to reason with them instead.

"I think you've got the wrong guy."

No response.

"I'm here to throw rocks like everyone else. Let me go punish that bitch for giving a speech. The nerve of her."

No response.

Try something else.

"You'll regret this. I'm a friend of Azrael. Let me go and I won't tell him what you did."

"Shut the fuck up, Ric."

Very few people remembered to call me Ric, no matter how often I insisted to the world not to call me Icarus, but recognition eluded me at first. I was never very good at the 'guess who' game. In fact, it usually pissed me off.

"Who's there?"

The hand holding my right arm tightened its grip, gave me a shake.

"Shut up and keep walking."

He'd spoken enough words for me to place the voice and, although most of the words I'd heard him speak through the years were alcohol-slurred, I knew who it belonged to.

"Is that you, Marty?"

A grunt.

"Dude, it's been months. How've you been?"

Truth be told, I didn't much care. The last time I saw him, he tried to beat me to death. Not his fault, I guess, being possessed and all, but he'd also said some uncomplimentary things about me when he thought I was dead, so I owed him. Asking a Hellbound dead guy how things are might be a subtle jab, but a jab nonetheless.

He didn't answer.

"Is Todd here, too, then?"

"Hey, Ric."

"Shut up, Todd."

I smiled beneath the bag. Todd had never been the smartest one in the group. Maybe I had a chance of figuring out what was going on.

"Where are you guys taking me?"

"Someone wants to see you," Todd answered.

"Will you shut up?" Marty's voice betrayed his annoyance. He shook me again. "You, too. No more questions."

"Okay." Not a question. "I'll just keep to myself under this stinky bag."

Someone wants to see you.

There were only a few people in Hell who might desire my company, none of whom I looked forward to seeing. They began with people I didn't like much and the list went downhill from there. I didn't get a good feeling from this.

Where's Piper?

We walked in silence for a long time, the scrape of our feet on the ground and my captured breath rattling against cloth the only sounds. I should have been nervous, scared, but distracted myself by watching my steps kick up puffs until the ash-covered sidewalk disappeared, giving way to parched orange earth scattered with black rock. I kicked at pebbles but quickly grew bored and my mind wandered back to my bleak situation.

Who wants to see me? Azrael? Probably. Father Dominic? Bad. Someone else I'd pissed off over the years? A long list. Red guy with horns and a tail?

I shivered a little and decided debating who wanted to punish me was detrimental to my state of mind. Time to find some other distraction.

"So, this Hell place is pretty nice. Warm little vacation spot."

No response but I thought I felt the angry look Marty shot Todd keep him quiet.

"I really expected it to be dirtier, nastier. All-in-all, it's not bad. No Disneyland, but it's not exactly third-world, either."

Marty shook me again, this time without words-of-warning, and I stumbled. Todd's grip kept me from going ass-over-tea kettle, as the British say. I don't even drink tea.

"You know, I feel bad about how you guys got here. Horrible what happened to you, but it's not my fault. What a maniac, that priest."

Feet scraping on ground.

"He tried to kill me, too, you know." Then, more to myself: "Of course you know. You helped."

"We had no choice, Ric," Todd's disembodied voice responded.

"Enough," Marty snapped and pushed me hard.

My one left foot caught behind my other left foot and down I went. Before I could recover, one of my escorts lashed my wrists together behind my back with something that felt warm; it pulsed and moved. My stomach churned.

"Marty—"

"Shut up, Todd. He's on his own from here."

"Whoa, whoa, whoa. What do you mean 'on his own'?" I scuffled my feet against the orange earth, pushing myself to a sitting position. Mission finally accomplished, I waited for them to respond.

No one spoke. A minute passed.

"Guys?"

The thing binding my wrists pulsed, slithered, held still. As if gym shorts over the face wasn't disgusting enough, I had to touch a snake, too. So much for all the good things I said about Hell.

"Come on, guys. Let me go. I promise I'll be good."

I thought I heard a furtive step, maybe a whisper, but couldn't be sure—blood pounded too loudly through my head.

"Guys?"

No doubt about the footsteps this time. Two sets of feet hurried away making no effort to conceal their movements.

"Marty! Todd! Don't leave."

The footsteps receded, leaving me alone.

I hoped.

From the beginning, I'd felt some fear being in Hell, but the longer I spent, the less it bothered me.

Until now.

I scrambled to my feet, blind and unsteady. The world swirled and tilted beneath me and I swayed with vertigo; the meager contents of my stomach tried to find their way up my esophagus and out, but I convinced them otherwise. I stumbled forward a couple of steps to keep my feet under me where they belonged.

The rank taste of the air I gasped through the stinking hood in an attempt to relieve my claustrophobia brought nausea back, but breathing eventually succeeded in calming me. I stood, head sagging, staring at the tops of my shoes. They needed polishing, but that would have to wait for a more opportune time—I had to get the hood off first.

I bent quickly at the waist and jerked back to standing. The stinking material slapped against my face but didn't come off. I bowed again, shook my head back and forth to work it free. It shifted a little but stayed put.

"Damn it."

Given the locale, it was probably too late for such a sentiment to be granted.

I lowered my ass to the ground and sucked a sharp breath through my teeth as a jagged rock dug into my left cheek. Hell gets you any way it can. A few seconds of butt-shuffling brought enough comfort for me to draw my legs up, lower my head and hold the edge of the hood with my knees. I smiled, confident and satisfied, and pulled my head back, but the shroud slipped from my grip.

Shroud.

An ominous word I hadn't thought of until this point.

They put shrouds on dead people.

The idea really shouldn't have bothered me—I'd already died once. But I didn't want to end up here for good.

I tried again, and again the material slipped from my grasp. I rolled onto my side, grunting, attempting to pin hood between shoulder and ground but only succeeded in banging my head on the same rock my ass met moments before.

"Get the fuck off me."

I rolled the other way, tossing my head side-to-side with the same result. When I rolled back, I hit something solid.

It felt like a leg.

I froze, panic coursing through my veins as I realized whoever or whatever stood over me had me at their mercy. Pictures of leering demons jumped into my head. I thrashed and pushed away but a hand on my shoulder stopped me.

"Icarus."

The voice was lyrical, familiar, female.

"Piper?" *Where were you?*

"Yes. Be calm."

"Untie me."

"Trevor's here."

I held my breath, mind swirling. *Did I hear her right?*

"Trevor?"

"Not *here*, but in Hell." She paused; my breath rasped in and out. "Poe brought him."

Any questions about where Piper had been fled my mind.

'Trevor's here. Poe brought him.'

The two fragments didn't seem to go together. Poe was an angel—my guardian angel.

Why would she bring Trevor to—

A memory flickered, something Piper said. I'd been angry at the time and didn't give her words much credence, but they came back full force as I lay on Hell's burnt soil with a bag over my head.

'Some are suspicious. They think Poe might be playing for the other side.'

"Where are they?" I demanded. "Take me to them."

"I can't, Icarus."

Ric, God damn it.

"Why not?"

She paused and it seemed like a wind blew across the scorched plain, a sigh of warm air bearing her words:

"Because I'm not here."

With the breeze and the whisper, a shiver shook my spine and the pulsating rope binding my wrists disappeared. Despite my anger at Poe for involving my son, I was shaken. I sat up cautiously, rubbing my wrists and expecting a ring of slime. Instead, I found them dry and raw, chafed like the hands of someone who's worked hard in their lives. I hadn't experienced it, but I'd heard of such a thing.

I brought my hand up to the hood, listening to the sounds around me as I did. A wind which no longer touched me rattled pebbles across hard ground; a flap of huge wings passed high overhead. Someone laughed—a low, mirthless, throaty laugh.

And it was close.

The hood slid off my head easily, making me wonder why I couldn't remove it before, but the thought evaporated like a drop of water on a hot pan when I gazed up at the man standing before me. His filthy coat hung in tatters, his bare feet were covered with blisters long burst and turned to weeping sores. He held his hands in front of his chest, rubbing them as if trying to clean them without benefit of soap and water. Streaks of soot obscured his face, hiding the crosses carved into his forehead and cheeks, but no amount of dirt could hide this man's identity, not after all our history together.

"It's hot enough down here to melt a man's wings, eh, Icarus?"

I frowned, my molars grinding against one another, and I wished they did so with him between them. The last things I needed while trapped in Hell with my son roaming the abyss with a rogue angel was this man and his corny mythological references.

I spat his name on the dry ground at his feet.

"Father Dominic."

Chapter Seventeen

TREVOR TURNED SLOWLY, BREATH held, and thought he felt Poe stir minutely in his arms. He glanced down at her, but her eyes remained closed, her limbs limp, so he raised his eyes and looked at the thing which plucked them from the abyss.

Trevor's mouth fell open as he looked into the face of a demon.

No horror movies could have prepared him for the thing; no amount of prosthetics, make-up, masks or latex could have created it. White maggots squirmed across its face, dragging themselves out of one fissure and into another; its black skin stretched to the point of breaking across misshapen muscles no body builder would wish upon their greatest rival. Leathery wings creaked as they moved, shifting slightly like a tightrope walker's pole as the thing stood on taloned feet not designed for the purpose.

Trevor's skin went cold with goose bumps despite the heat the creature emitted.

The demon's chest heaved as it gulped air in through its mouth and blew it heavily through flapped nostrils set in the middle of its noseless face.

Fuck me.

Trevor took a step back and found the mob of damned souls crowding behind him, their desire to be close to the angel greater than their fear of the demon. One reached out tentatively and stroked Poe's hair, pursed its lips and started the chant again, so quietly it may as well not have been there.

"P."

For a moment, there was no response. The demon's purple eyes darted back and forth across the wall of souls surrounding them, his gaze daring them to pick up the mantra. Trevor didn't think any would, not in the face of the monstrosity, but one was finally overcome.

"Oh."

A sigh, nothing more; or it might have been one soul breathing louder than the others. The demon needed no more provocation. It leaned forward, mouth open to reveal two rows of pointed teeth dripping saliva, and screamed, a sound part fog horn, part siren mixed with the roar of a lion. Deafening. Trevor flinched and cowered away as the beast grabbed the closest soul and flung it over the edge of the canyon. It went over without exclamation, the chains binding it to the next clanking then going taut and pulling its neighbor along with it, then the next and the next. A dozen or more toppled into the chasm in succession like the coils of a giant slinky but with no next stair to land on. The other souls backed away.

Poe stirred in Trevor's arms.

He looked down and saw her eyelids flutter then close, shielding her sensitive eyes from light. She shifted and Trevor became acutely aware of the weight in his arms, an awkward weight he'd been carrying a long while. His shoulders felt as though they might detach from his body and his arms drop to the rocky ground with the angel in them.

"What's happening?"

She whispered the words like a child waking, but it wasn't Trevor alone who heard. A gasp rolled across the crowd of souls; the demon reared back, wings spread in a menacing pose, its face twisting into further grotesque contortions. Trevor held his breath, waiting to see what would happen, whether he would survive.

The damned souls held their ground, undeterred by the possibility of following their compatriots over the edge of the canyon. The demon leaned forward, propping itself on its knuckles in a gorilla-pose, its head three feet from Trevor and Poe. The nostril flaps quivered and danced as it sniffed the angel. What passed for its lips pulled away from its teeth, a growl reverberated in its chest.

Poe's hand shot out and grabbed it by the throat.

·····•·•····

A dream. It's only a dream.

It was beyond hot in the dream—sweltering, scorching, burning—and dark. Sounds came and went; first the sound of feet walking, then labored breathing, a muffled shout she didn't hear. None of this made her afraid in the dream, they were simply there, like the people touching her which came next, the chanting of her name and finally the sensation of falling.

It felt nice, the falling. Wind whipped her hair and she imagined it to be flying instead of falling. She liked flying. It gave her the freedom and solitude she craved but never got. She only flew in her dreams.

The flying stopped.

Nothing happened for a minute. It wasn't that she was asleep and not dreaming—she was aware, but there was nothing of which to be aware. Darkness. Quiet.

Then the scream woke her.

She'd heard such a scream before, in a time she wanted to forget and place she never wanted to be again. A place to which she'd now returned. Without opening her eyes, she knew—the smell told her. She tried to stretch her aching muscles, felt arms supporting her and remembered everything: following the Carrion, the trip to Hell with Trevor, passing out. Her eyelids resisted opening but she caught a glimpse of the teenager looming above her.

Trevor.

"What's happening?"

She felt the reaction to her words as much as heard it. Trevor wasn't the only one here. She sensed thousands of presences, all of them lost and afraid, except one which overpowered the others with its rancor, its hatred. She felt it close to her, the rumble of its growl shook her core.

Poe opened her eyes.

The thing leered at her, rage gurgling in its chest, readying to spill out on her, on Trevor. It only took a glimpse to recognize the beast and the severity of the situation. She reached out her hand and grasped the demon by its throat. The movement unsettled her in Trevor's arms and he dropped her but Poe moved lithely, twisting herself to land on her feet without losing her grip on the demon.

"Abaddon," she said. "Angel of the Bottomless Pit."

"So it is you, Poe," the thing replied. "Thought never to see you again."

"You'll soon wish you hadn't."

The beast stood to its full height—easily nine feet to the top of its head—but Poe didn't let go. Her feet left the ground, dangled level with the creature's waist. It shook its head and shoulders sharply like a horse dislodging a fly; her grip remained strong.

What am I doing?

She looked up into the beast's face and terror filled her lungs, threatened to gag her. She wanted to let go, to drop to the ground and run, seek refuge amongst the damned souls watching with uncharacteristically agape mouths, but her fingers wouldn't obey her wishes. Their grip continued to hold fast when the demon stretched its wings and took to the sky with a powerful stroke.

"Poe!"

She heard Trevor's voice disappear beneath her as the beast shot them into the roiling sky. Hot wind rustled her hair around her ears and cheeks, stole the breath out of her nose.

Flying, really flying.

The demon clutched at her legs with its taloned feet. She twisted, avoiding their grasp, but a claw raked her leg, drawing blood. The panic in her chest flooded into her head, clouding her thoughts and blurring her vision as her free hand drew back, clenched into a fist. She looked down at her own hand, dimly wondered how it acted of its own accord, and watched in shock as it shot forward and penetrated the demon's chest.

The beast thrashed and contorted, spun in circles attempting to throw her off. Poe's fingers dug deep into the thing's chest until they found a hard, pulsing lump, then they squeezed.

The demon screamed, its cry high-pitched with rage and pain. It twisted again. Spun again. Thrashed. Clawed.

And then they fell from the sky.

•••••••••••

The force of the wind created by the creature's wings drove Trevor back a step. He threw his arm over his eyes to keep the dust it stirred up from blinding him but saw over the top of his forearm as the demon shot into the sky, Poe dangling in front of it.

"Poe!"

They climbed toward the clouds at an unbelievable rate, quickly becoming a black dot against the gray sky. He squinted and strained to see, but they disappeared. Trevor faced the crowd of souls and found they'd crept up behind him, pressing at his back.

"What happened?" he said to the closest of the slack faced things. It acted as if it didn't hear him. "Where did they go?"

All of the gray-skinned faces were tilted skyward, mouths open. They encircled him, all of them trying to fit into the place where the demon leaped into the sky with their angel, their salvation, dangling from its throat. After a few seconds, one a few rows deep from Trevor began the chant again.

"P."

"Oh," a second on his other side responded.

Then, without warning or apparent reason, the entire group of thousands turned and ran as fast as their shackles allowed. Trevor pivoted in a tight circle, searching the plain around them.

Nothing.

The cloud of dust kicked up by the souls' shuffling feet obscured the horizon, but through it he saw no others crossing the plain, nothing climbing from the misty-bottomed cavern. One other alternative dawned on him and he raised his eyes to the sky.

Immediately he picked out the black dot against the clouds, growing larger, coming closer, moving fast. Trevor took a step back, eyes steady on the falling object, then moved carefully toward the edge of the crevasse.

"Poe," he said.

Crazily, he thought about catching her, or at least breaking her fall, but the thought vanished quickly. The dot falling through the sky looked to be moving at the speed of a missile. Trevor glanced down to see where he'd stopped at the lip of the chasm, peered over the edge. The mist swirled faster than before, more violently, like a school of sharks circling, preparing for a frenzy.

When he looked up again, the dot was plainly the two figures he'd seen launch into the sky a minute before. A sound accompanied their fall—high-pitched, pained. The scream made the flesh on the back of his neck want to crawl up under his hairline.

"Poe!"

The demon and the angel plummeted past him in slow motion, twisting and spinning. He saw rage contorting Poe's features from the pleasant-looking face he'd grown used to into someone unrecognizable. At the same time, he discerned the pain on the demon's face. A thick, black ichor smeared all the way past the guardian angel's elbow from her hand planted in the creature's chest.

He watched them hurtle beyond the brink of the chasm, then fell to his knees, leaned over the edge, as time returned to its normal pace and the two combatants disappeared into the writhing fog. The demon's scream followed them and, seconds later, died away with them.

"Poe!"

Trevor fought the objectionable urge to jump in after them, realizing its futility.

But without Poe, how will I find Ric? How will I get home?

He stared into the smog for a minute, two, searching for some movement other than the eddy of the vapor itself, imagining Poe pulling herself out of the mist on the gossamer wings of angels of legend. She didn't. He saw no movement to stir hope in him. Eventually, he gave up, leaned back and surveyed the plain.

The dust cloud had settled and, in the distance, he saw the tiny figures of damned souls chained together marching to who-knew-where. Or maybe they were going exactly nowhere, spending their after-lives marching without rest or respite, without hope.

In that moment, he thought he knew exactly how lost and alone they felt.

"What do I do now?"

He felt the subtle change in temperature at his back before he smelled the pleasant odor of fresh baking. The words followed closely behind.

"I'll take care of you."

The unfamiliar voice held undertones of lyricism and harmonies, but the smell of fresh apple pie told who stood behind him.

"Michael," Trevor exclaimed jumping to his feet. "Poe is—"

He spun around to greet the archangel, not knowing whether seeing God's right hand in Hell was a good thing or not, but anything seemed better than the alternative. When he saw the black clothing and dark locks of the man standing before him, the hopeful smile disappeared.

"You...you're not Michael."

The man shook his head deliberately.

"No, I am not."

"Then who—?"

A thought interrupted Trevor's words: he stood in Hell, confronted by a man in black. He didn't appear to have horns or pointed tail, but he'd already discovered most things here weren't what they seemed.

"Are you...?"

"No, I am not him, either."

The man took two strides forward and placed his hand on Trevor's shoulder sending a jolt down his chest. With the gaping canyon at his back, the teen had no choice but to let him.

"My name is Azrael."

Trevor swallowed hard.

Chapter Eighteen

D ESPITE THE FOOTSTEPS I'D heard, Marty and Todd stood only a few paces behind the murderous priest. They looked like overweight dancers from the set of Michael Jackson's *Thriller* video, with decaying flesh hanging from their cheeks and pus oozing out of more places than my stomach could bear counting.

"Hey guys, looking good."

I went to stand but Father Dominic planted his foot squarely in my gut. Air whooshed out of my chest and I crumpled to the ground gasping for breath. Marty made his angry face and took a couple of steps forward like he wanted to add his size twelve to my midsection but the priest extended an arm to hold him back. I'd rarely felt thankful for anything that bastard did, but I extended him the courtesy this time, though I wouldn't have told him so, even if I possessed the ability to speak.

"Leave him," Father Dominic grated. "I had you bring him so I could make him pay for what he's done."

To put an exclamation point on his words, he kicked me again. The sliver of thankfulness I'd felt melted back into the pool of hatred I carried in my belly for the man. I promised to get back at him by groaning and drooling on myself.

Marty backed off a step and the three of them stood staring at me like I was some sideshow attraction at the local freak show. Slowly, I unfolded myself from the fetal position the priest's kicks put me in and clawed my way to kneeling while remaining wary of Father Dominic's feet. This wasn't the first time he'd kicked me—that distinction dated back to my childhood and had been renewed a few months ago—but I was determined to see it afforded a good chance of being the last.

While I was distracted watching for kicks, he reached out, grabbed the front of my shirt with both grubby hands, and hauled me to my feet. He stood a few inches shorter than me but still lifted me high enough the toes of my shoes scraped the ground.

"It seems like you're still upset with me, Father."

In answer, he shook me and showed his teeth.

"It's not my fault. I didn't make you kill anyone."

"If you'd taken my soul like you were supposed to, none of this would have happened."

His statement was a finger-poke to an open wound. If I'd done my stupid job, he wouldn't be here, Beth, Tony and the others wouldn't have been here, and neither would I.

Neither would Trevor.

The priest glanced over his shoulder at his two disheveled minions lurking behind him.

"Go find something else to do. Leave Icarus to me."

"Ric. I really prefer you call me Ric."

He shook me hard, rattling my back teeth together and leaving me a little dazed. As my eyeballs settled themselves back into place, I watched Marty and Todd slouching away. I raised my hand and waved bye-bye, but they weren't looking.

Father Dominic lowered my feet back to the ground and pulled my face close to his, then opened his mouth to speak. His breath smelled like Hell. I clenched my teeth and pulled my face back in readiness for his tirade, or perhaps a head butt to the face.

"Take me back."

I blinked twice rapidly and shook my head to clear it. Instead of swearing, cursing, calling me names or verbally degrading me, I thought I'd heard him say 'take me back.'

"What?"

"I know why you're here."

"Wish I could say the same thing."

"You're here to rescue souls sent to Hell because of you. I'm one of those souls. Take me back."

His grip on my shirt front loosened and he backed away a couple of steps. The expression on his face changed from leering menace to a look of desperation, longing.

"After everything you did to me, I'm supposed to be your salvation?"

For a second, he looked like I'd punched him. For years, I'd often wished I had, but I resisted the urge—it seemed like there might be better ways to hurt him right now.

"This could be your own salvation, Icarus."

He added a sibilance to the last letter of my name, highlighting the fact that he refused to call me Ric—one more reason to leave the bastard rotting away in Hell, like he deserved. I didn't regret letting Azrael take his soul because of what it meant to him, only because it caused harm to others.

I stepped closer, feeling like I possessed the power now. I had what he wanted.

"Forget it. You got what you deserved."

"Icarus. Please."

He grasped the front of my shirt again, but this time with no violence in the action, only pleading.

"You have to take me to Heaven."

"No, I don't."

"Please."

He released my shirt and sank to his knees looking up at me, clenched hands held in front of his chest.

Begging.

I suppressed a smile.

"Please take me."

I made a show of rubbing my chin, considering my options. I shifted from one foot to the other, scratched my head, then went back to my chin again.

"Heaven, huh?"

"Yes, please."

"And you think you deserve to go to Heaven?"

"I am God's servant."

"And God's servant kills people?"

"That wasn't my fault."

He looked over his shoulder like a man expecting someone behind him, listening in. I glanced around, too, but there was nothing but flat plains for miles in every direction—no way for anyone to sneak up and eavesdrop.

Paranoid bastard.

"He made me do it."

"Who?"

I had a pretty good idea who he meant, but I wanted him to say it.

"Who made you do it?"

The priest shook his head and dropped his gaze to the ground. He may have whispered something but, if he did, it was too quiet to hear.

"Tell me and I'll think about saving you."

He shook his head harder, refusing to speak the name. What's the big deal? I knew Azrael was behind it; he'd orchestrated Father Dominic's murderous rampage to steal my soul back from Mikey.

Why won't he just tell me?

"What's the big deal? Why won't you just tell me?"

Being afraid of the archangel in life, I understood, but when you're already in Hell, how much worse could it get? Not for the first time, I wondered if more was going on here than I realized.

Father Dominic's shoulders trembled and I thought he might be crying.

"Are you crying?"

He raised his eyes and glared at me, the tears on his cheeks shimmering in the red-orange light. The muscles in his jaw bunched and released, bunched and released.

"Take me with you."

His voice was low and firm, lacking the begging tone smothering it a moment before. He lowered his hands, held them at his side clenched into fists. He didn't stand.

I looked him directly in the eyes and saw the hatred he felt for me burning deep inside them. Pictures of me as a child being punished, degraded, abused seemed to flicker across their bloodshot surfaces. The look on my face must have given away the fact I'd seen them dancing in his irises because the bastard smiled.

Fuck you.

"No." I crossed my arms in front of my chest. "Burn in Hell."

The priest jumped straight from his knees to his feet like a child might have been made to do in P.E. class. I snapped into a fighting stance, ready for him and looking forward to kicking his ass all over Hell, but he disappointed me. Instead of coming at me, fists flailing, he threw his arms up in the air, hands open, fingers crooked. I stared, confused. For a second, nothing happened except for Father Dominic looking melodramatic, then the ground trembled beneath my feet.

An earthquake in Hell? A Hellquake?

Probably not terribly unusual but the timing to go along with the warped priest's gesture threw a scare into me. I stumbled back a step out of surprise and Father Dominic repeated the gesture. The ground shook harder. I looked around, frantic, searching for the nearest doorway under which to cower like we'd been taught as kids but, of course, there were none. There was nothing at all.

Until the rock walls rose out of the ground.

They pushed straight up toward the sky, each looking like a daisy growing in the spring, filmed in time-lapse photography on the nature channel. I blundered in a rough circle, buffeted back by the rock walls on all sides. They rose up twelve feet, fifteen feet, twenty, their sides sheer and smooth like unpolished marble. The rumble of rock grinding against rock rattled my eardrums and I threw my hands against the sides of my head to protect them.

Above it all, I heard the priest cackling like the maniac I'd always known him to be.

When the ground's reverberations ceased, I stood hunched with my hands over my ears for a few seconds, waiting to see if the ground would quake again. It didn't, so I lowered my hands and glanced around.

I wasn't surrounded on all sides, but close enough. The gray clouds roiled above my head, a misty whirlpool in the sky. A stone hallway stretched out before me, the demon-priest standing twenty feet away, leering at me, yellow teeth exposed, black eyes gleaming.

"What have you done?" I attempted to sound unconcerned. I didn't. I wasn't.

"You should have agreed to take me back."

"*What have you done?*"

The maniac smile clung to his face like a baby gorilla hanging on to its mother for dear life and, to really piss me off, he threw in an equally maniacal laugh. It did the job.

I lunged forward, legs pumping as my feet churned and slipped in the fresh scree created by the growing rocks. They found purchase after a second and I shot forward, determined to tackle the priest and show him how I really felt, in case I'd missed making it obvious up to this point. Dominic's evil smile broadened and he tensed, readying to receive whatever I threw at him. I decided on a roundhouse punch.

My fist looped forward and, at the last second, the priest waved his hand and the air in front of him shimmered then went opaque. My fist and face ran into the freshly minted rock wall at approximately the same instant and I fell back on my ass, dazed.

I lay on my back, watching the ugly sky as a trickle of blood ran down the side of my face from a nose I wouldn't need a doctor to tell me was broken. At least it distracted me from my throbbing hand. When the world stopped spinning, I saw Father Dominic perched atop the wall, staring down at me. With some effort, I climbed to my feet, though I must have looked like someone fresh off the Mad Hatter's teacup ride at Disneyland.

"What did you do?"

The priest spread his arms, gesturing at the area around me.

"Take a look," he said. "I think you'll find I've done a fine job."

I did as he said and glanced at the walls on all sides of me. The one I'd run into was solid, but the others all had openings. A long passage ran from one; the second had a short corridor which took a hard left and went out of sight; the third ran for fifteen feet finishing in a dead end. It took a few seconds for my addled brain to clear enough to realize what I saw.

A labyrinth.

"That's right, Icarus. A labyrinth. A maze. There's a way out, but it might take you eternity to find it."

He stood on the top of the wall towering twenty-five feet over my head, looming, laughing.

"I was your last chance. You'll never get out of Hell now, priest," I said feeling silly and impotent shaking my fist at him.

"Neither will you. Bet you wished you had wings now, don't you, Icarus?"

He jumped down to the opposite side of the wall, laughter trailing after him. I gritted my teeth and clenched my fist then cringed at the pain both caused. After a few deep breaths, I opened my mouth, intending to make fun of the priest for screwing up his mythology—the labyrinth was on Crete, a maze meant to keep the minotaur for King Minos. Nothing to do with Icarus. The words burbled near my lips when I remembered my own readings: Daedalus built the labyrinth—Icarus' father.

I hate Greek mythology.

Chapter Nineteen

P OE'S LEG HURT DESPERATELY; blood stuck her pants to her thigh. She wiggled her fingers, felt the rock she'd embedded them in grind against her flesh and, face pressed against the stone, looked up at the sheer cliff stretching above her. The stinking fog limited her vision but, as far as she could see, there were no knobs of rock or outcroppings to serve as hand and footholds. She looked down at the mist nipping at her feet. Somewhere below, the demon Abaddon waited, resting, licking his wounds. Somewhere above—Trevor.

"I can't stay here."

Her words echoed into the abyss, smothered by the mist, and she chastised herself silently for not being more careful. She didn't know if the demon thought her dead or alive—best not to announce the truth.

Slowly, she pulled the fingers of her right hand free, reached as high as she could, then rammed them against the rock. They sank in half-an-inch—enough of a hold to inch herself up. She repeated the procedure with her left foot, then her left hand. Each impact sent a jolt of pain along her arm, her leg. The gash in her thigh screamed in protest, but all of it was nothing compared to what Abaddon would do to her if he found her clinging defenseless to the cliff face.

Inch by inch she made her way up the cliff, concentrating on each handhold, each foot placement. When she looked up again, she saw she'd cleared the mist and the edge of the canyon taunted high above with nothing but the cloud-covered sky beyond it. The odd perspective made it seem like the climb would go on forever.

Right hand. Left foot. Left hand. Right foot.

Poe focused on the movements, struggling to put the consequences of slipping, of losing her grip and plummeting into the abyss, out of her mind. Sweat ran down her forehead, sticking her blond hair to her face, stinging her eyes. She craned her neck to wipe her eyes on her shoulder and felt her hold slip. The jolt froze her, sent adrenaline coursing through her veins. She hugged the cliff face, breathing heavily from the scare, then directed her attention back to the climb, ignoring the sweat irritating her eyes.

It seemed like a very long time before she'd drawn herself to within ten feet of the edge, the effort twisting all her muscles into granny knots.

Right hand.

She went to remove her fingers from the furrow they'd created but nothing happened. Again. Her elbow quivered; her hand and fingers didn't move. She tried her left hand with the same result. Her head lolled back, staring at the end of her climb so enticingly close, and a knot clogged her throat. She swallowed hard hoping to swallow the panic, the desperation, and breathed a shuddering breath through her mouth.

A screech rose out of the mist far below. Poe looked down between her feet and saw nothing but the fog. A wave of vertigo tilted her head and canted her gut forcing her to look back to the edge of the cliff above and the sky overhead. She willed her hands to move again, her feet, but they remained stationary, revolting against her wishes with the end so near.

She needed help.

"Trevor."

The word might have been whispered by a bullfrog. She swallowed what little saliva her mouth mustered in an attempt to lubricate a throat gone dry with effort and fear, coughed to clear it like an opera singer preparing to belt out an aria.

"Trevor."

Louder but still meek. No answer floated down from on high, no promise of help or salvation, no cry of surprise or concern. Poe rested her forehead against the rock wall, felt the hardness of it press directly on her brain.

I have to get out.

The screech again, but she didn't bother attempting to look. Her fatigued arms wouldn't go any further, though she thought her fingers would gladly let go and revel in the relief as she fell to her ultimate death or whatever waited in the mist.

She breathed deep and shifted her weight as far to the left as she dared. Her muscles screamed, but the action brought a crumb of respite to their right-hand counterparts. If she held herself like this long enough, maybe she'd be able to continue, maybe she'd be able to climb the last few feet.

As she controlled her breathing, something struck the top if her head, something small and light. She ignored it.

My imagination.

When it happened again, she couldn't disregard it.

"Trevor?"

She shifted her weight to look up and the muscles on her right side, moments away from finding enough reserve to continue, failed her. Her foot slipped first, her hand followed close behind. Her right side swung away from the cliff and she instinctively gripped tighter with her left. Searing pain shot through her left shoulder into her chest as she struggled to right herself. She saw the edge of the cliff above: still nothing.

"Trevor!"

She heard the chant begin first, quiet and tentative, growing as more voices added themselves.

"P."

"Oh."

"P."

"Oh."

The first gray face peered over the edge a few seconds later, then others gathered beside it. They stared blankly, thin lips moving with each syllable of their chant.

"P."

"Oh."

"P."

"Oh."

"Help," she whispered in response. "Please help me."

Two of the damned looked at each other, a cursed expression of questioning passing between them. One faced Poe and reached out a bone-thin arm, its long fingers stretching out. The attempt fell well short, though she doubted her ability to grasp it, anyway. She tried to right herself, dig the fingers of her right hand back into the stone wall, but the muscles in her arm refused her request.

The fingers of her left hand slipped out a quarter-inch.

Her useless right hand pawed the cliff face, the numb tips of her fingers brushing the indentations they'd previously made but finding no purchase. She settled her right foot back into a divot in the wall and a knot in her calf squealed its protest.

Above her, the soul which had been reaching out, attempting to help, dangled its legs over the side, its waist bent over the edge.

Not close enough.

It let itself down further until it hung from its fingers, stretched to its full height. Poe looked up at the bottom of its bare feet stained orange by its accursed march across the plains of Hell. She threw her limp arm toward it, missed by a yard.

With a jerk, the damned one moved closer by six inches. The movement startled Poe and her right foot slipped again, but she recovered, the knot in her calf feeling as though it would tear muscle from bone. Carefully she shifted to see past the pendulous soul. The second one had lowered it over the edge by the chain which bound them together. Poe saw the shackles digging into its wrists, shredding the flesh beneath the iron band. No blood flowed from the wound.

A warmth flowed through Poe, giving energy to her fatigued limbs, and she recognized the feeling as hope. Her would-be rescuer jerked down again, inches closer. She reached up, swiped at its foot. Her fingertips brushed the orange-tinted skin.

Somewhere below, an angry shriek echoed up out of the chasm.

The urge to look down, to seek the source of the screech, nearly made Poe shift her position again, but at the last second, she remembered the results of the last time she'd attempted it. Instead, she concentrated on those above her and their attempt to save her.

How do they know me? Why would they save me?

She didn't have the answers, truthfully didn't care right in that moment, but they served to distract her when a second howl reverberated up the walls of the canyon.

The second soul lowered itself over the side. The first jolted down three more feet, its knees coming even with Poe's eyes. She threw her arm up a third time, hand slapping against the soul's loose, gray flesh. Her fingers slid off without grasping. She did it again, concentrating all her will on her fingers, on being able to grab on. Flesh clapped against flesh, her fingers twitched but her energy, her strength, failed her.

The chains rattled and the soul plummeted another four feet, its slack face now even with Poe's. She looked into its bottomless eyes and saw the misery churning in them, felt some of the pain and hopelessness this one-time person must deal with for the rest of eternity.

"P," it intoned.

"Oh," the one dangling above added.

She smiled.

A sound like a sheet flapping on a clothes line on a blustery spring day sounded and a whoosh of air engulfed her. She wrenched around instinctively and saw the black shape shoot past, headed for the sky, when her hold on the cliff face gave way. Poe tumbled backwards.

So close. So close to making it.

And she fell into the damned soul's arms.

She hung limply in its grasp, cold radiating from it like its insides housed a million ice cubes. Relief flooded her, though she wanted to wriggle out of its grasp, get free from the icy, dead grip, but she let herself be saved.

Her shoulder scraped painfully against the jagged edge as they pulled her over. The gash in her thigh, almost scabbed over while she clung desperately to the rock face, reopened and started bleeding anew. A second later, she lay on solid ground, safe.

Safe from the fall.

The souls who saved her and their compatriots—it looked like hundreds of them crowded around to see her—backed away a few steps, giving her space to breathe, recover. She raised her head off the ground, pebbles and sand sticking to her cheek, but didn't have the strength to hold it up.

"Thank you," she said as her head sank back down to the orangey dirt.

"P."

"Oh."

The crowd of souls got through one verse of the chant before the demon landed on the ground between them and Poe. The earth shook as its talon feet struck, its wings flapped giving it balance and kicking up a tumult of dust into the air. It leaned forward on all fours and bellowed at the damned. They backed away a few steps, cowering, then the beast turned toward the collapsed guardian angel.

Poe blinked the dust out of her eyes, struggled to get her arms moving, to push herself to a sitting position, then to her feet to defend herself. All the aches and pains, knots and wounds protested collectively and she fell back.

The demon stalked toward her, covering the space between them in two steps. It leered down at her, huffing hatred through its flapped nostrils, saliva dripping off its double row of picket fence teeth. A split tongue flicked out and brushed Poe's cheek, tasting her sweat, and she cringed.

I'm so sorry, Trevor. Sorry, Icarus.

The beast reared up, wings spread for balance, and put the talon of one foot against Poe's throat. It threw its head back and screamed a victory cry toward the swirling sky, then glared back down at her. She swore the demon smiled.

The first of the damned—Poe thought it the one who'd come over the side to get her—hit the demon broadside and bounced off. Abaddon turned his attention away from his foe lying defenseless beneath his foot and drew back his thickly muscled arm to swat away the disturbing pest, but the rest washed over him like a wave on a beach.

A hundred damned souls swarmed over the demon, their collective force throwing him off balance before he struck back, before he could sink his talon into Poe's jugular vein. The mob flowed over the angel, feet brushing against her arms, her legs, her torso, but none of them doing damage. Chains clanked and banged, the demon howled, the damned chanted.

"P."

"Oh."

"P."

"Oh."

With effort, Poe turned her head in time to see the mass of gray bodies topple over the edge, a few patches of the demon's black skin showing through the throng as they rode him into the depths of the abyss.

The chant, the chains, the demon's howl receded into the pit.

"Thank you," Poe whispered, her breath stirring dust into the air, then she lowered her head and closed her eyes.

· · · · ·· · · · ·

The sky was dark when Poe woke, darker than before. She lay still for a minute, listening to the sound of nothingness, breathing quietly through her mouth. No sounds of feet shuffling, no wings beating the air, no accursed voices chanting her name. Nothing. After what seemed an appropriate amount of time and caution, she rolled on to her back and immediately regretted it.

Every muscle and joint in her body cried uncle. Her head throbbed. "Ohhh."

The groan escaped her lips without permission and she squashed it immediately for fear something might lay in wait for her in the silence, biding its time until she regained consciousness.

Nothing responded to her inadvertent lament.

She stared up at the clouds for a while. Every few minutes, a bolt of lightning jumped across them, flashing brief respite in the darkness before disappearing, leaving a green streak in her vision. She breathed deep, thankful to draw breath, thankful for life in spite of the pain in her body.

Trevor!

She sat up suddenly and it felt like her brain slapped against the inside of her forehead with the movement. Ignoring it, she struggled to her feet.

"Trevor!"

Poe circled, shuffling her feet, then remembered where she'd come to rest. She looked down, located the edge of the chasm, and shambled away a few steps to a safer locale. The leg of her pants was stiff with her own blood, the leg beneath stiffer with the gash the demon's talon had torn in it. She grimaced with the effort.

"Trevor!"

Her voice echoed across the empty plain and disappeared into the distant dark. Panic filled her head, pushing the pain aside. Concern roiled in her gut, energized her limbs. She hadn't wanted the boy to come but, truthfully, she'd been glad he did. She'd welcomed the company and the possibility he could convince his father to give up his silly ideas of coming to Hell to save a few possibly mistaken damned.

Would he have knowingly traded his son's life to save them?

The answer was no, but he hadn't brought the teenager, she had.

Her fault.

"Trevor!"

A flash of lightning punctuated her words, lit the sky and the bleak landscape, showed her its emptiness. Her gaze strayed to the edge of the abyss and she wondered if he'd gone over the edge.

No. He couldn't have.

Poe set her jaw, teeth clenched tight, and limped away from the precipice, injured leg dragging in the dirt behind her. She didn't know if Trevor still lived, if he wandered through Hell or ended up at the bottom of Abaddon's pit, but she couldn't stay here wondering.

If he was out there, if he lived, she'd find him.

"Trevor!"

A clap of thunder echoed across the plains of Hell.

Chapter Twenty

I TOOK A RIGHT and came within inches of walking into a wall at another dead end.

"Goddamn it."

Not the first dead end I'd encountered since Dominic trapped me in the maze and, unfortunately, probably not the last, either. I took a step back and peered along the corridor I'd most recently traversed and thought I saw movement.

I hurried toward it and came to another dead end where I stopped and looked at the wall, touched it, felt the solid stone.

This wasn't here before.

A surety that the labyrinth didn't play fair rose in me. It moved and changed behind me, manipulating the path I could choose. No matter what I did, the maze determined where I ended up.

It was herding me.

I thought back to the little bit of mythology I'd read—most of it stolen during furtive trips to the library when I sneaked away from Father Dominic's watchful eye. Daedelus built the labyrinth to contain the half-man, half-bull minotaur kept by King Minos. The king fed the beast by sending unsuspecting victims into the maze.

I shivered.

No way for me to know if a minotaur, or worse, lurked somewhere in the twisting, frustrating corridors, but I needed to get out. Somewhere else in Hell, my son might be in trouble. Once, not long ago, I'd have trusted Poe to have his best interests at heart but may have doubted her ability to keep him safe in spite of her designation as a guardian angel. Now I doubted both.

I went left—the only available option—trotted twenty yards, then came to a fork, deliberated for a second, and took the path to the right for no deeper reason than I had to go one way or the other. The fork led to a T, where I went left this time, followed it to a right hand turn, went ten yards to another right and walked into another dead end.

Frustrated, I slapped my hand against the wall and the pain it caused made me immediately regret the action.

"Damn you, Dominic," I cried toward the gray sky and the irony of my words perched me on the edge of laughing—I'd already taken care of that. If I could have sent him to Hell again, I'd have done it.

The thought did nothing to make me feel better about Trevor's safety.

I backtracked, ran into a wall which wasn't there before. Left, right, left, left, dead end.

"Fuck."

Went back, took a left where I'd taken a right before. Left, left, left. A long corridor of unbroken wall stretched before me. I jogged down it, ribs hurting with each stride, a reminder of the priest's shoe contacting my midsection. The corridor ended in another intersection. I decided to go left because it worked out the last few times. I went a few paces and stopped, listening.

Running water.

I thought the sound came from somewhere ahead but, with so many walls to bounce it around, the source might have been anywhere. With little choice, I continued on, the gurgling water making me realize I'd become thirsty, parched, without realizing.

Every step forward brought a new level of dryness to my mouth. I licked my lips with a tongue which felt like a dusting cloth. Swallowing became a labor. I stumbled down the corridor, pausing each time I came to another corridor to listen, attempting to discern from where the promise of water came.

Straight past two turns, then left. I lumbered fifteen yards and took a right. Each time I turned a corner and didn't find water, desperation built in me. The virtual desiccation of my mouth made me forget Trevor and his plight, Poe and her possible transgressions. Nothing mattered in my world anymore other than quenching a thirst which grew bigger by the second, overtaking everything.

My steps faltered. My right foot caught up in my left and I fell to the ground, face first. Dust kicked up and found its way past my lips making my impossibly dry mouth impossibly dryer. I hacked a weak cough but, without the aid of saliva, it did nothing to clear the grit from my tongue. The tiny amount of spit I developed turned the dust to sticky paste and I climbed to my feet, smacking my lips like a kid who'd jammed too much peanut butter into his mouth, and lurched forward.

My head spun as I tried to remember the last time I'd taken a drink: of water, of vodka, soda, anything. It had been so long, the memory escaped me.

Have I ever had a drink?

I must have. I wouldn't have made it to almost forty without drinking *something*. Whatever I drank, whenever it happened, eluded me completely.

I staggered around another corner, legs threatening to falter again, and saw it: a fountain carved of marble, its height and beauty worthy of a palace. I wouldn't have cared had it been a urinal.

I stumbled toward it, fell, swallowed more dirt, scrambled to my feet. The few yards between me and the water spouting out of the top of the fountain to careen into the first bowl, then the second and finally the bottom seemed impossibly far. I willed my legs to push on no matter how my thighs burned.

Waterwaterwaterwaterwater.

My swollen tongue sandpapered across chapped lips as I rushed toward the life-giving liquid without getting any closer. A dust cloud rose around me, churned into the air by my useless steps. This was exactly what Hell was about.

I stopped running, my level of frustration reaching the point of giving up. My eyelids slid closed and I attempted to breathe deep through nostrils clogged with dust. It didn't work, so I opened my mouth and sucked a breath down my constricted throat.

My tongue tasted the water.

My jaw snapped shut, cutting off the freshness that teased me, threatened to drive me mad. I drew another halting breath, filtering the temptation of the unreachable water with my teeth. It didn't help. A coolness flowed across my tongue with each gasp of air. Behind my closed eyes, I pictured the mist kicked up by Niagara Falls, a stream flowing through a forest, a bottle of water which, if you read its name backwards, spells naive.

My hands started to shake. My knees quivered. I concentrated on stopping these things without success; my mind resorted to any vision of water it could conjure: diving into a pool, brushing my teeth, fishing, flushing a toilet. In my head, I watched the water swirl around the porcelain bowl, round and round, until it disappeared and didn't refill.

"No," I croaked and fell to my knees. "No."

I tipped forward, expecting to fall to the ground and suck more dust and dirt into my esophagus, hoping it would be enough to put me out of my misery. Instead, my forearms struck a hard surface eighteen inches above where the ground should have been.

My left eyelid opened a crack.

The water shimmered like liquid silver, like mercury escaped from the thermometer. I opened my other eye and stared. Somehow, without moving, I'd arrived at the fountain, but now I didn't know what to do. I'd forgotten why I wanted to get to the water in the first place.

Until a drop splashed onto my hand.

The cool of it, the wetness, reminded me what water was for and I plunged my face into it, sucked it into my mouth. Nothing ever tasted so good.

I did my best to drink the entire contents of the fountain. My head throbbed with the cold of the water but I didn't stop. My belly bulged with the weight of it but I didn't stop. It seemed like I'd gone so long without it, I didn't want to take it for granted. What if I never saw water again?

Eventually I came up for air. I pulled my face out of the water, threw my head back imagining droplets flying from me, tossed into the air by my wet hair like supermodel Elle MacPherson doing a *Sports Illustrated* swimsuit edition shoot.

No one ever accused me of being a super model.

I remained on my knees, face tilted skyward looking at the dark clouds and wishing for sunshine. How good it would feel to have the sun's warming rays shining on my face, drying the water on my cheeks.

I closed my eyes to imagine the feeling and it suddenly felt like years since I last saw the sun.

"Icarus."

I opened my eyes at the sound of my name but didn't move as I attempted to determine if I'd actually heard it. Water splashed and flowed. My breath whispered through my lips. Nothing else.

My imagination.

"Icarus."

Definitely not my imagination. A woman's voice spoke the word, though it sounded indistinct and warbly, disguised by the sound of the fountain. I lowered my head slowly, my aching muscles tensing.

The water cascading down the fountain transformed the figure of the woman standing opposite me into a shimmering silhouette. I made out her dark hair and light skin but no other features. My mouth dropped open at her beauty. We stayed in that frozen tableau for a minute until she stepped out from behind the watery curtain.

"Piper?"

I jammed my fists into my eyes, determined to wipe her away if she should be an illusion. When I took them away, she remained. She raised her hand and twiddled her fingers in a gesture of hello.

"Piper!"

I jumped up, my overworked muscles suddenly feeling revitalized—by the water, by her presence, by both. I circumnavigated the fountain and threw my arms around the angel. She returned the embrace, head laid on my shoulder, hair tickling the tip of my nose. I breathed deep to have the aroma of her but smelled only water and dust.

After a minute enjoying her body pressed against mine, I leaned back and looked into her dark eyes. She smiled.

"Where have you been?"

Not to my surprise, she shrugged. It did, however, catch me off guard when she leaned forward and pressed her lips against mine. I didn't resist. An excitement built in my stomach as the kiss prolonged, turning from 'hello, I missed you, friend' into something more. She finished the kiss and pulled away leaving a tingle of excitement in my stomach but I quickly realized it resided there alone, the usual angelic jolt of her touch missing. My concerned eyebrows dipped toward the bridge of my nose.

"Is something wrong?"

Her smile withered. "Trevor."

"You told me: Poe brought him here."

In my desire to quench my thirst, I'd put thoughts of Trevor's plight and my anger at Poe out of my mind but the mention of his name brought it all back full force.

"It's worse, Icarus."

"Worse?" The statement made my heart beat faster, threatening to turn into an out of control train. "What happened? Is he okay?"

"Poe lost him."

My arms slipped from around her, I took a step back, dumfounded.

"Lost him? What do you mean?"

"He's gone. She doesn't know where he is."

"She doesn't know where he is?" The volume of my voice crept up a few decibels. "She brought my son to Hell and lost him?"

Piper put her hand on my shoulder—again, no tingle or shock.

"I sense he's unharmed for now."

"For now." I felt like a freaking parrot, but my distressed brain refused to find words of its own.

"I'm looking for him right now."

I stared into her eyes, finally understanding why her touch had no effect—she wasn't really here.

But what about the kiss?

My brain shook back into line and rediscovered how to form original sentences.

"I have to get out of here." I looked around at the fountain, the stone walls. "Help me get out of here."

Her hand fell away from my shoulder and she stepped back, head shaking side to side, her opacity fading the way a shadow begins to lighten as sun breaks through the clouds. I reached for her and my fingers passed through her hand.

"Don't go," I pleaded. "I need your help. Show me how to get out of here."

"I can't," she replied, her voice becoming ghostly the same way as her form. "I'll find him, Icarus. I'll make him safe for you."

She disappeared with a wave of her hand and I stood, jaw clenched in anger, shoulders slumped in defeat. I sagged down, sat on the edge of the fountain and hung my head. The water swirled and eddied into miniature whirlpools, capturing my attention.

A picture formed, became a scene.

In the water, I saw Trevor sitting on a rock, shivering with fear, alone. In the distance, Poe danced and cavorted, surrounded by others engaged in the same reckless dance. They disappeared into the darkness at the horizon, fading into Hell's night. Trevor called out weakly, the terror he felt evident in his voice. He stood and waved his arms in desperation. Behind him, great black wings spread out, enveloping the night.

They wrapped around him and the vision disappeared.

I stood abruptly, shaking off the shock, replacing it with anger at what Poe had done.

How could she desert my son?

I headed for the nearest corridor striding fast, purposefully, though I didn't know where to go. All I knew was I needed to find my son.

And Poe.

· · · ● ● ● ● ● · · ·

I stared down at the thread running between my feet.

Fine, black, barely noticeable, Hell's dirt camouflaged the tiny filament. I bent at the waist to get a better look, reached out and brushed away the dust partially obscuring it, careful not to touch it. It continued toward the corner ahead of me. I pivoted, looked back along my path, and saw the thread disappeared five feet behind me. Stepping carefully so as not to tread on it, I went to where I no longer saw it, moved a pebble and some dirt and found this was where the line of thread started.

Or ended.

More than two hours had passed since I left the fountain, in my best judgment—probably not great judgment given the lack of sun crossing the sky, the lack of difference between night and day, and not wearing a watch. Maybe longer, maybe less...whatever. I'd traversed the corridors desperately at first, convinced I'd find my way out through the sheer will to rescue my son. For the last while, I'd more or less wandered aimlessly, with no idea where to go, trying not to despair.

I was about to give up when I spotted the thread.

I picked up the end, brought it toward my face, and eight feet of it came up out of the dirt, dust falling from it like a builder's chalk line. I gave it a little tug and it stretched like any thread would, so I pulled harder.

It snapped.

"Shit."

I dropped the piece remaining in my hand and strode forward to find where the other end went. It coiled in a small pile ten feet down the corridor, the frayed end pointing toward me. I picked it up, stared at it running down the corridor out of sight and sighed. I felt manipulated, but did I have any other, better choice? For all I knew, I'd been wandering the labyrinth for days without a glimmer of finding an exit.

Fuck it.

I followed the thread, tracing its path hand over hand, careful not to tug too hard and break it again. It ran straight for a while past a couple of openings, then right, left, left, right. With each step, hope grew inexplicably in me, fortifying my effort, quickening my pace.

Two more lefts, a long straightaway and a final right brought me into a huge open space filled with people milling about like a crowd waiting for a train. They looked much like the people we'd seen in the city, though perhaps a little less dirty and aromatic, a little more confused-looking. The thread ran right into the middle of them.

I stared, incredulous.

All this time, they were so close.

I didn't see any way out of the ceiling-less room, so I decided following the thin, black guide line was the best course of action. A deep breath filled my lungs, my stomach gurgled reminding me that, though I'd quenched my thirst, I hadn't eaten in a while, but I could deal with hunger. I waded into the crowd.

The black thread slid through my fingers as shoulders and elbows jostled me. The ones who bumped into me didn't seem to notice they'd done so and I fought the urge to get angry at them like I'd have done in your average, earthbound mob.

"Hey," I admonished when one particularly solid shoulder spun me one-hundred-eighty degrees.

The man who'd bumped me turned toward the sound of my voice. I recognized him immediately as the steroid-gorilla I'd met watching the door at Rocky's 24-Hour Fitness Center. Even in Hell, his muscles were big enough to make it appear as though someone stuck two full-sized men together into one body.

I didn't know he died.

He looked at me with the same confused look all the others wore—they must have been handing them out at the door—and his lips moved without creating any sound. Unfortunately, I'm the world's worst lip reader, so I don't know what he said. Maybe checking to see if I remembered my club pass. I gazed into his defeated eyes and a vision came to my mind of him sitting in an empty bathtub, his shoulders shaking with sobs. It was the night Alfred died, and there was blood on the knife he held in his right hand, on his jeans, in the tub. My heart plummeted into my gut and I opened my mouth to say something but he lost interest and disappeared into the crowd as well as any man who stood six inches taller than everyone else could.

I shook my head and returned my attention to the thread but, in my distraction, I'd dropped it. I scanned the ground at my feet, but didn't see it. My shoes kicked dirt aside. Nothing. I circled, pivoting on my left foot like a basketball player. Still nothing.

I stretched to my tallest to see over the crowd. The walls seemed farther away. I saw no opening in them, no exit—not even the doorway through which I'd come.

I'm never going to get out of here.

I dropped to my knees and sifted through the reddish-orange dirt with the tips of my fingers but yielded nothing other than dirty fingernails.

It has to be here.

Suddenly, I felt like the thread was my last hope of salvation, for rescue from this holding pen for the damned. I didn't know where it led, or who or what placed it for me to find, but I had nothing else. My hope literally hung by a thread.

I shuffled forward on hands and knees as legs thumped against my sides; I dodged knees inadvertently or purposely aimed for my head. The crowd grew thick around me, slowing my search. Someone's foot mashed my fingers into the ground as they strode by and I cringed.

Where is the Goddamn thread?

I inched my way through the forest of legs, my stepped-on fingers throbbing. A pair of legs which looked different than the others—thick, green, scaly—went by and I fought the urge to look up—limbs so unattractive wouldn't be attached to anything good.

Where is it?

Too many people around me stopped my forward motion. I attempted to move forward, left, right, and finally backward but legs penned me in on all sides. My fingers, colored orange like the dirt I crawled upon, scratched at the tiny patch of earth in front of me. Nothing but dust and rock.

Defeated, I fell to my elbows, rested my forehead on my grubby hands. When I'd found the thread, hope filled me—here was my Ariadne leading me out of the labyrinth. But now, with the thread gone, hope was gone, too. I cowered on the ground, head hung in despair.

A hand touch the top of my head.

At first, I ignored it. Many hands, feet, elbows, shoulders had contacted me, so it meant nothing, didn't pull me from my wallowing. When it remained, it drew my attention. When it stroked my hair comfortingly, I looked up.

A black skirt which brushed the dirt hid the person's feet. I gulped around a knot which formed immediately in my throat, remembering the long, black trench coats favored by Azrael and his Carrion cohorts. My eyes traveled farther up, past a belt fashioned of a piece of rope, a wide sleeve concealing all but the fingers of the hand holding the end of my black thread.

I pushed myself back to my knees to look into the face of the woman holding my thread.

"Mother?"

A loose piece of black hair fell over her forehead and across her left eye but it didn't hide the sadness flickering deep within them in spite of her smile.

"Son."

Chapter
Twenty-One

S ISTER AGNES—BORN ALESYA, BUT no saints shared the name, so she became Agnes when she took her vows—sat on the edge of her bed reading the letter for the third time. She'd expected the news for a long time, dreaded it every time the mail came, so the contents shouldn't have surprised her. He'd been ill for months, but knowing the inevitable didn't make it hurt any less, nor did her learnings and beliefs about what happened, now he was gone.

Her father had been a good man, treated her like a princess, supported her when she was eighteen and announced her intention to become a nun. Her atheist father didn't waste a word talking her out of it, only told her how proud he was, that he secretly wished he shared her faith.

Five years later, he was dead without anything close to that kind of faith, and her worries began. Her belief in God and Heaven was unshakable, but on the fate of unbelievers, she felt lost. She wanted to believe a forgiving God would find a place in the firmament for a good and caring man like her father whose one sin was lacking faith or, more accurately, lacking proof to give him faith. But Father Dominic told her unbelievers weren't allowed into Heaven.

The paper slipped from her fingers, floated to the floor between her feet. She watched it settle on the carpet, the tear drops upon it discoloring the paper, smearing the words staring up at her. She buried her face in her hands and sobbed. Her shoulders shook as she did her best to stifle them lest she disturb any of the other sisters in their rooms.

When she heard the whisper of a footstep on carpet, she clamped her lips closed around the lament and prepared to apologize for the noise. She wiped tears away with the back of her hand, breathed deeply through her nose to collect herself and caught the aroma of cinnamon.

"There, there."

The deep rumble of the man's voice startled Sister Agnes. She looked up, too grief-stricken by the loss of her father to be confused by his presence in her residence, too overcome by sadness to be afraid. The man towered over her, his long, dark hair spilling past his shoulders, an oilskin coat hanging below his knees making him look like he'd wandered in from the Australian outback. She looked into his face and saw caring eyes, beautiful features; some of the sadness and grief which had settled into her body lifted, easing the heaviness in her limbs.

"Who...who are you?"

"My name does not matter, child."

He reached out and swept hair off her forehead, fingertips brushing her skin lightly. A sensation surged through her head and for a second it seemed like her room sparkled. She sat straighter, unconsciously pulling her face from his touch as her eyes widened, her mouth fell open.

"I am sorry your father's time has come."

She stared at the man, wanting to ask him how he knew, but her lips didn't attempt the words. If she opened her mouth to speak, she suspected they would produce nothing but a sorrowful wail. The man removed his coat, hung it over the back of the chair at her desk, then sat on the mattress beside her. Sister Agnes scooted away keeping three feet between them.

"I will not hurt you, Alesya. Do not be afraid."

"How...?"

The man stroked her cheek, halting the question. The electricity of his touch warmed her, comforted her, but it wasn't the electricity like she felt on her prom night when Kelly Booker slid his penis into her in the back seat of his parents' Cadillac—a brief shock of excitement and pain, over practically before it began. This was closer to how she'd felt later that night, when God came to her and beckoned her to be his bride.

A touch to change her life, calling her to Heaven.

"Am I dying?"

"Ssh, Alesya. You are not dying, you are very much alive. Perhaps more alive than ever before."

He slid closer and she felt heat radiating from him. His hand found her thigh and years of training and study, belief and chastity told her to move away. She couldn't. His touch comforted her, spoke to her. She looked down at his big hand resting on her leg where no man's hand had touched since Kelly Booker's and her breath shortened. The electricity of his touch swelled up her thigh, into her groin, her lower stomach, filling places empty for half a decade.

"I am here to tell you your father will be taken care of. You need not worry."

Grief and relief exploded in her. She let out one loud sob, then buried her face in the man's chest. He encircled her shoulders, held her tight, consoling her, and she felt the muscles of his arm against her back and found herself imaging what they looked like. The thought sent a shiver down her spine. She knew she shouldn't be enjoying his touch—she belonged to God, not any man—but something about him made her feel closer to God. Instead of pulling away, she settled into his embrace.

His hand inched further up her thigh. Unconsciously, her legs opened slightly as if making their own decisions. The warmth of his hand felt like it might burn her through her nightie but she didn't move away. Instead, she brought her arm up and across his chest, turned more toward him, hugged herself closer.

A part of her mind implored her to stop, insisted a nun didn't act this way, and she knew it was right, but she felt like the closer she got to him, the safer her father would be. She had the impression this man held responsibility for getting him to Heaven and he deserved whatever appreciation she gave.

A second later, his fingers found the place only she and Kelly Booker ever touched—him for pleasure and her only to wash in the years since.

When he laid her down and loomed over her she wanted to tell him 'no'. She was naked by then, though she didn't know how her nakedness happened, and he was, too. When he entered her—gently and firmly all at once—she gasped and bit down on her wrist to keep from crying out. She'd never felt ecstasy before, thought she never would until the day God took her into his kingdom.

After this, would she be allowed in?

Stars exploded before her eyes, a swirling cosmos blurring her vision of the man above her as he rocked his pelvis back and forth against hers. The movement, his touch, the sensations inside her transported her away from her father's death, from her life as a nun, into some unknown firmament where only herself and the man existed—nothing but the movement, the touch, the electric sensation. It grew and grew between her legs, extending into her belly and chest, down her legs and along her arms. She moved and bucked beneath him and, in this unknown place, this beautiful, empty firmament where they frolicked alone, she took her hand off her mouth and screamed her ecstasy to the Heavens.

After the man was gone—she still didn't know who he was but felt as though she'd touched a piece of Heaven—she lay naked on the bed, the sweat of their coupling cooling on her skin. She couldn't cry anymore, she couldn't smile, couldn't move. She luxuriated in the feeling between her legs, in her chest, permeating her body, touching her soul. Time melted into a blur she would never be able to fully recall. Later, she'd have a vague recollection of his electric touch exciting every nerve in her body.

Somewhere in the distance, she heard the sounds of insistent knocking, muffled voices calling out. In her state, Sister Agnes didn't hear what the voices said, couldn't answer, truthfully didn't care. The night air enveloped her as she lay listening to the sounds, frustration mounting in her that they should distract her from the lingering pleasure of the man.

Her hand crept across the smooth skin of her flat belly moving down, down until her fingers found the wetness between her legs, the heady mixture of her pleasure and his seed, and the feeling of her own touch drove the frustration and distraction from her mind. Somewhere far, far away, the door to her room burst open and three people spilled in. She saw them as if watching on television, the three sisters finding her lying on her bed: sweaty, spent and touching herself. They rushed to her side, speaking to her in concerned tones which she fought against taking her away from her place of pleasure.

As the sisters spoke to her, asked 'are you all right' and 'what happened', Sister Agnes—named for the patron saint of chastity—drifted off to sleep and dreamed about a child of Heaven.

Chapter
Twenty-Two

T HE CRAGGY HORIZON DREW no closer but the ground upon which Poe strode changed. It faded from red-orange to gray, then brown. Stunted shrubs and trees like over-sized bonsais popped up sporadically, their frequency increasing as she went. She never saw them in the distance but rather they seemed to spring out of the ground on her approach.

She did her best to ignore the pain in her leg, now dulled to a nagging ache, concentrating instead on surveying the area around her, watching the ground for footprints to show her the passing of a teenage boy. At first, she found no signs of anything passing. After a while, she came upon a set of footprints and, although she possessed no tracking skills, chose to follow them. She soon lost them among other tracks which seemed to appear out of nowhere, both human and otherwise, until enough prints covered the ground she thought she might be tracking Trevor along a parade route.

Wearily and losing faith, she pressed on.

Where are you, Trevor?

A few paces ahead she saw a tree which wasn't there before. It grew a few feet toward the chaotic sky, hooked to the left a few feet before bending skyward again. It stood taller than the others she'd seen, its trunk thicker; big enough to pass for an earthbound tree. She limped over to it, leaned on it to test its strength then, finding it solid, sat in the crook. It bounced under her weight, swayed as she settled in, but held her one-hundred-and-two pound frame without bending.

She sat staring at her feet, shoulders slumped forward, her determination waned. Hell was too big a place to find one person with no direction, help or idea of where to look.

Needle, meet haystack.

The corner of her mouth twitched at the thought which sounded so much like one of Icarus' sarcastic clichés but, given the circumstances, she didn't allow herself to smile. And the thought of her charge made the shadow of a smile disappear quickly.

What would Icarus think if he knew I brought Trevor here? What would he think if he knew I lost him?

She leaned forward, propped her elbows on her knees and buried her face in her hands. Too late to have those thoughts now, she should have considered them before they ever came here, but she'd been blinded by Michael's words.

'There have been rumors about you, Poe. There has been some question about your loyalties.'

Spoken by anyone, the words would have stung, but all the more so from Michael, the archangel, the hand of God, her savior. As soon as they left his lips, nothing else in the world mattered but proving herself to him, showing herself worthy of the gift he'd given her four decades ago. Now, sitting on a crooked tree in Hell, she knew she'd let Michael or anyone else think anything they wanted about her if it meant Trevor's safety.

The desiccated leaves rustled in the tree above Poe and she removed her face from her hands. She felt no wind to move the sparse leaves, the earth itself hadn't shaken, yet the sound came again. The guardian angel looked up to see a raven perched on the highest branch. She sat up straight.

"Where did you come from?"

Her muscles tensed and pain from the gash in her leg shot up to her hip. On earth, the question would have been rhetorical, but in Hell, the possibility existed anything might respond...or attack.

The raven fluttered its wings and stared at Poe. Black flesh showed through its patchy feathers in some spots; a divot in its head held the place where an eye should have been. Its pointed beak opened and closed once with a click, then opened again and it spoke.

"Caw."

Poe shook her head and allowed the corner of her mouth to curve up a fraction of an inch.

"So you are only a raven."

The bird flapped its wings again, bouncing the branch on which it perched, held them out to the sides for balance as it leaned forward stretching out its neck.

"What are you doing, silly bird?"

Poe's mood lightened with the bird here despite its motley appearance. Being in the presence of something else seemingly normal and alive, especially something not appearing to want her dead, made her feel so much less alone.

"Crawk!"

The raven drew its head back and extended it again, then did it a third time before Poe realized the bird meant the gesture as a way of pointing. A sliver of dread forced itself into her mood as she turned her head slowly.

Ten yards away, directly in front of her stood a decrepit shack. She blinked, shook her head, but the broken-down building—empty air seconds before—remained.

"What the...?"

Poe stood and took a step toward it, distrusting her sight. The broken-down wood building didn't waver or disappear. She rubbed her eyes and looked again. It remained.

"Caw," the raven croaked, startling her.

Poe looked back over her shoulder but the bird was gone. She searched the dark sky and saw no sign of the bird, no movement, no flapping wings silhouetted against the clouds.

She looked back at the shack.

Some of its boards canted at odd angles creating spaces wide enough to peer through into the interior. The door hung on one hinge; hastily nailed boards mostly covered the single, broken window. Improbably for a structure residing in Hell, green moss sprouted upon its roof.

Poe padded tentatively across the brown earth separating her from the small building. With each step closer, she felt she should recognize the place, though the reason eluded her. It felt like a place she might have seen in a dream a long time ago, a dream forgotten as others replaced it.

She crept to the window and peeked between the boards: empty. Nothing sat on the dirt floor, nothing leaned against the rotting walls, nothing hung from the splintered overhead beams. Empty, yet the sense of dread the raven's prompting brought blossomed in her thoughts.

Her feet took her to the door though she didn't ask them to. Her hand reached out for the rusted latch though she didn't want it to. The one hinge creaked as her arm pulled the door open though she pleaded in her head for it not to.

In the middle of the single room stood a woman with long, black hair, pale skin and a silver stud gleaming between her bottom lip and her chin.

"Hello, Poe."

Piper.

· · · ● · ● · ● · · ·

Trevor couldn't put his finger on the aroma in the room—there were too many mingling smells to identify any one of them individually, as if he'd been left in a kitchen cooking many foods, with the ingredients list including things like sulfur and roses. After a while, it began to burn the inside of Trevor's nostrils and he covered his nose to alleviate the unpleasant feeling.

Rich tapestries covered the walls of the opulent room, though they pictured scenes he'd rather not see—torture and death, souls writhing in excruciating pain. Antique furniture, ornately carved and decorated, sat around the room. He knew nothing about such things but even he realized these kinds of furnishings would make the old English buggers on *The Antiques Roadshow* salivate.

He got up off the couch and padded across the thick carpet, moving furtively as he searched behind three sofas, under a huge grand piano, in the space under a massive desk with a roll top. No one else inhabited the room and he found no method of exit.

"Shit."

The trip getting here was a blur. He remembered turning around and seeing Azrael; he remembered feeling fear at the sight of the banished archangel but exactly how he got here, or how long it took, he didn't know. It wasn't the first time he'd been in Azrael's presence and he didn't remember much of the first visit—the angel of death seemed to have that effect on him.

Maybe not such a bad thing.

Trevor moved to a blank space of wall: no pictures, no tapestry, just dark wood paneling taken from someone's nineteen-sixties rec room. He examined it closely, drew his fingers along the ridges where one sheet met the next, looking for but not expecting to find some hidden egress, the empty feeling in his gut growing as he went.

If I got in, there has to be a way out.

He moved to the next seam, then the next until the empty wall ran out and he stood in front of one of the tapestries.

There might be a door behind it.

He raised his hand, intending to grasp the tapestry and pull it aside, either gain his escape or prove himself a captive to stay, but the scene elaborately embroidered in dark colored thread across the curtain's surface caught his attention. It showed a long side-view of a cliff, a black winged beast pushed over it by a mob of beings who all looked the same, each of them bound to the next by a length of silver thread.

Trevor squinted and leaned closer.

"Abaddon."

Another figure knelt on the ground behind the group plummeting over the edge: a woman, petite, her hair sewn of yellow thread. Trevor stared at the depiction and the tiny figure seemed to turn its head and look at him. He recognized her instantly.

"Poe!"

He reached his hand out to touch the figure but, a fraction of an inch away from his fingers brushing the velvety cloth, a voice broke the silence, startling him.

"I wouldn't touch that if I were you."

The voice sounded more like multiple voices with a touch of discordant undertones ringing beneath the surface. The simple words held a tone of command and expectation which made him stop.

The depiction of Poe looked away, hung her head. Trevor pivoted toward the voice.

"Who are you?"

The boy looked a few years younger than Trevor, perhaps eleven or twelve years old. He smiled, the expression transforming his face into a thing of beauty despite a smear of dirt across his left cheek, the tousle of unkempt hair perched atop his head. The boy's face mesmerized Trevor, distracted him from seeking an answer to the question he'd asked.

"You need not be afraid, son of Icarus. I won't hurt you."

Without seeming to move, he was at Trevor's side, hand clutching the teen's. Trevor's mind told him to move away but his heart held his legs in check. The boy walked him toward one of the couches.

"Where's Azrael? He brought me here."

"He had things to do. You and I will be spending some time together instead."

Trevor sat on the sofa while the boy remained standing. His eyes held on Trevor's like they looked right into him, saw more than hair and flesh and muscle beneath. It made the teen squirm, but he didn't look away.

I shouldn't be afraid. He's younger than me, and smaller.

Trevor cleared his throat.

"What's your name?"

"I have many names," the boy said still smiling, though now it held the quality of a willing secret, happy to be kept. "You can't pronounce most of them."

"Why am I here?"

"Your father's looking for you, you know."

Trevor nodded. "Is he alright?"

"For now. Many trials await him."

He wanted to be concerned but the boy's voice flowed through his brain like syrup, slowing its machinations, making his head feel tired though his body felt awake and alive, practically vibrated in the boy's presence.

"Will he be okay?"

"We shall see," the boy said, the smile clinging tenaciously to his lips. "We shall see."

· · · ● · ● · · · ·

Behind Poe, the door clacked shut against the askance frame, but she ignored it as she gazed into Piper's face. The woman was beautiful, no doubt about it; her beauty made Poe feel embarrassed by her own plainness, a feeling which dogged her through her lives, both mortal and angel. An ingredient in her corporeal demise.

"Who are you?"

"You know who I am," Piper responded, smiling.

"I know your name. I don't know who you are."

"I'm like you, Poe. Only better."

Poe's eyes narrowed. "I don't think you are what you seem."

Piper threw her head back and barked a short, sharp laugh. The sound made Poe jump.

"Who are you to accuse me of not being what I seem? Does anyone know the truth of your past?"

"I—"

"Have you ever told Icarus?"

"I wanted—"

Piper laughed again, interrupting her, and the feeling of inadequacy and desperation she'd been fleeing for so many years took a big bite and held on. Her head drooped until her chin brushed the top of her chest. She stared down at her feet smudged with dirt and whispered: "I wanted to."

"Oh, poor thing. Of course you did."

Poe didn't know if she'd heard sarcastic tones in Piper's words or if she added them in her head. When she looked up, the supposed-angel stood immediately in front of her, her smile softened from border-line maniacal to sort-of-reassuring.

"Come, someone wants to see you."

She took Poe by the elbow and an electric shock quivered the muscle of the guardian angel's upper arm, not painful but not pleasant, like a bare wire brushed her bicep. The sensation remained with Piper's touch.

They moved toward the door, Piper having to prompt Poe on.

"Don't worry, muffin."

"Who wants to see me?"

"An old friend."

Piper pushed the door open and, instead of opening onto the bleak landscape of bare dirt and gnarled trees she'd left, Poe saw Arbutus trees and oaks. The roofs of houses showed through their branches, close enough to walk to but not so close the residents of those houses could hear.

She'd been here before, a long time ago. Seeing the shed out of context set against the backdrop of Hell's desolation had camouflaged the truth, but now that she saw it back where it belonged, in the empty lot behind the Baxters' house, she remembered it. She remembered everything she'd tried so hard to forget.

Piper's hand fell away from her arm and Poe looked at the shed. It appeared the same as it did more than four decades ago, right down to the weeds growing out of control around the base of its walls, the blackened boards to the left of the door where some teenager once attempted to burn it down.

Poe's mouth fell open, goose bumps prickled her flesh as she peered upon the place where she'd been raped. If she'd harbored any doubt before that she was in Hell, it disappeared.

Now she was in her own Hell.

Chapter
Twenty-Three

MY MOTHER'S SMILE DIDN'T falter as I stood and looked down into her eyes for the first time in my life, but neither did the sadness concealed behind them. My mind whirled. I'd never expected to be in this situation, so I never planned what to say. When someone dies the moment you're born, it's normally a waste of time thinking about the conversation you'll have when you meet them.

Welcome to my life.

"What are you doing here?"

Lame.

"You needed help. Why are you here?"

"Does Dominic know you came to help me?" I swallowed hard. "Azrael?"

I glanced around the crowd, looking for the priest's leering face, the angel of death's looming presence, but saw only the lost, confused-looking souls. I didn't recognize any of them.

My mother shook her head and put her hand on my cheek. Her touch didn't hold the tingle of Poe's or Piper's, the shock and threat of Azrael's or Mikey's. She wasn't an angel in the true sense of the word, but after wandering the labyrinth for God-only-knew how long, she was my angel.

"Did you do something wrong? Did you die again? Is that why you're here?"

"No."

The concern in her voice touched me. There were so few times in my life I'd had anyone who cared enough to be concerned about me: Rae, though I drank away any concern she'd had for me, and Sister

Mary-Therese. But this was different; this was the woman who gave me life.

She dropped her hand from my cheek and took my arm to lead me through the crowd. We walked in silence for a while, the unexpected reunion leaving both of us speechless. Other people in a similar scenario—long lost son reunited with his mother—might have many things about which to talk: how's life? What have you been up to? Tell me what's been going on for you.

'How's Hell been treating you, Ma,' didn't seem appropriate.

As for her, I got the sense she'd been watching me and knew about my life. When your son's been abused, berated, a druggie, an alcoholic, murdered and resurrected against his will, you probably also want to tread lightly around conversation.

We weaved our way through the crowd, her arm hooked through mine, neither of us speaking. I looked at her from the corner of my eye, saw her sharp jaw and high cheek bones and understood how even an archangel might give in to temptation. Understanding didn't make what he did acceptable. Thinking about it made me angry, and that anger transferred to thoughts about what happened to bring me to this unusual point in my life—strolling through Hell with my dead mother. I felt the time appropriate to attempt conversation.

"People died because of me."

"I know."

"I came here to get them back."

She didn't reply, looking at her feet as she walked. As I watched her watching her steps, a thought occurred to me. I stopped. She continued a step, tugging at my arm before coming to a stop. One of the lost walked into my back and moved on without excusing him or herself.

"I'll take you back."

Why didn't I think of that before?

She smiled and touched my cheek.

"But I'm not here because of you."

I shook my head. "You're the first person to die because of me."

"No, Icarus. I didn't die because of you." She tried to smile but the sadness in her eyes leaked into her lips, into her tone.

I thought about my first visit to Hell. I'd seen my mother as she gave birth to me, Sister Mary-Therese aiding her as Michael and Azrael loomed over the scene and a Carrion waited in the wings. Okay, given those circumstances, maybe her death wasn't my fault, but that didn't mean I couldn't take her back.

"That doesn't mean you can't come back with me."

She pulled on my arm to get me walking again; I complied, watching her features as we went. Her smile faded but her eyes looked sadder than before and I sensed a debate going on behind them. When she looked up, I knew one debating team had convinced the other.

"I don't deserve to be anywhere but here."

"What are you talking about? You're a good person. You shouldn't be here."

"You don't know what kind of person I am."

"You're my mother."

"Exactly. I was a nun *and* I am your mother. One doesn't go with the other"

Touché.

"That wasn't your fault."

A path through the crowd of milling souls cleared before us so readily, a cynic like me might have thought we were being herded. I looked up and saw a group of souls ahead of us gathered around something.

"Azrael didn't force himself on me, Icarus. I could have refused but didn't. I'm where I should be."

"But you have to come with me."

"I can't. For you to take a soul, one must replace it. Who would you leave? Trevor?"

"I..."

I didn't have an answer. I'd come to Hell to rescue souls, not trade them. Who was I to decide who should replace someone else in Hell? I suddenly felt relieved I didn't bring Tony McSweeny back. The thought of trading for a seeming pedophile churned my stomach.

'For you to take a soul, one must replace it.'

The words bounced around my head looking for a place to grab on so I could understand their impact. It took a few seconds; my mind can be a slippery slope at the best of times. When they finally found purchase, they brought a memory of the crowd I'd seen before Marty and Todd found me, the woman condemned to public-speaking-Hell. But it wasn't her, it was the face in the crowd.

Detective Williams.

I'd dropped him off to be taken to Heaven, yet saw him amongst the crowd in Hell. I didn't have time to think it through at the time—Marty and Todd's stinking bag being yanked over my head distracted me from discerning a reason for his presence—but my mother's words told the truth of it.

When I brought Elizabeth Elton back, Hell took the detective as payment.

Great. First I kill the guy, then I get him condemned. Nice work.

"Shit."

We drew closer to the group, close enough I saw they were gathered around another person, jostling to get close. The path to them lay clear before us, each side lined with more lost souls like well-wishers at a ticker-tape parade or the receiving line at a wedding.

"I must stay here, Icarus, but others need you."

"Ric."

She gestured toward the group of souls shuffling and circling twenty feet away and let her arm slip from mine. I stepped forward, looking at the faces, but I recognized none of them.

"What do you mean?" I asked looking back at her. "Who needs me?"

She directed me on a route around the small mob. As we came around, I saw who the souls were elbowing each other aside to get to: *Orlando Albert.*

In life, he'd been my supplier, and even after Father Dominic killed him during his murderous spree to cleanse the earth of everyone I'd ever known—the reason I'd come to Hell to recover souls—he showed up with drugs when I'd sunk to my lowest. If not for whoever pulled me out of that alleyway—a person *not* my guardian angel—I'd likely still be slouched in the grime doing anything to score more dope. Or, more likely, I'd be dead. Deader, I mean. Really dead.

The rickety-looking stool supporting Orlando creaked as he turned to face one of the lost souls who stepped in front of him, rolled up his sleeve and offered his bare arm. In response, Orlando reached into a doctor's bag on the ground by his feet and pulled out a syringe. He stuck the needle into the lost one's arm and depressed the plunger. Apparently Mr. Albert's Hell and his life bore a striking resemblance.

The lost soul leaned forward, bit off Orlando's ear, then stumbled away.

Okay, maybe a little different.

Orlando watched the man he'd injected as he teetered on unsteady feet. I could identify—Orlando always provided good stuff and it occasionally affected me the same way, at least up until the point when the soul bent at the waist and spewed a gush of vomit onto the ground.

I grimaced. The soul heaved again and puke splashed in the dirt. My own stomach did a small back flip as the smell wafted to where we stood. My mother made a small gulping sound at the back of her throat.

The soul vomited again and again. After the fourth time, I noticed his skin was tightening across his bones with each retch, turning him from a desperately lost but otherwise normal looking man to Vietnam prisoner-of-war physique in a matter of five heaves. One more made him a skeleton with skin. The seventh time he puked, it looked to be his heart he threw up, and his desiccated body folded to the ground.

The next soul stepped up, arm exposed, and Orlando obliged with another injection. The woman who received his wares took a bite out of his forearm, then turned and wandered toward us, apparently han-dling the drugs better than her friend. As she came close, blood began running first from her nose, then her eyes. Blood streamed down her cheeks, ran from her ears. Blood soaked her pants, dripped from her fingertips. Every possible opening in her body, and a few improbable ones, flowed with blood until she finally stumbled and fell at my feet, blood spattering my shoes.

I looked up and my eyes met Orlando's.

"Icarus? Icarus Fell? Is that you?"

I had the ridiculous urge to look over my shoulder as if he'd directed his comments to someone else. Instead, I stared at him, half-mesmer-ized by his missing ear, the bite out of his forearm, the bag of drugs.

He stood, grabbed the bag, and came toward me.

"That is you, Icarus."

"Ric," I conceded grudgingly.

"What are you doing here?"

I shook my head and shrugged as if I didn't know the answer. He raised an eyebrow like he didn't buy it and approached close enough his sweet odor of stale sweat wafted to my nostrils, overpowering the pukey stench his customer left behind.

"Orlando. Good to see you."

A lie. I didn't extend my hand. Good things never happened when Orlando Albert showed up in my life. He'd been one of the architects of my life's ruin; no reason to think it would be different in Hell.

He looked from my face to someone in the crowd of souls and back again. His fingers scratched his stubbly chin and he took another step closer, tilted his head like a dog deciphering his master's command.

"I saw you in the alley, you know."

My casual survey of him morphed into a glare.

"He sent me to give you drugs. I fed you enough to kill a horse."

The hair at the base of my head prickled. "Who sent you?"

"You should be dead. You don't look dead."

"Who sent you to give me drugs?"

A look of realization crossed his face. He stepped forward, grabbing me by both shoulders.

"You're alive," he said in a husky whisper. "You're in Hell, but you're alive."

His stink overpowered me, clawed its way up my nostrils into my brain. The feel of his fingers pressing against my shoulders and his words incited my anger.

He was sent to give me drugs. Someone sent him. To kill me.

My molars clamped down tight. Behind Orlando, the crowd to which he'd been dispensing drugs grew restless as they milled around his vacated stool. One of them spied him and stumbled our way.

"*Who sent you?*"

Insistent words spilled through clenched teeth and between tight lips. I thought I'd spoken loud enough, but he responded as though he didn't hear me.

"You have to take me back, Icarus. Take me away from this place."

"No."

"I was always good to you. I always gave you what you wanted, sometimes when you couldn't pay for it."

More of the lost souls gathered behind him, closing in but not close enough that he noticed them.

"You deserve to be here."

"No. I did what I had to." He grabbed the front of my shirt, resorting to begging. "Please, please. Please take me back."

"No."

"Icarus. I was your friend."

"My friend?" I swiped his hands off my chest. "My friend? You ruined my life."

"No. I gave you what you asked for. You came to me."

Anger exploded, coursing out of my chest, down my arms. My flat palms hit him in the chest, pushing him away. The impact surprised him and he stumbled backward into the waiting arms of two dozen drug-hungry souls; they engulfed him like an avalanche taking a skier.

Grabbing hands pulled him down, snatched the bag of drugs and ripped it open spilling syringes to the ground causing a frenzy amongst the damned.

My anger dissipated as I watched lost soul after lost soul scoop syringes off the ground and insert the dirty needles into their arms. Immediately after each one did, they stepped forward and took a bite out of Orlando Albert, consuming him like the slice of lime after their shot of tequila.

I should have been disgusted, felt guilty for causing this, but I didn't.

I should have looked away; I didn't.

Instead, I watched: interested, titillated, vindicated. I watched each bite, each piece of his soul gulped down the throat of one of those lost souls until roughly half of Orlando Albert remained.

"Icarus, please," he called from beneath the pile of desperate damned.

I didn't respond.

When the puking and the bleeding began seconds later, en masse, I remembered my mother standing behind me and decided to get her away from such a spectacle.

What kind of son am I?

I turned, intending to take her arm and lead her away much the way she'd led me here in the first place, but my fingers closed on empty air.

"Mother?"

The word felt foreign on my lips, an ill-tasting chunk of food ejected from my tongue, but I let it go without querying why it tasted so bad. I scanned the crowd around me, moved away from the Orlando Albert buffet in search of the woman who birthed me. Lost souls pushed by me, some moving to join the feeding frenzy, some milling in the aimless manner of the damned. I snaked my way between them and caught a glimpse of my mother heading for a door which hadn't been there before.

"Mother!"

I spat the word as loudly as possible but the tumult of damned feet shuffling in dirt and Orlando's screams as his tormentors got down to the good stuff smothered it. I jogged after her, squeezing my way through the crowd as she pulled the door open and stepped through. Halfway to her, a squat, dense soul which bore more resemblance to a sumo wrestler than to the others gathered here stepped in front of me. I hit the man's broad chest and bounced back a few steps. His deportment immediately suggested he didn't intend to let me pass. I held my hands up, palms toward him in a gesture of surrender.

"I don't want any trouble. Just let me by."

His lips pulled back in a growl revealing teeth a few decades beyond their best days. A ragged piece of meat hung between two of them. The way he looked told me reasoning with him might not be an option, so I didn't bother.

I deked right, then went left, but he didn't bite—exactly why I never played football. A massive arm shot out and caught me across the throat with a text book clothesline move right out of *Wrestlemania*. I hit the ground in a puff of dirt and felt the chance of catching up with my mother disappear like the dust dissipating in the air.

For a second I saw chaotic sky swirling overhead, but then the pseudo-sumo wrestler's figure moved over me, blocking it. The muscles in his arms and legs tensed giving me a fraction of a second to panic. I'd seen this move before: the Big Splash. Seasoned wrestlers didn't recover from a monster like this coming down on them.

He leapt impossibly high in the air, arms waving like he wanted to swim. I gritted my teeth, readying myself for the impact.

And then he exploded.

Blood and goop rained down, spattering me. I lay unmoving for a few seconds, not sure what happened, then climbed to my feet cautiously—Hell had proven unpredictable more than once. I took a few steps away and looked back at a perfect outline of my body painted on the dirt in blood.

Adds a whole new meaning to the name 'Big Splash'.

Under other circumstances, I might have marveled at the cartoon-esque nature of an exploding man, maybe laughed a little—or maybe lost my lunch—but the need to find where my mother had gone tied my intestines into a lasso. I wiped the sumo off my face and continued along the path he'd blocked. Ten seconds later I arrived at the door, threw it open and spilled through with no regard to what might be on the other side.

My first sensation was of heat, though my nerve endings and eyes quickly combined to rectify that to reality: cold. A dusting of snow shrouded the sidewalk at my feet and the parking lot stretching before me. I looked down, confused.

Snow in Hell?

No, not snow in Hell. And no footprints in the snow which wasn't in Hell. Wherever I'd ended up, it wasn't where my mother went. I pivoted on one heel, tore the door open and rushed through again.

And tripped over a stack of patio chairs.

I righted myself and looked around the dark warehouse which I'd now visited at least one time too many.

"No," I said aloud, the word dying against a plastic-wrapped stack of cushions. "No."

I went out the door into the same parking lot, realizing where I was. Thirty yards away, a couple strolled arm in arm through the pleasant winter night, content with each other and with whatever beliefs they did or didn't have in the existence of Heaven and Hell.

"No," I bellowed into the wintery night.

The man hugged his lady close, shot me a baleful look and crossed the street to a sidewalk safe from shouting lunatics. I wished I shared their uncertain beliefs, but I'd been to Hell and back in the realest sense of the cliché and, more disturbingly, my turncoat guardian angel lost my son there.

And I didn't know how to get back.

Chapter
Twenty-Four

T HE BOY WAS CAUCASIAN but of dark hair and complexion, as though another lineage combined to give his skin a shade two steps darker than olive. Or perhaps the unwashed nature of his face gave it its shade. In any case, his skin looked taut and smooth like most any twelve year old, and he stood a full head shorter than Trevor, but his demeanor made him seem older, bigger.

"Where's my father?" Trevor asked, the syrupy feeling in his head slowing his words as they exited his mouth.

"I'll show you, if you like."

Trevor's head bobbed like a cork floating on a lake. The many-named boy with no name gestured for him to follow as he strode across the room. Trevor struggled to his feet, dragging his heavier-than-usual head with him as he went, and followed the boy. Crossing the room, he noticed some odd ornamentation he hadn't seen during his first cursory glance at his surroundings. An ornate cage with bars made of intricately carved wood sat on a table, its bottom covered with fine-grained sand, a volcanic rock formation in one corner; a long, leafless branch extended the length of the cage. The skeleton of the gecko one might have expected to find in such a cage sat in the middle. Trevor stared at it as he passed the table; the skeleton-lizard snapped its jaws at him and shuffled to the bars to watch him go by.

On the wall behind the table hung a grisly rendition of the comedy and tragedy masks, each of them broad, stretched, as if peeled directly off someone's face. Trevor thought if he examined them close enough, he'd likely find them actually made of flesh and chose to direct his eyes ahead, fixing them on the boy's back.

The boy had reached the other side of the room and stood facing a tapestry, his back to Trevor blocking his view of the depiction upon the cloth. Something fluttered in the corner Trevor's vision, but he kept his on the boy.

"Hmm. This is interesting," the boy said. "Perhaps you should hurry."

He wiggled his fingers and the rubber cement which had filled the gaps in Trevor's brain evaporated, freeing his thoughts and movements. He made his legs go faster and propelled himself to the boy's side to see the scene woven in the tapestry.

The hanging showed a partial bird's-eye view, to the right of which was a complicated pattern, like the mazes Trevor used to do in the puzzle books his mother bought him in his youth. He'd never been good at them, and the one embroidered on the cloth looked like it might be the most complicated he'd ever seen, its complexity heightened by the fact its walls seemed to shift every time Trevor moved his eyes. He blinked rapidly to dispel what he thought must be an optical illusion and found it changed with each flutter of his eyelids.

"Look here," the boy prompted and Trevor shifted his gaze away from the labyrinth.

At the end of the maze was an open space in which hundreds of stick people milled about. No doubt about the movement of the depictions this time; tiny people walked back and forth aimlessly, bumping into each other, wandering to the wall bounding their holding area then turning around and walking back like scores of miniature zombies.

In one spot, the scene differed. A group of slightly more fleshed out stick men gathered around another who kicked and struggled on the ground amidst them.

They appeared to be eating him.

Trevor's lip curled in disgust. His eyes wandered back toward the labyrinth but the boy's hand on his arm diverted his attention back.

"Did you see this?"

He pointed at the two figures on the tapestry directly in front of him, one considerably thicker than the other, a detailed rendering of a man who, in life, would be well muscled and stocky. The second figure stood a bit taller, not as broad, but equally as well detailed.

"Dad?"

"That's him."

Trevor leaned in, squinted at the figures as Icarus gestured, held up his hands. The other man flexed in menace, his muscles visible even in the tapestry's thread.

"What's going on? Where is he?"

"Right there." The boy pointed at the hanging.

Trevor extended his finger, intending to stroke the lines of thread depicting his father, but the boy grabbed his hand, stopping him less than an inch from touching the cloth.

"Not a good idea," he said.

His grip was strong enough to keep Trevor from moving his hand forward or pulling it away. The boy held it in place as the stocky figure clothes-lined the miniature, embroidered Icarus to the ground. Trevor gasped. He didn't know exactly what he was seeing—an illusion? A portrayal of events happening now, past or future?—but he felt his father was in danger.

The stocky man bunched, crouched, then jumped into the air over the Icarus figure.

"Okay. Touch him."

The boy guided Trevor's finger forward and pressed it against the thread-man. It didn't feel of soft cloth, instead Trevor felt something alive squirm beneath the fleshy tip of his finger, like he'd trapped a bug. It wriggled momentarily then burst like he'd pressed too hard on a grape. He jerked his hand away and the boy released his grip.

Trevor stared at the tapestry. A red smudge tainted the cloth where the stocky figure was a moment before, the smear obscuring the miniature Icarus. Trevor's heart jumped. He leaned forward, breath held, examining the threads to see if both figures had been destroyed. When the tiny version of his father separated from the stain, leaving behind an outline of itself, Trevor stumbled back from the wall.

"What the Hell was that?"

The boy chuckled a laugh which didn't belong in the throat of a twelve-year-old.

"You just saved your father's life."

Trevor looked at the boy, then back at the tapestry where the thread-Icarus ran across the yard, opened a door in the wall and disappeared. The teen shook his head trying to rearrange his thoughts.

"What?"

"You saved Icarus. That man would have killed him. For real, this time."

"That really happened?"

"Mmm hmm."

"I saved my father."

"Yes."

"That means—"

"You killed the other man, yes."

"But...isn't he already dead?"

"Mmm. To a point. Now he is all the way."

Trevor's throat tied itself in a knot and he stumbled back a couple of steps, head spinning. He looked at the tip of his finger, then wiped it vehemently on his pant leg, wiping away debris which didn't exist.

I killed him.

"Sacrifices must be made, Trevor. Choices. It was him or your father. Would you prefer it the other way? I can change it."

The boy raised a hand toward the hanging but stopped when Trevor shook his head.

"No. You have already lost him once, haven't you? You would not want to be responsible for losing him again."

The boy turned toward him and took two steps. Trevor backed away until he bumped a piece of furniture behind him. He heard the click-clack of skeletal jaws snapping and knew he'd backed into the table with its caged lizard-thing.

"I told you I would not hurt you. Quite the opposite. It is by accident you are here, so I am keeping you safe."

Trevor glanced at the stretched flesh of the comedy/tragedy masks on the wall and doubted his safety. He wanted to go home.

"Don't worry. You will get home soon enough. I need to show you some things first, however."

He gestured for Trevor to follow again and the teen did despite an urgent desire to either stay put or flee—anything but follow the boy again. They went to the same wall, the same tapestry, but this time it showed a different scene. A church on a stormy night, a man not dressed for the weather seeking refuge beneath its eaves. Across the churchyard, two other figures lurked beneath a giant oak tree, a silver-threaded knife flashing in one of their hands.

"It is time someone knew the truth."

Trevor watched the thread-version of his father leave the protection of the church's eaves and head across the churchyard where two muggers waited to kill him.

Chapter
Twenty-Five

O PEN THE DOOR.

Close the door.

Open the door.

Close the door.

Open the door.

Each time, the door opened on the same darkened warehouse, the same stacks of plastic chairs and tables.

How do they do it?

After manipulating the door through its paces enough times to make my arm sore, I saw the futility in the venture and began wracking my brain: *where else did I see people go to Hell?*

I'd seen Hell the first time in my hotel room at the hands of the archangel Michael. Real as it seemed, I'd assumed it a representation of Hell, not that my hotel room hid a Hellish portal a la *The Amityville Horror* or *Buffy the Vampire Slayer*. The second time, I'd ended up there because of Father Dominic. That time it had been at the church.

The church.

When we'd brought Beth Elton back, Piper took me through the church, at least what remained of it. Makes one wonder about the nature of the church when it proves the best method of ingress to Hell.

I always knew something was wrong with that place.

I slammed the warehouse door shut one last time with authority so it would know I was done with this silliness, then took two steps across the parking lot and stopped. Before I went any further, I returned to the door and peeked through once more. Chairs and tables.

I headed for the nearest bus stop.

· · · · ● · ● ● · · ·

The crowd had grown since my last visit to the church. How long ago was it? A couple of days? Time loses its meaning in Hell and the battery in my throw-away digital watch gave up the ghost a few weeks before, so I threw it away.

I surveyed the situation from beneath the oak tree, keenly aware I stood bare yards from where two muggers killed me for a few bucks and an Xbox game: Halo—good game. Every time I came here, the memories sent shivers reverberating up my spine, partially due to the shock and pain of dying, partially because part of me wondered what life would have been like if I didn't bump into the guys with the knife that night. What if I never met Mikey and took this job? Where would I be? What would I be doing?

Good chance I wouldn't be hanging around here trying to find my way to Hell. Also a good chance I wouldn't have reconciled with Trevor. If nothing else, dying gave me back a relationship with my son I'd lost years before.

But now you've lost him.

Emerging from behind the oak tree's broad trunk, I headed across the churchyard toward the tents pitched there, studiously doing my best to avoid the police presence in place to keep the peace like it was some kind of 'Occupy Heaven' protest. At the edge of the crowd, I settled in beside a man with a wool hat pulled down to his eyebrows, his hands encased in thick mitts which matched the hat and looked like they'd been knitted by someone's grandmother.

"What's going on?" I asked, aiming for a friendly tone but barely hiding my impatience.

"What?"

"I said: what's going on?"

"Don't you watch the news?"

I shook my head and the man looked me up and down. I had no coat and wasn't feeling the cold—a by-product of being in Hell for a while, I suppose—but hugged myself against the chill and feigned a shiver to avoid creating suspicion.

"Jesus."

"Whoa, tone it down a bit, buddy," I said leaning toward him. "This doesn't seem like the kind of crowd that would approve of you using the big guy's name in vain."

"No. We saw Jesus last night."

I pressed my lips together stifling a giggle, though part of me felt jealous. I'd been dead for months, met angels, archangels, demons, but no sign of this Jesus fellow. Didn't seem right these people should see him before me. The thought bubbled a chuckle to the edge of my lips.

"What? He just came strolling up and said 'what's up, Doc?'"

"He was in the window."

The man's face remained serious, my poor humor lost on him.

"Has he been back?"

"No. But he'll come. I know he will."

I nodded, ending the conversation. My experience with people like this guy told me once they got talking about Jesus, getting anything else out of them was impossible. Probably he wouldn't be too helpful if I straight up asked 'have you seen a doorway to Hell around here?'

I skirted the outside edge of the crowd, hiding my face as I passed necessarily close to one of the police officers monitoring the gathering, but his eyes didn't waver from the stained glass window, apparently counting himself one of the flock. The way they all stared, faces blank with wonder, reminded me of the souls I'd seen in Hell, though their eyes held hope instead of despair. Doesn't the one often precede the other?

My circuitous route took me through the dilapidated graveyard with its tumble-down headstones. A rime of snow and frost lay atop the cracked and chipped stones, bringing more lightness and joy to the little cemetery than it had seen in years. I followed the wrought iron fence, checking over my shoulder frequently to ensure no one saw me, but the miraculous window held all the onlookers rapt. After a minute, I came directly behind the still-standing section of church and hopped the fence back into the churchyard, careful not to skewer myself on its black tines.

For some reason, the Jesus-seekers stayed away from this side of the ruined church. Maybe out of respect, or fear, or maybe the cops kept them away. Whatever. I crept across the snowy lawn, noticed a couple of sets of footprints mostly filled with new snow, and made it to the church unnoticed.

No snow dusted the ground within the ruins despite the explosion that left the church with no roof. The shattered pews and chunks of stone walls scattered around the one-time nave lay free of the white shawl of winter beautifying the cemetery. I scampered toward the window sending wayward pebbles skittering before me with each step, cursing myself in my head with each sound for fear someone would hear, but I didn't slow. The closer I got to the window, the more sure I became this would get me where I needed to go.

I felt Hell getting closer.

The pew Piper had man-handled against the wall still rested there, propped up to serve as an awkward ladder to the window. I boosted myself up, the smell of its charred wood entering my nostrils, but it didn't do so alone. Buried deep beneath it, a hair's breadth from being unnoticeable, I caught a whiff of cinnamon and fresh baking.

Mikey's been here.

I grabbed the sides of the bench to haul myself up and got a sliver in the index finger of my right hand. The quick jab of pain it brought made me realize the other injuries I'd sustained had all but disappeared—if I'd healed this well in life, maybe I'd have stuck with football and gotten better at it. Probably wouldn't have helped.

I stuck my finger in my mouth and chewed at it until I felt the tiny, intrusive piece of wood on my tongue and spit it out. A line of saliva dribbled down my chin; I wiped it on the sleeve of my shirt and continued my climb.

Reaching the pinnacle of the up-turned pew, I perched for a few seconds, my face inches from the stained glass. My breath fogged its surface like it would any glass and the surety I'd felt this was my path back to Hell took a hit. I touched it with my recently-slivered finger: solid, but not as solid as a window should be.

Breathed a sigh of relief, fogging the glass again.

Carefully, aware of the precarious nature of standing atop an up-ended pew leaned against a free-standing wall, I stood. To make sure my finger hadn't misinterpreted what it felt, I placed the toe of my shoe against the window. It passed through sending a tingling warmth flowing up my leg. I smiled and leaned closer to the glass. The thick, colored glass of the window hid the crowd gathered on the sidewalk from me, leaving me unsure whether they saw me or not.

What the Hell.

I spread my arms to the sides the way Father Dominic made me do for punishment as a child under his care, leaned my head back and hoped the man with whom I'd spoken got his view of Jesus.

I fell forward through the stained glass into Hell.

• • • • •• • • • • •

The shack's open door gaped at Poe like the toothless maw of a prehistoric beast. Why a building like this stood abandoned in the forest near the railroad tracks, she didn't know. The neighborhood kids told stories of a hermit who called it home decades before; a desperate, out-of-work soul banished from his home when the bank foreclosed during the stock market crash. The same kids said his ghost haunted the shack, appearing during the new moon with night at its darkest.

Poe didn't believe it, not when she was one of those kids and certainly not now. She'd always thought the shack had been erected as a playhouse for someone's beloved daughter, or perhaps as an over-sized shed which had outlived its use. None of these possibilities frightened her—not even the ghost story—but what actually happened to her here did.

She stared at the splintered boards, the rusted hinges, the weeds growing rampant at the base of its walls, and shuddered. More than four decades had passed since she last saw Hell's rendition of this horrible place, and two decades before that since she'd actually been there, but the latent memory lived in her body, festered in her mind.

"Piper, I—"

She turned to the woman, intending to ask her to take her away, but her words ceased when she saw the raven-haired Piper no longer stood beside her.

Instead, she looked up into the face of Aaron Baxter.

Poe was always smaller than the other kids, and in the spring of 1946—when the world still breathed its sigh of relief for the end of the war—she stood more than a head shorter than the older boy. She was twelve and Aaron was sixteen. His cousin, whose name she never knew, was older and bigger. He loomed behind Aaron, leering at Poe a look she hadn't seen before at that point of her life but had seen far too many times since.

On that spring day in 1946, she wasn't afraid, not immediately. Of all the kids in the neighborhood, Aaron Baxter was one of the few who was nice to her—maybe not nice, exactly, but not mean—and she liked him for it. His wavy blond hair and piercing blue eyes didn't hurt, either. His unnamed cousin looked like he hailed from a distant branch of the family tree: dark hair and dark eyes, thick chest, a crooked nose, a cruel tilt to his mouth.

"Hi, Aaron," she heard herself say.

Panic unfurled inside Poe because she knew it should, but resignation easily overcame it. She'd been to this corner of Hell before and knew it unchangeable—she'd tried a hundred times before.

"Hey, Paula."

Her name before she became Poe, a name she'd neither heard nor wanted to hear in a very long time.

"This is my cousin. He just moved to town."

"Hi."

The bigger boy tilted his head and grunted.

Poe gritted her teeth at the sound of Paula's voice, at the innocence it held and the underlying longing to be at least accepted, if not liked. Shrill, girly and joyous, but underneath it screamed to the boys to like her. The sound of it made Poe's stomach clench.

"I was going to show him the hermit's shack. Want to come?"

No. Nonononono.

"Sure."

They strode toward the shed, a boy on each side of her. Paula enjoyed their presence close to her; Poe saw their positioning for what it was: to keep her from running away. The thought never occurred to Paula.

She stepped through the doorway first and inhaled the smells: must, rotted wood, bare dirt. Aaron's cousin wore cologne, she remembered. Half-an-hour later, when the reek of the boys' freshly let blood overpowered the aroma of the wood and the dirt, she would still smell the cologne.

The boys stepped in behind her and one of them closed the door. With her back to them, she never knew which one shut it but hoped it was the cousin, not Aaron. It was easier to bear thinking the boy she knew had been there against his will, that somewhere under the violence he'd actually liked her. Poe suspected it wasn't the case.

"It's dark," Paula said.

She faced the boys and saw their expressions silhouetted in the daylight creeping through the cracks between the boards. They looked like they might have been in one of those monster movies: *Dracula, Frankenstein, The Wolfman.* Her mother didn't want her to see such things, but she'd sneaked into a matinee. By herself. Even with the light hitting their faces, highlighting their expressions that were neither joy nor friendship; Paula still wasn't afraid.

She didn't know what lust looked like.

Run away. Get out while you can.

The words raced through Poe's mind despite their futility. She knew they'd make no difference. In a moment, the knife would be out and they would be on her.

The next few minutes blurred into confusion for the young girl, but Poe relived every emotion, every feeling, every agonizing second. First, the surprise and concern at seeing the knife, but Paula brushed those feelings aside; surely the boys were playing. It was even exciting when Aaron grabbed her developing breast, though it hurt a little.

"No," Paula said, brushing his hand away like a lady is supposed to do.

Aaron pushed her and she tumbled to the ground, landing hard on her bum. Her skirt flew up revealing white panties beneath. Poe remembered choosing her outfit on that Saturday morning in the spring of 1946. She didn't have many outfits to choose from, but she always wore her best on the weekend, when she might see some of the other kids, especially the ones she wanted to like her, like Aaron Baxter.

A sliver of concern entered Paula's thoughts but she convinced herself it was an accident. Aaron didn't mean for her to fall, didn't want to hurt her. But she had no time to think before he was sitting on her, straddling her hips, leaning forward to pin her arms. The feel of him against her made her excited and the thought of crying out never occurred to her. He moved his face close to hers; she smelled the tuna salad he'd eaten for lunch, felt the warmth of his breath against her cheek. She fought the urge to stretch her neck forward and put her lips on his.

Paula reveled in the new feelings of the boy's attention until she felt the cousin's hands under her skirt tearing the white panties brusquely off. Panic rose in her—he wasn't supposed to do that. His hands groped her secret areas, his fingers found her places as Aaron Baxter sat on her, holding her down.

She screamed once, then the cold steel of the pocket knife against the flesh of her throat stopped her, threatened to cut her with every sob, every hard swallow.

The next few minutes came to Poe in disjointed snatches, like time lapse photography with some of the frames missing.

Bare flesh against bare flesh.

Aaron's forearm over her mouth; her tongue tasting the dirty flannel of his shirt.

Pain exploding between her legs.

Sobbing.

The knife carelessly on the ground beside her as the two boys traded spots.

Her fingers wrapping unnoticed around the knife; the blade sinking into the cousin's throat, into a vein called the jugular which Paula found by accident because she hadn't learned about it in school yet; cousin screaming; Paula jumping to her feet.

Aaron reached for her, pants around his ankles so she saw his thing—the first and last time in her life she'd seen one. His feet caught in his pants and he stumbled. The tip of the knife entered his eye and found its way into his brain.

Poe felt empty inside, helpless.

Paula stutter-stepped away from the two boys lying on the dirt floor. Their blood looked black in the dim light. It was on them, in the dirt; it covered the knife, her hands. It felt tacky on her face. She sank to the ground pulling shuddering breaths through her clenched throat.

"Don't do it."

Poe heard her own voice and Paula seemed to pause for a second as if she'd heard a whisper. Poe tried to repeat it but nothing came out.

Paula hung her head. Her private place between her legs throbbed and ached, her heart threatened to explode and add her own lifeblood to that of the boys muddying the shack's dirt floor.

"Why?" she squeaked. Snot bubbled at her nose, tears washed blood down her cheeks.

She only wanted to be liked.

Paula breathed a sharp breath through her teeth as the keen edge of the blade cut easily into the soft flesh of her wrist. She closed her eyes and drifted to sleep.

When Poe opened her eyes, she stood under the trees outside the shed. She looked down at her hands: they were clean. A slight spring breeze rustled the leaves on the trees overhead, stirred the skirt hanging around her knees and brought with it the scent of cologne.

Paula turned her head and looked up at Aaron Baxter.

Chapter
Twenty-Six

H ELL IS A PAIN in the ass.

I tumbled through the stained glass window-portal and hit the ground hard, jarring my shoulder and sending a jolt of pain down my arm. I laid in the dirt, groaning, cheek pressed against the ground, until I realized this probably wasn't the best way to be in Hell. I didn't know where I was or who was around, so I untangled myself and climbed to my feet.

No burbling creek ran nearby like the last time I went through the window with Piper. No ferryman to be paid, no city looming on a distant horizon.

On the bright side, maybe I won't get bit.

On the not-so-bright side, I had no idea where I'd ended up or how to get where I needed to go—wherever that was.

While there was no city set against the horizon, it didn't sit bare. A conflagration spewed billowing clouds of smoke into an otherwise colorless sky. Rough and rocky terrain stretched out before me—the badlands gone badder—and a cliff rose behind me; the mouths of caves dotted its surface. Uneven stairs hewn from the rock connected the openings, and pairs of glowing eyes shone from many of them.

"Shit."

Two choices: set out into the canyons and crags to find my way to who-knew-where using my limited rock climbing abilities and end up like the guy who got his arm caught and had to cut it off to survive, or chance the caves. Door number one or door number two? Behind one lies a tiger, the other a shark.

Some choice: die here or die there.

A lot of effort and wandering stood between me and the fires burning on the horizon, and, truthfully, Dominic's labyrinth had provided all the wandering I could stomach for a while. And I didn't feel like scrambling over boulders and through crevasses. Once again, like so many times in my life, I made a decision based essentially on laziness.

I wandered to the nearest set of stairs and put my foot on the first step. The precarious staircase climbed steeply, switching back on itself time and again to connect the myriad caves, each of its steps less than a foot wide. I took a deep breath and stepped up, shoulder brushing the gray cliff face. I'd gone five steps when I looked up and saw the man on the staircase blocking my way.

He might have been the man piloting the ferry across the river Styx, or perhaps a close relative. Same hook nose and lank hair but without the ferryman's eye patch. He didn't sport the patch, but the eye socket it should have covered gleamed with taut pink scar tissue.

"Uh, hey. What's happening?"

Not the cleverest thing to say, but even the best action hero runs out of amusing comments eventually. Hell, when Arnie Schwarzenegger and Clint Eastwood ran out, they went into politics. I hadn't reached that level of desperation yet.

The man didn't reply, only stared his one-eyed stare at me. Overhead, a huge raven circled. I watched it glide effortlessly through the air for a minute until it disappeared onto one of the ledges above. A second later, it cawed loudly and a woman screamed.

I went up two more steps and stood ten paces from the man. He smelled bad and the look of his hair suggested non-bathing the cause. Beneath the dirt and sweat, I whiffed a far more unpleasant odor I preferred not to identify.

"Don't mind me, I'm just going up the stairs."

More staring. Two more steps.

"Not going to bug anybody, just looking for a friend."

Frown. Two steps.

It shouldn't have surprised me when he lurched toward me, but it did. His head morphed into some sort of monstrous rooster; his body slammed into mine sending me sprawling down the stairs as his beak sank into my upper chest.

I'll admit it: I screamed.

The thing rode me down the stairs like a living snowboard until my back hit the ground at the bottom and my breath whooshed out of my lungs. I closed my eyes, teeth grinding with the pain, and felt a rush of air on my face, heard feathers rustling. The man-thing's weight lifted off me.

So much for not getting bit.

I didn't know what it meant in the long run to have some of Hell's denizens take bites out of me, but I imagined it couldn't be good. A question to ask Mikey next time I saw him. If he ever talked to me again after all this.

Minutes passed as I lay there, eyes closed, waiting for my breath to return. Over the last few months, I must have set a record for the number of times a guy's wind was knocked out of him. Where are the *Guinness Book of World Records* people when you need them?

My eyes jerked open when a shadow fell across me. I looked up at a figure with dark, wild hair, high cheekbones, a square jaw.

"Mother?"

"Are you okay?"

I am now.

• • • • •• • • • •

Trevor sat down hard on the wooden chair behind the huge desk and felt the empty eyes of the comedy/tragedy masks staring, heard the breathy hiss of laughs and groans passing their pulled-thin lips. He found himself wondering whose faces those expressions were peeled from, how they came to adorn a wall in the kingdom of Hell. Were their disembodied cheeks and mouthless lips pulled into those expressions, or were they alive when the flesh came off? Trevor shivered.

The boy remained by the tapestry where he'd revealed the events surrounding Icarus' death. Trevor didn't completely understand what he'd seen, but he realized it might mean something to his father.

"Make sure you tell Icarus what I've shown you," the boy said, a chuckle camouflaged beneath his words.

Trevor looked up at the boy, but the tapestry behind him snatched his attention. A rainfall of colors ran and melded across its surface: a crimson lava flow, a yellow sun dog. Blue flowed into green into black, but the predominant color was red—the red of blood and fire and hate.

The boy appeared directly in front of Trevor, blocking his view, though Trevor didn't see him move.

"Don't look at it too long. You'll see things you don't want to see. Eventually, you'll become part of it."

Trevor glanced at his face, at the mischievous smile on his lips, then attempted to look around him. The boy extended his arm toward the wooden cage holding the skeleton-lizard, blocking Trevor's view as he stuck a finger between the bars. The lizard scuttled over, snapped its jaws, and bit off his fingertip. The boy neither acted surprised nor jerked his finger away as the lizard chewed it with the relish of fully-fleshed lizard devouring a cricket. After it swallowed—Trevor couldn't figure out where the fingertip disappeared to—it took another bite.

"Someone will be here to get you soon," the boy said withdrawing his finger from the cage.

He walked out of Trevor's line-of-sight and the teen felt a surge of relief when the tapestry came back into view. Short-lived relief, however—a static depiction of a head on a spike, a bleak wasteland stretching out behind it, replaced the riotous colors. Droplets of blood hung frozen in the air below the ragged flesh of the neck; unmoving black flies buzzed around the wound, one sat on an eyeball rolled back to show the white. The man looked familiar, though he didn't know why.

Trevor shuddered and looked away.

"Who is that?"

His question found an empty room. He looked around, stood and paced the length of the floor to confirm he was alone. The boy had slipped out, or perhaps disappeared into thin air. Trevor glanced at the fleshy masks on the wall, the skeleton-lizard in its cage, sat back down on the chair and pulled his knees up to his chest.

Someone will be coming for you.

Now that he was alone, the words felt ominous—more warning than statement. Trevor clenched his teeth and suppressed a shiver; his eyes wandered back to the tapestry where he'd saved his father, where he'd been the first to find out the truth about his death.

Was what I saw the truth?

A vast blue sky had replaced the decapitated head on the cloth, the perspective making it look three-dimensional, like it stretched on forever. The sun hung high in the corner, its orange rays diffusing to yellow.

In the foreground, a man was falling from the sky, melted wings of wax trailing behind him.

· · · ●·●· · ·

I stood and brushed dust off my pants and shirt, each movement of my arm causing pain in my chest where the nasty chicken took its pound of flesh—okay, maybe only a few ounces of flesh, but it hurt. My mother watched my pained expression.

"Can you do anything about this?"

She shook her head.

"I am neither angel nor demon. I can't heal you."

I breathed deep, felt the taut pain of the wound, the warm flow of blood trickling down my meager pec. If she couldn't fix me, I'd have to deal with the pain until we found someone who could.

Where's Piper?

"How do you keep finding me?"

"You're my son."

It didn't seem like much of an explanation, especially since my reason for coming back was because my son was lost. If she could find me, why couldn't I find him? I looked at my feet, kicked at a Hell-rock.

"Trevor's safe," she said.

She couldn't heal me like an angel, but apparently she read my thoughts like one.

"How do you know?"

"I know."

She mounted the stairs before I said anything else and I followed. I had to pivot my shoulders sideways to fit up the stairs, the position making the wound in my chest ache and throb. Ahead, my mother seemed to practically float up the stairs with the ease of someone who's followed the same path a thousand times before.

We emerged on a wide ledge running the length of the cliff. More stairs ran up to a second ledge overhead. I paused, waiting to see where she'd lead me, but she stood in place like she waited to see where I'd go.

"Well?"

She looked at me, dark eyes gleaming, and a shadow of a smile brushed her lips like something was mildly funny that she didn't want to share. For the first time, I wondered if this woman who was not only my mother but had spent four decades living in Hell had my best interests at heart.

"Where's Trevor?"

"Somewhere here."

She swept her hand in front of her, gesturing toward the cave openings. I looked at them, counted them silently, stopping when I reached fifteen because each number beyond dampened my spirits.

How am I supposed to find him in there?

"How am I supposed to find him in there?"

"You will find what you are supposed to find."

I cocked an eyebrow. For someone who wasn't an angel, her response came off as a cryptically angelic answer.

"And what am I supposed to find?"

"Everything will work out as it should."

She stepped closer and encircled me with her arms, pulling me against her. At first, I stood like a punching dummy. I'd never been hugged by my mother before, so it took a few seconds for my brain to reconcile the action and figure out how to respond. I wrapped my arms around her shoulders and patted her on the back. She released me and stepped away.

"You will find what you are supposed to find."

If anyone other than my mother had repeated themselves like that, I'd have been compelled to toss out a sarcastic response. Since she gave birth to me, and died doing it, I gave her a pass.

I sighed and glanced at the cave mouths stretching into the distance. Dozens of openings, all of uniform size and shape with no doors, no street numbers, no welcoming potted plants sitting outside to distinguish one from another.

Mailman Hell.

I went to the closest cave and peered in. Darkness strangled the light out of the place a few feet down the rough-hewn walls. Unidentifiable smells floated to my nose; water gurgled somewhere in the dark. Or maybe it was the start of a growl at the back of some creature's throat.

"Shit."

I rubbed my chin, hesitated a second, then took a step in without asking my mother's opinion. Three more steps and the black enveloped me. I looked back over my shoulder; the light coming in the cave mouth appeared orange looking at it from a detached world of night. My mother stood silhouetted against it.

"Are you coming?"

"No. I don't like the caves."

Comforting.

I walked farther into the cave, moving slowly to avoid walking into anything. Each step brought deeper darkness. The temperature dropped. If I could see, I'm sure my breath would have been a cloud of white mist drifting ahead of me.

After a few more paces, the darkness began to wane. The change was almost imperceptible at first, but a definite difference. As I went deeper, the black lifted further. I made out the wall to my left, discerned the terrain of the floor passing beneath my feet, but the illumination didn't come from ahead; five feet further on, the night returned to impenetrability. Looking up, I saw no sign of light overhead. Hell, no sign of a ceiling.

I glanced right and the figure cloaked in light walking beside me startled me. The woman's long, dark hair visible within the luminosity made me think my mother might have lied about being an angel, but when the woman faced me and I saw her youth, noticed the stud below her lower lip, I knew who'd joined me.

"Piper? Where did you...?"

Her skin glowed with a dim yellow incandescence like a fish that lives in the deepest part of the ocean. I'd seen Poe perform a similar feat a couple of times, though her reasons were about enchantment, not illumination, and as I watched, the glow brightened. I diverted my eyes back to the path ahead, worried I'd be mesmerized.

"Where did you come from?"

"Around."

I practically heard her shrug with her answer. Not a satisfactory answer—her sudden appearance smacked of Hellish manipulation—but what's a man to do? If her presence aided me, I shouldn't look a gift angel in the mouth. Maybe some of the forces of good still chose to marshal on my side.

Sure.

"Well, it's nice to see you." I glanced down the rocky corridor ahead. "It's nice to see."

"Thanks," she replied and her fingers brushed my arm.

Her touch was what I might have expected it to be like if someone dragged a baby electric eel across my flesh—jolting, but not powerful enough to be painful or unpleasant. The tingle it created vibrated down to the tips of my fingers, up into my shoulder, then her touch disappeared.

We walked on, her glow brightening, allowing us to see farther ahead. My arm felt numb once the sensation of her caress waned and I considered amending my path to brush against her again but kept myself in check. Somewhere, my son was in serious danger—I didn't have time to dally. If not in this cave, then one of the others. Hell was an undeniably big place, but I had to believe something guided me, brought me to this particular corner of it on purpose. If I didn't hold on to that, nothing remained but despair.

And the angel at my side.

The tunnel widened until it became a roughly square room. It was empty except for a pile of straw in one corner. The three walls were bare and solid: no doorways, no windows, no cracks or fissures. We stepped into the room and Piper's iridescence increased to full-blown light, forcing away the darkness, leaving no shadows behind.

This is it?

I'd expected more from Hell, especially given my other experiences. Where hid the gargoyles? The tortured souls reliving their worst nightmares? Where was the nudity, debauchery, depravity and degradation?

Disappointing.

"What's going on here?"

I caught myself turning toward Piper as I asked the question but caught myself at the last second. Poe's glow had left the people at the hospital completely enchanted and unable to function of their own accord. Didn't need that to happen.

"What do you mean?"

Her voice changed, became the angelic choir I'd heard out of the mouths of other angels in the past: Poe, Michael, Raphael. Hers held a different tone, discordant, as though the mezzo soprano couldn't carry a tune.

"I mean: why is there nothing here?"

I stepped into the room, ran my fingers along the wall. It turned out to be cool, hard stone—exactly how it looked.

"What happened to you?" she asked.

I took a chance and glanced her direction. She was pointing at the patch of blood-soaked shirt clinging to my chest.

"Hell-beast got me again. Can you do something about it?"

"Depends."

"On what?"

I half-expected her to tell me we needed to find a handful of wolf's bane and a pinch of witch hazel.

"Whether you ask nicely or not."

She smiled coyly and tilted her head. Flirting while standing in a cave in Hell and not knowing where my son was made me uncomfortable, but you got to take it where you can get it. I diverted my gaze.

"Please?"

She put her hand on the wound, her touch immediately sending that tingling sensation through my chest, down my arm, racing to my brain. I felt warmth in my wound, imagined my skin knitting itself back together like some cheesy special effect out of a bad sci-fi flick. Visions of Piper unclothed replaced the thought as her touch lingered. I took a shuddering breath and stepped away before I embarrassed myself. When Piper took her hand away, some of the blood on my shirt stayed on her skin like she'd brushed her palm against a red ink pad used for rubber stamps.

"Good?"

I sighed. "Oh yeah. Never better."

She reached for me again but I stepped back.

"Maybe we better save that for later."

She shrugged.

"Perhaps this empty cave is here for us."

She whispered the words and, despite the space between us, it sounded as though she perched on my shoulder and spoke them directly into my ear. I felt her breath on my neck; it raised goose bumps on my arms. Difficult as it was, I took up my examination of the wall again, studiously looking for any deformity to show the cave was more than it appeared. Mostly I did it to distract myself from her.

"We have to...I need..."

My brain didn't seem to know what it wanted my mouth to say, so random words tumbled off my lips, the way I imagined my son would fumble for the right thing to say asking a girl on a date.

Trevor.

The thought of him brought reality back, focused my thoughts. I faced the doorway, purposely turning my head toward the wall and my back to Piper. Her hand touched my shoulder.

This time, the shock was immense but wholly pleasurable. My body stiffened and my feet ceased moving me toward the door; I imagined the glow emanating from Piper flowing into me. One finger of her free hand touched my chin, swiveled my head toward her. I tried to close my eyes but they weren't going along with the plan.

Piper's luminosity became almost blinding but, even in its brightness, I saw her clearly. Dark hair, sapphire eyes; the stud below her bottom lip; the milky curve of her chin.

Below that she was naked.

My eyes probably widened like a surprised child. My mouth must have fallen open like an old man in search of misplaced dentures. I became indistinct in my own mind as it filled with nothing but her: the beauty of her face, the smoothness of her skin, the warmth of her proximity. She stepped forward and pressed her body against mine. I felt her breasts against my chest and gasped.

The pressure of her against me forced me back and I let it. A moment later, I was supine on the heap of straw, the smell of hay the only thing I recognized outside of Piper's overwhelming presence. Her lips found mine, her energy flowed into me, and I felt like there was no me anymore, just us—two beings becoming one, our bodies merging, our essences. I lost myself and didn't care if anyone ever found me.

Somehow, in a dark cave of Hell, I found Heaven.

Chapter
Twenty-Seven

T HE SHACK WAS GONE, and the two boys. The knife, the blood, the feelings of anger, surprise, exhilaration, shame and despair: all gone.

Instead, Poe stood outside on a hot and sticky night, the kind of night that brings a sheen of sweat to your skin, leaves you feeling damp all the time. A night in high summer somewhere in a southern state.

Poe looked down at the railroad tracks beneath her feet and needed no more clues than the metal rails and the adhesive humidity to know where she was, and when—a place and time she didn't want to be.

No. Please not this.

Her lips moved to speak the words but they sounded only inside her head. Crickets hidden in scraggy bushes growing a few feet from the edge of the tracks chirruped, speaking to each other in their monotone rasps. Their night songs disguised the sound of a man snoring, a homeless man she knew she'd find sleeping on the tracks half-a-dozen yards from where she stood.

Soon, she'd hear the train.

When this really happened—in the real world instead of in the re-lived world of Hell—it was the second time they'd sent her out. The first time, she'd come back empty-handed and been returned to the shack to be raped over and over, to kill those boys and herself again and again until convinced to perform the work.

The rail shivered under Poe's foot and she wondered what would happen if she remained on the tracks, didn't move before the train came, bearing down on her with the cold light of its cyclopean eye.

She thought it, but her feet paid her no mind as she joined the crickets in the rough shrubs.

A minute later, the light appeared down the track; with it came the dull rumble of the train. The first time—the real time—she considered simply running over to the man and shaking him awake, but the shock of living her death over and over kept her from it. This time, she knew not to waste thought on it, it would make no difference to the outcome.

The train approached, sounded its horn at a crossing, the blast startling Poe like it had so many years before. The ground shook with its approach as the light shone down the track, illuminating the man lying half-on the tracks. The train's horn blasted again as it sped by the nearest road.

Get up! Get up!

The futility of her lips moving along with the words in her head brought a lump to Poe's throat. Things were about to end for the man, but it would get worse for her.

The distance between train and man shrank. Poe looked from one to the other. A few seconds, no more. The man stirred, a movement Poe didn't notice when this happened for real. He propped himself on an elbow, looked up at the train rushing toward him.

Poe's heart leaped into her throat as she clearly saw the man's face: dazed-looking with sleep at first, then slack with fear, his jaw dropping open comically. His feet pushed against the ground, searching for purchase to move out of the train's path, but they found none as the dry dirt gave way under his churning shoes.

That didn't happen. He didn't know.

The train hit him and flung him off the tracks, spinning him three hundred-sixty degrees on the vertical plane like a huge, awkward Frisbee. He landed in the brush ten feet from Poe as the locomotive and its cargo rushed past without noticing the life it ended.

Poe allowed her feet to carry her to the man. The impact had split his head open, dislodged its contents. She began to cry, like her first time here. Then the man sat up.

Not the man, precisely, but his soul. Poe knew it to be the case this time, but it shocked her the first time as she'd thought the man had survived. He looked younger, cleaner, and shimmered a little in the dark of the night.

"What...?" The man looked around him until his eyes settled on Poe.

"It's okay," she said, words choked with enough emotion he couldn't have believed them.

The man's expression was the same as when he saw the train: wide-eyed, gaping mouth. He scrambled away and his soul stretched like an elastic band caught on a twig. It detached and he jumped to his feet, stared down at the broken body he'd inhabited for decades, its limbs now twisted into unfathomable shapes, its head split open like a coconut with all the milk spilled out.

"What did you do to me?"

"No, I—"

The man took off, stumbling through the tangled shrubs, heading for the easier going of the railroad tracks. His foot slipped in his own blood, but he kept his feet, made it to the tracks, and ran.

Poe sighed. As bad as it was watching him die again, this part would be worse.

She darted out of the brush and onto the tracks behind him, boots clopping on the wooden ties as a black overcoat flapped against her thighs. The man stole a look back over his shoulder at her closing ground, and the sight of her gave him speed, but she was too quick. A moment later, she grabbed him by the shoulders and rode him to the ground.

They scraped along the tracks, the man groaning with the impact, but he twisted himself under her to end up on his back. He punched her in the throat, pushed her away, raked her cheeks with his nails.

Reliving the event, Poe fought the rage building inside her. It wasn't anger at the man or his attempts to be free of her, she'd have done the same thing if she suspected what awaited. This anger was at Aaron Baxter and his cousin, at what they'd done to her and what they made her do, at the time she'd spent in Hell. She raged at going through it all again, of repeating this, and at having lost Icarus' trust and his son.

I'm sorry. I'm so sorry, her lips said wordlessly as her fists flailed, hammering the surprised soul's face, pummeling him into unconsciousness, then she hit him some more.

Sometime later, Poe found herself kneeling in the corner of a room. She hadn't noticed the train tracks and the man's battered soul disappear from around her. Shoulders sagging, hands lying loosely in her lap, she stared at her fingers, at the chipped nails and the black buttons on her overcoat. She didn't look up, didn't want to. She couldn't imagine being anywhere that would make her feel better.

She gazed into her lap until she heard the grunt made by a woman's throat. It held no threat or anger but sounded more like the struggle of a pained beast.

Poe raised her head and saw a woman lying on a bed, propped on her elbows, her swollen belly preventing her from sitting up further. Another woman crouched at the end of the bed, the sleeves of her blouse rolled up, a towel draped over her shoulder.

Poe stood, pulled the hood dangling at her back up over her head, held her breath and watched.

· · • •• • • • ·

I plucked straw out of the hair at the back of my head and let it fall to the ground as we made our way to the next cave opening. The fourth. We'd exited the first cave onto the empty ledge and I felt something was missing, but my foggy brain refused to nail it down. I dazedly surveyed the area like a man retracing his steps trying to figure out where he'd left his keys but soon gave up in favor of searching the caves.

After finding our torrid lovemaking in the first, the second and third caves had proven disappointingly empty. If endorphins hadn't been racing through my body like a pack of greyhounds after a mechanical rabbit, I'd have been getting stressed by our lack of success.

"I don't think we're going to find anything here," Piper said.

The first words either of us had spoken since emerging from each other's bodies. It left me feeling a little disappointed the reverence had been broken. The spell was broken, the pleasure done. Back to business.

"Where to, then?"

She shrugged, of course, and I remembered why we were there.

"I have to find Trevor. Do you know where he is?"

"No. I haven't been able to locate him since your guardian angel lost him."

She practically spat the words 'guardian angel'. Right then, I didn't care what she thought of Poe. I'd have to deal with her later.

"What does that mean?"

"I don't know."

I thought about asking her what good she was, but my anger would have been misplaced. Piper didn't get my son into this mess; that distinction fell squarely on Poe's shoulders. Piper wanted to help. She deserved my gratitude, not my ire. Given the circumstances, controlling my emotions was proving difficult.

"Damn it." I looked up the next set of stairs. "You have no ideas?"

"Sorry."

"Then let's try up there."

My mind full with the smolderings of anger and the residue of desire, I took the stairs two at a time—for the first few at least, until I ran out of steam. I heard Piper's footsteps padding up the steps behind me, her breathing easy, not labored the way the climb made mine. At the next landing, I paused, bent at the waist to catch my breath. She stood beside me, watching with a sly smile.

"It's the altitude," I gasped. "The air's thinner."

"Down here in Hell."

I straightened and shrugged giving her a taste of her own medicine, then directed my attention toward the caves.

"Any idea which one?" I asked.

She shrugged and strolled past me appraising the nearest caves. After a few paces, she pivoted on her heel to face me, hair swinging around her head in a dark cloud, eyes sparkling. Any misplaced anger I'd been tempted to direct her way disappeared at the sight of her beauty, and I struggled to put the memories of the cave out of my head and focus on the task at hand.

"We've got to look somewhere," I said.

"How about this one?"

"Yeah, we should—"

I looked beyond her shoulder and saw a figure standing at the foot of the stairs leading to the next level of caves. Seeing another person cleared the cobwebs from my head. Although too far away to see their face, I sensed a familiarity. I stepped past Piper and squinted at the figure, my shoulder brushing the angel's, but I barely noticed the accompanying tingle. A couple more steps, a little more squinting.

A black frock clothed the figure but with some white around his or her head and upper chest. I recognized the costume: a nun.

"Mother?"

I realized two things at once: she wasn't dressed that way last time I saw her, and she'd been the unidentified missing thing when Piper and I emerged from our rocky love nest. The angel's touch and affection somehow affected me by erasing my mother's presence from my mind until now.

I broke into a trot leaving Piper behind and passing the yawning cave mouths. As I jogged, I got no closer to her. Cave openings went by, my feet pounded the red clay leaving dusty footprints in my wake, yet I made no progress toward my goal. I glanced over my shoulder at Piper watching me from the top of the stairs, her figure small with distance. I was moving but not going anywhere.

"What the fuck?"

I slowed my pace and, as so often seems to be the case in my screwed-up joke of an afterlife, chose exactly the wrong moment to do so.

I didn't see Father Dominic charge out of the mouth of the cave until too late. He'd built up a pretty good head of steam for an old, dead guy, and the impact of him hitting me square in the chest threw me to the ground like a poorly secured tackling dummy at a high school football practice.

My shoulder and hip hit the ground first and we skidded across the rocky dirt, coming to a stop with the top third of my body hanging over the edge of the cliff and the dead priest perched on my chest. I twisted to look down at the ground thirty-five feet below—maybe it wouldn't break my neck if we went over. The thought fled as Dominic's fingers wrapped around my throat.

"Take me back."

I grabbed his wrists to prevent him from strangling me but realized I could breathe—he held me but wasn't trying to squeeze my life from me.

Not yet.

I shook my head.

"Not a chance."

His fingers constricted the words, made them small and he must not have liked my response because he tightened his hold. I felt my cheeks go hot and red as the blood in my head achieved little success finding its way back to my heart. He rocked his weight forward bending me over the precipice. His eyes—the irises dark outlines in a sea of red—glared maniacally, his yellowed teeth clenched, and I noticed for the first time he was missing two. He'd had all his teeth when he died.

"It's because of you I'm here."

I tried to shake my head because I knew he was wrong. The first time I'd been to the underworld, I saw the priest's Hell, so I knew he'd made his own bed.

"Let him go."

My eyes flickered away from Father Dominic to Piper standing over his shoulder. A gust of warm breeze blew her hair back and her pale skin stood out in stark contrast to the orange-red cliff behind her. I momentarily forgot the priest's fingers gripping my trachea.

Dominic looked over his shoulder at her and snarled.

"What are you doing here?"

"It doesn't matter. Get off him."

"Does he know you're with him?"

The priest's words caught my attention or, more specifically, the way they spoke to each other did: as if they knew one another.

"He?" I wheezed but the word was too strangled—literally—to be heard.

She grabbed his shoulder but he shrugged it away and shifted his attention back to me.

"Take me back."

I looked from Piper to Dominic, Piper to Dominic, and felt my eyes rub against my eyelids as they bulged from the pressure the priest exerted on my throat. With my bug-eyed gaze settled back on Father Dominic and contemplating how badly someone needed to get the man a bottle of Visine, I noticed a shadow fall on the ground beside him.

Piper straightened and took a step away.

"Please let him go, Dominic," the new voice said.

The priest's eyes remained on mine, his grip stayed tight, but his expression faded like a photograph left too long in the sun. His lips sagged back to cover his teeth; his mouth dipped at the corners; the intense look in his eyes softened.

"S—sister?"

"Please, Dominic."

He unlaced his fingers from my throat and leaned back taking the pressure off. A wave of vertigo spun my head as it hung over empty space. The feeling increased when he rose from where he'd been seated on my midsection, removing the counter-weight keeping me from sliding over the edge.

I'd have gone over if Piper's electric touch on my arm didn't steady my disorientation. My wits began to gather back in my head as I struggled myself to a sitting position—with Piper's help—and blinked hard to reset my bugged-out eyes. My slightly doubled vision rectified itself and I saw Father Dominic kneeling before my mother, hands clasped in front of his chest as if in prayer.

"Sister Agnes," he said. "Please forgive me."

"Nothing to forgive."

I clamored to my feet and brushed orangey dust off the ass of my pants. My mother didn't look away from the priest genuflecting before her. I rubbed my throat and turned my head first one way, then the other, flexing the muscles in my neck as I watched the conversation. Piper wasn't at my side and I heard her shoes scraping ground as she crept away. The vertigo was gone, but confusion did a fine job of making my head lurch in its stead.

Father Dominic bowed his head to look at the dirt. His hands remained clasped in front of him.

"I failed you," he said. "I didn't defend you before the church. I didn't keep the bastard angel from taking you." He sniffed deeply. "I didn't do anything."

My mother put her hand on the priest's cheek.

"That isn't why you're here, you know that, Dominic. Icarus cannot take you back."

He looked up, tears gleaming on his cheeks in the tangerine light.

"Then why did you bring me here to him if not to ask for him to take me back?"

My mother may have answered but I'd stopped listening. I'd also stopped breathing, stopped having reasonable thoughts.

She brought him here. Him, the man responsible for all the troubles in my life. The man who nearly caused my son's death, the reason I'm in Hell now.

I took a step back, suddenly needing to be farther away from these two people. My mother looked up at the movement and spoke, this time I heard her words.

"Piper. I should have suspected you'd be involved."

Her words came out icy enough to send a shiver down my spine.

How does she know her? How does a resident of Hell know a guardian angel?

I looked at Piper, gazed into her wide eyes. She shook her head as if to deny my thoughts but didn't respond to my mother. My head spun as my brain worked its way through what unfolded before me.

My mother had brought Father Dominic to me, the man who'd been my enemy practically since birth.

Piper—a supposed guardian angel and my recent lover—was acquainted with both of them. And also with the ominously mentioned 'him', whoever that might be—I might have guessed, but none of the possibilities would be anyone I wanted to know. Anger and confusion combined in my already spinning head, picked up the remnants of fuzz left from my encounter with Piper to force all coherent thoughts out of my brain. I clenched my teeth, my vision blurred.

I looked at Father Dominic.

Asshole.

I looked at Piper.

Deceiver.

I looked at my mother.

My mother.

Traitor.

I couldn't stay there any longer. They'd all manipulated me for their own purposes. None of them cared about me. No surprise from the murderous priest, but my mother and my lover? Which was worse?

I darted into the nearest cave, plunging into darkness without knowing where to go or what lay ahead. Behind me, I heard Piper's voice calling me, then my mother's, their words bouncing against the sides of the cave, the echoes combining with the beat of my footsteps to drown their words.

In the dark, my shoulder hit the wall of the cave, spun me around, but I kept on. Ahead, I saw a light, dim but there, and kept it directly ahead of me. It became my beacon to take me away from the priest, Piper, and my mother. I raced toward it like a child to an ice cream truck, only the driver of this ice cream truck would likely be a ghoul or demon, maybe the devil himself.

The cave wall rushed past beside me and a minute later, I spilled into a room with no business being in a cave. A bed, a bedside table, a lamp; a nondescript bedroom with a wooden crucifix hung on the wall as the only decoration. It might have been anywhere but I felt I'd been there before. Plain white walls, gold shag carpet. I glanced around and saw nothing to indicate my location. I looked over my shoulder; the cave's passage was gone behind me, replaced by another plain wall, a wooden door to my left. I moved toward it when I heard the woman's voice.

I stepped back, listening to the unintelligible words. The voice grew louder and I knew it came toward the door so I faded into the corner, not sure if whoever it was would be able to see me.

Better safe than sorry.

Some strange things had happened to me, even in other people's Hells. I crouched, making myself as small as possible in the corner, and waited.

The door opened and two women stepped through.

Chapter
Twenty-Eight

"I HAVE TO CALL the doctor."

"No."

"But I can't—"

"Yes. You. Can." Each individual word a grunt.

Poe peered from under the hood of her black coat, watching silently. As it had been with the man on the railroad tracks, she'd been here before a long time ago. Everything was the same: the words they spoke, the golden shag on the floor, the crucifix on the wall. Sister Mary-Therese knelt between the legs of Sister Agnes—who the church no longer recognized as Sister Agnes by this time—the towel draped over her shoulder the lone tool she had to deliver her friend's baby.

Though she couldn't see them, Poe knew there were two other entities in the room, bickering like the siblings they were, arguing over how this would or should turn out. Neither of them realized her presence or knew someone else had sent her. With such a momentous event happening, larger forces than the two archangels were mobilized, and one used Poe as a pawn.

"But, Alesya—"

"There's no...time."

Breathing heavily, the woman on the bed fell back on the pillows, sweat standing on her brow. For a few seconds, it seemed like the pain subsided but then she tensed, came up onto her elbows again.

"Okay," Sister Mary-Therese said. "Okay."

Poe hadn't known these women in her life, had only been in Sister Mary-Therese's presence once before the priest ended her life by the pond. Despite not knowing them, she felt now as she did when she was here before: they were women of great power, women to be respected and loved. She felt she'd have been friends with them, given the chance.

Too bad her job was to take one of them to Hell.

Poe cowered against the wall. Living through the man on the railroad tracks again was bad, but this was worse. It wasn't Aleysa's fault she found herself in this position. Without intervention, Poe assumed she'd have remained Sister Agnes for the rest of her days, serving God until she lay on her death bed in old age.

Poe shook her head sadly—here Aleysa lay on her death bed, so much potential wasted by an angel's lust.

"Push," Sister Mary-Therese said.

"She will come with me."

The deep, melodic peal of words floated out of empty air, but neither of the women noticed. Poe scanned the room and saw the two figures in the opposite corner nearest the bed, their shadowy silhouettes outlined against the white wall. She'd felt their presence the first time she was here, but hadn't seen them.

Why can I see them now?

Strange things come to pass in Hell.

Sister Agnes let out a grunt worthy of a power-lifter surpassing his personal best.

"That's it, that's it. Keep pushing."

Sister Mary-Therese reached over her friend's knees and wiped the sweat off her forehead. The nun seemed understandably uncomfortable with her role as obstetrician. Poe imagined the convent teaching mentioned precious little about assisting a fellow nun giving birth. Spiritual birth, emotional birth, perhaps, but not the having a baby kind of birth.

The thought sounded so much like one of Icarus', it bubbled a nervous titter over Poe's lips. She clamped her hand over her mouth. The two women on the bed didn't notice, but the archangels—their figures filling in with shape and features and color—paused in their dispute and glanced in her direction.

She froze.

•••••••••••

My mother grunted and my gut twinged. Moments before, I'd mentally accused her of betraying me and now I was watching her make the ultimate sacrifice for me. She gave up everything. It would have been so much easier to don a disguise and find a back-alley abortion clinic than to be a nun carrying a baby to term. How different her life would have been.

She gave it all up for me. And what have I done to thank her?

The anger and confusion that drove me into the tunnel faded, replaced by the urge to rush to her side and comfort her. I tried, but my feet wouldn't move.

"That's it, that's it. Keep pushing."

I heard the giggle right after Sister Mary-Therese wiped the sweat from my mother's face. It was so small and quiet, I wasn't completely sure I'd heard it. Neither of the women made the noise—my mother too involved in giving birth to laugh and Sister Mary-Therese too considerate a woman to giggle under these circumstances.

There was someone else in the room.

It didn't surprise me, I'd seen this before and there had been a Carrion and a couple of bickering archangels in attendance at the momentous occasion of my birth.

And my mother's death.

I looked around the room. A vague bank of fog floated in one corner, like the way the faces of people in a crowd on a newscast are blotted out. I blinked and it faded, forgotten about when I spied the figure crouched in the other corner. A figure dressed in black with a cowl pulled over his head.

The Carrion.

· · · ● ● · ● ● · · ·

Minutes passed, the baby's first breath inching closer. Poe's apprehension increased with each second closer it grew. She'd attempted to change the outcome in the shed and couldn't. She tried to change what happened to the man on the railroad tracks without success. Everything pointed to her inability to influence the outcome to be anything other than what had already happened, but she was determined to try.

If I don't collect the soul, she may live.

The two archangels—solid now, though still invisible to the women—moved closer to the bed. They loomed over the nuns, shoulder to shoulder, like rabid fans attempting to glimpse their favorite celebrity.

But Azrael would take her to Hell.

Only a fifty/fifty chance things would turn out for the better if she didn't do something to influence the outcome. If she could. She needed to make sure Michael ended up with Sister Agnes' soul or, preferably, neither of them.

I have to distract Azrael.

Her feet carried her forward a step. Sister Agnes grunted, the tail end of it turning to a half-scream. Sister Mary-Therese's voice murmured beneath her friend's.

"You can do it. You can do it. Here it comes. You can do it."

The startling cry of a newborn gasping its first breath stopped both of them. Sister Mary-Therese guided the tiny body free of its mother, gently cradled it in her arms and did her best to hold the child up for the new mother to see.

"Aleysa. It's a—"

The first time this happened—the time it *really* happened—the newborn so enthralled Poe she hadn't noticed anything else go on around her. This time, knowing the outcome and being determined to change it refocused her attention. She looked over Sister Mary-Therese's shoulder when the gush of blood followed the baby out of Sister Agnes' womb, soaking the bed in crimson, and saw the new mother's face go white.

She saw Michael's hand on the woman's stomach.

"No."

She didn't mean to say the word aloud. For years, she'd worshipped the archangel Michael, hung on his words, strove to please the angel responsible for saving her from the life of a Carrion. To find out responsibility for the nun's death rested with him and not Azrael, as she'd been led to believe...

Both archangels looked up, unaware until now that she was there. They all stared at each other for an instant. Poe's heart thumped on her head.

How can this be?

She shook free of the shock first and grabbed Sister Agnes by the arm, wrenching her soul free of the earthly body before either angel claimed her. The threat of tears choked her throat closed, otherwise she might have paused to ask Michael why he had done this.

The spirit followed without protest as Sister Mary-Therese, oblivious to the others in the room, shouted for help.

She doesn't know it's too late.

The thought was welcome relief from the aching disappointment filling Poe's limbs. If this had been real instead of a Hellish re-enactment, she might not have made it across the room and out the door. The weight of knowing, of disappointment, might have dragged her to the floor, curled her up in a ball, knees hugged to chest. But it wasn't real, it happened nearly forty years before. Maybe what she was in wasn't reality but Hell manipulating her memory.

With the soul of the nun trailing behind, Poe reached for the door knob, the hood falling away from her face. Only then did she see the man standing to the right of the door.

Only then did she look into the eyes of Icarus Fell.

·········

The first mewling, high-pitched cry—the first sound I ever made—startled me and brought prickly flesh to the back of my neck. I reached up and rubbed the goose bumps as Sister Mary-Therese held the baby-me up for my mother to see and told her I was a boy. Her words stopped mid-sentence and I smelled the coppery odor of my mother's blood, like when I saw this in Hell before, but this time the Carrion stood between me and the bed so I didn't have to see her bleed to death.

Sister Mary-Therese screamed for help as the Carrion snatched my mother's soul and stumbled away from the bedside. I struggled to move and block the door, to stop this from happening again, but my legs only moved me two steps, positioning me beside the doorway.

The Carrion approached, his black hood hiding his face, my mother in tow. No choice but to watch. A step away, the Carrion looked up and reached for the door knob. The hood fell away.

My flesh went instantly cold.

"Poe?"

Our eyes met and hers widened. I opened my mouth to question her, to ask what she was doing here, what was going on, but breath failed me. Seeing her taking my mother to Hell took it away.

They brushed past me, opened the door and went through. I stood in shock for a few seconds, my eyes looking at but not seeing Sister Mary-Therese as she held me in her arms, comforting me even as she screamed for help. The archangels struggled behind her. The noise of the crying babe, the shouting nun, dragged me from my stupor and I turned to follow the Carrion. Conflicting emotions hammered my brain—anger and disappointment at Poe, whom I'd trusted, whom I very nearly loved, but also excitement. If I was here, if I could affect the outcome, then I intended to find a way to win my mother back. This was my chance to make up for all she'd sacrificed so I could live.

When I spun around, the rough-hewn wall of a Hell cave stood at my back. I stumbled forward, disbelieving my eyes, unwilling to give up the opportunity to make amends, but the rock remained. My fingers brushed the stone, felt its warmth and solidity, and my stomach slipped.

They're gone.

The crying and shouting had ceased. I looked back to where Sister Mary-Therese had been holding me in the first moment of my being and found her gone. No bedroom, no gold shag, no wooden crucifix. Instead, I gazed upon a roughly square stone room with a pile of hay pushed into the far corner. A wan light emanating from nowhere and everywhere illuminated the area; I saw a dark patch of crimson on the ground near the straw. Part of me wanted to go to it, but I already knew that the stain was a marker to remind me of and torture me with my mother's death.

She was in love against her will. She didn't deserve this.

I loped down the tunnel without knowing where it might lead. Would it take me back to the ledge I'd left or deep into Hellish catacombs I'd never find my way out of?

As I left the room behind, the dim illumination receded along with it. I slowed my pace, bumped into walls as the corridor twisted and turned leaving me in a darkness only experienced underground. Claustrophobia threatened the edge of my consciousness, but the roil of emotions twisting my guts and rattling my mind wouldn't let it in.

Azrael, my mother, Father Dominic, Marty and Todd, Piper and now Poe. Could I trust no one? Didn't anyone care?

The thought of Poe made my teeth clench. For these past months I'd trusted her, listened to her, only to find her a part of the machinations which ruined my life, the impetus which started the proverbial ball rolling. She told me once Michael rescued her from Hell, but she'd never mentioned being a Carrion.

She didn't tell me it was her who took my mother's soul to Hell.

I blundered down the dark corridor, seething and sad. After a while, light began to filter down from ahead of me. I quickened my pace, desperate to get out before my other emotions waned and the sickening feel of claustrophobia enveloped me, constricting my chest and wrenching my stomach inside out.

The light grew and I saw the tunnel ahead clearly, so I pushed myself to go faster. I filled my lungs with air likely no different than what I'd been breathing, but that tasted so much fresher. It revitalized me, gave my limbs new energy. I rounded a bend and saw the exit, the source of the light shining through the portal. I stepped through.

I collected comic books in my teens—one of the few normalities in which I engaged between street life and drug use. Neil Gaiman wrote some of my favorites: Sandman, The Books of Magic, and Death—now eerily appropriate reading. One of my favorite lines came from a Sandman story and went something like this: *Sometimes you wake up. Sometimes the fall kills you, and sometimes when you fall, you fly.*

As I plunged through the doorway and over the precipice of whatever drop I didn't know lay before me, I crazily wondered which would be the case this time.

Given my name, I didn't feel good about my chances.

Chapter
Twenty-Nine

P OE PUSHED BY ICARUS, diverting her eyes from the stunned expression on his face. Her cheeks went hot, like she'd been caught
watching a Paul Newman movie with her hand down her pants. The
urge to stop and explain that if she had a choice, she'd never have taken
any souls, least of all his mother, coursed through her, but the forward
movement of her feet couldn't be slowed.

She burst across the plane of the doorway with Sister Agnes' soul in
tow, but didn't find the nun's living room as she should have. Instead,
she entered a hazy, indistinct place, like she saw it through a heavily
frosted pane of glass.

Poe took a step forward and her toe contacted something solid. She
looked down, but her leg below the knee was as disguised by whiteness
as the area around her, like she looked at it in a misted-over mirror.
After a second, the haze cleared revealing the bottom of her leg, her
foot, the stone she'd kicked sitting on brown, loamy soil. The blur
around her foot disappeared as though sucked up by a cosmic vacuum
cleaner. When she raised her head, she saw her surroundings clearly:
Arbutus trees with their peeling bark and red, slick-looking wood
beneath; the broad leaves of oak and maple; the black-shingled roof of
a house showing through the branches. She turned slowly, hoping she
wouldn't see what she knew would be there: the shack.

It was.

"Oh no."

She spun one-hundred and eighty degrees, not sure why: to avoid
the rundown shack, to run, to find Icarus and beg his forgiveness and
help, maybe to explain to the nun's spirit what happened. But the nun

was gone, the door to the bedroom was gone, Icarus was gone. The path back to the old neighborhood snaked through the trees behind her and somewhere up the path she heard two voices talking as they came closer.

Poe's mouth went dry. She knew who the voices belonged to, knew Aaron Baxter and his cousin would soon come swaggering into the small clearing, then take her into the shed to rape her and lose their lives for it.

Not again. Please, not again.

She deviated off the path and willed her feet to take her toward the shed; it surprised her to find they obeyed this time. Her pace increased, carrying her across the short distance to the crooked door as the boys' voices came closer. She slid through the doorway and eased it closed behind her so as not to attract the boys' attention. Crouching behind the rickety door, Poe peeked through the crack between it and the door jamb.

The two boys reached the edge of the clearing and stopped, sly smiles crossing their faces. Aaron Baxter elbowed his cousin in the ribs and pointed. Poe's gaze followed his finger to the younger girl standing in the middle of the clearing staring directly at the door through which she peered. The slightly open door mesmerized twelve-year-old Paula Edgar so she didn't notice the boys creeping toward her.

I thought there was something in the shack. Someone...me.

The boys reached the girl and Aaron spoke, startling Paula and making her jump. She turned to engage them in conversation and Poe stood, backed away from the door. Hell already forced her to endure that awful day again, now it appeared she would have to relive it once more, this time as an observer, which might be worse.

Poe spun away from the door with its crack which would have shown her Aaron and his cousin coaxing Paula toward the shack. Though she knew the shed was empty, the guardian angel wanted to find somewhere to hide, or at least hide her eyes until the terrible event concluded, but she knew she wouldn't find anywhere to conceal herself. At least she thought she wouldn't until she found she was no longer in the shack.

The brightly lit room was opulently—if weirdly—decorated. Tapestries hung on the walls; a huge desk supported by thick wooden legs carved into the shapes of gargoyles with lolling tongues dominated one side of the room. She glanced back over her shoulder and found the cracked shed door by a wall covered with another tapestry. The scene on the hanging showed a copse of trees sewn with brown trunks and green leaves, a clearing, three small figures and a gray shack leaning to one side. The three embroidered people moved across the clearing toward the shed.

Poe closed her eyes and jerked away from the tapestry, returning her attention to the room. When she opened her eyes, she noticed a chair set close to the desk. Over-sized and made of wood, the chair looked as though it may have been carved out of a single piece, like a huge stump ripped from the ground and chiseled into a seat, back and four legs. A man sat in the chair, his feet on the seat, knees drawn up to his chest. Poe took a cautious step forward, eyes fixed on him. His shaggy hair hung down past his shoulders and his frame was slight. She realized, even without seeing his face, this wasn't a man but a boy, a teen. Her breath caught in her throat as she thought it must be Aaron Baxter or his cousin.

She took another step. On a table beside the teen, a skeleton lizard scuttled across the bottom of its wooden cage and clacked its bony jaws at her. The teen's head inclined slightly toward the cage, but then returned to the same position, staring at the tapestry on the wall in front of him. Poe followed his gaze but the tapestry was a blank sea of black velvet.

She approached the large chair; the boy still didn't notice her. She leaned forward, attempting to see his face, but his hair hung down by his cheek, hiding his features. She lifted her hand, reaching for his shoulder to get his attention, but stopped.

What if it is Aaron? What if it's his cousin?

She shivered. She'd never found out the name of the other boy who raped her, the young man she killed. Not knowing what to call him made it all the worse. Poe drew a halting breath and forced her hand to complete its journey.

Her fingers touched the young man's shoulder; he didn't react so she squeezed, lightly at first, then more firmly when he didn't acknowledge her presence. Finally, when she felt she must be gripping hard enough to cause pain, the teen faced her, their gazes met and she looked into the unmistakable eyes of the boy's father. It seemed like an eternity since the two of them traveled to Hell together, since she'd lost him at the edge of Abaddon's pit. Poe swallowed hard.

"Trevor?"

The teen stared back at her without recognition, eyes glassy and unfocused. Poe threw her arms around his neck and pulled him to her.

"Trevor. Thank God."

Trevor didn't respond.

· · · · ·· · ·· ·

Wind rushed by, flapping my hair against my forehead and temples. At first, I fell beside a cliff of orange, chalk-like stone, but it disappeared leaving empty air on all sides. I plummeted blind—back toward the ground—past strange creatures floating or flying through the air, some of them gargoyles on ragged wings, others wisps of smoke shaped like people full of holes. A fish, a turtle, misshapen birds, a clown with smeared make-up and pointed teeth. The only thing missing was the Stay-Puft Marshmallow Man from the movie *Ghostbusters.* Although I fell at an incredible speed, I saw each of the creatures clearly, saw every detail of their hideous faces and twisted bodies.

Eventually, the creatures disappeared. I braced myself for impact presuming I must be approaching the ground, but instead of hitting earth, a movie began to play around me as though I fell through the screen of an over-sized IMAX theater. The movie at this particular theater showed the story of my life.

I stifled a yawn.

Of course, I'd lived all this crap—the abuse at the hands of Father Dominic, the time on the street, the booze, the drugs, my sham of a marriage—but I also saw the first cut when those bastard muggers slid a knife into me in the churchyard a few months back. My life in syndication.

You'd think Hell would have more original tricks up its sleeve.

As I fell and watched, I noticed differences in the familiar scenes playing around me. The same happenings as before—same unlikely plot line, same unbelievable events, same hammy actors. The thing which differed from when I saw it last and from when I lived it hid in the background.

Standing off to the side, or in the shadows, or hidden behind a curtain in every event was Michael or Azrael, sometimes both.

The revelation startled me. If I could have sat up to take a closer look, I would have, but the act of lying on one's back and falling precludes the possibility of straining into a seated position. Or maybe I needed to do a few more crunches if I ever saw a gym again.

As I took stock of what seeing them meant, the movie ended with my murder and it seemed to me the faces beneath those hoods pulled up to block out the rain belonged to the two archangels.

And then I was no longer falling.

I didn't hit the ground with a bone-jarring jolt, I simply stopped. With no warning, my feet touched solid ground. More precisely, my feet settled on a scattering of dirty straw close to what looked like a large pile of shit which would have required a huge bowel. The thought of how big the beast which made the heap of feces must have been made me shudder as much as the smell of it did.

I glanced away from the mountainous turd at my surroundings. It was night and I stood in a lane created by a network of drab canvas tents pitched in rows on either side of me. Frayed ropes ran from their edges to wooden stakes driven into the ground. I took a few steps away from the mound of fecal matter leaving its smell behind and caught a whiff of the old canvas instead. Evidently the tents had been put away wet a few times.

Stepping over the lines anchoring tents to ground, I picked my way along the makeshift boulevard feeling like a youngster who sneaked into the carnival. I heard no sounds beyond the occasional snap of a corner of canvas picked up by a wind I didn't feel. No carnival music emanating from a Ray Bradbury-esque carousel, no pitchman barking about freaks, no screams of pain or pleasure.

Light shone between the tents, casting shadowy spider webs on the ground as it played over the cat's cradle of ropes, but the light prevented me seeing beyond the far edge of the tent. I pressed on, sometimes remembering to draw breath, always expecting some Hell-thing to jump out at me—something capable of leaving behind a bowel movement the size of a Volkswagen.

My eyes darted left and right, watching, and it seemed every time I looked right, I saw movement in my peripheral vision to the left. When I looked left, movement on my right. Nothing jumped me, and by the time I made it to the end of the canvas alley, all the muscles in my body felt like some demonic boy scout had removed them, used them to practice for his knot-tying badge, then replaced them.

The straw-strewn ground continued a couple of yards beyond the end of the tents, carrying on into blackness. And I don't mean it was dark: there was nothing. Like the artist drawing the scene ran out of ink or time and left the rest of the page a colorless blank. I crept to the edge and considered extending a toe out into the dark like a swimmer testing the temperature of the ocean, but decided against it. At the beach, you could pull your toe out if it was too cold—I wasn't so sure I could retrieve my toe if the void wasn't to my liking.

I stutter-stepped my way crab-wise along the edge, ducking under ropes disappearing into the dark which remained taut despite ending. When I reached the front corner, I peered around while trying to keep the majority of myself hidden behind the canvas pavilion. A broad, brightly lit avenue stretched between the tents on one side and the edge of a forest of trees taller than any I'd ever seen on the other. Cages lined the boulevard at regular intervals, exactly the type of enclosures you'd expect to see at a traveling zoo: gray metal bars ran vertically between wood fascias painted in one-time bright reds and golds now faded to dull pink and yellow.

The nearest cage held an animal I'd have to compare to an elephant, only bigger. It looked sort of like an elephant—wrinkled gray skin, stump-like legs, a writhing trunk—but the similarities weren't as similar as they appeared at first glance. The wrinkled skin looked wet, slimy, the way a snake's looked. The six thick, stumpy legs each ended with a huge hand like the foot of an orangutan. The writhing trunk protruded off the beast's forehead, three tiny, bloodshot eyes winking at me beneath it. It also had tusks: two great, curved, black tusks set atop its head.

It appeared to ponder me, then circled away, its attention drawn somewhere else. As its other end faced me, it lifted its tail, loosened a sphincter large enough to swallow a compact car, and proved beyond doubt this beast created the mound of dung I nearly landed in. I turned my head away in disgust.

Imagine cleaning that off the bottom of your shoe.

· · · ● ● · ● ● · · ·

The scene on the tapestry neither moved nor changed. The embroidered rendition of the mythological Icarus hung suspended in the blue sky, the wings strapped to him with a leather harness falling to pieces as the warmth of the sun melted the feathers composing them.

Trevor stared, waiting for the man to fall to his death or the scene to shift again, but neither happened. The man floated in endless free fall, head thrown back, his face hidden from Trevor, but he knew it was his father's face. He hugged his knees tighter to his chest, chewed on the inside edge of his bottom lip. What happened if the fall ended?

Is this happening? Can I save him?

Time the teen no longer felt capable of measuring passed and the man continued his fall. Trevor stared and, after a while, didn't know why he did, couldn't remember why he found it important. His vision blurred, his eyes hurt, and he forgot who was falling. Forgot why he was in the room, where the room was.

When the woman interrupted his stare, he no longer recognized the word she spoke.

"Trevor?"

He re-aimed his head toward her with great effort, as though a sand bag sat atop his shoulders rather than his head. He gazed at her blond hair, golden eyes, and recognition flickered somewhere at the back of his mind before the urge to return his gaze to the tapestry snuffed it out.

She put her arms around him, pressed herself against him, and her touch ran a shock through his shoulders, into his chest—a huge, living joy buzzer pressed uncomfortably to his entire body. When she released him and held him by the shoulders at arms' length, the vibration subsided to a tolerable level and he began to breathe again.

"Are you alright?"

The words made their way into his ears where he heard them but didn't comprehend. He stared back at her, his eyes open so long by then he no longer felt able to blink for fear his eyelids would be sandpaper scraping across his corneas.

The woman said something else he didn't understand and stood. His eyes didn't move, only stared at the same level, stared at her midsection now. Dirt streaked her shirt, and blood. A missing button left a gap in her blouse and he saw the pale flesh of her belly.

"Trevor."

The word again. It echoed in his head, bounced around his brain looking for a place to take hold long enough for him to recognize it. It circled like a marble dropped into a sink and quickly met the same fate: it disappeared. He swiveled his heavy head and caught another glimpse of the tapestry before the woman pulled him to his feet, jerking his gaze away. The falling man had landed, but not in a pile of broken bones and twisted limbs. Instead of a shattered body lying on the ground, he saw the man standing, a cage at his back.

And then the woman put her arm around him again, the sensation of her touch pulsing his teeth like he'd bitten down on a chunk of aluminum foil, and pulled him away.

· · · · · · · · · ·

Poe guided Trevor away from the chair and toward the door on the far side of the room, each step a struggle to keep him headed in the right direction as he sought to look over his shoulder at the wall hanging.

"Come on," she coaxed. "We have to get out of here."

She fought to keep her tone even, confident, though she in no way felt either. The shack where she died, the man on the tracks, Icarus' birth, and now this.

"Where are you?" she whispered to the teen. He acted like he didn't hear her. "Where did you go?"

She pushed him toward the door, wishing he'd snap out of it, silently making deals with God in her head for him to be alright.

But He can't hear me down here.

Fighting to keep her throat from closing with emotion, she reached her hand out and twisted the ornate door knob. As her fingers grasped it, she realized it was cast in the shape of a human head, mouth open, teeth bared in an expression of agony. She forced herself to work the knob instead of recoiling.

The door swung open and she pushed Trevor through in front of her, looking back at the tapestry which held him so enthralled as she kept herself between him and it.

It remained blank, a sheet of black velvet shimmering against the wall, wavering, rippling like waves upon a lake.

She closed the door.

Trevor pulled himself away and moved a step sending a trill of panic through the guardian angel. She pivoted to collect him before he got away again and quickly saw there was no danger of that happening; they'd emerged from the room into a cage.

The air smelled sweetly of the fresh-cut hay lining the floor at their feet. The red paint on the ceiling above their heads flaked, weathered wood showing through. She peered through the bars at a forest of huge trees, their bows shivering in an unfelt wind.

No birds sang. No crickets chirruped.

She pivoted to peer through the bars on the other side of the cage and saw a line of canvas tents which looked as though they'd been in use since long before the inside of the cage received its most recent paint job. But her gaze held on them only briefly as the man standing near the bars grabbed her attention.

Icarus Fell stared at them through the rusted bars.

· · · ● · ● · · ·

I took a couple of steps toward the elephant-thing's cage, carefully staying out of range of the trunk-or-whatever-it-was growing out of its forehead. Since things aren't always as they seem in Hell, it might have been the thing's dick, for all I knew.

It looked at me again, the three beady eyes winking independently of one another. Eyes fixed on the beast, I grapevined by the cage like in an aerobics class so I didn't have to turn away, and nearly tripped over a rope running from tent-edge to wooden stake. When I glanced away to see what booby trap almost got me, the creature made its move.

It reared up and stuck two of its stumpy legs between the bars, the long, ape-like fingers flexing and unflexing, grasping for me. The black tusks banged against the bars as it sent its trunk-thing lashing at me. I was out of its range, but fell back a couple of steps in surprise, heart pounding. With the elephant-thing upright, I gained confirmation that the thing on its head was indeed a trunk and not its trouser snake.

"Wow. You are a big boy, aren't you?"

I smiled a little and tried to return my breathing to normal as its long fingers groped empty air six feet from me. Its waving hands and trunk wafted air against my face and with it came the smell of its fresh load of dung. The odor reminded me again of the giant pile at the end of my fall.

The pile *outside* the cage.

If it got out before, it could get out again.

I tittered nervously and side-stepped away.

"It's okay, boy. I won't hurt you."

If the thing could understand my words, I'm sure it would have laughed. What could a measly little thing like me do to hurt the likes of him? Nothing. If it got free I'd be crushed, pulled to pieces and, if Hell is as bad as it seems, raped by the ridiculous appendage between its legs.

Time to go.

I stepped over a rope and the creature stopped flailing its arms, the fingers clenching into fists. I held up a hand and wiggled my own fingers at it, waving bye-bye, and the thing took the opportunity to flick its trunk at me. A glob of the shiny mucous-like shit covering its skin in a sheen flew off and struck me in the cheek.

I recoiled, wiped the substance off with the sleeve of my shirt, and gagged at the back of my throat.

Great, hit with elephant snot.

When I looked up at it again after settling my epiglottis, I swear elephant-thing smiled at me. I shot it the bird, showed it my back and walked away.

The next two cages were smaller and empty of strange animals or straw on the floor. The fourth cage was the smallest yet, perhaps big enough for a medium-sized dog, but too small for the human skeleton jammed into it, though I'd have put money it wasn't a pile of bones when the jamming began.

The next cage—a little bigger than the last—housed a golden-furred monkey with big, lovable eyes like they'd feature in an issue of *National Geographic*. The sharp-looking teeth protruding from its mouth and the way it twitched like a fish tossed on the wharf might have disqualified it from cover model status and prompted me to make a wide berth around it. The next cage stood empty, the one after occupied by a large parrot with a vaguely human face. It regarded me with a perfunctory look for about fifteen seconds, then began plunging its scimitar beak into its side and pulling out green and red feathers by the mouthful.

I walked past the next few cages without looking closely at their contents, but some I couldn't help noticing: a horse walking on two legs; the top half of a man using his fingernails to drag himself across the floor of the cage toward his bottom half standing in the far corner, foot tapping; a giraffe with the markings of a zebra and the body of a dog; a man with no arms and no legs sat upon by a grotesquely obese woman with stout horns atop her head, the woman rocking back and forth, moaning with pleasure as the man shrieked.

I looked away from that one.

I walked for a couple more minutes, gaze diverted toward the row of tents as I used the memory of the obese woman's sagging, hairy breasts to keep my curiosity at bay. My curiosity squashing approached its limit when I banged into the bars of a cage set directly in my path.

"Dammit."

I looked up at the rusted bars, rubbed my forehead where contact with said bars occurred, and found a goose egg already forming.

"Shit."

I took a step back to look at the cage in front of me. It was as big as the first one which penned the elephant-thing, but sat on a three foot high platform. It was empty except for the straw covering the floor—freshly cut, by the smell of it—and a galvanized steel pail of water. Another cage stood to my left. In fact, as I circled doing my surveillance of the milieu I'd neglected in my desire *not* to see more unattractive people engaged in sexual activities, I found cages encircled me, the corner of one touching the corner of the next, effectively penning me in the largest cage yet.

I stepped into the middle of the ring and turned two more circles to ensure my eyes weren't playing tricks on me, then went to the cage directly behind me and tested the solidity of its bars. I knew it hadn't existed a moment before because I walked through that spot, but the bars rattled proving themselves real. I was giving them a second shake, just to be sure, when I heard a sound from behind me like kids make by putting their finger in their cheek and pulling it out. Only this was loud enough the finger and cheek would have needed to be enormous. I spun toward the sound.

Two people stood with their backs to me in the previously empty platform cage: a woman whose blond hair cascaded down her back and a fellow beside her who looked about eight inches taller, his unkempt brown hair brushing the tops of his shoulders. I took a couple of steps toward the bars for a closer look.

The woman turned her head, sweeping her gaze over the line of tents, long hair falling across her forehead, beside her cheek, but I saw her profile and recognized her instantly.

My chest tightened and I took another step closer to the bars.

My movement must have caught her attention because her eyes flickered in my direction. When they fell on me, she turned and I looked into Poe's face. She raised her hand to her mouth, covering her lips, caught so completely off guard by my presence that she didn't know what else to do. I didn't react.

Not until Trevor looked at me.

His eyes met mine without recognition or comprehension. His blank expression didn't alter as his gaze swept over me, over the cages behind me. He looked lost.

"Trevor?"

I grabbed the bars, my heart suddenly beating so hard against my ribs I heard it in my ears. My hands squeezed the cold, rusty metal, the blood forced out of my fingers until my knuckles went white.

Trevor didn't respond, didn't so much as look at me. I switched my gaze back to Poe who still held her hand over her mouth.

"What have you done?" I demanded between clenched teeth. "*What have you done?*"

Chapter Thirty

I SHOOK THE BARS and Poe's eyes widened while Trevor continued acting like a man trying to figure out where he was and how he got there. The thought of Trevor as a man rather than a boy loosened my chest, as well as my grip on the bars. I breathed deep through my nose, inhaling the sweet smell of the straw scattered across the cage floor as the thought of my son growing up made me both proud and sad, distracted me until I recognized the look he wore. I'd seen it before when I met Alfred Topping, and when I'd accidentally killed Detective Williams.

It was the expression I'd seen on the faces of souls surprised to be free of their earthly bodies.

All hint of reminiscence and pride disappeared as fury overwhelmed me at the thought my supposed guardian angel had harvested my son's soul.

Like she'd harvested my mother's.

"What. Have. You. Done?"

I emphasized each word with a shake of the bars and had a momentary flash that, from Poe's perspective, I must have looked like a child having a temper tantrum inside my play pen. The idea she may have considered the thought angered me further.

"Icarus, I—"

"Ric, for Christ's sake. Why the fuck can't you call me Ric?"

Her hand dropped from her face. Her mouth quivered a little at the corners; her obvious upset fortified me. She stared at me for a full minute and I simply glowered back at her.

"Ric," she said finally, her voice a whisper.

Hearing her say my name the way I preferred gave me a sense of accomplishment, as though I'd won. With my slack-faced son staring vacantly beside her, the feeling disappeared quickly.

"What did you do to him? Who sent you for him?"

"I didn't do anything. I –"

"Did Azrael send you?"

"No. I—"

"Piper said you were working for them."

Her expression changed, hardened.

"Piper's a liar."

"Then how do you explain this?"

I gestured toward Trevor whose back was to us as he looked in the direction of the forest. His face was hidden from me, but I imagined him staring, awe struck by the size of the trees. I gritted my teeth and attempted to set Poe alight with my glare. It didn't work.

The look on her face sagged when she answered.

"It was a mistake."

"A mistake? A *mistake*? How do you bring a teenage boy to Hell by mistake?"

"I came to save you. He followed."

Her statement gave me a fraction of a second's pause before my response seethed between my lips.

"Like you saved my mother?"

She couldn't keep her eyes on me. She looked at her feet, shoulders sagging to match her expression. Trevor scuffled his feet as he turned to peer at the canvas tents. A breeze blew through the circle of cages, stirring the straw at their feet, flapping a corner of one of the tents. That seemed to grab his attention.

"Trevor. Trevor!"

No dice.

"I had no choice, Icar...Ric. I had to."

"Had to condemn my mother to Hell?"

She nodded, then shook her head like someone who couldn't decide how to answer.

"Yes, I mean no. I didn't condemn her. I only...I only took her."

"Took her to live for eternity here."

This time she nodded but still wouldn't meet my eyes.

"And now you've done the same with my son."

She responded immediately, shaking her head vehemently and finally meeting my eyes. Her gaze held mine for a second before straying past me, peering over my shoulder as if someone stood behind me. I fought the urge to turn.

It's a trick. If I look, she'll disappear and take Trevor with her.

That's what happens in movies—I wouldn't be so stupid. When Poe's eyes widened and her expression changed, I thought it might be a possibility I was either wrong or Poe was a really good actress.

I watched fear creep across the guardian angel's face.

· · · ● · ● · · · ·

"And now you've done the same to my son."

His words slammed against Poe like he'd thrown a glass of cold water in her face.

I didn't mean to bring him. I'm sorry. I don't want to hurt him. I'll do anything to make it better. Please forgive me, Icarus. We came to save you. I want the best for you and Trevor. I love you.

All the possible responses ricocheted through her mind, the last words surprising her. She didn't expect it, not here, not now, not like that. She shook her head and looked up, lips parted to counter his accusation, but nothing came out. She peered into his eyes for a moment and longed to tell him all—everything that had happened to her in life and after, to tell him she understood better than anyone what he'd gone through in the past few months, about her years being a Carrion against her will, of Michael saving her.

Michael.

All those things danced on the tip of her tongue but a movement behind Icarus caught her attention. Her eyes flickered to a spot over his shoulder.

Two figures stood in the center of the rough ring of cages: a tall man dressed in black and a boy younger than Trevor. The man towered over his companion like a huge pepper grinder sitting on the table beside a mismatched salt shaker.

A shiver gripped Poe. She knew both of them and wished neither of them were here. The man was Azrael, the angel of death, banished from Heaven for an act Poe now knew he didn't do. The responsibility for bringing souls to Hell belonged to him—the man who truly condemned the damned.

The boy was something far worse.

Behind them, figures populated the previously empty cages. To the left, two men squatted peering through the bars of one: Marty and Todd. She'd met them once before, and then in a fight, but knew Icarus' old drinking buddies because she'd hovered close by, watching out for him during his drinking binges before he knew he had a guardian angel. In the next cage slouched a man she didn't know, though she thought she'd seen his face before. The next held the man who used to sell Icarus drugs. Beside him, in a cage not quite big enough for him to stand, Father Dominic glared out between the rusty bars. From her vantage point, she found it difficult to tell if he directed the ire in his expression at Icarus or the back of Azrael's head.

In the fifth cage, Sister Agnes—Icarus' mother—sat placidly on the straw-covered floor. When she glanced in Poe's direction, the guardian angel looked away. The last enclosure held Piper. She paced the length of the cage like a beast at the zoo, eyes darting between Azrael and the boy, Father Dominic, Icarus and Poe, like she was searching for who to blame.

Poe saw all this in the moment before Icarus turned to see what captured her attention. As he turned his face away from her, she noticed his shoulders sag. It seemed he didn't want to bump into the angel of death any more than she did.

"Hello, Icarus, my son," the fallen angel said, his voice the perfect arrangement of an all-male choir. "We meet again."

Beside Poe, Trevor's body stiffened.

· · · ● · ● ● · · ·

A breeze played across Trevor's face, stirred his hair against his cheek. He blinked stray stands out of his eyes. Behind him, he heard words he thought he should know. He listened closer, concentrating. More than one voice spoke, but he couldn't pinpoint where the sound came from, who spoke them, because the trees forced themselves into his mind, pulling him back to them every time he attempted to turn his thoughts away.

They reached all the way to the sky, maybe beyond, those trees. He thought if he climbed one, it would take him the rest of his life to reach the top, but when he did, he would find himself in Heaven.

Heaven.

The word sounded in his head like the peal of a bell. His eyes flickered tree to tree surveying the brown bark, the green needles on the branches, moss on the trunks.

Beautiful.

Maybe this was Heaven and the trees led closer to God. The idea felt good to Trevor, but the concept seemed wrong.

The wind blew again, this time bringing a chill to his skin, raising goose flesh on his arms and making the hairs on the back of his neck stand upright. He shivered. The wind died but the chill remained and he realized without knowing why: *this isn't Heaven.*

As the thought entered his mind, the trees changed. The brown bark shriveled and peeled; velvety moss turned to slime; green needles lost their pigment, became the gray of ash. If another breeze blew, it would surely separate them from the gnarled branches.

All Trevor's muscles went stiff with realization, awareness.

This is Hell.

Memory flooded back in as if the pipe in his head channeling them past conscious thought had burst. He remembered Poe, the demon, the landscape of Hell. He remembered the strange room, the tapestry.

He remembered the boy.

Trevor pivoted slowly on one foot, like a basketball player in slow motion. He saw Poe at his side, a look of fear on her face. He saw his father standing outside the bars, his back to them. Beyond Icarus stood two more figures.

His eyes met the boy's gaze and the boy smiled.

Chapter
Thirty-One

WHEN I TURNED AWAY from Poe, I didn't know what to expect. For months, I'd thought of her as my guardian angel, always on the look-out for me, a being who'd put my best interests before all else.

How things change.

In retrospect, I saw her failings: the times I'd needed her and she wasn't there, the times she'd showed up to help and it led to more trouble, the Carrions who appeared whenever she did. And now I knew why.

Because she's one of them.

So when I pivoted to see what she stared at behind me, I expected it to be a trick, a way for her to escape with my son and lead me on a further merry chase through Hell. I didn't expect what was actually behind me.

Azrael was clothed as usual: black on black. His appearance made me think of an old-time gunslinger, someone about whom Zane Grey might have written in his old Western novels. As much as I loathed Azrael for everything he stood for and everything he'd done—from killing my mother to abducting my son—I'm sorry to say I also felt an unwanted tickle of pride somewhere down deep, though not deep enough to hide it completely. The man was not a man but an archangel and my father.

How many people can say that?

What's your father do for a living?

Mine? Oh, he's an archangel. The angel of death, to be precise.

Didn't Heaven banish him?

Shut the fuck up.

A boy stood beside Azrael. I recognized him immediately as the kid I'd seen at other times during my visits to the underworld and, though I'd never been in his presence exactly, his attention directed toward me stood the small hairs on my arms on end.

I decided I didn't like him.

The cages at their backs were occupied but I didn't dare take my eyes off the dynamic duo. I'd seen what I assumed was a small fraction of Azrael's capabilities and figured they'd be multiplied here in Hell.

"Hello, Icarus, my son. We meet again."

It felt as if his words made the ground quiver beneath my feet but it may have been my knees wobbling at the sound of his voice. At my back, I heard a distressed squeal from Poe's throat. Again the feeling of being tricked overwhelmed me, kept curiosity from turning me to see what prompted the sound. I gritted my teeth and forced my knees to keep still.

"What do you want?"

"Your freedom. Nothing more, nothing less."

My eyebrows must have come dangerously close to touching as I peered at him through slitted lids.

Why would he want my freedom?

"Why would you want my freedom?"

"You've messed up the balance and it must be restored."

My eyebrows inched closer together.

"What are you talking about?"

Azrael opened his mouth to answer but the boy at his side raised a hand, stopping him before any sound emerged. I suspected his gesture would have the same effect on any living thing.

"You don't belong here," the boy said, his voice the high-pitched, slightly girlish tone of a young man not quite through puberty. But it contained undertones, too: evil, discordant undertones loaded with menace.

"You're damn straight I don't."

The boy smiled.

"And you have attracted too many others who don't belong."

He gestured and I followed the wave of his hand, saw for the first time the people housed in the cages behind him: Marty and Todd,

Tony McSweeney, Orlando Albert, Father Dominic, my mother and, finally, Piper. All but my mother stared at me; her eyes were fixed on Azrael, an expression of adoration on her face.

"You must leave," the boy continued. "And you must take one of these souls with you."

I blew a single, sharp laugh through my nose.

"I'll do better: I'll take all of them off your hands." Father Dominic's expression brightened. "Except the priest."

"One," Azrael said, the index finger on his left hand pointing skyward in both a gesture indicating how many available for the taking as well as what direction I'd be headed with said soul. "You take one or you take none."

"But I thought you were over-stocked."

The boy smiled more broadly, as if I'd told a joke which he alone understood.

"Arrangements can be made, Icarus. Do you want to try me?"

I shivered and glanced at my feet—nothing interesting about them other than the fact I didn't have to look into the boy's blazing eyes. Exactly my goal.

"Okay. One."

The choice would be easy. I turned toward the cage behind me and saw Poe kneeling on the floor, Trevor standing beside her. His eyes stared beyond me, fixed on Azrael and the boy. It struck me that my son and the guardian angel would have made a cute couple; Poe only appeared a few years older than Trevor, a gap too big at age fifteen but more than acceptable in a couple of years. The idea felt good for the heartbeat before reality settled back in to my brain.

We were in Hell. They were in a cage. The woman stole souls.

"What did you do to him?" I growled.

Poe looked at me, eyes brimming fake tears, and shook her head.

Does she mean she doesn't know? That she didn't do it?

Part of me remembered the times she'd saved me and wanted to believe her. But too many other things crowded my head, too many times she'd been the cause of my problems. I'd seen her take my mother's soul. I knew she'd brought my son to Hell.

"I'll take Trevor."

"He is not one of the choices."

I spun around fast enough at Azrael's words I teetered on the edge of losing my balance.

"What? You said I had to take one of these souls. Why can't—"

The boy raised his hand again and I stopped talking. I didn't mean to, my mouth just stopped as though I was Achmed the dead terrorist and he had his Jeff Dunham hand jammed up my ass to determine my lips' actions.

"He is not one of the choices. The angel brought him here by mistake."

My heart jumped in my chest, beat faster like it wanted to break free. *He's not supposed to be here.*

My lips trembled as I said: "So, he can—"

Azrael stretched his arms out mimicking the pose of Christ on the cross then, with his arms still straight, brought his hands together in front of him hard. His hellish version of the clapper didn't extinguish the lights, but I heard the same popping sound behind me as when Trevor and Poe appeared out of nowhere. I pivoted back toward the bars, my head starting to spin with so much back and forth.

The cage was gone.

I stared, struggling to control my breathing and keep panic from rising in my chest.

It's Poe's fault this happened.

My son was gone, the Carrion disguised as a guardian angel to blame. I spun back toward the angel of death.

"Where are they?"

The other cages had disappeared, too, and the tents and the trees. I stood facing Azrael and the boy across a smudge of orange-brown dirt scattered with straw. Neither of them answered my question.

"Where?"

"It is time to choose."

Another thunderous clap echoed, the force of it buffeting my chest and forcing me to my knees. My head spun with the impact, my ears rang with the sound. I closed my eyes to settle my brain; when I opened them again, the ground under me was no longer soil and straw. Instead, my knees rested on a piece of soggy cardboard spread across pavement. I raised my head. Azrael and the boy were gone.

To my right was an over-flowing garbage bin sitting in front of a brick wall scrawled with graffiti. I recognized the place, or places like it, at least. A man sat across the alley from me, staring, a moth-chewed blanket pulled across his shoulders.

Orlando Albert.

"Icarus," he said.

His voice came out a croak, like a toad lived in his throat and needed to speak with me. No surprise given the damned souls who'd had a go at him at the labyrinth had done quite a job. Crooked, yellow teeth showed through holes in both cheeks. His breath wheezed through another hole in his throat; he lacked both ears; one eye bulged on the verge of bursting out of his head, the white tinted pink with blood.

"No."

I got to my feet, wobbled to get my balance right, then sidestepped away from him. I didn't know where to go—the alley appeared to stretch on pretty much forever in both directions—but I knew I didn't want to be there.

Orlando struggled to get up, propping himself against the brick wall to do so. When he finally made it to his version of standing—more the slouch of a man well into his centennial year—the tattered blanket fell off his shoulders. He was naked beneath, though the word doesn't do justice: no clothes and little flesh. Bone and muscle peeked through what remained of his shredded skin, bite marks showing at irregular intervals, pieces of meat hanging from his legs and torso where the job of rending his flesh was left not-quite-done.

"Please. I shouldn't be here."

"What are you talking about? You ruined lives, killed people. Why shouldn't I leave you here?"

"Because I gave you what you wanted."

I don't know where he'd been hiding the needle he waved at me—naked men have few options for concealing things. The one possibility I could think of made me shudder.

"Take me with you and you can have it again. All you want."

He shuffled forward a step, a loose bit of flesh flapping where his genitals once dangled.

I gagged.

"I don't need it anymore."

As the words left my mouth, a shiver pulsed beneath my skin, an itch. My gaze fell on the needle in his hand and stuck.

"Yes, you do."

The croak of his voice echoed in my head as he came closer, arm extended. Offering? Trying to stick me? Saliva filled my mouth, threatened to over-flow as though he offered a particularly appetizing meal rather than a substance which had stolen my life and came close to ending it.

I licked my lips, rocked back and forth on the balls of my feet. My body remembered the feel of the drug coursing through my veins, the way it made my head inflate. The rush, the calm.

I shook my head, dislodging the thought.

"No."

I turned my back on him, unafraid he possessed the energy or ability to jump me, and walked away.

"Please," he croaked after me. "Please, Icarus. Don't leave me here."

I ignored his pleas and the itch bubbling under my skin subsided. Six paces passed beneath my feet when the alleyway began to fade around me. I hesitated, waiting to see what was going on before I continued into the unknown. Unfortunately, the half-eaten man was more dexterous than I'd thought and he lunged, the needle piercing shirt sleeve and flesh as the last of the alley disappeared. I jumped away, rubbing my arm, and my thigh bumped against a chair.

Orlando was gone. The stench of garbage and excrement: gone. I found myself surrounded by tables and chairs, a wooden-topped bar. The place hadn't been aired-out in a long while and the smell of dried beer spilled by intoxicated hands permeated the room.

I'd ended up in a bar.

Sully's.

I let my hand fall away from my arm and took a step forward, wondering if I merely needed a tetanus shot or if he'd gotten some of the evil liquid into me.

A minute later, the feeling in my head, the sensation in my limbs, answered the question.

Shit.

Chapter
Thirty-Two

I GLANCED OVER AT the bar, expecting to see Sully's ever-present smile peeking out from beneath his bushy Ned Flanders moustache, but the area was vacant. Bottles sat lined up in orderly rows along the back bar, little galvanized pails of peanuts at regular intervals along the bar's dark wood surface awaited hungry fingers, but no bartender.

How's a guy supposed to get a drink?

For the first time in my life, I struggled against the feeling revving up in my brain, in the muscles of my arms and legs like a pencil wound at the end of an elastic. I took a few steps toward the row of stools at the bar, intending to peer over and see if someone hid behind it, but the clink of glass against glass caught my attention.

The room was empty of people except for the two men seated at a table by the big screen TV in the corner. Images flickered across the screen, a contest which might have been considered a sport in ancient Rome involving men dragged behind horses and skeletal beings with over-sized axes, but I didn't let my gaze linger once I saw the first man beheaded, choosing to scrutinize the men at the table instead.

The growing feeling in my brain made it more difficult than it should have been, but I eventually recognized Marty and Todd.

"Yah," Marty cried out and pumped a fist in the air at an event on the TV. "I told you they'd take it this year."

I took a careful step toward them, thinking I'd succeeded at being quiet until they whirled around as if I'd stepped on a cat.

"Look. It's Ric Fell," Todd said.

"Hey, Ric. Come sit with us."

Marty pushed a chair away from the table with his foot by way of invitation and I felt drawn to it. Hell, I needed to sit down. They watched as I crossed the room and settled my ass onto the chair's faux-leather seat.

"Ain't seen you in a long time," Todd said and raised his half-empty beer glass in toast. Marty did the same but paused before drinking.

"Wait a second, Todd. Ol' Ric doesn't have a drink. Hey barkeep." He raised his other hand and gestured. "Bring my friend a drink. Vodka soda with lime, right Ric?"

My brain said yes—exactly what I needed to calm my increasingly jangled nerves—and I thought it told my head to nod, but the damn thing shook side to side instead and my mouth followed suit.

"No, I—"

A man placed a drink on the table in front of me, interrupting my renegade words. Ice and clear liquid filled the tall glass, sweat ran down the side, a quarter lime perched on the rim. The man's presence startled me—I thought only the three of us occupied the bar. I looked up to thank him out of habit and, for a second time in a row, it surprised me not to see Sully. Instead, I looked up at the man I'd last seen ogling teenage boys in a Hell-bound locker room.

"Tony? What are you doing here?"

He wiped his hands on the short, white apron around his waist as if he was normally a bartender rather than a borderline-pedophile high school coach. In life, I'd never seen Tony at Sully's or any other bar, but this wasn't life, this was Hell.

At least, I assumed it was still Hell. In a bar, with a drink in front of me and a major buzz brewing in my head, didn't seem like such a bad place to be.

"Never mind him," Marty said. "We need to talk."

I looked from the misplaced Tony to Marty as he leaned forward, smiling. His nose seemed to have grown, his ear lobes flopped at the side of his head. I repressed a giggle and looked at my drink as Todd pushed it toward me. The droplets of water running down the side of the glass looked so refreshing, the lime so tempting. I swallowed hard and licked my lips, trying to concentrate hard enough to shrink myself down and dive right in.

"Yeah, we have to talk," Todd repeated.

"So talk."

I reached for the drink and tried to imbibe its refreshment through the fleshy pads of my fingers as they touched the cool glass. When that didn't work to my expectations, I went to pick it up, bring it to my mouth, but Todd held its base and wouldn't relinquish his grip. My tongue lolled across my bottom lip.

"You're our ticket out of here," Marty said, voice hushed to keep our conversation from Tony standing at my elbow. "You can make things right."

I started to shake my head but Todd interrupted.

"We wouldn't be here if it wasn't for you."

I glanced from Marty to Todd. If not for the drugs distorting my perception, he'd have looked much like he did in life: red veins stood out on his nose, dark circles colored the area below his eyes. In my current state, they stood out comically, like he was a caricature of W.C. Fields.

"But I—"

"You don't have to answer yet," Marty said. My eyes floated back to him and his gaze flickered to Tony looming behind me. "Why don't you move on, pal. My friend's got his drink."

I sensed Tony shift his weight from foot to foot but he neither left nor responded. Marty's face darkened to the unusual shade of pink it tended toward whenever he angered—usually when his team lost and Todd poked fun at him. Or a server took too long getting him a fresh beer. He pushed his chair away from the table.

"Did you hear me, bub? Time to go."

Todd also moved his chair, fulfilling his role of wing man if things went bad, but he'd never fight, that was Marty's domain. The sound of chair legs screeching on pockmarked linoleum floor deserved a cliché comparison to fingernails on a chalkboard, but even with the drugs circling my brain, I wouldn't be so trite.

Tony ceased wiping his hands on the apron but still didn't leave. Marty's eyes bulged a little in his head, then he leaned against the edge of the table, readying himself to stand. I got to my feet before he did.

"Waitaminutewaitaminutewaitaminute. You don't need to do this."

Marty remained seated, hands on table. I glanced at Todd, then Tony who stood close enough to make me uncomfortable, all of them awaiting a good reason not to come to fisticuffs. I waited along with them, my brain wondering what the Hell my mouth would come up with. Luckily, Tony finally spoke up and took the pressure off.

"Icarus is taking me back," he said. "He already tried once."

Not helpful.

Marty stood, chair tipping behind him, clattering to the floor. I rolled my eyes—it seemed like Marty couldn't stand without knocking over his chair for melodramatic effect.

"Ric's our friend," Marty said, face red, fists clenched. "He's taking me and Todd."

"Whoa, settle down, boys. For starters, I can only take one back. Secondly—"

"One?" Todd reiterated. "Only one?"

My brain cursed my mouth.

Todd looked at Marty. Marty looked at Todd. Before I could react, Todd jumped out of his chair and grabbed the front of my shirt, pulled my face way too close to his. The veins on his nose looked like cracks in a sidewalk.

"Get me out of here, Ric," he said, spittle striking my cheek. I flinched, but probably about two seconds after it hit. His voice dropped to a husky whisper. "Marty never liked you."

"Not true."

Marty shoved Todd sending him stumbling. I lurched from the table, backing away in time to avoid Marty jumping across it to get at his friend. In the process, Tony grabbed me by the shoulders and dragged me from the scuffle. He released me when we got to the bar.

"Thanks," I said begrudgingly—the memory of him watching those boys in the locker room clung to me like dog shit to the bottom of a shoe.

"Thank me by taking me with you."

I shook my head and almost lost my balance. I giggled and immediately felt bad for doing so.

Child molesters are no laughing matter.

"But you were going to take me before."

"It was a mistake."

His expression changed as if I'd surprised him with a punch to the gut. It reminded me of Droopy, the morose-looking cartoon dog. I giggled again.

"A mistake? How could it be a mistake? What did I ever do to you?"

I glared at him, anger building in my muscles as the smell of the dog crap stuck in the treads of my runner wafted up to my nostrils forcing back the mild euphoria.

"You coached my son."

He looked at me, the hurt still in his eyes, and opened his mouth—probably to beg me to take him with me or ask forgiveness for being a pervert—but I stumbled past him, headed for the door.

I made it halfway before being tackled.

Maybe Marty and Todd had settled their differences over which one should go with me and which would be left behind, maybe they hadn't. Either way, it seemed they recognized that if I left, neither would go with me.

My elbow struck the floor and rubbed the threadbare carpet near the bar hard enough to leave a burn on my flesh. That made me laugh, too. Marty's big hand grabbed my shoulder, flipped me over, shook me. The combination of shaking and laughing made drool run down my cheek.

"Take me with you."

"No, take me."

Tony joined in, forcing his way between them so their trio of desperate faces pleaded from on high like a group of pathetic gargoyles. Through the haze of Orlando's syringe-full-of-fun, I recognized that none of them were really my friends. I'd barely said a sober word to Marty and Todd—ours was a friendship of the bottle. And Tony deserved a spot in Hell for his unwholesome appetites.

Here's the problem: the three of them had me pinned. No possibility of escape and, in that moment, I didn't care. But something deep down inside me realized this called for desperate measures, a complicated plan. I formulated it quickly and put it into play.

"Come on guys, let me go."

This time it was my mouth's chance to be disappointed with my brain's choice of actions.

"Not until you tell us who you're taking."

Marty elbowed Tony, then shouldered Todd aside. He had size on both of them so if it came to a contest of strength, he'd win. But Tony proved plucky and the two of them stared down at me as they forced Todd back.

"Guys—"

Marty leaned forward suddenly, the proximity of his nose to mine startling me. The pink tinge in his face deepened to red, his eyes bulged in cartoonish fashion. Looking up at him, I wasn't sure whether Orlando's injection made him look this way or if this was the real Marty.

"I got an idea," Marty said, sour breath warm on my face. "Maybe if Ric doesn't go back there'd be room for one more."

I stared up at him without comprehension. To clarify, Tony shouldered his way past Marty's leering face and wrapped his fingers around my throat. I had the sinking suspicion they'd rehearsed this.

Tony's fingers clamped around my windpipe, squeezing until breath couldn't find its way into my lungs. I knew I should struggle, and part of me wanted to, but Marty perched on my chest and a chemically-induced sense of security and euphoria kept me from bothering.

The edge of my vision went fuzzy, like I viewed the world from inside an aquarium in need of cleaning. I waited for a school of fish to swim by, or perhaps an octopus propelling itself forth on a tangle of legs. No such luck. Instead, the fuzziness went gray. I stared up at Marty and Tony, found myself wondering if one of them or Todd would be left behind when Tony finished wringing out my life. I'd been killed before, so I didn't know if their plan would work or, if it did, whether I'd get to find out the outcome.

The point became moot when the water splashed down over me and my attackers.

To me, it served as a cool, refreshing slap in the face. It cleared my vision and sent the drugged-out feeling running for the hills. I felt like a new man.

The same couldn't be said for Marty and friends. They reacted as if splashed with acid. Tony screamed and relinquished his grip on my throat; Marty fell backwards, rolling painfully on my lower legs before tumbling off. I'm not sure what happened to Todd, he seemed to have disappeared completely. Maybe he melted.

I pushed myself up on my elbows, coughed to clear my pained esophagus, and blinked to clear water from my eyes. The world before me smeared, blurred for a moment, but I made out the figure standing in front of the bar.

Todd?

I blinked again.

Maybe Sully dropped by.

The last of the water cleared my eyes and I looked at my son, hair hanging in his eyes, the galvanized steel pail I'd seen in the cage with him dangling in his right hand.

"Trevor?"

He looked at me through his bangs and twitched his mouth into an almost-smile. The pail slipped from his fingers and clanked against the floor. Somewhere nearby, my attackers continued screaming and cursing, but I ignored them as I climbed to my feet. They didn't sound in any condition to be of immediate danger. My joints creaked as I made my way toward Trevor. The effects of the drug were gone, washed from me by the water like they'd been mud on my skin, but the experience left my body a little worse for the wear.

Trevor's eyes followed my approach, though he didn't move. It reminded me of how he'd been in the cage with Poe: there but not there. Anger at the guardian angel brewed in my gut again but I suppressed it; more important things beckoned my worry.

"Trevor? Are you okay?"

When I was steps away from him, Trevor slumped as if all his bones dissolved. I caught him before he hit the floor, the effort of it straining my fatigued muscles.

"Come on," I grunted. "Let's get you out of here."

Let's get you home, I wanted to say, but didn't, unsure if the possibility existed.

I regarded Marty and Tony, both of them in varying states of agony. Marty writhed on the floor like the world's worst break dancer while Tony sat at a table banging his head rhythmically on its surface. Neither looked like a threat, and still no sign of Todd.

The effort of dragging Trevor toward the door took all my remaining energy, but we made it. I leaned him against the wall, using my shoulder to prop him up as I spun the knob and swung the door open.

Cool air which smelled of neither alley-waste nor spilled beer wafted against my face. It held a flowery odor. I threw Trevor's arm over my shoulders, wrapped mine around his waist and wrestled him through the doorway taking care not to bump his limp body or lolling head against the frame.

I watched my feet to keep from tripping over anything as we crossed the threshold. Instead of stepping onto the sidewalk outside Sully's Tavern, my loafers touched yellow carpet of the durable variety designed to withstand the tread of many feet. I looked up.

The room we'd entered made me realize the smell wasn't the fresh aroma of spring flowers, but the manufactured scent of burning incense.

We were in a church.

No, not a church. *The* church.

Crap.

Chapter
Thirty-Three

H ALF-A-MINUTE HAD PASSED SINCE Icarus faded from sight and Trevor disappeared from the cage with a pop of rushing air and a slop of water from the pail he'd picked up a second before. Poe stared at the wet spot on the grubby straw; it was the first time since she'd found Trevor that he'd seemed remotely lucid. She was thankful but worried and prayed silently that he'd end up with Icarus.

Ric. I have to remember to call him Ric.

After Trevor disappeared, Poe killed time pacing the cage. She kicked straw aside, looking for a trap door in the bottom of the pen through which she might escape but found none. She wandered to the bars and looked out at the gray-white mist roiling in the space the other cages recently occupied, the blank spot where a forest grew not so long ago. If she did find a trap door or another way out of the cage, she'd likely be safer staying put.

This was limbo, a place where she'd been put on pause. She'd been in places like this before and knew the mist held far worse places than the confines of her cell. The same mist as this lurked at the bottom of Abaddon's pit, the same mist concealed horrors too much even for the residents of Hell.

Poe shuddered and strained to keep her teeth from chattering.

With the straw-kicking and mist-searching done, both yielding nothing, she sank down to the floor and sat cross-legged. Waiting.

Waiting for what?

She didn't know.

She hung her head and looked at her hands in her lap, watched her fingers fiddle with each other like a science experiment over which she had no control. To prove to herself it wasn't the case, she made them stop.

How did this happen to me?

Her life—or, more accurately, her after-life—went from misery to elation on the day, years ago, when Michael rescued her from Hell. During her time serving as a Carrion, she'd felt like every soul she retrieved and sent to Hell ripped away a piece of her own to go with it. The years spent doing it came close to ruining her. Then Michael came along, took her away, and she thought Hell done with. Never expected to be back.

Michael.

She closed her eyes and replayed the harvesting of Sister Agnes' soul. All these years she—and higher powers, too, it seemed—thought Azrael killed the nun to keep her soul for himself. Clearly, Michael's hand touched her, released her from the mortal world.

But why?

"You're not crying, are you?"

The words startled Poe. She drew a surprised breath and looked up at the woman standing in front of her. Even in the dreary, overcast world of the limbo, the silver stud shone from the spot between her lower lip and chin.

Poe stood. "What are you doing here?"

Piper shrugged. "Don't know. One minute I was in my own cage, then the mist came and I ended up in here with you, watching you curled up on the ground, mewling."

"I wasn't crying."

"I would be if I were you."

"What does that mean?"

Piper sauntered to the bars and looked out at the swirling fog contemplatively. "Think about it: he can only take one soul back."

Poe stood erect, muscles tensed and teeth clenched, waiting for the other woman to continue.

"Forget the priest and his flunkies. And those other two fellows, whoever they are."

"Tony was his soccer coach," Poe said, a surge of pride swelling her chest because she knew this about Icarus and Piper didn't. "The other is named Orlando. Like the city."

"Whatever. He wouldn't choose any of them over his son."

"Azrael said he wasn't one of the choices." Poe's voice trailed off at the end of her statement, saddened by its content.

He's here because of me.

"Maybe, but we both know he'll be the first choice if he can be, which leaves us here."

She gestured toward the fog.

"If it means Trevor is safe, I'll stay."

"How noble. But what should worry you more is if the boy really is off the table. How will you fare when Icarus' choice is between the treacherous bird Poe, his mother and," she faced Poe, her lips pulled up in a devious smile, "his lover."

"His—?"

Piper nodded, raised an eyebrow as if daring Poe to argue the point. She didn't. Instead, her shoulders drooped and she looked away.

Michael. Trevor. Icarus. I've lost them all.

Piper laughed, the sound dull and lifeless as the mist surrounding the cage deadened it. Hearing the sound made Poe look up. Seeing the mirth on Piper's face—in this place and at her expense—drove the despair and feelings of loss from her instantly. Anger filled the spaces it left behind, sending energy down her limbs and coursing through her head.

She remembered the boys who started her along this path, the things they did in the shed in the woods and hated them. She recalled Michael's hand brushing the nun's stomach. Not knowing why he would do such a thing frustrated her. Trevor's face came to mind and what the boy had been through because of her brought embarrassment.

I had no choice. I was pushed into it.

Piper's laugh continued, the sounds falling from her lips to be stomped into submission by the mist.

If she didn't bring Icarus here, none of this would have happened.

A vein at Poe's temple pulsed. The chords in her neck tightened. Her hands clenched into fists. Her next thought caught her off guard.

And now Icarus loves another, not me.

The anger and hatred, frustration and embarrassment exploded a scream from her lips and her legs launched her at the so-called angel.

Piper's breath left her lungs with a satisfying whoosh as Poe's shoulder contacted her midsection. They collapsed to the floor of the cage, rolled in the straw jockeying for position and leverage and came to a stop with Piper on the bottom struggling for breath. Poe grabbed her by both wrists, pinned her to the floor.

"Why? Why did you do this? Why didn't you just leave me alone?"

Piper glared up at her, silent and seething.

"You're no angel," Poe said, anger smothering her words. "You were never an angel."

"Maybe not, but neither are you anymore."

Piper's words hit Poe like she'd slapped her across the face. She stared down at her, shocked at the thought, before shaking herself free of the other woman's words.

"Icarus will take me back, not you."

She let go of Piper's left wrist and cocked her arm back, her slender fingers—what Icarus once called 'piano-players fingers'—curled into a fist. Piper brought her arm up across her cheek to protect herself from the impending blow.

"That is enough, ladies."

Poe looked up, fist still pulled back ready to strike, and saw the man standing outside the bars of the cage. Mist swirled around him, partially concealing his face, but Poe had spent enough of her time over the past years staring at that face to recognize the archangel under any conditions.

She bared her teeth and leaped from Piper, hands grasping for Michael.

Chapter
Thirty-Four

THE CHURCH LOOKED TO have recovered from the explosion which left it a pile of rubble. Neat rows of wooden pews lined the room; the marble altar gleamed; the organ sat awaiting a talented set of fingers to coax hymns from its pipes. Even the bibles and hymnals I'd seen burned and shredded were intact and interspersed at regular intervals. I wondered what might be written on the pages of a bible in Hell.

"Hello?"

My voice echoed into the high ceiling but no one answered. I put my arm around Trevor's waist and dragged him across the threshold. The stoup on the wall by the door contained a fluid looking more like blood than holy water but I didn't stop to examine it. Other things around the church were not quite right, either: the pipes of the organ stood askew, shadows of dirty footprints showed on the carpet, and termite trails marred the wooden pews.

Hell's version of the church.

I hauled Trevor to the closest seat and set him down as gently as possible. His head lolled to the side then fell forward until his chin rested on his chest. I laughed a little to myself thinking about how many people spent their Sundays looking exactly like this at the back of the church drooling on their Sunday best. My amusement dissipated quickly at the sound of a step behind me.

Here we go.

I straightened, fists clenched at my sides, and turned expecting to find Marty or Tony had followed me from Hell-Sully's. Instead, I looked into my mother's face. She wore the whole nuns' get-up—black hood, white bib, black dress—and the sight of her startled me. When you're expecting a fat, drunk guy and you get a fully decked out nun, it catches you off guard.

"Mother?"

She looked past me at Trevor slumped in the pew. I glanced back at him, too. He'd slid down a little but held his own.

"Is this...?"

"Trevor."

She touched her lips with her fingers and stared, eyes wide.

"My grandson?"

I nodded.

"Yeah. I guess not many nuns get to say that, do they?"

I felt bad for having said it as soon as the words left my mouth. Would it remind her of how awful it must have been for her to have me? What must a pregnant nun have gone through? She probably had it worse than a priest accused of abusing a child—at least they were used to that. The thought made me look over my shoulder for a quick survey of the church.

Where's Father Dominic?

"I wouldn't change a thing, Icarus."

Did she read my thoughts or infer them from my sarcasm? Could have been either. In my after-death, my thoughts had been read by more people—angels—than I felt comfortable with, one more didn't matter.

My mother stepped forward and crouched in front of my son.

"Trevor," she whispered into his face.

He didn't react.

She shifted herself to perch on the edge of the pew beside him and put her hand on his cheek. Nothing happened for a few seconds and impatience built in my gut—Azrael and the boy hadn't given me a deadline, but I felt like time grew short. My lead was shrinking, my deficit growing; I felt the need to get away as soon as possible.

I opened my mouth to hurry her along, but the flutter of Trevor's eyelids interrupted me. His eyes opened and he gazed at the nun seated beside him as she took her hand away from his face. Trevor licked his lips like a man desperately in need of water, then pivoted his head toward me. His eyes lit up at the sight of me and his lips moved.

I'm not a very good lip reader but the lack of words coming from his mouth forced me into the role.

"Dad," his lips said without sound.

I smiled.

"Trevor," I replied, though I chose to actually make a noise.

He looked to my mother and back. His lips moved again but still made no sound.

"What's wrong with him?"

My mother shook her head minutely but said nothing, leaving me feeling either deaf or the only one amongst us with the ability to speak. I knelt in front of Trevor, hands on his knees, and looked up at him.

"Say something."

I gave him a gentle shake as if he was one of those toy cows that moo when you jostle them. His lips moved again but he neither mooed nor spoke.

"Trevor."

My mother put her hand over mine, and when I faced her, she was looking at me with even more sadness in her eyes than usual.

"He has been through much."

At least I'm not the last guy in the world with a voice.

Trevor's eyes flickered back and forth between us with the smallest hint of realization showing in them. Worry fluttered in my chest.

What have I done to him.

"It'll be okay, Trev. I'll get you out of here."

I stood and a knot threatened my calf but I shook it out before it took hold. After another survey of the church—the image in the stained glass window showed a distinctly more pornographic version of a not-so-virgin Mary and the Christ-on-the-cross leered like the Joker in a Batman comic—I offered Trevor my hand.

"We have to get out of here."

He accepted my help while my mother remained perched on the edge of the pew looking up at us. Her lips pulled into a smile tinged with pain.

"Come with us."

She shook her head, the white cotton bib of her habit brushing against the black tunic.

"No, I told you already."

"But why not?"

She looked down at her hands in her lap, studied the way her fingers smoothed the creases in her tunic before looking up again and answering.

"I don't deserve to be anywhere else."

"Bullshit."

She fixed me with a look that reminded me of Sister Mary-Therese, the kind of look meant to remind me nuns don't like swearing.

Too bad.

"What happened wasn't your fault," I said.

"Wasn't it?"

"No, it wasn't." I hesitated, examined her expression. "Was it?"

She shrugged, looked back at her lap again, then forced herself to keep her eyes on mine.

"One can always say no."

"To an archangel? Do you really believe that?"

Trevor shifted at my side but I dismissed the movement as an active teen tired of standing in one spot. Instead, I concentrated on my mother, awaited her answer. I thought of my encounter with Piper in a cave in Hell. Could I have said no to her?

I didn't want to.

Maybe I knew what she meant more than I wanted to let myself believe.

"Guilt isn't the only reason, is it?" I asked.

She shook her head. Her eyes looked glossy, as though she teetered on the edge of tears but held them back.

"You love him."

"Yes."

The word held laughter and happiness, a joy I didn't expect in her voice. The bastard angel-of-death took her from the world and condemned her to live for eternity in Hell, and here she was, happy. Didn't make sense. Shouldn't she be angry? Pissed off in the highest degree? I was.

Trevor shuffled his feet beside me, runners rubbing on stained carpet.

Neither my mother nor I shifted our gazes and the longer I looked into her eyes, the more I saw the love she felt for Azrael. I didn't understand it, but there it was. I began to understand my anger came from how I felt about her being taken from the world, and her feelings had nothing to do with mine. I might go to the end of my days hating Azrael for taking my mother away, but in the end, she was happy. Probably happier than if he hadn't. I sensed an apology bubbling up at the back of my throat so I clamped my lips shut to make sure it didn't escape.

I wasn't quite ready to give up my anger.

Trevor moved again and this time my mother glanced away. When she did, her eyes widened and the flicker of love I'd seen in them disappeared. Not what you expect from a grandmother gazing upon her grandson.

Crap.

I felt the hand on my shoulder and caught the whiff of singed hair before turning my head. With the pressure of the touch on me and the odor in my nostrils, I didn't really need to look to see who'd taken Trevor's place beside me.

"Father Dominic," I said doing my best to sound nonchalant. He stood close, invading my personal space. Trevor looked on from the other side of him, safe for now, it seemed. Dominic smiled his sharp-toothed, blood-smeared smile. "What are you doing here?"

"You have to take me back."

"Haven't we already had this conversation?"

His grip tightened; I gritted my teeth, determined not to show pain.

"Let me rephrase," the hellish priest said through clenched teeth. "You *will* take me with you."

I glanced past him at Trevor who had backed away a couple of steps, increasing his margin of safety slightly.

Good boy.

"Let me rephrase, also: no."

The muscles of his jaw flexed beneath the medium-rare skin of his face and I swear the bumps on is forehead—horns doing their best to force their way through?—grew a little. If he'd been a cartoon, steam would have spewed from his ears. The thought almost made me giggle but the way he grabbed me by the front of my shirt and shook me like a rat in the jaws of a terrier loosened the expression from my face.

"Take me," he screamed, spittle flying against my cheeks.

The sides of my mouth pulled taut in an expression I probably wouldn't have characterized as a smile. Nasty smirk maybe. Vengeful grin, perhaps.

"Fuck you."

His forehead crunched against the bridge of my nose and pain exploded through my face. I jerked my head back already feeling warm blood on my top lip and had to blink a couple of times to clear my suddenly fuzzy vision.

"You will take me back with you. It's your fault I'm here and you will fix it."

I didn't feel anything like smiling this time but I did manage to shake my head which felt like it belonged to someone else. Given the pain, I wished whoever it belonged to would take it back.

The priest shook me again, rattling my teeth. I grabbed his wrists, tried to pull his hands from my shirt but his hold on me was too solid.

"Take. Me."

He punctuated each word with a solid jolt. My nose throbbed, blood ran into my mouth, I felt my brain slap against the inside of my skull. If I didn't make him stop, it might end up falling out of my ear. Turns out having your thinker rattled around against your cranium isn't the ideal situation for coming up with clever plans, so I continued attempting to pry his fingers away.

No luck.

The priest's eyes bulged in their sockets, his lips pulled back from his teeth far enough to reveal tattered gums and shit stuck between his molars. He breathed rotten breath into my face making me gag.

"Icarus Fell," he said with an ominous tone. "Take me to Heaven or face the consequences."

My mind flashed back through all the consequences this man had doled out in my youth: locking me in the lightless closet, forcing me to stand in the sign of the cross for hours, the slender switch he used to punish me when I did something against God. Once he fashioned a crown of thorns out of a length of barbed wire he'd purchased for the purpose and made me wear it all day.

Enough of his fucking consequences.

"Kiss. My. Ass."

The expression on his face took on a fleeting aspect of surprise, but rage quickly overcame it. Saliva spilled from the corner of his mouth and I watched it trace a path along the line of his jaw and down his chin. I shouldn't have allowed myself the distraction.

The priest threw me across the room where I slammed into a pew, tipping it backward and banging my nose. Pain blinded me. I righted myself and tried to blink away the throb in my face as Father Dominic bore down on me. My faulty vision clouded his features into a smear of flesh punctuated by dark holes where his eyes should have been. He held something I couldn't make out in his hand, something he brandished in the manner of a man meaning to strike.

I brought an arm up defensively, already knowing it wouldn't be enough to protect me but unable to do anything else. He loomed over me, probably enjoying the moment, until arms wrapped around him—one around his neck, one around the top of his head. Even through the cotton filling my head, I recognized the sleeper hold from my years enjoying the entertainment provided by the likes of Hulk Hogan and his wrestling cronies.

At least it was a sleeper hold until the arms twisted Father Dominic's head violently and snapped his neck with the dry pop of an old twig. The arms slipped away and the priest's limp body slouched to the floor.

I blinked again and stared into the startled face of my mother.

"Do I deserve to go to Heaven now?"

She lowered her eyes to look at the crumpled body of the priest. Did she know he'd loved her in a way a man-of-the-cloth isn't meant to love anyone? Did she know the things he'd done to me?

I scrambled to my feet and looked past her at Trevor leaning on the pew, watching with wide eyes. He shivered but looked otherwise unharmed. I breathed a relieved sigh and looked back at my mother still staring at the priest.

"It's not your fault. None of it." I reached out to touch her shoulder but she pulled away. "I can still take you."

"I don't want to go."

She'd already made it clear, but hearing the words stung anyway. I'd finally met my mother and she didn't want to be with me because she'd found someone else more important to her. Difficult to accept, even given the small amount of time we'd been together. I opened my mouth to protest, to beg, but she cut me off.

"You have to go now."

She finally looked away from the body of Father Dominic but wouldn't meet my eyes. Instead, she glanced around the church as if looking for someone hiding behind a pew or crouched behind the altar. I followed her gaze and saw no one, but the church had changed. A crack appeared in the wall, the pews showed signs of charring. While Christ's shit-eating grin remained, his cross hung askew.

"But we—"

"Go," she shouted and the ground shook beneath my feet.

Quite the special effect.

But it wasn't. The church walls quaked, pews rattled across the floor. Bricks toppled onto the keyboard of the organ, hammering out a desperate, discordant tune. I pushed aside the throbbing in my face, pushed past my mother and grabbed Trevor's arm, but I didn't know where to go or how to get away. The whore-Mary in the stained glass window laughed at me, the joker-Jesus toppled to the floor. Without thinking, I pulled Trevor past the altar and headed for the rear entrance—it saved us once before, why not again?

As we passed through the tapestry, I glanced back. My mother stood over Father Dominic's body watching us, making sure we got away.

And then the roof of the church collapsed.

The concussion of it hitting the floor pushed us into a hall no longer a hall. We stumbled and fell, skidding in red-orange dirt, scraping our palms. I quickly collected myself, got to my feet and pulled Trevor up.

I looked around at the circle of cages and saw Michael standing by Poe's. Azrael and the boy stood twenty feet to his left. Two archangels and that damn kid, together in Hell.

This can't be good.

Chapter
Thirty-Five

MICHAEL STEPPED AWAY FROM Poe's reach and her chest slammed painfully against the bars forcing a grunt from her. The tips of her fingers brushed the front of his red shirt and electricity crackled through the air.

"Now, now, Poe. Be calm."

She bared her teeth, a small growl rumbling at the back of her throat.

"I saw what you did," she said, tears threatening at the edge of her words. "I saw it."

"You have gotten yourself in quite a pickle here, haven't you?"

Poe stared at the archangel, seething as he spoke as if he hadn't heard what she said. Michael looked past her over her shoulder.

"Hello, Piper."

"Michael."

Poe looked back at the woman. She sat on the straw rubbing her wrists where Poe had gripped them.

"You know each other?"

"Yeah, you might say that," Piper responded as she stood and brushed straw off her backside.

Poe looked back to Michael.

"How...?"

"Piper followed a similar path to yours, didn't you Piper?"

The woman grunted in response.

"Similar but different," Michael continued. "The same but opposite."

Poe considered asking him to clarify but didn't. More pressing things needed clearing up.

"What are you doing here?"

"Oh, I am not here. An angel cannot be present in Hell."

Poe's breath caught in her throat.

If an angel can't be in Hell, doesn't that mean—

"Yes. Unfortunate, is it not? I really did like you, Poe. You were not the best guardian, but you followed orders with enthusiasm."

"Told you," Piper muttered.

Poe suppressed the urge to cross the cage and slap her. Instead, she remained pressed against the bars, arms hanging loose between them.

"But I—," she began before the archangel interrupted.

"Where is the boy?"

Poe paused a second, confused.

"What?"

"The boy, the son of Icarus. Where is he?"

"I...I don't know."

"She lost him again," Piper said. She moved to the side of the cage but kept out of Poe's reach.

"Again?"

"She's made a habit of losing him down here."

Poe glared at Piper; the woman smiled back.

"Truth hurt?"

One step of straw-littered cage floor passed beneath Poe's feet before Michael's angel-choir voice stopped her.

"Ladies, I do not have time for your quarrels. Do either of you know where the boy is?"

Poe looked back at the archangel, her stomach doing flips in her midsection. For years she revered this being, loved him in the way one loves an idol, but what she'd seen in Sister Mary-Therese's apartment—a touch she didn't see when it actually happened—brought an edge of nausea and suspicion.

"Why?"

Michael smiled. "The boy does not belong here. His time has not yet come."

Some of Poe's tension waned. Perhaps he'd come to take Trevor to safety. Still, the lingering memory of his touch on the birth-giving nun's stomach clouded her thoughts. Could he be trusted?

"Why did you do it?"

Michael raised an eyebrow but said nothing.

"I know you can read my thoughts. Why did you do it? Why did you kill Sister Agnes?"

The archangel didn't answer immediately and Poe clamped her jaw tight to keep nerves from chattering her teeth together. She wanted him to say she'd mis-seen the events in the apartment, tell her Azrael killed the nun to steal her soul for himself. She wanted Michael to return to the perfect picture she carried close to her heart: the tall, lambent doer-of-good who stood at God's side representing everything moral and righteous.

Pleasepleaseplease.

She stared into his face, at his golden eyes and his hair draped over his shoulders. So many times she'd looked at him like this and been mesmerized, unable to speak, move or form independent thought. She felt some of that now but a feeling approaching disgust tempered it.

Michael smiled and said nothing, but she thought she heard his answer in his lack of words.

"He didn't kill her," Piper said derisively. "You did."

Poe looked at her, surprised, mouth agape.

"No. I saw him."

"Everyone knows you took her soul."

"It was my job. I had no choice."

Piper took a step away from the bars toward Poe, lips curled in a smirk.

"Really? Is that what you tell Icarus?"

Poe's lips pressed into a colorless line as she struggled not respond to Piper's baiting but found herself unable to stop.

"He doesn't know," she said, her cheeks flushing at the memory of him standing by the doorway.

It wasn't real, it was an illusion, part of my Hell.

"Or so you think."

"No." Poe stepped away from the bars, closing the gap between her and Piper to less than ten feet. "I've never told him. I never told anyone."

"And yet he was there, wasn't he?"

"How do you know?"

Piper shrugged. "I know what he knows. If you'd refused, none of this would have happened."

"I had no choice," Poe said and glanced back at Michael for help. His smile was gone but his eyes shone as if he enjoyed their exchange. He offered no assistance.

"There's always a choice," Piper chided.

"No. They'd have punished me."

"Instead you allowed Sister Agnes to be punished. And Icarus. And Trevor and the others."

"No, I—"

"It's your fault. All of it."

"No." Poe forced the word through her gritted teeth.

"You could have stopped it. You could have saved them all."

Each woman took a step forward, further closing the gap. Piper glanced over Poe's shoulder at Michael, then looked back into her eyes, the smirk on her face expanding.

"Why don't you admit you fucked up. Your selfishness cost people their lives."

Piper's words poked Poe's heart, the truth in them catching her off guard. She may not have caused all this on purpose, but her actions—her own or those she was made to perform—were the first in a long string of cause and effect leading them all here to this place, this moment.

Poe's resolve quaked, her lip quivered.

She's right. I could have stopped it.

"It's my fault," she said, her voice merely a whisper.

"What?" Piper prompted.

"It's my fault," Poe repeated, louder this time. "I took the nun's soul. I could have kept all of this from happening."

"So it's true."

The familiar voice at her back made it feel as though her heart sank into her gut where the acid in her stomach immediately began the job of digesting it.

Icarus.

She didn't face him. The mish-mash of feelings in her—embarrassment, anger, sadness, love—made her head spin. She couldn't bear to see the look on Icarus' face, the disappointment she imagined in his eyes. Her head lolled forward in despair as she tried to sort through the emotions and use them to decide what to do next.

Then Piper laughed, not with humor, but a heartless, hurtful laugh. One emotion burst to the fore, making her decision for her: hatred.

Poe's fist connected with Piper's mouth driving the stud piercing the spot below her bottom lip hard into her teeth. Piper stumbled from the blow and Poe jumped her, driving her to the ground.

· · · ● · ● · ● · · · ·

"It's my fault. I took the nun's soul. I could have kept all of this from happening."

Poe's words entered my ear and echoed around my head, each ricochet adding to my anger. Michael looked toward me, then his eyes found Trevor and his expression changed.

"So it's true."

Poe didn't turn but I saw her body tense, her head droop. Next, I expected her to face me with apologetic puppy dog eyes seeking forgiveness but Piper laughed and Poe snapped. Her fist looped out and caught Piper in the jaw.

"No," I shouted as Piper staggered back a step.

Poe launched herself at my one-time lover and rode her to the ground. I took a step forward, thinking I might reach the cage and stop Poe before too much damage was done to either of them, but I walked directly into the brick wall of the archangel Michael. I didn't bother asking how he got from there to here so quickly—understanding the dynamics of angels was worse than figuring out quantum physics.

I bounced off his chest and looked up at him but his eyes were on Trevor standing behind me. A second later, I felt Trev's hand on my arm, pulling at my sleeve. I looked at him and the expression of fear on his face surprised me. Until now, he'd seemed unattached from the goings-on around him, but now he stared up into the archangel's face with a look like he thought the right hand of God was about to cuff him.

An alarm bell went off in my head and fatherly instinct I hadn't paid much attention to in far too long made me step between the angel and my son. I opened my mouth to ask Michael what he was doing here but was caught off guard when it sounded like someone else's voice came from my mouth.

"Michael."

It took a second to register someone else must be here—my voice didn't usually carry the deep resonance present in the word. I hadn't noticed Azrael standing a few yards to my left. I looked from one to the other, astounded by how much they looked alike. Other than hair color and attire, they could have been the same person.

Maybe they are.

"I was just leaving, brother." Disdain smothered his last word.

"Then leave."

I looked back toward Michael, but he'd already disappeared. Trevor's grip on my sleeve tightened, yanked at me once, then let go. I spun around and found out where Mikey went. He hugged Trevor around the chest, not a bear hug, but the way an uncle might embrace his favorite nephew. Only, in this case, the nephew looked terrified.

"What are you doing?" Some of Trevor's panic showed up in my voice.

"Keeping him safe from the likes of him," Michael answered gesturing toward Azrael with his chin.

"It is not me Icarus need worry about, is it, Michael?" Azrael said.

I glanced at the angel of death who'd moved closer without looking like a man who'd moved. His eyes gleamed like he knew something I didn't.

No shit, he's a deposed archangel. He knows a lot you don't, idiot.

"Worry about yourself, Icarus, not your son," Michael said. "I will take care of Trevor."

Behind me, I heard the sounds of fighting—scuffling, grunting, flesh contacting flesh—but ignored it. Trevor shook his head at Mikey's words, his look of panic holding steady as he reached out a hand toward me. His lips moved and he finally found his voice.

"Dad, he—"

Three things happened at once: I stretched out my hand and my fingers brushed Trevor's. In that instant of contact, a flash of shadowy figures in a churchyard came to my mind. It was my death, but this time there were four men. I recognized myself and the two hoodlums who killed me, but the fourth face eluded my view. It might have come clear if the second and third things didn't happen: Azrael jumped at Michael, diverting my attention from my son, and the blond archangel disappeared.

Trevor disappeared along with him.

Azrael's arms swung through empty air instead of grabbing Mike. I jumped forward irrationally thinking I might somehow grab hold of Trevor and bring him back. It didn't happen. Instead, my shoulder bumped Azrael's and the now-familiar shock which accompanied an angel's touch shot through me like someone soaked me with a hose and hooked me up to a car battery. My back teeth chattered together and I fell to the ground in a heap. I closed my eyes for what seemed like a second but might have been closer to eternity. When I opened them, I looked up into the face of the angel-of-death looming over me.

"The time has come," he said. "It is time to choose."

He offered his hand, but I wasn't falling for that again. When someone tricks you into touching a nine-volt battery to your tongue once, you don't intentionally do it again. Not without someone daring you or offering money, at least.

I climbed to my feet, all my muscles aching, and brushed orange-red dust off my clothes.

"Where did Mikey take my son?"

"I am sure he will be safe. I told you he did not belong here."

"But it's not his time to go to Heaven yet, either. Is it?"

Azrael acted like he didn't hear me. Typical archangel. Instead, he gestured toward the cages encircling us. They were all populated again, though every one of the occupants looked a little worse-for-wear.

"You can choose only one."

I breathed deep and ground my teeth together as I glanced from cage to cage.

Chapter Thirty-Six

FATHER DOMINIC SLOUCHED IN the farthest corner of the first cage, though it hardly appeared he needed anything to keep him from leaving. He looked more like a heap of old clothes than a man. I peered in at him, curious to see what damage he'd taken and only slightly disgusted with myself to find I hoped it was real bad. It was. His left arm was twisted at a grotesque angle, the dent in his skull was big enough to keep a small melon from rolling away.

"Not him, take me."

Marty's voice. He occupied a cage by himself rather than sharing with Todd like before. It seemed odd they weren't together, they'd become a package deal in my mind: Marty and Todd, Todd and Marty. Where you found Marty, you found Todd.

"You wanted to kill me," I said amending my path to take me to Marty.

"I was doing what I had to."

He glared at me, hands gripping the bars, drool running down his chin, the skin on his face reddened like he'd spent way too long at the beach. The man before me resembled the Marty I'd spent nights drinking away my life with, but in a distant-cousin kind of way. Like someone peeled his face off for a souvenir and left behind vague remnants. I cringed at the thought and started to walk away.

"Ric, come on. You don't know what it's like down here."

"Don't listen to him, Ric. I'm the one who was always there for you."

Todd populated the cage beside Marty's. It appeared he'd escaped the effects of Trevor's bucket of water, which explained why I'd lost track of him at Hell-Sully's—he'd been hiding.

"What the Hell did you ever do for me? You were a puppet. Marty may as well have taken a ventriloquist course to keep me from seeing his lips move every time you spoke."

My comment made Marty spew an abbreviated guffaw, but Todd looked as though I'd spit on the love letter he handed me.

"I didn't try to kill you."

"You didn't stop them, either."

His mouth opened and closed a couple of times like a suffocating fish. I moved on to the next cage while he found his voice and found Tony McSweeney slumped in the corner. He scrambled to his feet. I flipped him the bird and moved on.

Orlando Albert looked like a man clinging to life. The holes in his flesh had begun to rot around the edges; brownish blood and green-tinged pus oozed from his open wounds. The smell emanating from him made me crinkle my nose in disgust, reminding me of the head butt the priest so kindly gave me without asking for recompense. Considerate.

I touched my poor nose and flinched at the pain as I moved past the half-eaten drug dealer without pausing to make rude gestures at him. He was a bad man, but he already looked to have gotten what he deserved. Why waste a good bird flip?

The next cage must have been designed for a small animal, because it wasn't big enough for an adult to stand in. My mother sat cross-legged in the center, the black and white nun's garb she'd been wearing when I last saw her replaced by a gray, shapeless dress streaked with dirt. Her chin rested on her chest, her long hair was fallen forward hiding her face. I stopped in front of her and gripped the bars with both hands. The cage was small enough I could have reached in and touched her. I didn't.

"Mother." She didn't look up. There was blood on her hands. "Please."

She raised her head. As her hair fell away from her face, a few strands stuck to the tears streaking her cheeks. She peered into my eyes for a moment before speaking.

"Your face," she said reaching between the bars.

At first I pulled away. My nose hurt incredibly—much thanks to the drug dealer for reminding me—and didn't want her to touch it and remind me further. But, for some reason, I couldn't keep myself from her touch.

It might be the last time.

I leaned in and allowed her fingers to brush the bump that wasn't there before Father Dominic's introduced his forehead to the bridge of my nose. Pain shot through my face, but I didn't pull away. She moved her fingers to my forehead and laid her palm over my nose. My face throbbed. Beneath the pain, unnoticeable at first, a warmth kindled and spread, filling my nostrils, my sinuses. It overtook the pain until my mother's hand resting over my face felt like a gently applied hot water bottle.

When she took her hand away, I brought my own fingers to my nose, tested it. Both pain and bump were gone. I smiled at her and she did her best to return it but looked like she dealt with her own pain, though I expected it wasn't physical.

I felt it, too.

"Come with me."

She shook her head like she did before. "I belong here."

"She wants to stay," Azrael's all-male-choir voice sing-songed behind me.

I pivoted toward the sound of his voice and was surprised to find he stood only a few paces behind me.

"You did this to her," I said feeling a familiar anger building in my gut. "She's here because of you."

Azrael didn't answer. His eyes glowed, his hair moved as if blown by some unfelt breeze, but his expression remained neutral, unreadable. I felt my mother's hand on my shoulder.

"Don't blame him. Why I'm here is of no significance. I'm here and I shall stay."

I looked back to her, at the sadness in her eyes. This wasn't an easy decision for either of us, but it was out of my hands.

"Will I ever see you again?"

"Who knows what the future holds."

She drew her hand back through the bars, settled back into the tried and true 'criss-cross applesauce'. It made me smile a little.

"Take care of yourself, M—." I realized I didn't know what to call her. All the forms of 'mother' felt unfamiliar and uncomfortable on my lips.

"Azrael takes care of me."

I nodded and reluctantly moved on to the next cage.

Poe had climbed off Piper, allowing her to regain her feet. They stood on opposite sides of the enclosure, eyeing each other warily. A trickle of blood ran down Piper's chin from her swollen lower lip.

"Icarus," she said, the word distorted by the swelling.

I didn't respond, instead looking at Poe before turning my attention to Piper. Memories swirled through my head, confusing me, throwing a haze over my ability to make a decision. Only two possibilities remained: my guardian angel whose loyalty was in question and a woman who'd come out of nowhere with uncertain motives.

How can I decide?

Chapter
Thirty-Seven

I STARED AT THE two of them, blank faced. Behind me, I felt Azrael's presence as he looked on, waiting for me to choose who would go back with me and who would remain in Hell, and I wondered if he preferred one choice over the other. Did one soul hold more value to him? Should that be part of my decision?

"She killed your mother," Piper said pointing across the cage at Poe.

"She's a Carrion," Poe responded.

I stared at Piper for a few seconds then moved my head without taking my eyes off her so Azrael would know I spoke to him.

"Is that true?"

I heard a movement, a brush of fabric, and the cage in front of me disappeared. I stood at the corner of a busy street, traffic rushing past me. I'd been here before, when Mike showed me what happened when I wasn't available to do my job. Directly across the street, the woman gripped her son's hand while the boy held a red toy car concealed in the other. I wanted to look away but couldn't.

I've seen this before. Why send me here?

Curiosity kept my eyes on the woman and child.

The boy moved his hand to look at his prize and it slipped from his grip and fell into the street. He released his mother's hand, leaned forward, and I saw something I didn't see before—he could have reached the toy safely. A black-clad figure I hadn't noticed standing behind them pressed a finger to his back, over-balancing him.

I knew what happened next but found myself rushing across the busy road anyway, avoiding cars as the mother threw her son to safety and took the impact meant for him. She hit the post, spun a circle, the collision jarring her soul free of her body. Within seconds, the Carrion appeared at her side, gripped her arm to lead her away, but his time I was close enough to see the Carrion's face.

This time I saw Piper.

I reached out to wrest the woman's soul from her, my fingers brushing the back of the soul's arm, then I was back in the clearing surrounded by cages, my arm stuck between the bars, reaching for Piper. She stared at me, a look of confusion on her face.

"It's not true," she said. "Whatever you saw, it's not true."

I glared at her, not knowing what to say or believe. Even with the fat lip, her beauty touched me, triggered pleasant memories of the cave, her body, her flesh pressed against mine. I remembered the straw stuck in her hair when our lovemaking concluded.

And I remembered the choice wasn't completely mine.

I'd been a willing participant who didn't really have a choice. I remembered how Piper appeared out of nowhere, both that time and others, like someone who knew their way around Hell. I thought of how often she'd come with news of Trevor yet did nothing to stop it.

"It's true."

"No!"

She rushed me, taking me by surprise. I stumbled back but she would have gotten her hands on me if Poe didn't intercept her. They toppled to the floor and rolled, bodies slamming against the bars of the cage.

And then Piper's head slammed against the floor.

The fingers of both Poe's hands intertwined with Piper's hair as she pistoned the woman's head up and down. Piper grasped at Poe's wrists, writhed and fought beneath her, but the guardian angel's strength proved too much and her efforts diminished.

"Stop it!"

My words had no effect and I wondered if she controlled her actions or if other influences made her act this way. I turned to Azrael.

"Stop this," I hissed.

"I am doing nothing."

He looked right into my eyes when he said it and I believed him. I didn't want to, didn't think I should, but something sold me on his sincerity.

But that would mean...

I didn't want to finish the thought. The pile of evidence against Poe grew and grew and an increasing part of me believed it. Still, a chunk of my brain—and my heart—fought against the evidence, refused to accept my guardian angel as anything other than the innocent, sweet-faced being she professed to be.

"Poe. Stop, please."

This time she stopped and looked at me, her expression far from innocent. Her lips were pulled back from her teeth; the look in her eyes bordered on maniacal. The face of a person doing violence with intent. I gasped at the sight and the sound of breath entering my lungs seemed to bring her back to the world. The hardness in her expression disappeared. She looked down at Piper's head in her hands and immediately removed her fingers from her hair as if she didn't realize they'd been there.

Poe stood and stumbled back a step.

"What...? I..."

"Poe."

She faced me. Her blond hair, usually neat but without style, in disarray; sweat stuck her shirt to her chest heaving with the effort she'd expended. She glanced from me to Azrael, then Piper, then back to me again. Realization crept across her face, then sadness.

"Fair is fair," Azrael intoned behind me and suddenly I was standing on a street corner, watching as a man fell from a ladder and impaled himself on a garden gnome.

When I returned to the clearing, I stared at Poe and she looked back it me knowing what Azrael had revealed.

"You could have taken him to Heaven."

As I gazed upon her, memories of the other things she'd done came to me without the help of the angel of death, beginning with her not ensuring I did my job when sent to harvest the priest's soul and ending with her taking my mother's soul to Hell.

"It is time."

This time, the voice wasn't Azrael's. I turned to see the boy standing beside the archangel. Behind them, the others all stood at the front of their cages, hands gripping the bars in anticipation, all except my mother who remained cross-legged and regarding her lap.

"Who are you?"

The boy smiled and, for an instant, looked like any other mischievous ten-year-old.

"You know who I am, Icarus Fell. Decide."

I looked away, worried that if I didn't take the opportunity when I had the chance, I may never look away. My gaze swept across the cages: the priest, Marty, Todd, Tony, Orlando. Three of them deserved Hell no matter whether I felt responsible for their presence here or not. This was the consequence for being an abusive priest, a pedophile or a drug dealer. An argument might be made for the other two, at least up until they tried to kill me.

And would the world really miss a couple of drunks?

My eyes passed over my mother, her head still hung refusing to meet my gaze. I'd already beat that horse to death, which left the two so-called guardian angels.

I turned to look at Poe standing over Piper's prone form.

· · • •· • • · ·

Poe's heart jumped when Piper rushed at Icarus.

Ric.

Her body reacted without thought, without prompting, tackling her before Piper got her hands on him. They hit the floor then slammed painfully against the bars, Poe ending up on top of the woman.

She didn't remember much after that.

Her vision smeared to a blur and she saw nothing through the mist it created in her brain. The world disappeared, sounds disappeared. She pumped her arms up and down, vaguely felt something in her hands, the tremor of impact shaking its way up her wrists. The world seeped slowly back into her mind and she realized there was a person at the end of her arms.

Aaron Baxter. Or his cousin.

The world remained fuzzy enough for her to convince herself she gripped one of the hateful boys until words finally penetrated the veil.

"Poe. Stop. Please."

Her vision cleared and she looked down into Piper's face, her lip swollen, eyes rolled back into her head. Poe looked toward the voice, snarling and defensive until she saw Icarus standing outside the bars. His expression showed shock, disgust, disappointment, and it pulled her completely back to reality.

Poe jumped to her feet and faltered back a step, eyes on the woman lying pressed against the bars of the cage.

What have I done?

"What? I..."

"Poe."

She looked at Icarus. Azrael stood behind him, arms crossed, a frightful, impatient look on his face. She glanced at Piper who hadn't moved since Poe removed herself from atop her and wondered how badly she'd hurt the other woman. Not wanting to think about it, she returned her attention to Icarus, but Azrael had said something and Icarus' face went blank. All the blurry anger disappeared from her, shouldered aside by regret and sadness. She knew what Azrael was showing him.

"You could have taken him to Heaven," Icarus said a moment later.

Poe blinked and a tear ran down her cheek. She wanted to wipe it away but resisted.

Ric. Remember to call him Ric.

Somehow, during the fraction of a second she'd closed her eyes, the boy appeared beside Azrael and told Icarus it was time.

Time for what?

Icarus and the boy exchanged words but Poe didn't understand what they said, then Icarus looked at the people in the other cages. She knew them: the priest, the drinking buddies, the soccer coach, the drug dealer; all of them people from his past who ended up in Hell because of Icarus' actions or inaction.

Except his mother. She's here because of me.

The elements came together in her head like the answer to a puzzle finally becoming clear. These people, her and Piper, Azrael.

Decide, the boy said.

Icarus was to choose who would remain in Hell and who returned with him.

Poe breathed a shuddering sigh and peered down at Piper again. The woman's eyes were closed, breath shallow; a line of blood ran from the corner of her mouth. Poe's gaze followed the thin trail of blood as it etched the edge of her jaw line and disappeared into her hair. Any hope she'd held of returning with Icarus, of escaping Hell a second time, seemed to follow a similar path: thinning, fading, disappearing.

Why did I do that?

She'd been protecting Icarus, didn't he see? Did he know she'd done it for him?

Would it matter?

She raised her head and saw Icarus looking at her without forgiveness or understanding of what she'd done for him, now or in the past. For decades she protected him, watched over him, kept trouble from him time and time again before he knew she existed.

But you couldn't keep muggers from killing him, could you?

He continued to stare without speaking.

"Decide," the boy said again.

It's not my fault, Poe wanted to say. *I did as I was told. Forgive me. Forgive me.*

"Trevor is safe?" Icarus said over his shoulder, eyes on Poe.

"Your son is no longer in Hell," Azrael replied.

Icarus nodded.

"Then I've made my decision."

The hair on the back of Poe's neck prickled and goose bumps crept along her arms. She attempted her sweet smile, to appear the shy young woman Icarus met in the coffee shop, but so much had happened since then. Even Poe had to admit that girl no longer existed. She tried anyway.

Icarus turned his back on her.

"I'm not taking any of them."

Poe's heart sank.

Chapter
Thirty-Eight

T HE BOY RUBBED HIS chin like a man considering what to do—an action not often seen from a ten-year-old boy.

"If you do not choose, I will," the boy said. "And you may not like the soul I send back with you."

"I didn't say I wouldn't choose. I said I'm not taking any of them." I gestured toward the cages in case the little bastard didn't know who I meant by 'them'.

"I see. You have someone else I mind."

No shit, Sherlock.

I held my tongue and nodded instead.

"Who?"

"A policeman who shouldn't be here, a good man you took as payment when I rescued another soul."

"Stole another soul, I believe you mean."

"Whatever. Let him go."

"I know the man of whom you speak."

I glared at him, awaiting his answer. When it didn't come immediately, my eyes wandered to the cages behind him. All my past acquaintances were gone, the cages empty but for straw scattered on the floors. Rusted bars, flaking paint and straw—no priest, no mother, nothing. Behind me, I thought I heard a sob escape Poe's throat, a small sound that might have been my imagination.

After a few more seconds, the boy tilted his head toward Azrael. The archangel strode between two of the cages and disappeared, the cages fading away immediately after. I spun around to see if the cage holding Poe and Piper disappeared, too. It hadn't. Poe's glistening eyes held mine, resignation plain on her face.

"Icarus," she said, a tinge of pleading in her voice. I turned away.

Azrael stood directly in front of me, Detective Williams at his side looking disheveled as always, but now surprised as well.

How does he do that?

"Detective," I said and gave him a nod.

"What's going on?"

"I'm getting you out of here."

His expression changed instantly to relief, but it didn't stay long. It must take more than death and a visit to Hell to squeeze the police-ness out of a man, because a look of suspicion crossed his mug next.

"Really?"

I looked at Azrael and raised my eyebrows, passing the question along to the fallen archangel. He nodded once then returned to the boy's side.

"Really," I said.

Azrael and the boy watched us in silence and I swear a little sadness dulled the usual glow in Azrael's eye. But why? He said he wanted my freedom and now I had it, and he got two Carrions to add to his stable in return. Nothing to be sad about, right?

It's your imagination. Take the detective and get the fuck out of here before someone changes their mind.

The boy, on the other hand, waited with excited impatience, like he'd woken early on Christmas morning and had to wait to open his gifts, though I'd guess Christmas was one of the less popular holidays in Hell.

"Come on."

I strode away, careful not to look into the cage at Poe and Piper as I did. Detective Williams fell into step beside me.

"Icarus."

Poe's voice. I ignored her, my choice made. What's the old saying? You've pissed in your own bed, now you have to sleep in it, or some such thing? Still, it wasn't easy walking away. She'd been the most constant person in my life since I died.

"Icarus. Please."

The desperation in Poe's voice sank into my chest, compressed my heart until it became difficult to breathe, but I neither stopped nor slowed.

She's the reason why all those people got sent to Hell. She set me up.

"Icarus."

She nearly got my son condemned to Hell for eternity.

"Ric."

Detective Williams caught me by the sleeve, stopping me, and pointed back toward Poe, her desperation apparently affecting him. I gestured with my head, indicating we had to go. He must have seen my anger at my one-time guardian angel, my determination not to look back. I felt the detective's eyes on me but he said nothing.

"If I take her, you stay."

The first time I met the detective, I felt he was a good man despite the fact he'd wanted to see me in jail. To take Poe back, I'd have to give the devil his due, and there was only one other soul left. He'd seen enough of Hell to stay prudently silent.

"Ric, please."

She was crying. It almost made me look back and reconsider my options. Trevor was safe—I had to trust he was—and the others were gone. I was leaving Hell with a man who'd hunted me for months, determined to make me pay for crimes I didn't commit.

Didn't I?

I didn't wield the knife that killed Marty, Todd and the others, but I may as well have. If I'd done what I was told, none of this would have happened. If Poe did her job and kept me to my task, they'd be alive and I wouldn't have come to Hell to save a bunch of people who, for the most part, either didn't want to be saved or didn't deserve to be.

Which of us deserved blame?

Both. If she'd done her job, if I'd done mine. I could play the game in my head for eternity, but I didn't think Azrael and the boy would let me.

I gave in and glanced back. Poe stood against the cage, hands gripping the bars. Piper lay on the ground behind her, unconscious or maybe dead for good; Azrael stood beside the boy to her right. The expression on my one-time guardian angel's face did its best to convince me not to leave her. And it came close. Pain and desperation, a look like her best friend died while running over her dog.

She didn't say anything. She didn't use her angelic abilities to sway my decision, didn't beg or plead or illuminate with the golden glow capable of making people do anything she wanted. She just looked at me with eyes reflecting hurt beyond description. For a split second, I saw her shy, endearing smile; I remembered her love of all things sweet and the way she was always nervous, unable to look me in the eye.

No problem doing that now. She'd changed, the charade gone. But even after all the wrongs I'd uncovered and all the blame I found to lay on her, I knew I'd miss sitting in the Denny's watching her struggle a thick chocolate shake through a straw.

It would pass.

"You deserve to stay," I said and led the detective away.

He dragged his feet to slow me but I kept him moving. I heard Poe sob once.

"Icarus," she called, the sadness and tears gone from her voice. Instead, resignation and disappointment weighed her words down. "Everything I did, I did for you."

I pulled Detective Williams along by the sleeve of his rumpled suit jacket, his resistance fading, and did my best not to listen to Poe's words following us like desperate puppies.

"Things aren't always what they seem."

We increased our pace, not knowing where to go but feeling the necessity of getting away: from Poe, from the angel-of-death and from the boy—especially the boy. We kept walking, Poe kept talking, her words fading with distance. She said something about Michael that I ignored like everything else, something about my mother that piqued my interest. We walked on, the detective silent at my side.

After a while, the ground shivered beneath my feet. I stopped.

"Did you feel that?"

"What?"

Nothing for a few seconds. I thought it either my imagination or a volcano erupting in Chile. An instant before we began moving, it happened again, more noticeable this time.

"Felt that."

We set out and the ground shook a third time, a fourth. We increased our pace to a speed walk.

"Icarus Fell."

The words boomed around us, echoing in spite of the lack of anything for them to echo off.

"Ric," I corrected.

Something made me stop, literally. I didn't want to, but I had no choice. Detective Williams skidded to a halt beside me. With no desire to do so but with the same feeling of having no control, I spun around to look back.

No more cage holding Poe and Piper. Azrael and the boy stood twenty yards behind us, as if they'd been sneaking along, following us. Behind them, the elephant-beast I'd seen after the conclusion of my fall stomped its feet periodically, waved its trunk.

No elephant-thing cage, either.

"You didn't think it would be easy leaving Hell, did you?" the boy asked.

I saw the twinkle in his eyes, the shift of expression from the boy waiting to open the gifts to the satisfied look after decorative paper is torn to shreds. Bitter saliva filled my mouth and I gulped it around a lump forming in my throat. I searched desperately for a flippant remark, a vaguely funny quip to relieve the sudden feeling of dread permeating my muscles. I came up short.

Small gestures can say much: Azrael's eyes darted toward the boy and he shook his head. The boy ignored him and dipped his chin to his chest, nodding in our direction.

"Run, Icarus," Azrael yelled, his eyes on the boy. "Run."

I hesitated a second, stunned, then the beast charged, orangutan-like hands at the ends of its six stumpy legs beating a rhythm on the ground that shuddered up my legs and into my soul.

Detective Williams grabbed me by the arm and dragged me toward the forest.

Chapter
Thirty-Nine

WE HUNKERED DOWN BEHIND the biggest, strangest fern I'd ever seen. Each of its leaves splayed out at least six feet long and three feet wide, their surface such a dark green it might have been black, spattered with spots of red like drops of blood. I didn't touch them to find out.

It felt like we'd been pursued by the elephant-thing for hours but time and perception in Hell are skewed. And not in our favor. We crouched silently behind the fern, finding ways to deal with its putrid, wet-towel-left-in-the-washing-machine-too-long smell as the beast crashed through underbrush and knocked over trees looking for us.

At least we knew where to find it.

"We can't stay here. It'll scent us eventually," I said.

Detective Williams turned his head toward me, eyes wide and bottom lip quivering. This wasn't the way I expected a seasoned cop to react to a challenging situation.

"Where do we go? What do we do? You said you'd get me out of here. Take me home. Take me anywhere. Just get me out of here."

"Sshh."

I put my hand on his shoulder to calm him but he stood and backed away a couple of steps.

"I can't do this. We have to get out of here."

The sound of the beast rooting through the forest stopped and I imagined its head cocked to one side, listening. Did it hear him? Nothing happened for a minute. I remained crouched behind the fern, struggling not to gag on the odor penetrating my throat. Williams stood shivering, knees practically knocking together.

"I can't stay here," he said, his voice high-pitched. "You have no idea what they did to me."

The creature moved again, this time with no doubt about the purpose to its steps. The ground quivered under me and the detective's cheeks lost their color as he stared past me between the fern's enormous leaves. He'd seen it.

"Dammit."

I sprang to my feet, grabbed Williams by the arm and dragged him away. The frequency and rhythm of the footsteps shaking the forest floor increased reminding me of a scene out of *Jurassic Park* when the T-Rex chases everyone and then eats them. One thing in my after-life I knew for sure: I didn't want to end up an ingredient in one of the steaming mountains of dung the elephant-thing produced.

Anything's steaming pile of dung, really.

Williams' feet didn't want to cooperate with my escape efforts at first; his lack of help nearly pulled me off balance. I stopped to encourage him to get-the-fuck-going and saw the beast bearing down on us.

It thundered through the brush, galloping along on four of its six legs while using the other two to clear a path. What brush and smaller trees it missed with the hands it easily shouldered aside with its bulk. The trunk-appendage snaked out on front of it and the twisted black tusks atop its head crashed through the lower branches of trees, splintering wood and sending a shower of dead leaves in its wake.

"Come on!"

I yanked the cop's arm and this time he got his legs moving. I forced my way through brush and brambles, felt thorns claw my flesh; without any doubt the plants were purposely slowing our progress. Behind us, the beast kept coming, undeterred. We ducked under a fallen tree, swam through a dense swath of bushes, clambered over an expanse of deadfall and emerged onto a short plain. Thigh-high, gray grass stretched to a sheer cliff face that went up and up forever. I glanced at it, formulating a plan of action before the elephant-thing trampled us or worse, and thought I saw a crack in the rock. At this distance, it looked like it might be wide enough to allow a man passage but too narrow for the thing hot on our heels.

Williams must have seen it about the same time I did; he sprinted into the grass leaving me with my mouth open, about to tell him to make a break for the fissure.

Bastard left me behind. See if I save him next time.

I shook the thought from my mind and set off after him, resisting the urge to glance back and gauge how close the thing was to overtaking me. Judging by the quaking of the ground, it couldn't be far behind.

I can't believe those fuckers sent that thing after me. They said I'd have my freedom.

Did it really surprise me? I was in Hell, dealing with the deposed angel-of-death and a kid with a big attitude problem.

Maybe I'm a little too trusting.

Kinda what got me here in the first place.

I crashed through the grass, narrowly avoided an obstacle lying across my path as I saw it at the last second. I jumped it, spared it a quick glance, and thought I made out the shape of a corpse which may or may not have begun life as a human. It definitely smelled dead, but I'd passed the odor before it had a chance to penetrate.

Williams was thirty yards ahead of me, nearing the crack in the wall. About the time I felt relief at his safety, my foot caught on another hidden obstacle. My elbows scraped against rough grass, my shoulder struck a rock, and my nose came to a stop an inch from another corpse.

Dead, yes. Human, no.

The sickly-sweet stench of rot wafted up my nostrils making me gag. Decay blackened the thing's head; maggot-like bugs crawled out of one hole in its putrid flesh and into another. I rolled over and scrambled away coming within inches of burying my hand in another corpse. I struggled to my feet and took a step back. Bodies littered the area near the cliff, all of them rotted beyond recognition, most of them contorted in odd positions suggesting they'd plunged to their deaths from the cliff top.

"Shit."

Williams stood at the opening in the rock face. He didn't speak or gesture, only stared. I didn't realize the elephant thing was right behind me until I felt its breath on my neck.

"Fuck."

I closed my eyes.

How did I forget about that?

Its snake-ish trunk huffed another breath against the base of my skull, stirring my hair. A glob of beast-snot slapped against my neck but I didn't have the time to register disgust at it before I broke into a run.

I'd never been much of a football player but realized my opponent was faster than me, so running straight for the fissure might not be the best idea. Williams hadn't moved. He didn't so much as wave encouragement, offering only an expression of unfathomable terror.

Thanks.

I faked left, went right, and got one full stride in plus half of another before the thing's trunk slapped me in the side and sent me flying through the air. I landed on one of the corpses and it exploded in a cloud of black dust that adhered itself to the sweat on my forehead and cheeks. It didn't smell as bad as the others—must have been dead longer—but the dust clogged my nose. I sneezed once, twice, each time sending a puff of dead-guy into the air.

I wiped my nose on my arm to clear it and managed to stem the sneezing—little consolation considering I still needed to deal with the Hell-beast. And, unlike the other creatures I'd bumped into during my visits, I figured this thing wouldn't stop at one bite. I scrabbled away on hands and knees, a huge, pathetic baby desperately dragging itself from one place to another.

Elephant-thing was having none of it.

Its trunk coiled around my left ankle and jerked me off the ground hard enough to wrench my hip. I bent at the waist doing my first sit-up in years and clawed at the snake-like appendage but my fingernails slid off its slimy surface.

It dangled me upside down, blood draining from my extremities and collecting in my head, then it lifted me high into the air until my head was level with the three bloodshot eyes lined up under the base of the trunk. The eyes didn't concern me as much as the mouth.

Somehow, the first time I'd seen the beast, I didn't notice the mouth slashing across what passed for its face. Hard to believe about a maw containing so many teeth. Pointy, sharp-looking teeth designed for tearing flesh off bones.

"Okay, calm down, big boy. We can all just get along."

It didn't agree. It gave me a shake, presumably the elephant-kind's way of saying 'shut up'. I did.

It waved me around for a minute, twisting me back and forth like a feather on a string blown by the wind. I'd see a flash of the forest then the expanse of dead grass, the black corpses, the cliff.

Williams no longer stood at the crack in the rock wall.

"Williams!"

The beast took exception to my uttering a sound when it clearly didn't want me to and shook me harder, twisted me more violently. I grimaced at the pain in my groin and wondered if the thing could shake me hard enough for my leg to part with its socket. Some questions you don't want to find out the answer to, this being a prime example.

Forest, grass, corpses, cliff, the twisting continued. Corpses, grass, forest, person, grass, corpses.

Person?

I twisted and saw a figure approaching through the grass. A brief flash, not enough for recognition, so I waited for another chance.

And the beast ceased its twisting.

I wriggled and gyrated but couldn't see past it. I did another sit up, pounded my fists against the trunk. It squeezed tighter and I felt the bones in my ankle grind together. I sucked a pained breath through my teeth and stopped hitting it.

"Bastard," I said hoping it would bring the same result as before.

It reacted as predicted, but more violently. My leg screamed in pain, the tendons in my groin stretched like the elastic of a slingshot. My head swam; I concentrated on breathing and holding on to consciousness. It twisted me, swung me. At first, I couldn't think about looking to see who approached. When I got my wits back, I concentrated on looking for the figure when it swung me back toward the forest.

There.

My glimpse showed me wasn't Detective Williams come to my rescue—no rumpled suit jacket, un-pressed shirt or tie pulled askew.

The person wore plain clothes of drab colors. I saw no horns or wings or claws and decided to take a chance.

"Hey! Help!"

The elephant-thing had had enough.

It whipped me over its head, then forward, sling-shotting me to the ground. I hit with a crack of ribs and bounced once before coming to rest in a puff of dust. The thing may have released my ankle, but the pain enveloping my body precluded me from noticing such details. One of its hand-feet came to rest beside my head, but I couldn't move my head to see, only my eyes, and even they hurt. I felt its breath on my face—it had circled around in front of me. Its breath was different than before, firmer, stinkier. Mouth breath, not trunk breath.

I forced my head to move, pushed my eyes as far as they'd go, and peered up into the creature's toothy mouth.

So close. I was so close to getting out of here.

I wanted to close my eyes, a last gesture of surrender to the inevitable ingestion of my head, but my eyelids fluttered and remained wide open. Apparently, someone wanted me to bear witness to my own demise. Again.

Nice.

The elephant-thing's maw edged closer, closer. Saliva spilled over its teeth and down its slimy, gray, wrinkled chin, dripped onto the ground by my head. Closer. Closer.

Then it stopped.

The mouth closed. The thing pulled its face away, back to the edge of my vision, and tilted its head like a dog does when it's listening. I listened, too, but heard nothing.

A second passed, two. The beast remained unmoving. I struggled to quell the pain ringing in my ears and eventually made out a faint hum. Not the sound of someone who forgot the words to a song, but the kind of humming you feel as much as hear, like when you ignore the caution signs and jump the fence into the power station.

The humming grew, expanded. It seemed other sounds added themselves to it, voices doubling the volume and thickness of it, trebling it.

The beast reared up and let out a growl that transformed into a screech I wouldn't have expected from the creature, a sound more appropriately emitted by a giant parakeet. I winced at the noise as it drowned out the hum. When the beast paused to take a breath, the other sound was still there, louder, more powerful.

Then it stopped. My ears rang with it even after it ceased.

The elephant-thing took a step out of my view so I felt rather than saw when it leaped over me. I wanted to twist myself, see it happening. No chance of that—even the thought hurt.

The ground shook and shook again. The beast screeched and then the ground shook once more before everything went silent. No hum, no screech, no tremors beneath my pained chest.

I held my breath, waiting, listening without knowing what to listen for or what to wait on. Nothing happened for several seconds, then I felt a touch on my back.

I stiffened and sucked a breath between my teeth, tensing in readiness for the snapping of my spine. The two actions shot pain through my limbs suggesting the damage the creature caused wasn't limited to my ribs.

What now?

I opened my mouth to inquire. If I was in this bad of a shape, how much worse would speaking make it? The pain proved too much to form words through. The pressure of the touch on my back increased, causing more pain at first, but then a warmth began flowing, sending an electrical pulse along my back.

A buzz flowed through me, filling my torso first, spilling into my arms and legs until all my muscles tingled to the point of numbness. My teeth chattered, my eyelids fluttered. I tried to curb them, to wrest control back with no success. My breath came in short bursts, sucking dust from the ground which I longed to cough from my lungs. Just when I thought the dust would choke me and the electricity would squeeze the air from my chest, the touch disappeared and the buzz vanished. I regained control.

First I coughed and spit to clear my mouth.

After a moment recovering from my hacking spasm, I tested my limbs and ribs, found them pain free. Carefully, I pushed myself to sit, wiped gritty spittle from my chin, and faced my rescuer.

When I saw her while hanging upside down, her blond tresses had been hidden beneath a hat. It had fallen from her head during her confrontation with the elephant-beast. Her hair fell across her forehead, hung in her eyes hiding her expression.

Poe.

Behind her, the creature lay on its side, one leg stuck up in the air like a swatted fly.

"Is it...?"

After the words came out of my mouth, it occurred to me I should have thanked her first. She responded without giving me the opportunity to correct my oversight.

"Stunned. Go before it wakes."

"Poe, I—"

"Go."

She tossed her head to clear the hair from her face, and I saw a hardness in her expression that wasn't there before. Her jaw was set, her eyes unreadable. No timid smile or caring look. This was a different woman, and yet it was Poe.

I condemned her to Hell yet she saved my life.

"Why did you—"

"Go!"

The force in her word startled me to my feet. I stumbled back a step and then opened my mouth again, determined to ask my question, determined to get an answer. Her eyes flashed, silencing me, and she pointed past me. Behind her, the elephant-beast stirred. Its trunk flicked toward her.

"Poe—"

"Go now."

Her words spun me around against my will, made my feet carry me toward the fissure in the cliff. I wanted to look over my shoulder at her but needed to concentrate on my footing as I navigated the corpses. I jumped over the last one and reached the opening, then stopped and looked back.

The elephant-thing gripped Poe around the waist, its trunk cinching tight, yet she continued staring at me, eyes urging me to go and not look back. As I turned away, I saw the beginning of the glow I'd seen her utilize before, though it wasn't golden this time, but gray. I knew I didn't need to worry about her, at least not when it came to what would happen in her struggle with the creature.

I jammed myself between the sides of the fissure, forcing myself in, and tried not to think about it as I wriggled my way through, stranding my guardian angel in Hell.

Chapter Forty

T HE PATH THROUGH THE fissure twisted and turned, switching back on itself uncountable times, sometimes running straight for miles. It widened to the size of a banquet hall and narrowed until damn-near impassable. At one point, damn-near impassable and switchback came together as one and I got stuck for a panicky minute. I wriggled and gyrated, eventually working my way around the corner to find the path widened and straightened beyond.

And, not too far ahead, it ended.

The green-painted door set between the stone walls sported a push bar worn silver with use and might have been the exit door out of any school in North America. I slowed my pace to sneak up on the door, untrusting.

How does that come to be here?

It's Hell, stupid. What do you think?

Twenty feet away. It didn't move, only stood placidly, keeping me on this side away from whatever lay on the other. I stopped and listened: no electric hum, no screams, nothing. I moved closer.

Ten feet. The ground didn't become quicksand; dead hands didn't scrabble through the rocky ground to grasp my ankles and pull me into their graves.

Five feet. The earth didn't quake; rocks didn't tumble from above to crush me before I escaped. No voice boomed warning me away; no ancient runes scrawled in the rock promised a grotesque and hideous fate if I crossed the threshold.

Something's wrong.

Closer.

I reached out with shaking hand. My finger brushed the push bar where the paint was worn off. I pulled my hand away immediately like a child touching a hot stove.

Cold metal.

It didn't shock me or burn me. No man-eating slime leaped onto my flesh. If felt exactly the way it looked.

Someone's fucking with me.

I touched it again, wrapped my fingers around the bar—smooth except where a stubborn chip of paint clung tenaciously to the metal. I traced its edge with my finger and wondered why the bar was so worn, how many years the door had been here. The fact the bar was on this side suggested its job was to keep things out rather than to keep me in.

I filled my lungs with warm, gritty Hell-air, using the breath to collect enough nerve to push the door open and find out what lay on the other side. My pause stretched on for several seconds as I thought about Poe, the elephant-thing's trunk wrapped around her waist, squeezing, squeezing. I glanced back over my shoulder, down the path to the impossibly narrow switchback. No way to get back to her, not before one of them destroyed the other, or maybe both. Even if I could, she didn't want my help, not now, not after my betrayal.

And I had to consider Trevor.

I turned back to the door, took another breath, and did what a push bar is designed for.

Nothing happened.

I jiggled the bar, the metallic squeak echoing off the sides of the miniature canyon. Still nothing, so I examined the door frame for a lock or something jamming it shut. Everything looked fine. I tried again, this time throwing my shoulder into it as I pushed the bar. The door flew open. I stumbled through, light streaming through with me, briefly illuminating the room before my feet caught and I tumbled into a stack of green plastic patio chairs. The door closed, leaving me in darkness.

At least I knew where I was.

I untangled myself and clawed my way up the stack of chairs to my feet. A minute passed as I leaned against them, waiting for my eyes to become accustomed to the dark. Soon, I discerned the large flat boxes containing tables broken down into parts, the stacks of cushions and bunches of umbrellas. I looked back at where I'd come through and saw a set of shelves stacked with boxes reaching to the ceiling. No door. Was this the warehouse I knew or was I still trapped in some fiendish Hell?

A fiendish Hell where they enjoy patio furniture.

I made my way through the maze of boxes and shelves and, after a few turns, realized I could see the color of the cushion fabric, read the letters on the sides of boxes even though the lights weren't on and I'd seen no evidence of windows. The light source lay somewhere ahead; I decided it should be my goal, for better or worse.

A few more corners, including one leading to a dead end, and I emerged into an open area cleared of boxes and shelves. It took a second for me to realize something other than Detective Williams standing in the center of the room cast the glow.

Michael, resplendent in white leisure suit and crimson shirt, leaned against a stack of lawn chair skeletons. The suit itself looked crisp enough to cause the glow. I glanced at the archangel but chose to ignore him for the moment, directing my attention to Williams instead.

"Are you okay?"

He lifted his tired eyes and his mouth twitched into an approximation of a smile. Not much of an expression, but he squeezed volumes into it: relief, appreciation, desperation, embarrassment. I wondered which of the above he'd choose to express in words.

"Yeah," he said after a couple of seconds. "Thanks."

I considered prompting more out of him about the way he'd acted, or to chastise him for leaving me behind like in those rapture books by Tim LaHaye and Jerry Jenkins, the *Left Behind* series, but more important matters demanded my attention. I regarded the archangel and his misguided attempt at fashion.

"Where's my son?"

He smiled, the shine of his teeth matching his jacket, and raised an eyebrow. A shiver of worry ran down my spine. Maybe it wasn't Mikey I'd seen in Hell, maybe it had been an illusion. Maybe Trevor wasn't safe.

"Trevor. Where is he?" I demanded.

"The boy is safe," God's right hand answered finally. I suspected he enjoyed the moment of worry his pause inflicted on me. "He awaits you outside. Where is your guardian?"

His eyes flickered to the detective and I looked, too. Williams had slouched down onto a small pile of cushions and sat with his elbows propped on his knees, head hung like a man too tired to hold it up anymore. When I looked back at the archangel, his smile was gone. He glared at me, forcing me to answer.

"I left her."

Hearing the words come out of my mouth drove home what I'd done—I'd left my guardian angel to an eternity of torture and despair. Mikey's forehead creased, he pursed his lips.

"And you brought back this one instead?" He gestured toward the detective.

I nodded and steeled myself for the archangel's wrath. He looked at me a moment longer, then nodded once.

"I will take this man where he needs to go. Collect your son and get him home. It is cold outside tonight."

The archangel walked to the detective, put his hand on his shoulder. Detective Williams jumped at the shock of Mikey's touch, then looked up, the exhaustion in his expression replaced by wonder.

"But what about Poe?"

"What about her?"

"I left her," I said, struggling to look him in the eye. "I shouldn't have."

"No?"

"No. She doesn't deserve it."

"But you chose to leave her. No one else but you."

I looked at my shoes but they did nothing to make me feel any better. Never do.

"It might have been the wrong decision," I said, keeping my voice quiet enough Williams didn't hear.

"What is done is done. We will all have to live with the consequences."

He tugged on the detective's shoulder, directed him down an aisle between a stack of table boxes and shelves full of umbrella stands.

"Consequences?" I called after them. "What do you mean, consequences?"

"There are consequences to every action, every decision, Icarus Fell. This is no different. There will be consequences for the guardian and for you."

I opened my mouth to request more clarification, what kind of consequences I might watch out for, but a shiver beginning at my knees and working its way up to my shoulders shook the intent right out of me. By the time the shaking ceased, the detective, the archangel, his angelic glow and poor fashion sense were all gone.

I remained standing in the middle of the open space, staring down the aisle at the emptiness where the man and angel were seconds before. My gut roiled like I'd recently consumed a meal of rotten meat and maggots.

Perhaps I'd made the wrong decision.

"There will be consequences for the guardian and for you."

Murdered by muggers, back and forth to Hell, watching friends butchered and nearly losing my son. Twice. Hadn't I endured enough consequences over the past six months?

"Trevor."

I shook myself free of regret and remorse and took the sickened feeling in my gut in search of an exit to find my son and take him home.

Chapter Forty-One

I T TOOK A WHILE, but I finally found a door not marked with the words:

Fire Exit
Alarm Will Sound When Opened

I stumbled through the door into a night filled with swirling snow. As the door clicked shut, I stopped, face up-turned, and allowed flakes to land on my cheeks, my nose, cooling my burning flesh. In Hell, I'd gotten used to the increased temperature, so the feel of snowflakes landing and melting, the cool water running across my skin, confirmed I'd made it home. Such as it was.

I reveled in the feel of it for a minute before the scrape of a footstep made intentionally to draw my attention did exactly that. I lowered my face to see Trevor looking at me, a bewildered look on his face.

"Trevor."

I closed the space between us in five strides and threw my arms around him, held him tight. He patted my back.

"Hey, Dad," he said. "W—Where are we? How'd we get here?"

I loosened my bear hug and leaned back to look at him. His shaggy hair hung in his eyes and, wearing a short sleeved t-shirt, he was obviously resisting his body's desire to shiver.

"It doesn't matter," I said and turned to leave, arm around his shoulders. "Let's get you home."

We walked for a while listening to our footsteps crunching in the fresh snow. My mind replayed the events of the last few hours, and I cringed at what I'd put my son through. Again. Eventually, my thoughts came to the moment Mikey took Trevor, and I remembered he was going to tell me something.

"Hey, what were you going to say when Michael rescued you?"

His shoulders rise and fell in a shrug and I thought of Piper. One more thing to feel bad about.

"Who?"

"The big blond guy. You wanted to tell me something."

"I don't remember. When was that?"

"A few hours ago."

He snorted through his nose and shook his head. "I haven't seen you since the toy store. Thought you forgot me again."

My stomach clenched and I stopped walking. He continued two paces, my arm falling from around his shoulders.

"We were just together. In Hell."

Trevor's eyes widened, but he quickly got himself under control. He knew enough about my situation not to think me crazy when I said such things.

"Don't know what you're talking about, Dad."

"You and Poe came after me. You got lost. Don't you remember?"

He shook his head. "Poe? I read *Telltale Heart* in school. He's dead."

"No. Well, yes, he's dead, but that's not who I'm talking about. I mean Poe, my guardian angel."

Trevor laughed. "Maybe being dead has made you a little batshit." He gestured over his shoulder. "We're here. Better not walk me to the door; Mom wouldn't be happy to see you."

I looked up and saw Rae's house, the porch light reflecting off the falling flakes of snow.

"How—?"

Her house should have been another hour's walk, yet here we were. I surveyed the area, saw the leafless stick-trees, the row of houses identifiable from one another only by the color of their doors. Trevor watched me expectantly, as though it wasn't unusual we'd arrived so quickly.

"Thanks for bringing me back, Dad."

He threw his arms around my shoulders and gave me one of those teenage boy hugs which said he loved me but would rather not display it in public. I returned it, half-hearted with disbelief, then he started down the snow-dusted path to his mother's house.

He doesn't remember what happened.

Maybe it was for the better. Did a fifteen-year-old really need to know so much about Hell? Was that the kind of knowledge he needed to carry around for the rest of his life?

No.

"But Trev, what about—?"

"Don't know what you're talking about, Dad. Haven't been drinking, have you?"

He shot me a look that told me he was kidding, then sauntered to the door and gave me a wave over his shoulder.

"No," I answered after he disappeared inside. "Not yet."

· · • • • • • • · ·

The sidewalk was clear of people; the yellow police tape had been removed. I observed the wreckage for a bit, seeking refuge from the snow under the oak tree only a few steps from a spot of ground that tasted my blood a few months back. The place gave me the shivers, and not because it was chilly out.

Snow has a way of beautifying things. The cemetery bordering one side of the churchyard with its rusted iron fence and canted headstones wearing wintery white stoles looked worthy of a painting. The white stuff even loaned a certain charm to the blackened chunks of stone fallen from the church's walls. No footprints marred the snow blanketing the churchyard except mine. Pristine, calm, beautiful.

I stepped out from under the oak tree's shelter toward the church. I hadn't come to admire the winter elegance of the ruined church, I had other things in mind.

I crossed the yard toward the fallen building, intentionally dragging my feet as I went, leaving ugly lines in the snow. As I came close, I saw much of the mess was cleaned up. The splintered pews were gone, the fallen crucifix and broken altar removed. The pipe organ, split in two last time I'd seen it, was also gone, and all the remnants and scattered pages of bibles and hymnals. Salvaged by the church, gathered as evidence or taken by souvenir seekers and religious fanatics, I couldn't say, but they were all gone. Only the larger chunks of stone not so easily moved remained.

My snowy-silent footsteps carried me past the sections of fallen wall toward the one still standing. The pew we'd left leaning against the wall as a makeshift staircase was gone along with the others, so I scanned the area looking for another way up, but the clean-up crew had done their job well. I walked the building's perimeter, got cold hands searching under fallen pieces of wall, stubbed the big toe of my left foot on the one bible they'd missed, and eventually found myself searching the area below the window.

I don't know what I expected to find, but the more I searched and the less I found, the more desperate I became. Things weren't right—Trevor not remembering, Poe looking so guilty then saving my life. The suspicion I'd made decisions without all the pertinent information had nagged me almost from the moment I first met Michael. The thought that I didn't know everything going on or I'd misinterpreted things I'd seen kept me awake at night.

And I could only think of one way to set things right.

My foot crunched on something beneath the window. It wasn't the satisfying crunch of compacting snow, but a breaking sound. I crouched and dug my near-frostbitten fingertips into the packed snow of my footprint. Whatever I'd stepped on was too small to help me climb up, but I'm too curious by nature to break something and not see what.

My fingers cleared snow away from a smooth, blue piece of glass. I stared at it for a minute, uncomprehending. When it dawned on me what it meant, I looked up. I couldn't see the window beyond its ledge, so I stood and stepped back.

Snow blew through the empty window, swirling through the place where the virgin Mary should have been.

"No."

I stared at the hole, wondered why I didn't notice it was gone before this.

How did this happen?

People had gathered here seeking solace from the miraculous virgin, begging for money and miracle cures, good fortune and guidance. How could they let it break?

How will I get back to Hell?

I resisted the mental urge to blame some surly teen for throwing a rock through it as a 'fuck you' to religion and society because I might have done exactly that in my youth. Letting Azrael take Father Dominic to Hell was just that kind of rebellion.

"Damn it."

I had to try.

I backtracked to the largest chunk of wall I thought movable and jammed my fingers under its edge. The snow nipped at my cold fingertips. I clenched my teeth and grunted aloud trying to budge the hunk of stone. It didn't move.

Lift with your legs, not your back, dope.

I squatted, jammed my hands further under and used my legs, not my back. This time, the piece of wall moved. I struggled and grunted. It slipped back, threatened to crush my near-frozen fingers, but I caught it and propped it on its edge. I rested a minute with it leaned against my leg and tucked my fingers into my arm pits to warm them. Too bad being dead didn't afford me protection from cold, pain or discomfort. What's the point of being dead if it feels exactly like being alive? According to centuries of literature, zombies and vampires didn't have to deal with this.

When some sensation returned to my fingertips, I went back to the task at hand. Luckily, I'd chosen a vaguely round hunk of broken wall. On its edge, I rolled it to the wall. It wobbled and threatened to fall over, but I kept it upright until it leaned against the wall below the empty window.

I rested against it, catching my breath, snow caked to the stone's edge like it would become the base for a huge snowman. I hunched forward, elbows propped on my knees—not the best breath-catching position, really—and wondered if all this work would prove worthwhile.

You deserted her. She saved you. You suck.

'Nuff said.

I knocked snow from the top of the stone and climbed unsteadily onto it. On top, I could stretch high enough my fingers extended beyond the edge of the window ledge. I reached until my fingertips found the channel in which the stained glass had been set. Not much to grip, but a grip nonetheless.

With some effort, I inserted my fingertips firmly, and somewhat painfully, into the groove. I huffed a preparatory breath of mist and hoisted myself up, feet scrabbling against the wall. It felt like the tips of my fingers might come off, but I made it up. It wasn't pretty, but I made it.

I perched on the edge, resting, legs dangling above the chunk of wall which aided my climb. This was so much easier with pews to climb and Piper at my side.

Piper.

She'd used me, I saw that, but I missed her anyway. How often does a man have a woman who looks like *that* act like she's interested? In my case, not very fucking often. Oh well. I shrugged in tribute to her memory and stood.

I faced the spot where the stained glass rendition of Mary had been and looked out across the churchyard at the snow-swept street beyond. No traffic at this time—somewhere south of three in the morning, I figured—and no one on the sidewalk since the miraculous window was gone. I closed my eyes and took a breath, held it a second, released. My eyes fluttered open and I stepped across the groove marking the spot where the window had been and hoped to Hell I'd end up in Hell.

My foot slipped in the snow. My foot went from under me and I landed on my ass, grabbing the edge of the window frame to keep from going over and—knowing my luck—breaking a leg or my back.

Nothing else happened. The churchyard didn't become some Hellish landscape; no ferryman-beast took a bite out of me in exchange for passage; no deposed archangel, demon or damned soul greeted me.

It didn't work.

I righted myself and looked out over the churchyard, flakes collecting in my hair. The snow gave the night a preternatural glow, a lightness not seen at any other time. I raised my eyes toward the sky and the gray clouds dumping their cargo on the quiet city.

"I'm sorry, Poe."

The snow deadened my words. I wiped melted flakes from my face and looked back at the churchyard, the cemetery. The beauty of the wintery scene did nothing to quell the tightness in my chest, the band squeezing my heart.

"I'm so sorry."

Chapter Forty-Two

T HE BELL OVER THE door of the Chinese laundry tinkled. Chan Wu stopped counting the day's receipts and looked up, ready to serve another customer or, if need be, snatch the bat from under the counter if whoever came through the door had other things in mind. In all the years Chan Wu ran the laundry—more than anyone in the neighborhood would have been able to recall—a dozen times someone had come through the front door with theft on their minds. They never left with the old man's money, but usually got something very different than what they expected.

The door closed and the latch clicked. No one there. Chan Wu sighed, returned the receipts to the till and leaned forward resting his elbows on the counter, playing the part of a weary old man relieving his aching back. His back didn't ache.

"What are you doing here?"

No answer for a moment but the old man didn't doubt his ears. He waited patiently until the boy stepped into view. There was nothing in the shop for him to hide behind yet he appeared to have revealed himself from behind cover. Chan Wu wasn't surprised. It wasn't the first time the boy had come to his shop and it wouldn't be the last.

"Still playing the old man, are you?"

"It suits me, I think. Need I point out you are an immature little boy?"

"Your opinion," the boy scoffed.

"What brings you by? Surely you do not need me to do your laundry."

The boy looked down at his t-shirt streaked with orangey-red dirt and jeans with holes in the knees.

"Nope. Looking good."

"Then why are you here? You only come when you have something about which to gloat. That is obviously not the case this time."

"Isn't it?"

Chan Wu stood straight and came out from behind the counter. His black tunic hung to mid-thigh over black pants which stopped mid-calf above his sandal-clad feet. He paused to straighten the suit jacket on the mannequin in the window display before responding.

"It does not seem to me you ended up with what you wanted."

"Do you know what I wanted?"

"The harvester, of course. But he is home safe. Depressed and confused, but safe."

"Hmm."

The boy looked at a display of products: fabric glue for quick repairs, travel sewing kits, plastic cases containing a variety of different colored threads. He picked up one of the cases of thread, examined it briefly, then put it back in the wrong spot.

"If you aimed to achieve depressed and confused, then I guess you won this round. But I must tell you: we can get him through it."

The boy set his finger against the stack of travel kits and pushed it over. They fanned out across the shelf. One hit the floor.

"I didn't want the harvester."

"No?"

"No."

The boy smiled and the old man felt a sinking in his chest. He knew the game would go on forever between the two of them, and he knew one set back meant little in the grand scheme. No matter—he didn't like to lose. He went back behind his counter and reopened the till, removed the day's receipts again feigning disinterest.

"Well it seems we have stalemated, then."

"Oh, I don't think so."

"But you—"

"The guardian, old man. I took back my Carrion and you never saw it coming because you were so concerned with your precious harvester."

"Ah yes, the guardian. A shame."

Chang Wu looked down at the slip of paper between his fingers. He didn't want to give the boy the satisfaction.

"That's it? That's all you have to say about it?"

The receipt in his hands was for dry cleaning a three piece suit, Harold Bittner the name on it. Chan Wu knew Mr. Bittner would die of colon cancer in under three years. His wife would survive ten years beyond his death. He knew Mr. And Mrs. Bittner's son would become a surgeon like they dreamed he would, but his career would be cut short by arthritis. He'd go into teaching and live into his nineties. All this he knew, this and more, but he didn't know what it would mean that the boy had the Carrion back. He raised his head and looked at him but said nothing.

"Say *something*."

The boy punctuated his words by sweeping his arm across the shelf and knocking its contents on the floor. The packages of fabric adhesive bounced against one another; one of the plastic containers of thread broke and sent spools rolling under the counter.

"I won this time. I won and you didn't see it coming."

The old man looked across the counter at the boy and a smile crept across his face, deepening the wrinkles in his cheeks.

"Never has the dark managed to extinguish the light," he said, obviously enjoying the opportunity. "But no matter how dark it may become, the tiniest spark of light has the power to vanquish the night."

The boy stared, his brow creased. A few seconds passed as he formulated his response.

"Fuck you, old man."

And the boy disappeared as the old man chuckled to himself and returned to counting the day's receipts.

####

Also By Bruce Blake

Curse of the Unnamed epic fantasy:

The Book of Shadow
Shadow Scarred
A Shadow Upon the Land
In the Shadow of the Dragon - coming July, 2023

Khirro's Journey epic fantasy:

Blood of the King
Spirit of the King
Heart of the King

The Books of the Small Gods epic fantasy:

When Shadows Fall
The Darkness Comes
And Night Descends
When Ravens Call
The Twilight Fades
And Kingdoms End

The **Icarus Fell** urban fantasy series:

On Unfaithful Wings
All Who Wander Are Lost

Secrets of the Hanged Man

Visit Bruce on-line at www.bruceblake.net for free stories, to stay updated on news and new releases, and to purchase signed copies

Blood of the King (Khirro's Journey Book 1)

A kingdom torn by war. A curse whispered by dying lips. A hero born against his will.
With a vial of the king's blood in one hand, and a sword of legend in the other, one soldier sets out on an odyssey that will change his life... or end it.

Forced into the army, Khirro never wanted to fight. And with the monarch dead, any hope for the kingdom's survival hangs by a slender thread. But when the king's shaman charges Khirro with a curse, he's compelled to undertake a journey to the haunted land in search of the outlaw necromancer. And if he fails... the very walls of the fortress itself will fall to the blood-crazed undead.

Can Khirro complete his quest in time to save his realm from a brutal end?

"Blood of the King is a masterpiece. It is as close to perfection as I would consider a book to be."- Ella Medler, author of *Blood is Heavier*
"Blake has a knack for bringing you into the story"
"Mr. Blake's writing is masterful and clear, he draws you into his story and when it's finished you feel like you're leaving an old friend."

The Book of Shadow (Curse of the Unnamed Book 1)

Llyris Fildarae is an outcast tainted by a sliver of magic in a world terrified of the supernatural. Loathed and distrusted, she uses her ability to control a magical Unnamed to survive.
Caedric Carpera is desperate to save his son from a deadly illness. He enlists Llyris to locate a lost tome containing secrets capable of healing

him, but its location is a mystery that's already claimed lives. Thrust into a hostile world, Llyris and her companions risk everything to find the relic and return before the child's sickness prevails. But who is the enigmatic old man who appeared out of nowhere to set them on this dangerous expedition? And what does he really want?

Only a perilous mission to an untamed land can save the boy and reveal the truth.

Except some truths are too shocking to be exposed.

"Bruce Blake has written a hell of a book and I am eagerly awaiting the sequel!"

"I'm usually a chapter per night type, but I couldn't put this book down."

When Shadows Fall (The First Book of the Small Gods)

A hundred times a hundred seasons have passed since the Goddess banished the Small Gods to the sky, stripped them of their power, and erased their names from history.

Cast out but not forgotten, they bide their time awaiting the opportunity to exact their revenge.

While exploring a forgotten chamber, Prince Teryk and Princess Danya uncover an arcane scroll that speaks of impossible things--a barren mother, a man from across the sea, and the return of the Small Gods. After discovering the prophecy, Teryk believes himself the one chosen to save the kingdom, but Danya isn't so sure. Despite his sister's doubts, Teryk sets out on a dangerous quest to unlock the secrets of the scroll, risking everything to prove his worth to their father, the king. As he delves deeper into the prophecy, unaware of the powerful forces he's set in motion, he discovers his destiny may not be what he expected and his fight for the kingdom's salvation may cost him more than he ever imagined.

As the prince questions everything he thought he knew about himself, his destiny, and the Small Gods, will he be able to save all he holds dear, or will his quest for glory cost him everything?

"When Shadows Fall is one of the best fantasy books I have ever read. Its characters are memorable: you adore them, you want to strangle them, you cheer them on."

""It rained fire the day the Small Gods fled" Thus begins When Shadows Fall, the first book in the Small Gods series by Bruce Blake and what a terrific start to one fast-paced and completely engrossing new fantasy it is."

Visit Bruce on-line at www.bruceblake.net for free stories, to stay updated on news and new releases, and to purchase signed copies

About the Author

Award-winning author Bruce Blake lives on Vancouver Island in British Columbia, Canada. When pressing issues like shovelling snow and building igloos don't take up his spare time, Bruce can be found taking the dog sled to the nearest coffee shop to work on his short stories and novels.

Actually, Victoria, B.C. is only a couple hours north of Seattle, Wash., where more rain is seen than snow. Since snow isn't really a pressing issue, Bruce spends more time trying to remember to leave the "u" out of words like "colour" and "neighbour" than he does shovelling.

Bruce has been writing since grade school but it wasn't until the mid-2000's he set his sights on becoming a full-time writer. Since then, his first short story, "Another Man's Shoes" was published in the Winter 2008 edition of *Cemetery Moon*, another short, "Yardwork",was made into a podcast in Oct., 2011 by *Pseudopod*. Since then, he has concentrated on writing novels, publishing the **Khirro's Journey** trilogy (*Blood of the King, Spirit of the King,* and *Heart of the King*), three books in the ongoing **Icarus Fell** urban fantasy series (*On Unfaithful Wings, All Who Wander are Lost,* and *Secrets of the Hanged Man*), and the **Books of the Small Gods** series (*When Shadows Fall, The Darkness Comes, And Night Descends, When Ravens Call, The Twilight Fades,* and *And Kingdoms End*). *The Book of Shadow* is the first book in the **Curse of the Unnamed** series, to be followed by

Shadow Scarred, *A Shadow Upon the Land*, and *In the Shadow of the Dragon*.

Bruce has many more projects simmering on the back burner, so stay tuned.

Visit Bruce online at **www.bruceblake.net** for FREE SHORT STORIES, signed copies, and to keep up to date with new releases